Project Timeslip

Project Timeslip

A Novel

Randy S. Tanner

iUniverse, Inc.
New York Bloomington Shanghai

Project Timeslip

iUniverse books may be ordered through booksellers or by contacting:

iUniverse
1663 Liberty Drive
Bloomington, IN 47403
www.iuniverse.com
1-800-Authors (1-800-288-4677)

ISBN: 978-0-595-51219-5 (pbk)
ISBN: 978-0-595-61807-1 (ebk)

Printed in the United States of America

Dedicated to my wife, Betty, for her loving support over the last 37 years, without which this book (and my successful Naval career) would not have been possible. She is my guardian angel.

Prelude

As he stepped into the early morning sunlight, Daniel Thomas also stepped one hundred years into the future. He squinted through eyes still accustomed to the gloom of the underground complex. Everything looked the same as it had yesterday and the day before.

The Permian Basin was still a dried out, prehistoric seabed whose former inhabitants had turned into black, Texas crude oil millions of years ago. A barren land where thorny weeds struggled to survive. The harsh climate had forced their roots deep into the hard caliche soil that had sat for centuries under the same West Texas sun that the Pueblo Indians had used to bake adobe mud bricks. Daniel Williams shielded his eyes, searching for any sign of change, but even the sky seemed to feather off to the same dirty shade of tan where it touched the horizon. Everything looked the same—except for the tall Saguaro cactus standing across the highway; it hadn't been there that morning.

The silent cactus raised a spiny arm in greeting as it pointed another down the edge of the crumbling highway whose faded blacktop showed no signs of tire marks.

Daniel shivered and rubbed his arms against the fleeting chill of morning. The day was young and brisk, but a few hours of sunshine would soon alleviate that. He waved back to the friendly Saguaro and decided to take its advice.

The sun bleached asphalt stretched out in front of the time traveler as he followed the westerly road toward the city of Newtown—or at least where Newtown used to be. He wondered just how far into the future he had come, and he thought about the steps that he'd already taken, the steps that had brought him to … wherever he was.

The long walk gave him plenty of time to reflect. The past six months had been full of demands. The Timeslip Project, Chief Todd's unreasonable proposal, and then the tragic affair with Christina. He hadn't thought of her, or allowed himself to think of her, for a long time. That was another memory that deserved to stay buried. Her demands had been the hardest of all. He still wanted to blame her for the accident, for pushing the issue of commitment, and for running out on him. But he couldn't. He had pushed her away. He tried to convince himself that all that was far behind him now, buried in the past. He now walked in a different time, freed from the past-present to explore this future-present. Only he wasn't sure whether he was here to explore a different future, or to run away from his own.

Chapter 1

The journey had begun seven months earlier, when he was sitting in The Chair, the one directly in front of Chief Todd's desk. Chief Administrator Alexander Todd was probably the only individual with full knowledge of the many research projects and cutting-edge ventures conducted in the underground complex. He seemed to know everything. Sometimes, he knew too much. The chair was designed to be uncomfortable, and Daniel couldn't help shifting his weight under the Chief's penetrating gaze. He had been there before. Often. But this meeting was not about glow-in-the-dark toilet seats or unauthorized life forms.

"Asynchronous temporal displacement?" the administrator asked, meticulously pronouncing each word.

"I see you've read my proposal," Daniel answered. "Fascinating isn't it?"

"It's time travel nonsense!" As a seasoned Chief Administrator, Todd could bellow alongside the best of drill sergeants. Lingering cigar smoke drifted in layers above the administrator's balding head as he tossed the report into Daniel's lap like yesterday's stock tips.

"It's theoretically sound." Daniel said. "Validate the Einsteinean effect of velocity and gravity on time while postulating quantum properties of time flow."

The Chief Administrator continued to stare blankly and Daniel tried not to squirm as he adjusted his posture for a more sincere pose. "And the twelve-pound brains in Theta Phy donated a dozen pages of physics calculations to support it. Actual time travel is, well, just a hypothetical ramification of the theory."

"Hypothetical?" Chief Todd bit down on his cigar and leaned forward to focus his all-knowing stare. "You submitted a twelve million dollar funding request. I'd call that a sizable chunk of reality, wouldn't you?" He stopped to clear his throat.

"I'm only following procedure," Daniel said. "Before proposing any new project, a feasibility study is required, then a filed report including funding estimate."

"Don't quote policy to me, son. I wrote it."

Daniel shrugged. "I think the possibilities justify the expense. It may sound fantastic, but it's still worth investigating."

Chief Todd leaned back with an almost audible growl as if studying Daniel's superficial veneer. The proposal was worthy enough, at least from a technical standpoint. He seemed bothered by something else. Daniel knew that he had more chair time than anyone below the rank of Department Head. He might have become one already if not for his occasional irritating pranks. Daniel wondered if he was going to hear the maturity speech again.

"According to the personnel office, you've been at Theoretical Physics barely two months. Hardly enough time to comprehend everything going on. You can't seem to stay in one place for very long."

"It's long enough for a fast-tracker. Isn't that the purpose of the program?"

"Two months?" It was more of an accusation than a question. "Everyone has to pay their dues around here, even you."

Daniel couldn't help giving a smirk. "I think my Q-FET design is paying a couple of million a year, isn't it?"

"Closer to a billion," Todd answered. "But I'm talking about gaining a broader overview of this organization. Understanding how the various parts affect the whole. Displaying some evidence of commitment to supplement that immature genius."

Daniel grin widened. "A billion? Nice, and I'm not a genius. I'm an intuitive mastermind with a high I.Q."

"What's the difference?"

"Geniuses don't get laid."

Chief Todd rolled his eyes. "It wasn't meant as a compliment. Regardless of where your IQ hovers over your social development, I had planned to discuss your upward mobility. I suppose you do need some experience at running a project. So I'll authorize funding for temporary research, but only three months."

"Three months?"

"That's a month longer than you needed to learn the operations of an entire department."

Daniel shrugged. "Good point."

"But I want hard evidence of progress within three months, or you'll be back in Theta Phi in a heartbeat. Next time as a Department Head."

"I'll still need Tom's assistance." Daniel stood to leave. "And, for the record, it's only one-seventy five."

Chief Todd rubbed his temples. "Limited assistance. Not to interfere with his current projects."

Daniel wanted to press for more, but knew better. This arrangement had been predetermined before the meeting began, so he nodded and made his way out of the office, past the stone faced receptionist, and into the hall where he could no longer hear the conversation that followed.

# # #

"Do you really believe that twit could ever assume your job?"

Chief Todd did not bother to look up as he continued massaging his diminishing headache. The skeptical Ms. Anita Jenkins was his secretary, though she preferred to be called an administrative assistant. Assistants made more money.

"Eavesdropping again, Ms. Jenkins?"

"I never eavesdrop," straightening her business suit. "You left your inner door open again. I couldn't help but overhear."

"Of course not. And you never file my memos in the waste basket, either."

She stoically ignored the accusation. "So do you?"

"I fervently hope so." He reached for the next stack of reports waiting to be reviewed. "He has the talent and the drive. Something tells me that his future holds more of a destiny than most men. He just needs a little more maturity. He reminds me of another gifted scientist."

"Who's that, Dr. Frankenstein?"

He glanced up with one of his rare smiles. "Me, Ms. Jenkins."

"Does he know of your retirement?"

"Nobody knows! Nor will they, until I decide to announce my successor."

Ms. Jenkins had heard that reprimanding tone often enough to recognize it. She had also learned to ignore it. She placed the important papers that required his attention in his top basket and casually dropped the others into the trash can.

Chapter 2

Daniel peeked around the corner into the darkened room looking for his friend. He wasn't spying, only being cautious. Thomas had been known to throw things when he was interrupted at the wrong time. So Daniel eased silently into the dark room.

Thomas Caudle was perched atop his lab stool; his once white labcoat was spotted with week-old chemical stains. Wrinkles of concentration, illuminated by the phosphorescent glow of the scanning electron microscope, trailed the corner of his eyes as he stared intently at something.

There was no way to gradually interrupt someone; however, Daniel did scan for breakables on the table to prepare for a resulting high-speed projectile before announcing his presence.

"Hey, Tom, let's go eat. I'm starved!"

Thomas bolted upright and spun around angrily. "Don't you ever knock?"

"Why? It was open."

Thomas had reached for a flask of viscous green solution. "What do you want?" he said as he considered its value and set the beaker back on the bench top.

"It's lunch time and I thought you might be hungry."

"It's barely eleven o'clock, and I'm busy. Besides, I'm not sure being seen with you is such a good idea."

"Why? We're still friends, aren't we?"

Thomas turned back to the microscope and re-adjusted the targeting reticle. "I don't enjoy sitting in The Chair like you do."

Daniel couldn't help grinning. "Are you still pissed about that? A four-pound amoeba seemed hilarious to me."

"No. An amoeba is a microscopic organism. That crap was self-propelled vomit that I had to clean up after the Chief found it!"

"Sorry, I didn't think the Chief would go snooping through your desk."

"That's what I mean," Thomas said with a frown. "I can't afford the price of your pranks. Some of us still have to worry about funding."

"You always get your funding. And you're always busy." Daniel took his reluctant friend by the arm and pulled him into the corridor. "Come on, you need some fresh air before you turn into a mushroom."

# # #

The corridor was four stories below ground level, one of many in the brightly-lit labyrinth known as the S-RAY Complex. A mixed crew of workers and technicians scurried past them along both sides of the wide passageway. Like an endless line of worker ants, they carried their burdens of test tubes, Petri dishes, and stacks of computer printouts. The diverse community of this underground warren operated under a caste system borne of technology. The dingy coveralls of a laborer walking beside them marked him as one of the unskilled workers, an assist-tech. Presiding over the assist-techs were the specialized technicians in their freshly starched lab smocks of green, or pink, or blue. The color identified their particular area of expertise. Thomas and Daniel, wearing their white lab coats, were at the top of the social system. They were engineers, answering only to God himself. Actually Chief Administrator Todd filled the omnipotent position.

Daniel turned to follow the movement of an assist tech, admiring the natural sway of her hips. Long, curly lashes peeked out under blonde ringlets too pure to be true. She smiled invitingly, but kept walking.

Thomas gave a disapproving look. "I'll bet her personality washes down the drain with her make-up."

Daniel considered the possibility of finding out. "It's too late, you've already turned to a mushroom. It's a direct result of not enough light and too little sex."

"I get enough! It's called subdued lighting. And it's easier on my eyes, so less fatiguing. And I'm not exactly a monk."

"Oh, I almost forgot. Is that cute little tech still clinging to you like a vine?"

Thomas looked around. "Who?"

"Stephanie, who else?"

Thomas ignored the question and continued to the elevator.

The ground floor of the huge Complex was what CIA officials referred to as a front and appeared to be nothing more than an ordinary office building for some small pharmaceutical company. Several small offices were rented to some oil field geologists to add to the cover. The smoked glass windows of the foyer almost cut the glare of the West Texas sun. A smiling receptionist waited behind a contemporary style desk to direct guests and the occasional visitor while a lone security guard ambled along the polished tile floor in semi-retirement, occasionally glancing at access badges. His presence was expected in any modern office building, and entirely unnecessary. High above him, a dozen cameras, laser scanners, and RFID sensors silently verified bar codes embedded in the badges, and sent the data to the VAL-2700 security computer. Daniel resented the little tracking devices, but the company insisted they weren't using any capability beyond building security. He also resented the computer's eternal presence, while Thomas only saw another fascinating toy to play with. He hoped one day to look inside the Verified Artificial Logic series bio-processor and discover how it really worked. Daniel just wanted to take it apart.

# # #

Inside the company cafeteria, they joined the line leading to the buffet counter. The smell of fresh coffee drifted down the row of glass panels that displayed an assortment of freshly baked pastries. Tempting slices of ham sizzled on a blackened grill. Daniel also noticed other aromas, a variety of perfumes. He recognized some of the brand names and quickly placed a woman's name, or at least a face, with each scent.

"So what's big worry over funding this time?" Daniel asked.

Thomas was known throughout his technical fraternity for having a long face; he always seemed to be concentrating on something. But his expression suddenly brightened.

"Didn't I tell you? You won't believe it. The whole electronics industry will have to start from scratch. This idea is bigger than the quantum transistor."

"I don't think so," Daniel answered, a little defensively. He had designed the revolutionary Quantum Field Effect Transistor which had firmly established his worth to the company. The royalties from its sale to Litton-Intel Industries continued to support a score of company research projects. To Chief Administrator Alexander Todd, however, Daniel was a priceless pain in the ass.

"Well, it's bigger than the IC chip and fiber optics combined," Thomas continued. "It's a whole new field of science. We can grow complete circuits on a crystal!"

Daniel tried to look impressed. "So, what's this new science called?"

"Crystaltronics. Sounds catchy doesn't it? We're growing circuit chips, whole integrated circuits, from an encoded solution. You see, I discovered this macromolecule encoding technique for a mineral solution …"

"Sorry I asked." Daniel scanned the crowded tables as his friend lapsed into a monotone that could put any Washington bureaucrat to sleep. He was looking for Christina.

The cafeteria was a cauldron for ideas; engineers from different groups gathered for a quick meal or a needed break during the day's work, but couldn't sit long without talking shop and sharing the latest news or gossip of someone's research. The synergistic effect produced more breakthroughs than the company's generously funded think-tank. The tactical oversight in security, which had resulted in a total absence of surveillance cameras in the cafeteria, ensured the process would continue.

Thomas was saying something about space savings, high current loads, and obsolete micro lithography. Daniel took a tray and peered over a shoulder to preview the morning's selection of sweets: plenty of Danish pastries, two blondes, and a redhead. But no Christina, so he interrupted his friend.

"I'm going to be working on time flow."

"Huh? Time flow?" Thomas adjusted his glasses. "What a coincidence. You know there are several theories debated today. The consistency of time is debated heavily among the theoretical physicists ..." The clatter of trays and jingling of steel serving ware, mixed with the chatter of a dozen abbreviated conversations almost drowned out Thomas. Almost, but not quite. "... we have a new relational model. Next month I'm planning to present it at the Department Head symposium."

Daniel nodded. "I know. I read your report."

Thomas glanced up. "I haven't published yet."

"So? I know where you keep everything, remember?"

"You did what?"

"Relax, I wasn't poking around in your lab drawer or anything. VAL mentioned it during a topic search. Pretty good stuff, except for the part about trying to join all the known forces of the universe into one relative equation called the Unified Field Theory."

"I know what UFT is," Thomas said. "I wrote it. Are you sure you understood it?"

Daniel covered his grin and continued. "What got my interest was your suggestion to merge the old Linear Wave theories with the current Quantum String postulates. I have an idea to try and prove it with physical evidence." He paused to evaluate Thomas' expression. "What's wrong?"

"I don't know if I should feel flattered or violated."

Daniel handed his identicard to the cashier whose rich, sultry accent dripped with Southern hospitality.

"Hi, Daniel, missed you at the party."

Daniel looked up slowly, enjoying the stretched surface of her beige cafeteria smock that served to highlight more than conceal what nature had blessed her with. Gloria was the currently-blonde that everybody knew, or at least almost everybody claimed to know. Daniel had considered the pleasure of her company, but veered away. She was as cunning as she was cute. Many of the female engineers that worked in the Complex were savage competitors for promotions and funding, but Gloria was a different kind of predator in this techno-jungle. She was stalking a man who could afford her tastes. Today her bait included a faint trace of body glitter that made her cheeks sparkle with each smile.

She leaned closer in a whisper. "I really enjoy a stimulating conversation with a man who has more than one talent."

Thomas leaned over to join them. "I'll ask Christina if she minds sharing."

Daniel shot a frown and quickly paid for both trays. As they sat at an empty table, Thomas looked up over his glasses.

"That poor creature doesn't have enough I.Q. to fill out a credit application."

"She's smarter than you think. And I wasn't interested in her credit rating. In fact I'm not interested, period, at the moment."

"What about Christina?"

Daniel's frown deepened.

"On the skids, huh?"

"We're letting things slow down for awhile, okay? Let's get back to your paper. You mentioned that in UFT everything has a basic unit of measurement, including time."

"You drag me out of the lab for lunch and now you only want to talk shop?"

Daniel sighed. "All right. Christy and I had a little disagreement. Satisfied?"

"You asked her to move in, didn't you?" Thomas' smug look portrayed that he had already surmised the problem, knowing more than he would ever let on, and more than Daniel could ever admit to.

"The theoretical particle you're talking about is the chronoton. It carries a measurable quantity which is supposedly the shortest amount of time in which the primal event occurred."

"Primal event?"

"The Big Bang when the universe began. That very first instant between no universe, as we know it, and an exploding super mass of energy and gas filaments. A chronoton is calculated as the time lapse between the instant of the initial explosion and the moment when the macro ball of matter actually moved. And since the laws of physics were solidified during that primordial instant, then the individual ticks of time can be no smaller than that."

"That sounds so boring when you say it," Daniel interrupted, "Is tick the official techno-term?"

Thomas looked over his glasses. "Did you read the entire paper?"

"More like the Cliff notes version. I think the bottom line is that this chronoton, which is approximately 3.2 times 10^{-43} seconds, carries the ticks of time flow. It sounds like an old fashioned movie film, which is actually made up of thousands of individual frames, and the passage of frames is perceived as a single continuous, moving image."

"Movies?" Thomas pushed away from the table as if ready to leave. "Thank you for summarizing so many weeks of exhaustive scholastic work on notional physics to such a simple analogy. Now my mother won't have to strain her eyes trying to read my long, boring paper."

"That means that our time continuum may have invisible gaps in it."

"Yes, Captain Obvious." Thomas stood. "Can I go now?"

Daniel glanced over his shoulder and lowered his voice. "What if time flow is like a convoy of trucks moving down the highway, with these chronotons speeding through the space/time continuum. And what if we were able to match the speed of the trucks. Could you slip between and zip through them to reach the other side? Would it happen outside the confines of Time?"

Thomas lowered his glasses. "Don't ever call me a mushroom again. And I think that you should never again try to read one of my papers. Why don't you focus on something useful, like a global flu vaccine or a cure for navel lint?"

"I've got funding."

Daniel had saved releasing that bit of information for just the right moment and maximum effect. Then he waited for the inevitable reaction.

"You got funding? For this?" Thomas took a deep breath. "Okay, theoretically it might be outside of time itself. But if something could slip out of continuum, that would mean …" he sat back down and leaned forward. "Time travel?"

"It's not travel actually, more like a time slip. The Chief gave me a green light to put a team together, but I've only got three months for phase one. I might need some engineering help later on, nothing much. And you are the best gadget maker I know. It may sound crazy, but who knows where it'll go? It's good to know I can count on you, right? Tom?"

"What!"

"I can count on you, right?"

Thomas leaned back in the chair. "No jelly looking, crawly things this time?"

Daniel flashed his most trustworthy smile. “I promise.”

“Okay,” Thomas answered. “But I mean it, if anything comes slithering out of a lab drawer, I’m gone to the movies.”

Chapter 3

Three months had seemed like a long time to Daniel when he had started, but like a secret military shuttle flight in the night, they were gone before anyone had noticed. Already Chief Todd was awaiting his findings.

Daniel entered the darkened lab looking for his friend, and found him sitting on the lab stool like a mushroom worshiping the dim glow of the scanning electron microscope. Although staring quietly at the screen, Thomas seemed oblivious to the flickering image floating before him.

"Why didn't you answer?" Daniel asked, moving the closest beaker out of the way.

Thomas looked up blankly. "What?"

"I actually rang the buzzer this time, before I bypassed the lock. And you ignored me!"

"Sorry, didn't hear it." Thomas' face seemed even longer than usual.

"Come on, you look like you need a break."

"No, just thinking. Something came up with Stephanie and I don't know how to handle it."

"Don't tell me she found out you're not gay."

"Not funny."

Daniel shrugged and offered a feeble, "Sorry."

Thomas had gotten a reputation that was hard to live down. It wasn't from anything he did, but more by what he didn't do. He just didn't date any of the women in the Complex. Most of them were too busy proving themselves equal, or superior, to their male counterparts to appeal to him. Stephanie was the one exception, an innocent flower in a world of weeds. As a low paid assist-tech, she had no career to be concerned with, and nothing to compete for. She also had a most unnerving effect on Thomas.

"Let's take a walk," Daniel suggested.

"It's okay. Besides, Bio is waiting for me to finish this test, and I'm getting nowhere."

"Good, then it won't hurt to take a break. Let's take a walk," Daniel repeated. "In the garden."

"I said I was okay."

"Not for you." Daniel motioned for the door. "For me."

Thomas gave an understanding nod, and then turned the scope off. Bio Engineering would have to wait.

# # #

The "garden" did not exist inside the research complex. Just a mile away from the cluster of office buildings, out of sight from any road, laid a patch of green grass with seasonal wild flowers. Two young trees huddled together within the damp circle formed by a leaky underground water pipe. That small leak deep in the sand had transformed the normal desert mesquite and scrub brush into their private oasis. It was a good place to get away for awhile and just think, especially when one of them had a problem.

Thomas had plucked a slender grass shoot to chew on while he waited. His friend stood silently on the grass carpet as he stared out at nothing in particular. Both men needed their periodic visits, though neither would ever admit it. Finally the moist green of their surroundings had relieved the synthetic stress of the laboratory, and Daniel broke his silence.

"Tomorrow is deadline on my Timeslip proposal."

"So?"

"I don't know if the Chief will buy it or not. All I have to show him are theories."

"You brought me out here just to tell me that?"

Daniel shrugged, but waited a few seconds before saying anything. "I think I'll transfer to Physics and work there a while."

"Why don't you just give her a call and get it over with!"

"Who?"

Thomas plucked the grass stem from his teeth. "What are you trying to prove? You've dated almost every girl at the Complex. Found what you're looking for, yet? Don't think so."

"I don't know what I'm looking for."

"I do and you ain't been worth spit since you let her get away."

Daniel stared out over the dry plains as he searched for a denial. Christina was a beautiful, if not elegant, technical apprentice whom he had met last spring after running over her in the cafeteria. He had enjoyed her sense of humor almost as much as his own. She shared his assessment that the Complex frequently became too stuffy and serious, like some underground monastery. A practical joke was necessary once in a while for everyone's sanity. No one knew that it was Christina who had come up with the idea of the giant amoebae. Daniel just put it in Thomas' desk drawer—a task not easily accomplished for something that behaved like self-propelled vomit.

Daniel remembered how, after that, the two of them had spent a lot of time together, continually finding excuses to be with each other. They drove to work together and often met for lunch, when they would take long walks on the surface or just sit alone, enjoying the warm breeze and sunshine of the West Texas plains.

As their relationship grew, they spent evenings together; either for dancing, or the latest holo movie where they shared stolen kisses like adolescents, oblivious to the three dimensional scenery and virtual reality images moving around them. In a flippant moment he had suggested that "to save money," she could move in with him—a suggestion she had flatly rejected. She wanted "more." Like any other decent woman she wanted commitment. And that's what scared him.

"How come you know so frigging much about women when you don't even … you know?"

Thomas grinned. "It doesn't take a rocket scientist. Maybe I stay away because I do understand them." He waited for a barbed comment, but got none. "So how about it, are you going to call her, or do I have to?"

Daniel started back toward the car. "Let's go. I have to talk to the Chief."

# # #

The Chief Administrator's office was brightly lit, decorated in rich oak paneling and nostalgic office furniture from the early Nineties. A green banker's lamp glowed softly beneath the harsh room lights. His unlit cigar dangled rigidly as he stood before the window—actually a holographic viewing screen that displayed an image of a window scene.

"I've been expecting you," he said as Daniel entered. "We have something important to discuss."

"I know. It's three months tomorrow and my report is due. Substantial evidence and all that stuff."

"Substantive," he corrected, turning away from the hologram, "but that's not the point. Daniel, my health is failing."

"I know all I have so far is theories, but they're good ones. And it looks promising."

"I won't be able to fulfill my duties as Chief Administrator much longer. And it's a tradition for the incumbent Chief to select his own successor."

"Successor? I don't understand. What does your eventual retirement have to do with my project?"

Chief Todd took a deep, wheezy breath. "How do you feel about leaving research to take on the role of Administrator?"

"Me, as Chief? Get serious. And get a check-up."

"Daniel, for some time now I've been considering you as my replacement."

"No way! This outfit needs an old man, I mean an older man. You know what I mean. It needs someone mature and stable. Ten years from now, or maybe fifteen, and I might settle down enough, but not now."

Chief Todd eased himself into the large chair with a sigh. "I became the second scientist ever to assume the Administrator's title when an accident in the Nuclear Physics lab left me with, well, let's say an extreme sensitivity to radiation. Now it seems the same incident will force me to retire even sooner than I had thought. Besides, it will be nice to spend more time with my family." He picked up a hologram of a young woman with jet black hair and wistful smile. She seemed to smile directly at him.

"Your daughter?" Daniel asked.

"My wife." He set the picture back on the desk. "The accident didn't injure me, it changed me." He stopped to cough. "How old do you think I am?"

"I don't know," Daniel answered. "Sixty or sixty-five I suppose."

Chief Todd forced a cynical smile. "I would be in poor health even for sixty-five," he said, running a hand over the remnants of gray streaked hair. "The fact is, I'm barely forty-five. Forty-five and dying of old age."

Daniel stared in disbelief at the man who claimed to be so young. His appearance demanded two more decades. Furrowed lines crept from the corner of his eyes like a freshly plowed field and thinning hair receded quickly from a pinkish scalp.

"I, I don't know what to say."

His ironic smile seemed painful. "Neither does our illustrious Medical Department. I'm told it isn't a disease proper, but more a space-time anomaly. I guess you could say that my time is not the same as yours."

"So you're getting old faster than you should? I appreciate the confidence. Really. But I'm sure you're good for another year or two, or ten."

"I'm afraid not. The prognosis from Medical is that the effects may be accelerating. So I must train my replacement before it's too late."

"Your replacement? Look at me. I'm not the one you want. For Heaven's sake, don't you know how screwed up my life is? I'm thirty-two years old and, according to Ms. Jenkins, still in adolescence!"

Chief Todd shook his head and almost smiled. "Believe it or not, Ms. Jenkins does not run this front office. And I have the utmost confidence in your abilities. You have the qualities of a true leader. And it is something that even you can't hide."

"Now I know you're getting senile."

Chief Todd's stare became suddenly penetrating. "You have tapped only a small portion of your talent, Daniel, and yet you have displayed bursts of creative genius unparalleled in your peers. What could you accomplish if you really set your mind to it?"

"I might push beyond the barrier of time," Daniel said, trying to get back to his original goal.

Chief Todd picked up the status report and scanned it nonchalantly. "Yes, it looks interesting, and if anyone could find a way, you would be the best bet. But the decision has been made."

"You can't do this to me! Dammit, I'm close to major discovery, really close."

"This discussion is over, Daniel." Although sounding much older, the voice of the experienced drill sergeant still retained unquestionable authority.

"I have waited and watched and groomed you for the past three years. I gave you the freedom to explore. I allowed you to transfer from one department to another to learn as much as possible about this organization. Your every endeavor has been under my guidance. I've studied the records of a dozen contenders, and I have chosen you to be my replacement. How dare you doubt my judgment? By Jove, you'll do this or be terminated. Q-FET royalty and all!"

"Chief Administrator Williams?" Daniel waited for a bolt of lightning to obliterate him for blasphemy.

"It's Friday," the Chief said in a near whisper as he sat down to catch his breath. "You have two days to give me your answer Monday morning."

Daniel had never questioned the special favor he had enjoyed with the Chief, nor suspected an underlying motive. Still struggling to accept the concept of taking over the old man's position, he slowly realized that he had no options.

"Okay, but give me six months. Not to think about it, you've left me no choice. Just give me six months to try my Timeslip theory, that's all. And then I'll agree to whatever you want about, you know, taking over."

Chief Todd smiled as he contemplated the impossible challenge. "There is no way to complete such a complicated project that soon."

Daniel didn't return the smile. "Then you have nothing to lose, do you?"

Chapter 4

Daniel placed the compact note reader back on the conference table and poured another cup of coffee. He didn't get much sleep the night before; he had been too stressed. Six o'clock in the morning was too early to hold a meeting. It was too early to hold anything, except maybe Christina. And she was deliberately keeping far from his reach. Normal people didn't get up before the sun, but department heads weren't normal people. If Daniel were going to impress them, he had to play their game. And the next play started in another thirty minutes.

He nursed his second cup and reexamined his plans for the meeting. He'd never addressed the Department Head meeting before. He'd never been forced to do so. And today he had to face them with no support from Chief Todd who intended to sit back and watch the heir apparent. Daniel tried to concentrate. He only had six months to finish the project and he would need the combined resources of every department to pull it off. He checked his watch again.

"VAL, did you notify everyone on the list?"

"Yes, Daniel," the pseudo human voice answered. "Every member whom you requested has been contacted and instructed to be present."

He was about to query the VAL 2700 terminal again when the heavy oak doors to the conference room flew open. Thomas walked in.

"I had a bad dream last night," he said. He looked irritated. "About someone asking me in the middle of the night if I was hungry."

Daniel gave his best innocent look. "I don't know what you're talking about." It had seemed like a good idea at the time. He had worked till three in the morning the night before and was hungry, so he had given his friend a call. Thomas hadn't appreciated the invitation.

Two more representatives walked in, one was the department head of Nuclear Physics and the other was Biomedicine. They squeezed past Thomas and grumbled a "good morning," before taking a seat at the end of the long table. Thomas remained in the doorway, still awaiting an explanation, but the doors flew open again. A dozen Department Heads and senior technicians poured in, counting the chairs to find their assigned seats. Swept along in the flow of bodies, Thomas aimed a loaded finger.

"We'll talk later."

Chairs squeaked on the polished teak floor as the coffeepot drained into eagerly awaiting cups. Finally Chief Todd arrived and took his seat at the head of the table.

"Looks as though we're all here," he said, scanning the table. "Daniel, this meeting is yours. Proceed."

His unexpected announcement brought a few curious looks and some belligerent stares, but Daniel quickly took his queue.

He explained the details of his plan, officially named Project Timeslip. Each department represented at the table was given a task. He outlined their responsibility then presented a chart of planned milestones with their corresponding completion dates, each task preparing the way for the next. The individual assignments would fit together like pieces in a puzzle, perfectly interlocked to form his goal of breaking the time barrier. He hoped.

Logistics offered Room 601 to be designated as the construction site for the main unit; 602 would contain the control and monitoring equipment. Nuclear Physics would provide and install a graviton field generator and anti-magnetic shield to surround the main unit and contain the violent radiation. They would also construct the tachyon power plant, the heart of Daniel's proposal. Thomas's group from Special Electronics was tasked with the design work, something Thomas had not warmly accepted since interrupted his own research. Daniel planned to work closely with the "Bubble Heads" in Theoretical Physics who would calculate and verify each parameter of the construction. And Bio Med would assign personnel to act as safety and hazard monitors. Chief Todd had insisted on the last detail.

Upon conclusion of Daniel's brief, growing murmurs filled the room. They were obviously not thrilled with Daniel's plan. Some resented the newcomer who wasn't even a department head yet. They wanted to know how someone so junior could be placed in charge of a major project. Many were unconvinced of any lucrative technology spin-offs. Most objected to the arbitrary time constraints which they were unaccustomed to.

"This design calls for the construction of prototype equipment," one engineer pointed out to the mutual agreement of his peers. "Two years at least!"

"We have six months."

The murmurs grew into a roar.

"Six months? That's absurd!"

Daniel stared slowly and deliberately at each obstinate colleague.

"There will be a successful Timeslip event within six months," he said with emphasis. "This project has been fully sanctioned by the Chief Administrator and I now speak for him. If you can't complete the task, I'll find someone who can. Any questions?"

The room was silent enough for Daniel to hear the beating of his own heart as he scanned the faces around the table. When he reached his friend, he was surprised to find a smug grin. Then he realized that Thomas had never seen this side of him before.

"Review your files in the computer. You should find all the information you need to begin. As you can see by the Milestones Chart, we meet again in two weeks; I expect you to have some answers by then. I suggest we adjourn now and get to work."

The group broke up slowly with hushed grumbling. No one knew whether to call his bluff or just accept their assignments. As they shuffled out of the room, Thomas worked his way forward and approached with a lingering grin.

"That was pretty impressive for someone who doesn't like to assume responsibility."

"It's only temporary insanity," Daniel said with a shrug. He was trying to reassure himself. Only temporary. He had no intention of becoming the next Chief Administrator.

Chapter 5

Daniel attempted, for the third time, to gain Thomas' attention and waited impatiently for his friend to come over and join him. It was taking too long.

Weeks had stretched into months. Minor complications had become time consuming obstacles. And Daniel's project escalated into a major effort for the company, the only effort, involving more resources and people than he'd ever imagined. Too many people. The larger it grew, the slower it progressed. It had taken forever to install the tachyon drive. One division always had a complaint or excuse aimed at another for not completing an assignment. Daniel was surprised that many divisions cooperated long enough to complete anything.

He hated the delays, but he hated dealing indirectly with the problem even more. It left him very little time for actual "hands on" work. Most of his workday had become consumed coordinating, motivating, and encouraging the multitude of team leaders. And solving disputes between work centers. Most of all he hated the people problems. That was supposed to be the duties of a Department Head.

Thomas' crew had been assigned the simple task of power transfer, and they were past deadline. He waved again, trying to get his friend's attention over the chaos of construction.

Assist techs were dragging equipment, in periodic lurches, across a congested floor that squealed protests under the massive weight. Dozens of laborers in blue and green smocks danced around them shouting conflicting orders across the room. From the corner of the room, thready fingers of white metallic smoke curled upward from a laser spot welder as a goggled technician joined bundles of gold plated fiber optics.

Thomas finally looked up and nodded with a proud smile. He pointed to the center of the room where three men were inserting a finned, ceramic object into the bullet shaped capsule.

"There it is!" he yelled. "The thyratron for the Tachyon generator!"

Daniel wanted to take a closer look, but didn't have time. "Will it work?"

"Of course! Don't know about the generator. Nukes are building that, you know."

Daniel nodded his relief and turned to leave. The Nuke shop was his next stop and the reason he didn't have time to stay and give proper recognition of Thomas' success. Meanwhile he knew more work delays were piling up on his desk.

His antique wooden desk was covered with scratches buried under layers of yellow lacquer. It was also covered with unfinished work. Daniel attempted to resort the piles of paper: misplaced mathematical equations scribbled on the backs of week old production reports, forgotten appointments, and broken dinner dates.

He plucked a wrinkled reminder note from the clutter and tacked it to wall. Three times he had called Christina to set a time and place to sit down and just talk, explain everything. Each time something had come up. Maybe she had sensed his desire to open up; at least she was talking to him again, and had even offered to fix dinner. She'd chosen his townhouse to make it as easy as possible for him not to screw up.

He decided to reevaluate the complementary equations, again, and pushed the rest to the side. For the last four months he'd been trying to calculate which time frame he would arrive in, whether past or future. One series of equations were based on velocity, gravitational effect, and duration of the event which predicted the faster you go, the sooner you'd get there. If he went fast enough, he should theoretically arrive before he actually left.

The other treated time as an infinite dimension with a finite length and suggested that a Timeslip event would merely release an object from its present/past coordinate. At the end of a Timeslip, it could then slip back into a new "present" of random coordinates.

He didn't like the "random" part. It was like being a cork stuck in the bottom of a running stream: while resting on the bottom, the water of time flowed past. If the cork could free itself it would float up to the top, then drift along with the water over the riverbed. When it once again sank to the bottom, it would be in a different place. A different time.

As he massaged his temples, the door to his office slid open revealing Jake, the sour faced security guard.

"Got another visitor," he said, then as an afterthought added, "Mister Williams."

"Why didn't you let them in?"

"Ain't got the access level, that's why. Dern fool's wearing a Level THREE badge."

Daniel rubbed his forehead. "Tell him ... tell him I'll get back to him later."

"Suits me." Forty years of retired street cop lumbered down the hall. "I'll tell her to scat. Nice looker though."

"Her? Wait a second. Is it Christina?"

"Beats me," Jake grumbled, continuing down the hall. "Badge says Newark. Don't worry, I'll run her off."

Daniel gritted his teeth and hurried to catch up. He didn't need Jake's charm refining his relationship with Christina.

When they arrived at the security office, Christina was waiting with crossed arms. She aimed a stare past Daniel to the guard. "Am I interrupting something? Mr. Personality said I couldn't come in."

"No, of course not." Daniel glanced over to Jake who seemed unconcerned, writing something down in his logbook. "It's just, well, you could get in a lot of trouble being so far from your work center."

She fondled the bright red THREE emblazoned on her badge. "What, this? Don't sweat it. I'm an F.T."

Daniel's jaw dropped. "I didn't know."

He knew the term. Fast Tracker described the accelerated apprenticeship program used to prepare "specially gifted" individuals for placement in high tech positions. It was reserved for those few who displayed exceptional potential and drive. He new all about it because he had been an F.T., shuffled from one department to another, gaining an overall knowledge of each specialty before finally joining the elite think tank of Theoretical Physics. He just didn't know that she was one.

"Why didn't you tell me?"

"We never got around to talking much." She crossed her arms again. "I just wanted to remind you about tonight."

"Why didn't you page me on the intercom? I could've met you upstairs."

"I did. You didn't answer."

"Sorry. But don't worry, I won't forget."

She peeked over his shoulder at Jake as if she might kiss him on the cheek. "Please don't be late," she whispered. "It's going to be a special night."

"I know."

"I mean very special." Her blue eyes sparkled with implied promises.

# # #

The company gym was always crowded before lunch with well toned bodies glistening with perspiration. Amid the sound of clinking weights, some ran on treadmills that lay invisible in the floor. Others danced aerobics in front of the wall length mirror. A particularly energetic trio stood off in the far corner, alternately trading bruising punches and kicks and then bowing to each other.

While some came to the company gym to lose or control weight, most of the individuals around Thomas did not appear to need it. From their appearance—Grecian gods and goddesses of eternal youth with firm stomachs and bulging chests—they were instead working to improve already impressive physiques. Some, like his friend Daniel, came to practice at the archery tunnel, one of the few sports which had not been replaced by computer simulation. He had won the tournament two years in a row, then quit. Thomas suspected it to be due to a lack of any serious competition. Most came in a vain attempt to maintain their youthful appearance. Thomas simply came occasionally to relax. Becoming buff had never been a goal, but the exercise seemed to clear his head.

He strained to squeeze the padded bars together. Beads of perspiration trickled down his forehead, stinging his eyes. One more inch and the bars would touch together. One more push, then he relaxed letting the two mechanical arms snap back to their original position. He took quick breaths and continued, his concentration oblivious to the hard bodies around him as he focused on the pale beige wall before him. Just outside his field of view, a familiar figure entered and came straight across the room.

"I've been looking for you. Lab boys said you'd be here."

Thomas answered with a grunt.

"I'd like to talk to you."

"So talk. You look a little tense. Sit down and join me."

"It would be nice to have your full attention. Besides, I don't want to be late for dinner. Christy's fixing something special."

"Oh, sit down and loosen up. You're too nervous and high strung since you quit your running exercises."

"I'm not high strung!" Daniel lowered his voice and straddled the second machine. "I'm not high strung. Besides," he thumbed the lapels of his lab coat, "I'm not exactly dressed for it."

"So what's on your mind?"

"I haven't seen you for a week or so and wanted to get an update."

"Nothing's changed," Thomas said between breaths. "Still have a few minor details to work out, but everything's moving right along."

Daniel noticed a well-filled blue, spandex suit. Smooth, moist thighs. Bouncing hips. And a flat stomach. "Is that all?" he said, returning his attention to Thomas.

"What do you want, an in depth report? My weekly summary's been filed. Ask VAL if you want the details."

"You know I don't like reading those dry reports. It makes me gag to have to send one in myself. Chief has to threaten me every month."

"They're due every Monday."

"I know."

One of the trio of kickers was waving for Daniel's attention. He ignored him and pivoted on the vinyl seat for a better look at the blue spandex.

"So, how's Christina doing?" Thomas asked.

"Well, I'm no longer the bug on her windshield of life."

"Does that mean she's talking to you again?"

"She never stopped!" He lowered his voice again. "She never stopped talking. We just decided to cool things off for a while."

"You're crazy you know, she's everything you could ever want. Nice looking. Young. Intelligent. She's probably still a virgin, too."

"What do you know? Your idea of a great evening is curling up in front of the fireplace with a tech manual!"

"I know you," Thomas replied. And he did, better than anyone else at the Complex. Perhaps better than he knew himself. "I also know you haven't been very attentive. Your friend over there wants to talk to you. I think he's one of the security guards."

Daniel ducked. "Don't point, he'll see you. Jeesh, look at the size of him! He's big as a mountain. I knew I shouldn't have come in here."

"Why don't you go and see what he wants?"

"I know what he wants and I'm not going over there to accommodate him."

Thomas shrugged. "Looks like you won't have to. The mountain is coming over here."

A tall, broad shouldered figure rambled across the room, leaving heavy footprints in the resilient foam flooring. Bulging arms, resembling short tree trunks dangled rigidly. He stood tall and proud glaring down at Daniel, his over developed torso loosely wrapped in the silky black Gi.

"I hear you're purty good in the martial arts." He spoke with a strong Texas drawl and sounded like an old Western gunslinger, calling the sheriff to a showdown.

Daniel looked to his friend for advice.

Thomas shrugged. "Might as well get it over with."

"Let me guess," Daniel said, "You'd like to impress your friends over there with a short bout. I feel like I've said this before, but I'm not exactly dressed for it."

The burly figure grinned, then stepped back and stretched ceremoniously. With impressive speed, his tree branch arms whirred through the air as he performed a flamboyant Kata. Square fists of iron rapidly punched imaginary targets, then he spun full around, snapping a massive punch that stopped less than an inch from Daniel's face.

"A very short bout," he agreed.

Daniel gritted his teeth. He had survived several energetic challengers who wished to test their skills against his reputation. When they were sincere in wishing to learn, Daniel would always offer a little instruction, but when they were like this one—brash, aggressive, and overconfident—the lesson was usually quick and painful.

"Maybe I do have a few minutes to kill," he answered.

# # #

Christina stared out through the dining room window with dwindling anticipation as she finished her glass of wine. Two hours preparing dinner. She didn't even like mutton, but it was Daniel's favorite. Now it was drying in the oven while the mint gravy congealed on the table. Finally she turned away and blew out the remnant of the candles. She tossed the remaining log in the fireplace, and drained the bottle of expensive Merlot. Fine wine was supposed to be sipped. She didn't care.

She had opened it earlier to let it breathe as she recalled their first date. He had driven her to an obscure little restaurant in his convertible. Government approved "safe cars" weren't supposed to go that fast. But his car wasn't one of the late model cookie cutter G cars. It was an antique convertible, a restored relic from an era when fossil fuel was cheap and abundant. She had loved the thrill, the passing blur, and the cool, evening wind pushing in her face.

She had wondered what kind of place he would choose. An image had popped into her mind: a white horse, a shining knight, and a royal ball. It was a girlish thought, but that was how he made her feel, giddy and adolescent.

The pathetic "restaurant" had squatted at the end of a row of dilapidated warehouses, leaning precariously to one side. It resembled more than anything else an abandoned farmhouse sitting by the side of some rural road with warped and sun bleached boards dangling off a splitting porch choked by a sea of neglected weeds.

Inside, it didn't seem quite so deteriorated. Only because of the poor lighting, she remembered. He'd led her across the smoke filled room to sit at a table she could barely see. Soft romantic music hid in the background, blanketed by subdued conversations from shadowed couples.

"I hope you like it," he had said with an almost apologetic look.

She had loved it, an international mixture of French, German, and Moroccan delicacies. She had leaned close, enjoying the faint aroma of his cologne. He had tried for a candle-lit dinner, but the wrinkled little owner had objected, afraid of offending the other guests who apparently desired to be more discreet than they.

His closeness had excited her. The nervous butterflies were back in her stomach. It had been a long time since any man had caused that feeling. She liked it.

That evening had passed quickly. All too soon, they were standing in front of her apartment saying good bye. He squeezed her hand before leaving. He had tried nothing more than to hold her hand all evening. Not the Daniel she had heard about. Although she had been at the company only a few weeks, recruited from Cal Tech during the final weeks of her doctorate, she had already heard plenty of interesting gossip. And most of it concerned Daniel. She had wondered how much of it was true. Fidelity didn't seem to be his strong point. Well, she could change that, she had thought.

She had been wrong. It seemed the white knight had silently ridden away. She finished the glass of wine.

# # #

The headlights of the oncoming car glared through the windshield. Daniel squinted with his good eye until the car passed, trying to follow the blacktop that still glistened from the last thundershower. More storms and a possible tornado watch were predicted later that night. He checked his watch. The burly challenger with tree trunk arms had not fallen as quickly as planned, or as painlessly. By the end of the match, Daniel had needed more than just a quick shower to placate Christina. As he pulled into the driveway, he glanced at his watch again and cursed under his breath for being late again.

He was reaching for his keys when Christina opened the door.

"Hi. Sorry I'm late."

"I knew it. I just knew you couldn't make it home on time."

"I recognize that tone of voice. You're pissed aren't you?"

At least she didn't slam the door before she walked off.

"Sorry, honey. I really am. Something came up at the last minute and I had to take care of it. You understand," he said as he reached out to hold her. She needed to be hugged.

"You're wet," She said as she brushed his hands away. "Dinner's cold. And so am I. Good night."

"Where are you going?"

"To pack."

"You don't have anything to pack. You never moved in, remember?"

"There was tonight," she said softly. She picked up the cotton nightgown from the sofa and reached for her overnight bag.

He ran to catch her. "Christy, wait. I really am sorry. Let me make it up to you."

"How?"

He glanced at the nightgown and looked genuinely into her eyes.

"What about tomorrow?" she asked. "And the day after? There's more to a relationship than sex, you know. Or maybe you don't."

Daniel winced. "I never made any promises. If you don't like the way I am, why did you bring that?"

She surveyed the elegantly prepared meal and then studied him for a moment, the dying flicker of the fireplace bouncing off the moistness of her eyes. "I honestly don't know."

"Look," he said, still trying to touch her. "It's late and we're both tired, too tired to talk about this calmly. Why don't you take the downstairs room and we'll talk about it in the morning."

"You're right," she said. "You never made any promises."

Daniel started up the stairs. "You've been drinking too much for what I want to say. We'll talk about promises tomorrow."

He was lying and he knew it, but it was easier than facing the truth. He went to his bedroom and fell on the empty bed just as a peal of fresh thunder rattled the windows. This isn't how he'd planned to spend their evening. He had intended to be completely honest with her, perhaps even tell her about the rainbows. He closed his eyes and a haunting childhood memory returned: His father shaving in the mirror. Steam clouding the cold glass while his mother stood nearby. Yelling. It was the first time he had seen them argue.

"This is the last time!" his mother had yelled. "D'you hear me? I won't put up with it. You're not going to run around on me, I'll leave first." He didn't understand any of their conversation, what had happened, what had caused the fight. But he knew she was mad. She wanted to leave. And it scared him.

He had run out of the house to get away from the yelling and sat on the porch, staring at the schoolyard across the street. A growing emptiness made his tummy hurt. What was going to happen? He loved his dad, but he loved his mom, too. He didn't want either one to leave. He rubbed his burning eyes. He was a big boy (his father had told him so); he wouldn't cry. But the tears wouldn't stop. And the warm sunshine sparkled through his bleary eyes, casting prismatic reflections. Hundreds of tiny rainbows. Rainbows of love. Rainbows of fear.

His mother had never left, but every time she threatened, young Daniel would hold his breath and close his eyes, hiding from the rainbows. A lousy way to grow up, he remembered. He'd never take the chance of doing that to his son. Not even with Christina. Why couldn't he live in a different time. A time when life was simpler. A time with less complications, less responsibilities.

Christy would never say the word, but he had acted like a real sonofabitch. He'd apologize to her in the morning, he decided. He closed his burning eyes against the lightning and went to sleep. When he awoke the next morning and came down for breakfast, he had his apology all worked out, including a partial explanation of rainbows. But the kitchen was empty; she was nowhere to be found. Her clothes, her personal belongings, even the scent of her perfume was gone.

The sunrise drive in to the Complex would have made a great postcard as the awakening orange glow of the clouds stretched their pink-tipped arms over the morning's sky. The storm's deluge had been greedily absorbed overnight by the parched land, making the high plains seem greener. But to the side of the road, Daniel recognized something that made his heart stop. A pair of deep skid marks was gouged into the soft rain-soaked caliche. Where the skid marks ended, a battered car rested on its side. It was Christina's.

Daniel would never find the opportunity to apologize. He raced to the Trauma Care emergency room, then to the county's Medical Center where he found Chief Todd. The look on his face explained it all before he said a word. The coroner's office had called him to identify the body and notify next of kin.

"It's all over," he said softly. "It happened late last night. During the storm. I'm sorry, Daniel, but there's nothing you can do here. She's gone."

# # #

The graveside ceremony was simple and short. Her parents, who flew in from Atlanta, sat on the front row of thinly padded folding chairs. When it was over, Chief Todd shook their hands and praised their daughter's talent, complimenting them for her strong moral integrity.

"She will be missed," he had assured them.

Daniel had watched silently. He had not joined the small group of seated observers, but had stood behind them in the bright afternoon heat. And although the weatherman had delivered a typical sunny day with only a few scattered white puffs of cloud lost in the clear Texas sky, Daniel had watched the final moments of the ceremony through gathering rainbows.

Chapter 6

Daniel returned to work the day after the funeral.

It was a little calloused, some thought. Chief Todd had cautioned against trying to bury his grief in the Project, but Daniel didn't want to listen. He had spent the days before the funeral trying to remember: the good times with her laughter, the arguments with the apologies he'd never given, and the explanation he'd never been able to reveal. He tried to remember what had gone wrong. Then he tried even harder to forget. But he couldn't.

He seemed different to many, more serious and reserved, a man driven toward a single goal. The program manager who came back to work after the accident was aggressive, prone to pushing his crews without mercy, sometimes regarding a minor problem as a personal attack. Daniel tried to focus on the unrelenting deadline which loomed ever nearer. It was the only way to forestall the image that haunted him. Christina standing in front of the fireplace, its glow bouncing off the tears in her eyes. He was running out of time. And choices.

Chief Todd's condition steadily deteriorated. His voice lost its ring of bullish authority and he stayed more in his office to hide the debilitating changes that were occurring. Using the VAL-2700 central computer to keep track of the company's daily operation, he was amazed at Daniel's progress. He was demanding, but he was very efficient and the first functional test was soon at hand.

# # #

Thomas stood on a steel grate ladder, supervising calibrations for the support equipment, when he noticed his friend watching sullenly from the door. He waved a half-eaten doughnut.

"Danny, glad to see you. Come on in and take a look. The guys at Physics almost have this speed demon ready for a test drive."

Daniel gave a cursory nod. "Good, I want to send the first specimen next week."

"Next week?" Thomas jumped down. "Get serious. We've just barely put all the pieces together. What did the Chief say about an extension?"

"I didn't ask him."

"You know it has to be calibrated, who knows how many parameters are affected? We need at least a week for system checks—"

"And double checks and triple checks," Daniel interrupted. "Then what, a long, drawn out series of tests using every conceivable lab specimen from white mice to primates?"

"Well, yeah. I guess that's a fair, if not over simplified summary of the test plan. We have to make sure it's safe."

"The Chief could die of old age in less time than that!"

"You mean because of that strange disease?"

"What do you know about that?"

Thomas shrugged. "Exponential Aging Syndrome or something like that."

Daniel was surprised.

"I like to go through the files occasionally. So what's the big deal? He'll get a nice medical retirement. I doubt if the next chief administrator would try to cancel your project."

"I guess that part wasn't in the files, yet."

"What do you mean?"

Daniel backed out into the hall and glanced around. "No one's supposed to know, but the old codger is trying to force the administrator's title on me."

Thomas' smirk died before it started. "Are you serious?"

"Tom, you've got to help me. And you've got to cut a few corners. Work them all night if you have to. Kick 'em in the butt if it helps, but we have to finish this."

Thomas removed his glasses. "What kind of cuts are you talking about?"

"We have to make the test run with the calibrated mass next week, then one more with a live subject."

Thomas almost dropped his glasses. "Only one?"

"Why not? If the monkey can survive the trip, I'm sure I can."

"What happened to the safety factor? Have you forgotten what we're working with here? One small leak and you'll have more gray hair than a Geritol convention. Jeez, just look what it did to Chief Todd!"

"I know all about it. I just came from his office and he looks like crap."

"So do you," Thomas added.

# # #

The following week was the longest Daniel had ever endured. One problem after another threatened to delay the test run. Daniel had bribed, coaxed, or bullied solutions from his team leaders, refusing to accept any delay. Thomas and his crew had worked continuous shifts through the weekend to finish. They were nearly exhausted, but no one wanted to leave and miss seeing they "baby" turned on. Some even made up excuses about last minute items that had to be monitored as a reason to linger.

The control room was packed, a mass of blue and brown smocks speckled with the white lab coats. Next door in the Launch Room, as someone had named it, two technicians in sterilized surgical gowns made final checks of the main unit. Maintaining the Chief's required safety conditions had not been easy. A nervous medtech shadowed their every move, trailing along like a curious puppy, wagging his biomonitor and as he tried to observe everyone and everything.

Daniel stood impatiently on the steel ladder that led up to the capsule. He was waiting for some idiot assist-tech to deliver the test load. The precisely engineered twelve inch globe was composed of exactly one kilogram of titanium gold alloy. Its exact mass had been verified with the National Bureau of Standards. Its hollow design made it extremely sensitive to stress and would give graphic proof of the kinetic balance of the anti-magnetic field, or lack of it. He had decided to send someone to find the lost moron when he was startled to see Chief Todd approaching the base of the ladder, carrying the test load.

"Chief! Glad to see you could make it."

"I'm not a complete hermit yet. I wanted to bring your pilot myself." Chief Todd carefully handed the highly polished sphere to Daniel.

"I understand the engraving was Christina's idea."

Daniel shuddered when he touched it. He had almost forgotten. Christina finished it just before the end of her apprenticeship.

Chief Todd took an awkward step back. "It's a greeting in several languages. It seems the lads couldn't agree on where it was going. Future or past. Or if it's going anywhere. Since she didn't know who might read the message, she used English and Latin."

Daniel stared silently for a moment, then placed the sphere on the contoured seat. The inscription wished a blessing of peace and prosperity to whoever finds it. It was signed, "Friends From Afar." To fill the surplus of blank shiny space, she had apparently borrowed Da Vinci's pictogram—the same one NASA sent on the Voyager probe—just in case it went somewhere they couldn't read yet, or still.

Daniel closed the hatch and gave the first genuine smile in months.

"What is it?" the Chief asked.

"Huh? Oh, nothing, just thinking about Da Vinci's original picture. I wonder if he'd appreciate Christy's humor. Evidently she decided to improve it a little."

"What do you mean?"

Daniel grinned again. "Didn't you notice? Da Vinci's picture was a man."

In the adjoining room Chief Todd had hobbled in to peer over Thomas' shoulder to inspect the flickering control panel. "How does it look? Energy readings, I mean."

Thomas shrugged. "All readings nominal, so far. Lunch Room's clear!"

Daniel glanced up at the monitor for confirmation.

A hush blanketed the room during the final minutes of automated system checks. Imperceptibly the room filled with a low humming sound as huge transformers built up their tremendous store of power. Then an angry whine raced through the room as the Tachyon drive screamed to life, propelling the capsule along its circular track.

The capsule spun around the evacuated doughnut tube, whirling faster and faster until it could reach the theoretical velocity so extreme it would actually complete one revolution before it started. That was the moment it would slip out of the flow of Time. Hopefully. After that, nobody knew.

The reinforced concrete room shuddered with uncertainty as the next room struggled to contain energies and forces which most people couldn't even imagine. Drawing enough electricity to power a small city, they were creating magnetic fields strong enough to warp steel beams, and forming a spatial disturbance capable of bending temporal flux lines. Daniel could almost see the anti-magnetic flux field surrounding the tube, repelling and canceling the colossal inertial and temporal effects.

He looked closer at the monitor. He could see it! A pale blue corona glittered with indigo flashes. The wisps of plasma reached out in twisted streaks, whipping about the surrounding equipment with the vehemence of a hundred writhing snakes flailed by some ghostly Medusa. He ran to the thick alloy viewport to look directly at the apparition, but saw no apparent damage where they touched.

A smile of pride and achievement reflected off the viewport. He could almost feel the searing, time distorting cosmic static; feel the throbbing, pulsing energy coursing through his body. The smile vanished and he looked at his feet in surprise.

Chief Todd looked quickly around the room. "What's that?"

Everyone could feel it, an ominous vibration that crept from the floor through their shoes. And it was growing.

"Harmonic vibrations!" Thomas yelled, trying to explain what any first-year physics student already knew.

"I'm not sure the building can stand the stress ..." He saw Chief Todd's mouth moving, but his voice disappeared in the uproar.

Someone nudged Daniel and pointed to a dial.

The delicate instruments, which had been steadily climbing in unison, were now pegged past maximum, straining to move even farther with another energy surge.

The noise stopped instantly, exploding with a silence that left ears ringing with nothingness, as if the giant power dynamo had suddenly disappeared. For a moment no one moved. Then a white faced technician, who had been monitoring the control panel beside Thomas, broke the silence.

"Shi-yut! I mean, condition normal," he corrected. "Readings are nominal. Event duration was, uh, only seventy two seconds? Confirmed full power shutdown now complete."

Daniel bolted for the heavy double doors connecting the two rooms. Medtechs hurried to catch up, fumbling to adjust their radiation monitors on the way.

He pawed awkwardly at the latching mechanism to open the capsule. Questions filled his mind as he swung the cover up and open. Would Christina's sphere still be there? What if it was damaged? If it was still inside, how would he prove it ever left? He froze in mid-thought, staring open-mouthed at the object before him.

Thomas stood on tiptoes behind him, peering over his shoulder. "Well, what is it? Is it gone?"

In the cushioned seat sat a round, engraved golden wafer whose engraved letters had become melded together into distorted glyphs. Something had smashed it thinner than a compact video disk. He lifted the engraved disc out of the capsule and turned around.

The room was filled with curious faces gawking in awe. No one spoke, except Bill.

"Jasper, that's flatter than Aunt Emma's chest!"

Daniel curiously examined, then handed the yellow disk with its misshapen caricature of a woman to an assist tech standing behind him.

"Yep. Flatter than a silicon fart," Bill concluded.

Daniel looked up to his friend and flashed a cold stare of command that Thomas understood. He pushed his way through the crowd, summoning his calibration crew.

"Double check everything," he ordered. "I want every measurement verified."

Daniel returned to the control panel where a chart recorder had transcribed a wide band spectrum of energy levels during the brief event. A pile of fanfold paper lay on the floor. He ripped the graph paper from the printer and started to take it away. He paused to frown. It wasn't what he had expected to see. The chart's squiggly line formed two jagged mountain peaks that leaped off the edge of the paper. The twin peaks of power surge were separated by a narrow valley where the recorder had measured nothing, no energy at all.

The Chief barked a raspy command from the back of the crowd before limping away. "Preliminary report. My desk in two hours."

It took Thomas more than two hours to feel certain, but when he entered the teak and mahogany office where Daniel and Chief Todd were waiting, he nodded with confidence. He sat in the empty chair next to Daniel directly in front of the administrator's desk.

"Main unit's been verified," he said. "And it all checks out, every parameter measured up to specs." Thomas felt a little too close the administrator's desk and leaned the chair back on its edge.

"So it wasn't centrifugal, or centripetal, forces that flattened the ball." Daniel concluded.

Chief Todd did not seem convinced. "Then what did?"

"Beats me," Thomas answered.

"You sure the machine's all right?" Daniel asked.

"Sure."

Daniel's smug look returned. Thomas had confirmed what he had already felt inside, and what he'd just asserted moments before to the Chief.

"We don't know for sure where it went, but we can assume the damage was done at its interim destination before it returned."

Chief Todd bit down on his cigar. "We don't know that it ever left."

"Yes we do," Daniel said. "Timeslip definitely occurred. Those graphs prove it."

He had spread several sheets of fanfold over the Chief's desk and had been explaining their significance before Thomas arrived. The first chart depicted what the actual power curve should have been, a standard bell curve shape depicting an increase of power from zero to maximum, back to zero.

Thomas peered over the desk. "That's not what I saw."

"He's right." Daniel pulled another sheet from underneath. "Here's the actual printout. See the double spike in the middle? There's the proof."

Thomas studied the graph a moment, and then nodded. "You're right. It is a power curve, actually two parts of the same curve back to back.

"Are you both out of your minds?" the Chief suggested.

"Look, they're plotted in relation to time. The tachyon energy from the drive went through a time phase distortion."

"A what?"

Thomas ripped the paper in half and rearranged the pieces. When he did, the familiar bell shaped curve was reformed. "The first spike is actually the second half of the projected power curve at the moment of Timeslip. So it appeared before the first transition."

Daniel nodded. "It's the classic indication. The decaying tachyon particle appears before the parent element has decomposed."

"Exactly," Thomas agreed. "The instruments could only record the total energy sensed at a specific time. They couldn't distinguish between the present energy and the past future energy produced by the capsule's return."

Chief Todd shook his head. "Past future? Tom, do you two really understand what you're talking about?"

Thomas shrugged slowly. "Maybe not all of it, but the sphere obviously left our time and was damaged by some outside source."

"Even if I buy your double spike theory, you haven't substantiated any outside force."

"Tom, did you, or anyone you know, handle that thing with bare hands?" Daniel asked.

"Of course not, it was clean room environment the whole time."

"Then how do you explain the fingerprints?"

Thomas and Chief Todd looked to each other in surprise. "Are you sure?"

"Dozens of them. And they don't belong to anyone at the Complex either. It was an outside source," Daniel continued. "That makes it only a fluke, an accident beyond the experiment's control. We can send the monkey tomorrow."

Chief Todd leaned back and chewed his cigar. "I don't know."

Daniel lunged forward to lean over the startled administrator's desk. "If you stand in my way now, it's over and you know it. Keep your word on this, or the deal's off."

A younger Chief Todd would have backhanded the insolent subordinate and carried on casually. But he was too old now for that, and too much was at stake.

He rubbed a sweaty forehead, looking as though he found it difficult to even remember all the details of his "deal" with Daniel.

"If that chimp returns in any condition less than perfect, you're grounded. Permanently. Understand?"

Daniel's stomach tightened over the startling image of a primate pancake. He nodded. One way or the other, they would both know tomorrow.

The day began early, too early. After weeks of lost sleep Daniel's body craved rest, but he had been unable to get much the night before. Too many unanswered questions kept returning.

He stared into the mirror of the washroom as he splashed more cold water on his face. Bleary eyes with puffy circles stared back. He peeled off his old contacts and threw them away, replacing them with a new set of DisposaLens. Then he slicked his uncombed hair with his wet hands and took two more pills, dry. They were necessary, he thought. Just a little while longer, then he'd be able to get enough sleep and he wouldn't need them.

Bio Med had certified Sam, the rhesus, to be in perfect health. The telemetry electrodes, attached to his scalp, chest, and inner thighs, would closely monitor all bodily functions during the first phase of Timeslip. The launch room belonged to Bio-Med today, and they were treating it like an operating room, including sterilized gloves and gowns for everyone. For the first time, Daniel noticed that all of the workers, assistants, engineers, and med-techs wore the same color garments as they moved around the equipment. He smiled. Equality can be a good thing, he thought. But it might be a dangerous concept to introduce to the peasants of this little techno-serfdom.

Daniel walked over to where Thomas was guarding the system console with an almost motherly instinct.

"You ready?"

"Ready as I'll ever be. I installed a buffer on the power sensor. It might protect it from overload, but I wouldn't bet on it."

Daniel glanced up to the video monitor and saw the last technician leaving the launch room. His pulse quickened; the moment of launch was only a few seconds away and with it the Chief's final approval, or disapproval, for his attempt.

"Let's get this monkey on his way." He tried to sound relaxed, but didn't mask his nervousness very well.

Thomas nodded and set the controls to auto for the final phase of countdown. Three minutes later, the familiar low pitched hum once more filled the air.

Daniel was the last to slip the "mouse ears" over his head. He hated the twin, cup shaped hearing protectors which Bio Med had issued for everyone. They were uncomfortable; they made his ears itch. And they messed up his hair. With a little imagination, the bulbous attenuators did give everyone the semblance of the old cartoon character. They didn't fit his image. He was more suave than that. He looked at Thomas and grinned; the mouse ears looked good on him.

"His pulse rate just jumped over ninety," announced the medtech who was monitoring Sam's vitals. "A little excited but that's understandable."

Sam's was not the only rapid pulse. Daniel stood at the viewport knowing too well how much his ride through the frontier of Time depended upon the success of Sam's trip. Discovering a squashed primate in the capsule would be more than just messy, it would permanently ground his project.

The vibration grew more intense than before. He anxiously watched the glowing tube, squinting as the noise became unbearable even with the hearing protectors. He clenched his teeth against the raging intensity that soon passed beyond the distinctions of sound and touch.

Thomas sat at the console, no longer able to read any of the instruments before him as he squeezed the attenuators against his ears. The souls of his feet tingled from the painful, high frequency buzz that came up from the floor like a clawing animal. Then came a penetrating snap, like the crack of a high powered rifle. The tempered glass covers that protected the gauges had shattered, spraying jagged slivers onto his lap.

Then, as suddenly as the first time, it was over. The noise evaporated, leaving a dead calm in the room as if the center of the tremendous storm had passed over with eerie stillness. Fine, silvery particles of ceiling tiles glittered in the dusty air like weightless snowflakes.

"I think this slip was worse than the last!" someone said.

Thomas ignored the obvious comment as he brushed the shards of glass off his lap and inspect the damaged control panel. Glass slivers sparkled everywhere. The newly installed power sensor buffer was now only an acrid charred smell in the air. He shook his head. Something was wrong. His calculations, which had been based on the original one kilogram launch, did not predict this much energy being released for only 10 kilograms of monkey. What would happen on Daniel's trip?

In the next room two medtechs, Bill and Fred, clambered up the steel ladder to remove Sam from the capsule. As one swung open the hatch, the other reeled away covering his nose.

"Jeez-zus, what a smell! Look at all this crap."

"Shut-up, Fred, and catch the little hairball."

Fred managed to corral the over-excited rhesus, but couldn't decide how to best hold him. "Damn, who's gonna clean this up? Not me, I'll tell you that. I'm a medtech, not a friggin' zoo keeper!"

Daniel waited at the base of the narrow ladder. "What's the matter? Is he all right?"

"I think so," Bill answered as he brought Sam down to the medical cart. "But look at what he did all over your capsule."

To look inside, Daniel had to hold his nose too. Dumpy brown piles littered the cabin, and paw marks smeared the padded seat and window.

"What happened?"

"He crapped all over everything!" Fred answered with a nasal voice. "That's what happened. Just look at it, monkey crap everywhere."

"I can see that." Daniel backed away to cleaner air. "But why?"

"Damned hairballs. That's all they're good for. If they can't eat it, or screw it, they'll just crap on it!"

"Maybe the ride scared it out of him," Bill said. "He looks okay. We'll let you know for sure in about an hour. Chief wants a full set of tests, ya know. Come on, Fred, let's get this hairball out of here.

"You're giving the little shithead a bath, not me."

The medical team was given a wide berth as they wheeled Sam out and headed to Bio Med. Thomas walked up and tugged on Daniel's arm. "Buy you a cup of coffee?"

"Thanks, but I need to …"

"You need a cup of coffee," Thomas insisted, "while Medical checks out our little friend." He pinched his nose. "And in his case I think it'll take a while to make it a clean bill of health."

Even after three cups of coffee and a doughnut, the Bio-Med Department had still not called with their report. Daniel decided to see what he could do to speed them up.

The discourteous medical assistant stood determinedly in the entrance.

"I said no!"

"It's all right, I can come in. I'm Daniel Williams, the new assistant administrator."

"And I'm Fred the frigging medtech with monkey crap all over me!" He pushed Daniel back into the hall to close the door. "We'll call when we're through."

He wandered back to his office. There were other things to worry about, and he had to organize for the following day. Thomas would repair the damage to the console. His crew was already inspecting the generators and Tachyon drive. What does one wear to the Future? Or the Past? Should he pack an overnight bag?

The couch was soft and inviting. He could sure use a few minutes rest, but there was still so much to do. The long months of grueling meetings, planning sessions, design reviews, personnel squabbles that arose from interdepartmental rivalry, and the resulting stress had taken its toll on him in recent weeks. It felt so good to close his eyes. Too good.

He awoke, instantly alert at the sound of his door sliding open.

"Sorry, I didn't know," Thomas apologized. "I'll come back later."

"No, it's alright. I don't have time to sleep anyway."

Thomas entered reluctantly. "I just wanted to let you know. Sam's fine."

"Are you sure?"

"I know one of the assist-techs in medical who just sent the full report to the Chief. He's looking it over right now. Sam's a little dehydrated, and apparently half-starved, but he's okay. No side effects!"

Daniel bounced off the couch. "Yes! Yes! I knew it. We're all set to go."

"Hey, slow down." Thomas reached out to grab him as he darted for the door, but missed.

"Tomorrow, it's my turn. I finally get to go!" Daniel sighed with relief. For a moment, the burden of responsibility eased. His goal was in sight. Soon he would be rid of all the responsibility and headaches of running such a large project.

No. He wouldn't. He remembered the Chief's plans. He still hadn't figured a way out of that one, yet. The tightness in his forehead returned.

"It's good to see you happy about something. It's been a long time. But I wanted to talk about something else, too."

"What? The machine will be ready, won't it?"

Thomas sat down on the couch and removed his glasses. Daniel hated it when he removed his glasses.

"Danny, about the support equipment …"

"What's wrong? A few broken meter lenses maybe, but you can fix that."

"So far the damage is minor and easily repairable, but …" Thomas fidgeted with his glasses.

"But what?"

"It's the power level. Today's trip generated so much more power than before." He spread his hands to indicate the difference and then gave up. "You remember that buffer I put in? To protect the power sensor?"

"What about it?"

"That buffer was heavy duty, good for a full megawatt of normal power with ease. And you scorched it. Do you understand what I'm saying? I can't even begin to guess how much energy was dissipated this morning. But do know this, it's completely out of proportion for the difference in mass."

"And I weigh more than a monkey, is that it? Just put in a bigger buffer."

"They don't come any bigger. Besides, that's not the point. It doesn't take a rocket scientist with a precision power meter to see what's happening."

"So what's the problem?"

Thomas stood up in a rarely seen intimidating stance. "What happens next time? My last calculations were off by a factor of ten. If your trip releases the same logarithmic increase over the last, it's going to shake the hell out of this entire Complex."

Daniel nodded understanding and lay back on the couch. "Whether it's successful or not, tomorrow will probably be the last time that machine is used. So, that means it'll have to be successful, won't it?"

# # #

Thomas stayed late into the night installing his prototype crystal buffer and giving the equipment one last look over. His untested device would now get a perfect chance to prove itself against the capsule's tremendous energy. However, there was nothing he could do to protect the rest of the equipment. Once started, the capsule and its self contained drive unit would perform independently. Any malfunction in the console would have little effect. He hoped.

The impatient assist tech made the last ceramic solder connection and hastily began cleaning up to go. "It won't do any good, you know."

"What's that?"

"This power buffer. It's like stuffing cotton into his ears before juggling the nitro. Odds in the crew lounge are three to five against."

Thomas nodded agreement. "You're probably right. It'll shake itself to pieces from the harmonic vibrations alone."

"Probably so," echoed a voice behind him. Chief Todd stood with two crutches locked rigidly around his forearms.

"I'm not as old as I look," he continued, as Thomas tried to cover his look of surprise. "I saw what happened yesterday. And again this morning. I'm afraid tomorrow's launch may well destroy this wing of the Complex."

"You're not going to scrub the mission, are you?"

The Chief studied the control panel with its dangling wires, then glanced at the video monitor and the empty Launch Room. He turned to make his way out.

"No, we made a deal. Even if it kills him." He paused in front of the assist-tech who was hurriedly cleaning up the debris of wire clippings and solder splatters. "You said the odds were three to five against. Against what?"

The embarrassed assist-tech stuffed the collection of bills in her pocket. "On coming back, Sir."

The old administrator seemed to consider her answer for a moment and then answered. "I'm sure you know I don't condone gambling."

"Yessir."

"Good." he started out of the room. "Put me down for a hundred." He stopped by Daniel's office to find him sprawled on the couch, one leg dangling above the floor. He scribbled a quick DO NOT DISTURB sign, signed it, and attached it to the outside of the door.

# # #

The next morning, Daniel stumbled furiously into the Launch Room. "It's almost ten thirty! Why didn't someone wake me?"

"Relax," the Chief said casually. "Have some coffee."

"But look at the time!"

"We managed to get along remarkably well without you so far. And I decided you needed rest more than anything else."

Thomas nodded. "Sorry, but he threatened bodily harm to the first person who disturbed you."

"Here." Chief Todd held out a cup of coffee. "Take this and keep quiet. There's doughnuts in the corner."

Daniel took a sip of the relaxing hot coffee. It was good, but he tried not to show it. The old man had been right about needing the sleep, too. He grabbed a cinnamon roll and followed him into the launch room.

"So how's it going?" he asked. No one answered.

Several technicians passed by on their way out. Soon only Thomas, Chief Todd, and Greg, who was Thomas' first assistant, remained. Daniel could see the medtechs waiting next door.

"What's going on?"

Thomas took his arm and escorted him to the capsule. "It's time, Danny. T minus five minutes and counting."

Daniel choked on the dry doughnut and gulped the remainder of the coffee to wash it down, singeing his tongue in the process.

"Sure you don't want to change your mind about this?" Thomas fastened the restraining harness, giving it a solid jerk. "You can't change your mind once that tachyon motor fires up."

"Not a chance. I've got to go."

"Yeah. I know." Thomas stepped out of the way of an assist tech securing the hatch on the capsule. "Don't forget to write!"

The capsule's hatch slammed shut and Daniel squirmed to get comfortable on the thinly padded reclining seat. It was slightly contoured for an anatomical fit, but not exactly his contour. He scanned the capsule's Spartan interior. Only a few instruments. Most of the connections dangling from the dash were leftovers from Sam's telemetry electrodes. Daniel had refused to wear them.

A precision G Meter, calibrated in milligravs, huddled in the center of the panel. Below it sat a hydrogen maser clock which had been added as an afterthought to Sam's return. How simple it would have been, he thought, to send an accurate clock along to measure the actual time spent out of the present. It was too simple for a group of genius scientists. The janitor probably suggested it. He'd been too worried about whether or not Sam would make it back alive to think about the clock.

He picked up the intercom headset, adjusted it to fit, and tested the voice-activated microphone. "Testing, testing. One thousand, two thousand, three thousand years."

Thomas' voice answered through the headset. "Toto, this is Dorothy. Standby to leave Kansas."

"Leave the jokes to me, okay? You're supposed to be the professional."

"T minus two minutes. Computer shows all systems nominal. And who told you that you that I don't have a sense of humor?"

Thomas ignored a stern look from Chief Todd. "Welcome to Trans Spatial Airlines; this is your captain speaking. We hope you enjoy your flight this morning, wherever … or should I say whenever you're going. Please return all trays and seat backs to their full upright position. And enjoy your trip."

Not to be outdone, Daniel added, "And please keep your arms and feet fully inside the capsule at all times …" The Tachyon drive activated with crushing vengeance, snapping his head back against the seat as the capsule lurched forward, molding his body into the cushioned seat.

He began to spin faster and faster around the tube. The whine heard earlier next door became a thundering roar like the old freight trains he had seen in the holomovies. Only this one was rumbling by only inches from his ear.

"What a ride!" he shouted into the microphone, but no one answered.

The capsule spun faster, pressing him deeper into the padded seat. He forced a swallow to keep his ears open. The rumbling, whining maelstrom increased, threatening to deafen him as his velocity approached the boundary of normal physics. The cabin changed color as the room's light transform from amber to dull red. The plastilloy viewport seemed to take on an iridescent quality. When he looked forward he saw red; when he strained to look toward the rear through the window he saw blue. Then the window became totally black, as the capsule's velocity went beyond hyper—where even absolutes became relative. Inside the absolute blackness, he felt a crushing surge of acceleration. Approaching ludicrous, he thought, gritting his teeth.

The capsule shuddered. Then came the silence. His senses dulled, leaving only the pressure and the ringing in his ears. He started to wonder if he were unconscious and floating in the dark nothingness of cosmic eternity, when he suddenly slammed forward against the harness, his chest straining to rip the straps from their hinges like a dentist pulling a stubborn molar.

He was beginning his deceleration back into the flow of time. Thomas should've programmed a more gradual braking sequence, he noted painfully. His eyes felt as if they were bulging out of his head; his neck strained from trying to hold his head straight, and he felt nauseous. He thought he smelled excrement. His stomach quivered like a subterranean geyser about to spew. He felt sorry for Sam.

A dim light penetrated the murky blackness, taking his mind away from his stomach. Slowly he turned his head to watch through the viewport as the light changed from a flickering glow to a pulsing series of flashing streaks that passed the window like speeding cars on a dark rainy night. Gradually the tugging of the chest straps subsided. Slowly, the capsule skidded to a grinding stop.

Chapter 7

Escaping gas hissed like an angry snake as compressed air, stored inside the nose of the capsule, as it equalized the vacuum of the tube. When the hissing subsided, Daniel reached for the hatch. The bolt was stuck. He jerked on it repeatedly, realizing the precision fit had allowed no tolerance for warping under stress. Finally the stubborn bolt crept far enough to open the stubborn hatch and wiggle through.

He crawled hurriedly through the still warm tube till he reached the outer seal. The seal, which was held in place with non-metallic bolts and designed to hold a vacuum, not pressure, gave way to a firm kick and dropped to a dusty floor.

He scanned the room. The room appeared to have been abandoned for some time. Most of the ancillary equipment of the launch room was now missing, vanished in seconds. Only the tube and its huge power transformer remained. The streaking light that had greeted his arrival was a dim emergency exit sign over the door. Everything else sat quiet and lifeless as a grave, blanketed under a powdery layer of fine dust. As he crawled out, his hand left wavy pairs of parallel tracks on top of the gritty tube. A dry, musty smell lingered in the air and he didn't like the silence.

"VAL?"

No answer, only an echo.

He followed the dull reddish glow of exit signs that dotted the corridors like a string of measles. Everywhere, fine dust covered the floor, giving the abandoned corridors the murky appearance of catacombs filled with dead memories. And stale air.

He cued an elevator, but it too was dead, forcing him to grope his way up five flights of unlit stairs. He fumbled upward through the blackness, running his hand along the gritty railing and feeling the dust cake to sweaty palm.

The top floor seemed almost normal in the filtered twilight. Desks, room dividers, and computer terminals sat peacefully undisturbed as if it were any other empty office building on a deserted weekend. But the tranquil view disturbed him as he walked the corridors of his past and found no evidence of a lasting contribution. Nothing remained of himself or the others. He tried not to think about it as he hurried to an exit.

Then he stepped into the cool desert air, squinting against the morning sunlight to investigate the surrounding landscape.

Chapter 8

Ten kilometers away from the Complex, Daniel heard a high-pitched whine approaching from behind. He strained to make out the object concealed by the heat waves jumping off the simmering blacktop. It seemed to be following, but not quite touching, the road. Minutes later, a scratched and dusty vehicle floated to a stop and hovered beside him. A door screeched open and lowered a rusty red boarding ramp with patches of bare metal polished by a generation of shuffling feet. Daniel gratefully accepted the ride.

The airbus was filled with passengers, all blacks, including the driver who closed the door almost before Daniel was in. Since the driver paid no attention to his boarding, or the fact that he hadn't offered to deposit any fare, Daniel did his best not to look out of place. As the driver resumed his hasty journey with a jerk, Daniel stumbled into the nearest seat, beside an elderly woman on the first row.

Being alone among a different ethnic crowd had always given him a feeling of insecurity, but he felt extremely self-conscious at the moment as though he was being stared at.

He looked around. He was being stared at. A dozen black faces glowered at him, offering feelings of disgust, contempt, and even hate.

"Get in the back, Bios!" the driver ordered.

Daniel turned to the black lady beside him. "Is he talking to me?"

"You Bios know your place!" she answered. Her nose wrinkled as if violated by some evil smell. She nodded to the rear of the airbus. "In the back."

He waded through the waves of penetrating stares to the back where he noticed some other passengers, lighter skin color than the rest, crammed together in the last two rows of seats.

"S'down here, son," an old man offered, patting the seat without looking up.

Daniel offered a friendly smile, but it wasn't returned.

They weren't blacks, but they weren't Caucasians either. They had high cheek bones (smudged brown), pronounced nose ridges, and thick black hair which the men wore braided or tied in a long wiry ponytail. A pair of women, sitting quietly by themselves, wore theirs only slightly combed, trailing straight down their backs. He also became quickly aware of their cleanliness, or lack of it. The odor of skin untouched by water for days, maybe weeks. It wasn't difficult to understand why they would be positioned downwind from the other passengers. But why him?

He tried to get a better look at them without noticeably staring. Unlike the black passengers up front, with their nice clothes in well-kept condition, the backseat class looked a little worse for wear. Their clothes were dirty, showing mended tears and frequent patches.

A pair of intense black eyes met his. He turned away to look out the dust covered window, wishing he had chosen a place closer to the window, closer to fresh air.

The scenery whined by, kilometers of dry Texas plains punctuated by occasional patches of irrigated greenery.

"What Clan?" the wiry man beside him asked in broken English.

"What?"

"What Clan you from?"

"I'm not from a Clan," Daniel answered.

"Skin's fair, chalky," the wrinkled man commented. "Not work outside."

The old man's skin, darkly tanned and heavily creased like a pair of worn out shoes, had spent a lifetime outside. Daniel's hands seemed pale in comparison. It had been a while, Daniel thought, since he had spent some time sunning at the beach. After all, the nearest beach was five-hundred miles away.

"Where we going?" he asked, trying to keep the awkward conversation alive.

The old man turned to look at him for the first time. It was almost a stare of suspicion. "Work."

Daniel fidgeted in the seat, uncomfortable under the man's close examination. "I just got here this morning," he explained, trying to satisfy the man's curiosity.

"Got no Clan. Got no job. You one, poor Bios."

Daniel wanted to ask what a Bios was, but decided not to display all of his ignorance at one time. Asking what year it was seemed totally out of the question. Instead, he shrugged his shoulders in agreement and waited to see if the old man would offer any hints.

He didn't.

The airbus slowed to a stop and then hovered while four black passengers disembarked. Daniel's heart jumped at the thought of the old man getting off and leaving him alone. When the airbus took off again he relaxed a little, but when five or six more front-end passengers descended the exit ramp at the next stop, Daniel sensed the man becoming restless.

"Are you getting off soon?"

"Yup. Next stop."

Should he follow him? Where should he start first with his exploration? He had hundreds of questions. The old man wasn't answering any, but at least he was friendly. Almost.

"I don't suppose I could find work there with you, mister ..."

The man leaned over with a grunt, his brittle skin almost crackling. "This one is Ben-on." He examined Daniel's hand, rubbing it between stained fingers. "This one looks for herbs today. Pick some, buy some." He turned Daniel's smooth palm over and rubbed a scratchy finger across it. "Got no calluses. Soft like wo'ams."

"Wo'ams?"

"Must be houseboy. Too softs for nothing else. Talk smooth like one, too. Talk almost like Perf."

"Perf?" Daniel echoed.

The old man's look of confusion returned and Daniel dropped his question as though he had never asked it.

"What kinda worker permit you got?"

"I uh, I don't. Where do I get this permit?"

Ben-on's face once more wrinkled into a frown. "From social worker, where else?" He pointed to three men who sat across the aisle.

"If want job, follow them," he said. "Their boss need houseboy. But she don't hire no lily whites. And best have permit, or won't get spit round here."

The airbus slowed again and Ben-on stood to leave. His attitude hadn't exactly been cordial, but Daniel felt obliged say something.

"See you around."

Ben-on raised his hand to a near wave as he shuffled to the exit ramp. The three younger men acknowledged the old man's departure, but seemed unaware of Daniel's existence.

"Excuse me," he said to get their attention. "That gentleman said you all might know where I could find work."

They turned, their dirty faces looking him up and down as if unsure what to make of him. Their lingering gaze made him feel like an alien with a sign hung around his neck.

"You gardener?" one of them asked.

"Uh, no. Not exactly."

"Don't know, less you be houseboy."

"That's right," he said, remembering the old man's comments. "I'm a houseboy."

"Le'me see permit."

"Well, I don't exactly have one yet."

"No permit, no work for her. That's law."

"Her?" Daniel perked up. "You got a woman boss?"

The tallest of the three seemed upset. He shook his head. "Ain't got time for him. You wanna be late and make Miss Lillian mad?"

"No, brother," the first boy answered. "Not mad, she wants houseboy real bad. Maybe we get bonus for bring'n him."

The third dirty face nodded agreement. "Bonus sounds good to me."

When the airbus stopped again, the three lanky boys stood up. They resembled a group of scarecrows with black straw hair. Daniel followed them off into the street. They were in the city of Midessa, somewhere. Maybe the outskirts, or what used to be the outskirts of town; it must have grown outward, annexing Newtown. Tall buildings, the distinguishing trait of the city in his time, were still plentiful but displayed a markedly different style. Geometric shapes protruded from the otherwise sleek lines, looking like odd growths or tumors of architecture.

He followed the trio along the nearly empty sidewalk past two intersections before they stopped at one of the more modest and unadorned buildings, plain gray adobe with bars over the windows. Government buildings would always look the same. Drab and run down.

The three waited outside while Daniel went in and waited in line to get a ticket. He waited in another line to get it stamped. Finally he sat in front of the social worker's desk, a fat black woman who sweated too much.

She smiled in a condescending way that was almost friendly. "What can I do for you?"

"I need a permit, I guess."

"I'm sorry. We don't have any open positions for employment at the moment. However, I can arrange for some food stamps."

"You don't understand, Miss …?"

"Delilah," she said, readjusting the nameplate on her desk.

"You see, I have a position waiting, as soon as I get the permit."

"You do? For what kind of employment?" She keyed something into her terminal.

"The position of houseboy, Ma'am."

"I see. Well, that's different. A good houseboy is always in demand." She held her hand out. "Your green-card, please."

"My what?"

"Your green-card," she said slowly. "From Immigration."

Daniel shrugged.

Mrs. Delilah wiped her moist face and rolled her eyes to the ceiling fan that turned slowly overhead. "Look, I can't help you people if you don't cooperate. You know you must bring all of your paperwork or my hands are tied."

He stood in another line for his green card to certify non-fugitive, non-dissident status. The clerk insisted that he shouldn't have given Daniel a green card without his sponsor, but he seemed like a nice boy. It was also near quitting time for his shift and too hot to work overtime. They took his picture, not very flattering, and issued a number on the green plastic. He took it back to the social worker who inspected it with less enthusiasm than she did the clock on her desk before typing frantically on her keyboard.

"Name?"

"Williams. Daniel Williams."

She paused to stare at him. "Are you sure?"

"What? Yes, I'm sure. I haven't forgotten my name for a long time now."

She resumed typing. "Employer?"

"Miss Lillian. Sorry, I don't know her first name."

The fat social worker seemed to sneer. "Not necessary. I'm sure I know which one."

# # #

The three boys and Daniel rode the lavish elevator to the penthouse. Golden thread—he touched it to make sure it was real—glittered in the soft lighting. The extravagance made him wonder. This Miss Lillian's got to be rich to live here, he thought. And good looking.

During the ascent, he learned the names of his fellow workers, three brothers from some place called the Grotto Clan. Allon was the oldest even though Banion stood half a head taller. Dillon, the youngest of the three, had little to say and never smiled. Constricted black pupils, like pebbles of coal resting in a brown puddle, stared endlessly back at the white newcomer.

The elevator opened to reveal a small, carefully manicured forest with trees, grass, shrubs, and wild spices that colored the moist warm air with fragrant hues. A cobblestone path led from the elevator into the lush verdure. Two fluffy-tailed squirrels scurried across the path. They raced to the nearest tree, climbed the backside, and then peeked around to study the intruders.

Allon called out with a high voice that sounded almost timid. "Miss Lillian? Miss Lillian, you up, Ma'am?"

A dark figure stepped from behind a neatly cropped rose bush. Short, kinky hair accented her broad nose and slender neck. Her hands rested on firm, round hips.

"Two hours late?"

Allon stammered a little, as if arranging his lie. "We uh, we know'd how you was looking for a houseboy, Ma'am."

"You've brought me a houseboy?"

Daniel stepped forward.

"Well, I shall have to review him before I decide whether or not to excuse your tardiness." She approached the group with long graceful strides. He couldn't help but admire her slender beauty, its well-proportioned curves only slightly concealed beneath the translucent evening gown. Her legs seemed to go up forever. She was tall, Daniel noticed, taller than he. She stepped close to inspect him. The closer she got, the more beautiful she became. And the stronger her perfume became earthy sweet and exciting.

"My name is—"

"You best mind your manners," she said, cutting him off. "Proper etiquette is as important, if not more so, than handsome grooming and good breeding." She circled him, looking up and down. As her soft hand moved over his shoulders, they left behind a sense of detached coldness.

"In which house did you last serve?"

"House?" Daniel's mind went blank. "Williams, the house of Williams, Ma'am."

"Williams? I have never heard of any Williams around here." She fingered the collar of his jumpsuit, as if judging the material. "Show me your papers."

He held up the new green-card and permit which she hardly glanced at.

"No references, I see. Well." She smoothed the delicate lace of her gown. "I frequently entertain guests, important and influential guests. And I would do well with a properly trained servant who knew his job. You do know your job, don't you?"

"Of course! I—"

"And your place," she added. "I shan't allow any insolence."

Daniel waited. Maybe his proper place included silence unless spoken to directly. He could handle that. For a while.

"Very well," she said. "I shall allow you to work, conditionally, for two weeks. A kilo per week, I think. Yes, that should be more than enough."

"A kilo?" He wasn't sure how much money a kilo was, but it didn't sound like much. "Perhaps by that time, Ma'am, you'll have realized I'm worth twice that amount."

Allon groaned as if kicked in the stomach. His brothers shuffled back uncomfortably. Miss Lillian's eyes widened into ebony diamonds of skepticism, preceding a cold smile.

"We shall see. Now as for you three ..." She waved her hand as if shooing away flies. "If you desire continued employment, you had best be off to your duties!"

The brothers vanished. She turned silently away, her slippered feet gliding over the path with an almost regal stride. Daniel followed, awash in her perfume, as she led him through her private garden.

Glass and steel stretched high overhead forming a greenhouse skylight that protected a wealth of shrubs, flowering legumes, and occasional carnivores. In the secluded shaded spots, bright red and black petals sprouted from decaying fungus-like stalks nestled in dark crevices of damp wood.

As Daniel studied the passing flora, he paid little attention to where they were going, until he found himself in a formal living room. Plush, green carpeting blended the transition from the outside to the interior where Grecian columns climbed to a lofty, arched ceiling of rich wood and stained glass windows. He studied the strange windows. They seemed to portray scenes of suffering and dying, dark scenes of mass burials, and cremation fires.

"In here, boy," she called. "This is your dayroom." She picked up a black bracelet lying on the counter and fastened it snugly around his wrist. "The intercom will keep you in touch at all times. By the way, what is your name, boy?"

"Daniel, Ma'am."

She paused, giving a judgmental smile. "Interesting. How long has this been?"

He couldn't resist smiling back. "Since birth."

Her look deepened. Suddenly she reached down between his legs with an unexpected squeeze.

"Hey!"

"Hush," she commanded, her curiosity apparently satisfied. "If you wish to be called Danielle that is your business, and it should not affect your service. But I think I shall, simply call you <u>boy</u>."

Daniel rubbed his groin and studied the wristlet on his arm, a simple design of black anodized metal, its glazed oval center marked by three red glyphs. He fingered the seamless manacle looking for the latch but there wasn't one, no way to remove it.

"I see you appreciate the design," she said, smiling. "I think my brand displays far more artistry than most, don't you agree?"

"Brand? Uh, guess so. I mean yes, Ma'am."

"Let's be along now. You must become familiar with the premises."

She pranced off to an adjoining room lavishly decorated in red satin and black velvet. A large canopy-topped bed dominated the center of the room which had a dozen wall-length mirrors stationed about like silvered sentinels. Wherever she stood, at least one or two reflected her stunning figure.

She pointed through another door, down a long golden tiled hallway. "In there is my bath. Oh, by the way, I prefer forty-one degrees exactly. It's a trifle warm, but so relaxing. Be sure to remember now, forty-one degrees. Do you understand?"

He forced a smile. "Yes, Ma'am. Forty-one degrees. It's a little tough, but I think I can remember that." If he had the brains of a mushroom he could handle her simple tasks. Did she think he was a moron?

He followed her through the house, absently listening as she introduced each room and explained the responsibilities associated with the upkeep of each, giving simplistic, detailed instructions. He pretended to pay close attention each time she turned around to look at him, parroting her last comment to assure his comprehension.

This was a different experience for him. He had never actually worked before, not unskilled physical labor. College, postgraduate school, and a short internship at the research institute had preceded his involvement with S-RAY. It could almost be fun, he thought, not to use his education. Instead he found himself taking orders from, and acting submissive to, this woman of obvious affluence. And a darkly beautiful woman, no less.

Shortly after noon he went into the garden as instructed to serve lunch to Allon and his brothers.

"I hope you like my cooking, All."

"What is it?"

Daniel looked down at the pot. "I'm not sure. Stew, I think. But it smells good."

Dillon and Banion gave a doubtful look, but Allon dropped his tools and plopped down with a hungry grunt. He sniffed at the pot, waiting to be served. "You crazy or what?" he said.

Daniel looked at the stew again. "What? Does it smell that bad?"

"Thought we was dead when you told her you wanted twice as much."

"How much is a kilo, anyway?" Daniel asked as he served the brothers.

"A kilo's much as we gets put together." Banion downed the stew in slurping spoonfuls, raking a trickle from his chin with his sleeve.

"Why are houseboys paid so much more than gardeners? I've done very little so far."

"You know why, boy," Dillon said, holding up an empty bowl. "Cause you cleaner than a dirt worker. And talk fancy, the way them Perfs like."

Daniel twisted the intercom/brand around his wrist. "How does this thing come off?"

"Don't, o'course. Not till she unlocks it."

"Why?"

Allon looked up guardedly. "Thought you said you's houseboy. You'd know how master tags house servants."

"Why?" Daniel repeated.

Dillon groaned. "There goes our bonus."

"In case they wants to leave with some of her fine jewelry or silver. No other master'll hire houseboy who still wears old brand."

Their discussion was interrupted by a sultry voice from the intercom summoning him.

"Dan … elle," she said with her peculiar intonation. "I'm ready for my bath now."

"Yes, Ma'am." When he was sure the intercom had gone dead, he looked back to Allon. "Now about these brands, and masters and servants …"

"You best run along. She don't like t'be kept waiting."

Banion grinned, wiping his chin again. "Special when it's bath time."

Daniel stood to leave. He looked back over his shoulder as he trotted off to see the three brothers nudging each other amid muffled snickering.

# # #

He adjusted the gold-plated fixtures on the large tub until the pearlescent thermol lining had shifted colors from pink to red. Miss Lillian had explained how to tell the correct water temperature. Then he laid out several perfumed towels and started to leave.

"Your bath is ready, Ma'am!"

She entered straightway, before he could exit, carrying her scarlet velour robe casually draped over one arm. His eyes immediately riveted on her body, admiring her taught, firm midriff that flared smoothly to bare, round hips. Full, pointed breasts with dark brown nipples stood like chocolate drops staring back.

"Oh, you're still here. Did you want to wash my back?" Her smile seemed teasing.

"Beg your pardon?"

"No? Oh, yes. I see. You probably wouldn't be interested in that too much would you, Dan … elle?"

"Yes, Ma'am. I mean no, Ma'am." His heart was pounding, either from arousal or nervous surprise. An uncomfortable position. He wanted to stay and scrub that beautiful black backside. No. He wanted to leave. He didn't know what he wanted to do. "I—I'd better leave now," he said fumbling with the door latch.

The door closed slowly, giving one last narrow peek as she bent over to step into the tub. She was a black woman, he thought, a beautiful black woman. From head to toe.

He had been in the dayroom only a few minutes when the intercom buzzed again, tickling his wrist.

"Danielle, fetch me some white wine from the store. They won't deliver so you shall have to pick it up. And be quick about it, I feel like a massage after my bath."

"Yes, Ma'am."

"The credit voucher is on the valet. Don't forget to use my access code. Seven, seven, seven. Can you remember that? I'd rather you not write it down anywhere."

"Yes, Ma'am. Seven, seven, seven. I won't forget." He wouldn't forget the massage, either. This job was getting better.

On his way out of the garden he found Allon standing behind a shrub, slowly working the pruning shears. No hurry. He seemed to be making a life-long career of that one bush, nipping one shoot at a time.

Daniel walked over and whispered, "Where's the liquor store?"

Allon gave a blank expression.

"I have to pick up some wine."

"Oh, you wants pilque vendor. Out the door to the left. Two blocks down on right," he said, waiving his hand like a flag in the breeze. "Is named Chartiel's."

Daniel jumped into the elevator to leave as Allon added, "Best be proper. He don't cotton much to business with Bios."

Before Daniel could ask for clarification the doors closed, cutting them off with a dropping lurch.

He paused in front of the stained-glass doors of the lobby before walking outside. The scenes on the glass were similar to the ones upstairs in the master bedroom. What was their significance? It seemed curious that something so gruesome would be a popular for decoration.

He walked outside.

The white sidewalk flowed with a rush of people. He dove into the stream of traffic, dodging careless elbows and clumsy shoulders that obviously didn't want to let him in, and slipped into a drifting bare spot in the crowd. He walked past store fronts and residence entry ways.

Many of the buildings had signs posted in front stating BLACKS ONLY. He followed along with the crowd, but he was getting that uneasy feeling again. Something was wrong. Something was out of place. As he studied the ocean of faces that bobbed up and down around him, he noticed something that made his spine tingle. Although he counted several different ethnic groups in the mostly black tide of frowns, there was one which he did not see. He found Asians and Hispanics, even a few Native American Indian faces. What he couldn't find was one, single true Caucasian. He was the only white face in the crowd, a ping-pong ball in a bowl of chocolate pudding.

He suppressed a cold shiver and kept walking. Finally, across the street he spotted a large window with CHARTIEL'S painted in large port-red letters.

He passed in front of the large plate window, gazing through the streaked glass at the line of customers inside, and stepped into the entrance way where he stopped to read a small sign to his left: PERFECT CLIENTELE PREFERRED.

The door flew open in front of him. A burly black man, the size of an ox, came lumbering out of the door. With narrowed eyes he lowered his head and charged straight into Daniel, knocking him flat on his butt.

"Inconsiderate oaf," Daniel grumbled, staring up from under the shadowed awning. He started to rise, but the man moved directly over him.

"You got something to say, Bios!"

Daniel glanced up to the pedestrians who stepped out around him on the sidewalk and continued casually on their way, apparently indifferent to his trivial conflict. He looked back with indecision.

"Well?" repeated the very large inconsiderate oaf.

"No … Sir."

"Learn your place, boy. Decent folk come through that door all the time. You got no business blocking it with your Bios ignorance!"

Daniel sat on the cool concrete until the man left. As he started up, a prunish hand reached down from the crowd.

"Y'alright?" The short, plump Asian almost seemed concerned.

"Sort of. Thanks." He shook himself off, brushing off nonexistent dust, and tried to regain his dignity. "Nobody stopped. Nobody seemed to care."

"Why should they?"

"Because." It was expected, he thought. It was the civil thing to do. It was what anyone would do. "Because, that's why!"

The man's sympathetic look disappeared. "You know's they don't, son. Don't give a damn 'bout a Bios. Never did. Never will."

"Things sure are different here."

"New here, huh? Shows. He's right, y'know. Best learn your place if you plans to spend much time arounds. Perfs here 'bout the most bigoted bunch I ever meet. They don't take with no defiance. No sir, not a'tall."

"What defiance? I didn't do anything."

"You knows, boy." The plump little man leaned close as if sharing a valuable secret. "You was standing in his way! That's enough. Last thing one of us wants to do round here. Cuss'em all you wants at night round the fire, but here in the city you best stand out of their way and never get noticed. Don't even look 'em in the eye."

"Sounds like a lousy way to live, if you ask me."

The little man's face wrinkled; slanted eyes narrowed into slits. "Where you from, the moon?"

"No, I'm new in town. Skip it, and thanks again."

"Member what I said," he advised, turning to step into the passing wall of faces. "Don't get noticed."

Daniel went into the store. He waited at the back wall while the remaining black customers made their selections before stepping forward to order the wine. The man behind the counter, his bald head shining like a polished eight ball, leered down at him while scrutinizing the markings on his wristlet. He straightened after recognizing the brand logo.

"You got a voucher, boy? Don't carry no credit with—"

"White wine …" Daniel pulled the thin plastic voucher from his pocket and tossed it on the counter. "The code is 7-7-7."

The clerk's jaw tightened as his eyes focused into obsidian look daggers.

Daniel lowered his eyes and gritted his teeth to keep from saying anything. Finally the clerk shuffled away to look for his selection.

The room's walls were full of plastic bottles and shiny aluminum-looking containers with no prices posted. A drinking fountain stood in the corner with an inviting stream of crystal water bubbling out of its top. A small sign posted on the wall above it stated *Perfects Only*.

His throat was dry. He wasn't perfect, he thought. Pretty good, but not perfect. He eased toward the fountain.

"Don't even think it!" The clerk set the container of wine heavily on the counter. "Even if you can't read, you know what it means."

Daniel judged the distance. He knew he could connect a spinning round house and kick the bastard through the wall. But he resisted the urge. He'd been in the future for less than eight hours, and he'd already seen enough bigotry, and discrimination to be permeated by its bitterness.

The clerk tossed a bottle over the counter. "You tell your mistress this's my finest domestic white. Five yars old and guaranteed quality vintage."

"Thanks you, suh." He glanced through the plate glass window to make sure no one was approaching from the other side of the door.

The trip back to the penthouse was punctuated with more elbows and bumping shoulders. But Daniel didn't really notice; he was thinking of Miss Lillian. She'd probably be through with her bath by now and waiting for her massage. He could see her lying on the long table, her firm legs beaded with moisture. That would be an interesting diversion for half an hour, maybe longer with a little luck. He adjusted the pants of his tunic. They seemed to be growing a little tight.

Chapter 9

Daniel did not see Allon or his brothers.

He went to the dayroom, unwrapped the wine, and searched for a place to stow it, but he was still unfamiliar with his new surroundings. Had she pointed out the wine rack? He couldn't remember. But he wasn't going to let her know; that would only give her another opportunity to belittle him with moronistic instructions.

He searched everywhere he could think of: the dayroom, the kitchen, the den. He still couldn't find it. He tapped lightly on the wristlet intercom whatever-it-was.

"Miss Lillian?"

"Yes, what is it?"

"I can't find, I mean, where should I put the wine?"

"In the stow, of course. Where else would one put wine! And the stow is always located in or near the den, as any well-trained houseboy should know."

"I knew that," he mumbled.

"What was that?"

"I said thank-you, Ma'am. I'll try and remember that."

"See that you do. I expect quite a lot for two kilos payment."

Daniel gritted his teeth. He was forced to play out the role of submissive servant, at least until he could discover what had happened to this crazy, future present. As he slid the cylindrical bottle into its rack he stopped and stared at the label: Mohammed Ali Winery—bottled 2125.

A rustling sound caught his attention. Miss Lillian stood at the far end of the room. Her black, lace-trimmed evening gown plunged to her belly button in front and trailed behind her along the carpeted floor. Static made it cling revealingly to her swaying hips and inner thighs, revealing dark patches of temptation.

"Very nice. If you don't mind me saying so."

Her expression softened. "Do you think so? I had planned to wear it tonight at my gathering, but wasn't quite sure."

"Gathering?"

"Oh, didn't I tell you? Since the estate now has a proper houseboy, I have decided to invite a few guests. Just an informal thing to maintain status and social recognition. They're all Uppers, so you understand the importance of doing a good job tonight. "By the way, what took you so long? I tired of waiting for my massage. It's much too late now."

It didn't matter; Daniel's pants were no longer tight.

"I didn't see Allon or the others ..."

"Of course not. They've been dismissed for the day." She cringed with disgust. "Can't have those filthy dirt workers around when the guests begin arriving, now can we? You had no plans for tonight, did you, Danielle? Of course not. You should then, begin your preparations."

"Preparations?"

She paused to admire her reflection in the hall mirror. "For eight or ten guests, or maybe a dozen. And they are especially fond of Cartesian hors d'oeuvres."

"The Senator may show up, so you do me proud. Understand?"

"Yes, Ma'am." *Hors d'oeuvres?*

She turned, her gossamer gown loosing most of its static, billowed outward at her slightest movement. He caught himself admiring the dark shadows that hid beneath the midnight lace.

"Before you leave?"

"What is it now?" she said, rolling her eyes. "Oh, yes, the gathering will no doubt last late into the evening. You might as well stay the night. Wouldn't want you out on the streets after dark, would we?"

"No, I guess not. Thanks. But you spoke earlier about a 'perfect' society. Is that the Perfs?"

Her sudden stare chilled him. "You will not use that Bios word in this house. Understand? You know perfectly well our society exceeds that of the past. So don't play dumb with me. Or dumber than you really are. Why should I explain the natural order of things to a Bios? It's not like you're capable of being educated." She ended the pointless conversation by leaving the room.

# # #

Daniel set the trays of snacks—a collage of items found in the pantry—in the refrigerator. He'd been too proud to admit he didn't know how to make Cartesian hors d'oeuvres, or any hors d'oeuvres. And although the alphabet hadn't changed much during the last century, it seemed that brand labels and names had. Completely. He figured he was safe, however. He hadn't seen any pets around the house, so hopefully what he had identified as goose pate wouldn't turn out to be cat food.

Whatever they were, they smelled like hors d'oeuvres—mushy piles of temptation that never tasted as good as they looked. Admiring his appetizing display, he decided that it was going to be a good party. He could pull this off, be the unseen attendant, and probably discover a lot about this strange society during her cocktail party *gathering*.

The door chimed for his attendance. Someone was waiting in the elevator. Time to snivel and grovel. He took one of the trays and headed for the door.

He greeted the arrivals with as much humble servitude as he could muster. "Good evening," he would say. "Please come in. Miss Lillian will be with you presently."

She was dressed and ready, but waiting until enough of her guests had arrived to warrant her appearance. They were all blacks, but somehow that didn't surprise him. The elevator opened again and a foursome emerged. He lowered the polished silver tray with a cursive bow. "With her compliments …" If Thomas could only see him now.

"Not now, boy. Bring us some 'tails."

"Cocktails? Certainly, sir." *Bigot!* he added silently. He nodded to the couple immediately behind them. "Would you—"

"Ooh, tasties," the lady squealed, her exposed breasts wiggling. "I just love tasties."

She took a pink one and popped it into her mouth, then a black one, then a brown one. Her escort smiled with embarrassment and pulled her into the garden, but her squeaky voice echoed down the cobblestone path.

"Ooh, they're so good …"

Daniel glanced down at the tray. They did look good. He glanced around to ensure no one was looking, then stuffed one of the puffy morsels into his mouth, and bit into its creamy texture of putrid grit.

"Crap!"

He tried to spit out the soggy cracker and greasy filling, looking for something to wipe his tongue on. The taste from the nasty remnants lingered, glued to the roof of his mouth. He started to dump the entire tray's contents into a nearby rose bush, but the chime sounded again. More guests. He wiped his tongue on his jacket sleeve, but it didn't help.

The door opened and a party of five, dressed in formal gowns and tuxedos, paraded into the garden.

"Good evening," Daniel began. "Miss Lillian will—"

"Here, boy." One of the men stuffed a golden crested walking cane into his free hand while draping a topcoat over his other.

I'm not a damn coat rack. Daniel held up the tray of colored dung drops. "Care for an hors d'oeuvre?"

"Not now, boy."

"The brown ones are quite popular tonight. They're Cartesian."

"They are?" The man stopped. "Well, in that case maybe I will."

The second man was also draping his coat over Daniel's arm. "The brown ones you say? I'll have one, too. And bring us something to drink, boy. I'm parched."

Daniel bowed and turned to leave like the perfect gentleman's gentleman as the two guests bit into his horrible creations. Miss Lillian announced herself from the main house and glided over to greet them. The two men cringed and glanced around for a discreet exit, but it was too late, and they were forced to swallow. They desperately needed a drink now.

Miss Lillian greeted each of the guests. She danced charmingly about from one to the other while smiling, complimenting, and graciously laughing at each "funny" story told.

The last guest to arrive was a squat little man who flashed a sculptured smile of gold-capped teeth and waved his stubby cigar around like a campaign promise while his satin cummerbund strained to contain his basketball belly.

"Senator!" Miss Lillian made the announcement loud enough to ensure everyone understood the status of the late arrival. "I'm so delighted you could come."

"Lillian, my dear." The Senator took her hand and pretended to kiss it. "You're even more ravishing than I remembered. Absolutely stunning gown."

Daniel needed a drink and looked for an inconspicuous corner to stand in. He'd noticed her beauty, too, and how much beauty the gown revealed. In spite of her shallow personality and bigoted outlook, he'd noticed a recurring desire to take her. Each time she came near him, the feeling returned.

The party continued late into the night. Daniel waited dutifully by the door as the guests departed, handing them fur coats, gold-knobbed walking canes, and other trinkets which the affluent always seemed to acquire. As the procession slowly passed, Miss Lillian trading token kisses and empty salutations. When the last guest had disappeared into the elevator, Miss Lillian trotted off into her bedroom.

"Wake me up at ten," she said. "I'm absolutely exhausted. Try not to stay up too late cleaning the mess."

The dining room was a shambles. Discarded dishes of cold food, dried wine glasses, and the Senator's damp stogies littered the room like a battlefield. Even the plush carpet was blemished with scattered stains where her "Upper" guests had dropped or spilled their refreshments.

Daniel shuffled off to the dayroom and looked for a soft place to lie down. He'd finish it tomorrow.

Lying on his back, his feet drawn up on the uncomfortably short wall shelf, he reviewed the events of his first day after timeslip. He wasn't impressed. He had learned very little about this new world, or why it was so different. Becoming a houseboy had been a bad idea. He tried to stretch. Tomorrow he'd try something different.

# # #

He opened the door to the bedroom and peeked in. "Miss Lillian? Are you awake?" No sounds came from inside the elegantly decorated room, so he stepped in further. The air was thick with perfume. On top of the mattress lay a jumble of scarlet satin sheets and black pillows. The twisted bundle moved as she stirred.

"You wanted to be awakened …"

"What time is it?" She yawned, clawing the air with long, purple fingernails.

"A little after ten, Ma'am. I have some breakfast ready."

"Draw my bath," she said as she stretched again. "Then I shall require a full massage before I can enjoy brunch."

"Yes, Ma'am." The role of servant was no easier for him to play today than it was last night. This plan wasn't working out; therefore, it was time to leave. After the massage, of course.

The skylight diffused the afternoon sun, casting its soft glow over the garden. Daniel returned from the main house to check on the progress of the "dirt workers." They were almost finished planting seedlings for the new herbal patch. He was supposed to be supervising them, but he felt useless. Allon and his brothers knew much more about gardening than he, but Miss Lillian had been very specific; he was to oversee their work. As soon as they were through, he could dismiss them for the day.

"Dan … elle."

It was peculiar the way she constantly mispronounced his name. And irritating.

"I have clients arriving soon." She freshened the perfume on her wrists. "And some business to attend to this afternoon. I shan't be needing you anymore today." Her expensive perfume blanketed the delicate herbal scents of the freshly planted spices like a heavy cloud. He turned to the three boys covered with dirt.

"Allon, when you and your brothers leave, I'd like to go with you."

"Why? We go to Clan."

"I know. I want to follow you home, to your clan. Maybe I could stay there for a while."

"Stay with your clan." Allon said.

"I don't have one."

Banion dropped his spade to join the conversation. "Every mano has clan."

"Well, I don't. I'm new here, remember? I come from a long ways off, a very long way." He waited for an answer, but they only stared.

"Please?"

Allon and Banion looked to each other, as if waiting for the other to decide. Finally Dillon spoke out.

"You can follow us, but May'r say yes or no if you stay."

"Who's May'r?"

They stared again.

# # #

The ride out of town seemed even longer than before with the brothers content to sit like mute statues. By the time they stepped off the airbus, it was almost sundown. Daniel looked around. They were not far from where he had originally caught his first ride. "Where's your clan?"

"Close," Dillon answered, pointing over the open land toward a small hill. "Have to walk rest of way."

Following a worn path that threaded its way between small cacti and waist-high scrubs, Daniel followed the brothers to the almost barren outcropping of rock. Only a sprinkling of stubby mesquites and desert sage grew on the thin topsoil covering the crest of limestone.

"There," Allon announced. "Home of Grotto Clan."

Daniel looked incredulously at the dark opening in the rock face. "You live in a cave?"

"Grotto Cave," Dillon answered, ducking his head to clear the rock overhang.

"This used to be called Sonora Caverns," Daniel started to explain, but no one was listening. He recognized the entrance tunnel, having visited part of the caverns when they were a tourist attraction. He remembered that, once long ago, the place had been a Civil Defense shelter. But why would anyone want to live here instead of in the city?

They descended the mouth of the cave entrance. In contrast to all the drastic changes he had witnessed, the entrance seemed completely unchanged. It was exactly the same as when he was here last—a century ago, he remembered. The only innovation was a row of blue-white panels that lined the tunnel entrance and flooded it with an eerie blue glow.

The narrow ramp opened into a large bottle-shaped cavern where thousands of glistening water jewels clung from a jagged icicled ceiling of stalactites. The beads of moisture gathered to fall into a crystal clear pool twenty meters below. Daniel stayed back from the ledge, hugging the wall as he studied the damp room bathed in the blue twilight of more lighting panels.

"It's kind of nice," Daniel commented.

The brothers did not respond as they kept walking along the narrow rim. They slipped between two large boulders and disappeared. Daniel followed between the boulders which guarded the entrance of a huge cavern. Behind them a vast, domed room exploded into enormous dimensions. Far below the long, descending ramp lay a village with hundreds of people of all ages. He stood in awe.

"This is incredible!"

"No," Dillon corrected, "this Grotto Clan."

Chapter 10

As Daniel followed Allon and his brothers into the village, a trail of curious children gathered behind him. They tagged along with hungry curiosity over their new visitor like a pack of yelping pups. Some reached out to touch him and squeal, while most kept a timid distance behind, giggling and chattering all the way.

The troupe passed several small campfires where large pots hung from wooden tripods. Daniel leaned over one of the smelly concoctions, which emitted an acid smell somewhere between tanning leather and boiling lard. The wrinkled women who tended the pots paid little attention to the stranger's passing as they tended the fires and stirred the contents. One woman with sunken eyes glanced up, twirling a chewed snuff stick between brown teeth. She studied him for a moment, spat on the ground, and went back to stirring her pot.

The dwellings along the way seemed little more than crude, leaning shacks; some only tents of drawn canvas or what looked like partially cured animal hides. Several younger women peeked out from the shabby dwellings to investigate the commotion of the excited children. The soft, high-cheeked faces were almost pretty, he thought, except for the smudges. Dirt and greasy soot seemed to be cosmetic of choice.

He passed a group of elderly men sitting cross-legged on the ground. They puffed contentedly on long wooden pipes and gave no recognition of the group's passing, hardly turning their snow-capped, wrinkled faces to look. The bittersweet aroma of cannabis leaves explained the far off, distant glaze over the black pools of their eyes.

He had trouble keeping up as the brothers worked their way between the crowded dwellings, following a well-known path. That path was a narrow patch of bare dirt that twisted between the shacks and tents. The density of the packed dwellings increased as they pressed deeper into the village. The acrid smell of smoke and unwashed bodies also increased. An orchestra of human sounds: laughter, muted conversations, distant shouts, and the clatter of cooking utensils echoed off the stone walls of the cavern.

Dillon stopped abruptly at the edge of a clearing while his two brothers walked on. "Is Lodge," he said, pointing ahead. "Wait here. May'r send for us when ready."

The clearing extended in a circle around a single, large dwelling the brothers simply called the Lodge. Around the edge of the clearing, the squalor of packed dwellings halted abruptly, contrasting the cleanness of the inner circle. He noticed multiple paths that funneled into the central clearing like the crooked spokes of a wheel. Allon had emerged from the Lodge and was waving for them to come forward.

The entrance of the structure was draped with a large flap of hide. A somber looking guard, wearing black leather breeches and a salt-crusted vest, pulled the flap out of the way for Daniel to enter.

Inside, the air was dank and heavy with earthy incense, but still an improvement over the odors outside. Overlapping patches of mismatched carpet almost concealed the earthen floor. He squinted through a haze of tobacco smoke laced with more cannabis alkaloid stimulants. Through the smoke he found Allon sitting against the far wall. Beside him sat an older man, quietly observing the pale-skinned visitor. The man sat with an air of dignity and pride. He wore a red, black, and white checkered shawl draped loosely over his broad shoulders.

"Nathon is May'r of Lowman clan," Allon said, with obvious respect. "I told him you want to stay here."

The man introduced as May'r Nathon motioned for Daniel to sit. "Why do you come here?"

"I have come from afar," Daniel started. May'r Nathon leaned forward as if suddenly interested. "Customs and circumstance make me a stranger in your land. You see, I have no place to stay."

"Then you are poor." Nathon folded his arms. "Is much room in Grotto Cave, but Clan is large. Many mouths. We have little to share with outers."

Daniel waited. He figured he knew what Nathon's answer was going to be and he couldn't argue with it. From what he'd seen on the way in, poor wouldn't adequately describe the Clan's condition. Poverty would be a better choice. But Nathon didn't say no. He didn't say anything. He just sat quietly with his arms folded in contemplation like an old cigar store figure. Finally he continued.

"What can you contribute?"

"I've found work in town," Daniel answered. "Allon says that two kilos a week is considered a large sum for payment. Whatever it is, I offer it as a token reimbursement for your hospitality."

May'r Nathon turned to Allon with a questioning look.

"One kilo was offered," Allon corrected. "He claimed to be worth two."

Nathon rubbed his short chin. "One kilo can feed many children. If you can bring two, Clan would gain strong provider." He nodded acceptance of Daniel's terms. "You are called what?"

"My given name is Daniel Williams, but you can call me …"

Nathon sat upright and glanced to the three brothers. They only shrugged. He looked intently at Daniel. "This one does not understand. Your name is Danielle?"

"That's not exactly the way I say it, but yes. Why?"

"Is most strange. You dress like mano, and wear hair as mano."

"Mano, you mean man? Of course. I'm a man!"

Dillon leaned over to Nathon and whispered, "He is houseboy. Maybe explain odd name."

"It is strange," Nathon replied, "even for houseboy." He looked back to Daniel. "You are from place with different customs. Is your name is common among your people?"

"Well, sure. I guess. What's so unusual about it?"

Nathon rubbed his chin again to hide a smile. "Mano's name say much about him. His status, his lineage, his role in life. This name is not warrior, not provider. This sounds like …"

"Wo'am," Dillon interjected. "Is wo'am name."

"Wo'am? You mean woman's?" Daniel stood up. "Now look here! I've been knocked down, insulted, and even groped by the arrogant blacks of this culturally mixed-up Wonderland ever since I got here. I expected a little more empathy from a fellow Bios."

Nathon rose slowly to his feet like a darkly tanned obelisk extruding from the ground, and the temperature in the meeting room dropped about five degrees. The guard from outside appeared directly behind Daniel with Dillon and his brothers closing ranks.

"Did I say something wrong?"

"You not speak like that to May'r," Allon said with a tone of warning that was far different from the timid way he talked to Miss Lillian.

Daniel swallowed, wishing he hadn't used the new ethnic term. Evidently one didn't use it unless they were smiling, and he hadn't been. He tried to smile now.

"No insult meant."

The leader of the Lowman Clan studied Daniel's defensive posture. He seemed very experienced at detecting the subtleties of innuendo and hidden intent. Evidently he saw none and motioned for the others to sit.

"We will call you anything you wish. But maybe you consider more common name if stay with us. Name of Dan-on would cause less problem."

"I can stay?" Daniel began to breathe easier.

"Is finished." Nathon stood and draped the shawl over his arm. "Will introduce Danon as visitor at night's council for all to know." He looked to Dillon and added, "Show him round village. Where good water and communal places can be found. And tabuli."

Dillon turned with a curt nod and hid a frown on his way past Daniel. "Come on. Hurry, I show you now."

Daniel caught up with his reluctant guide who was still grumbling, louder now that they were outside of the Lodge and away from Nathon's hearing.

"Know'd I have to shows you round if Allon brought you back. Cause I'm youngest, that's why." He took one of the crooked paths without looking back to see if Daniel followed.

"What did he mean when he said that I'd be welcomed at the council tonight?" Daniel asked after catching up to him.

"Council will want to see you."

"What kind of council?"

"Is council of Elders. You see tonight." Dillon led him to a wall of stone and pointed. "We climb now."

"Up there? I thought you were going to show me around the cavern."

"This faster."

"Great," he mumbled. "I have to get a mountain goat for a guide."

Daniel struggled to follow his nimble escort, clinging tightly to handholds the size of thumbnails while he tried to wedge the toe of his boot in the shallow cracks and indentions. He didn't like heights either. If he made a list of the things he hated, heights would be at the top. Right under dark places and kissing skunks.

He paid close attention to follow Dillon's path. He didn't want to think about the result of falling, or even worse, having to ask Dillon to pull him up.

He was breathing deeply by the time he scooted over the precipice to rest on a narrow ledge. It was a fairly good climb, but not too rough. He'd handled worse. Nevertheless he kept a strong grip on the ledge as he took a look around.

The cavernous room swallowed the tiny village. The uneven floor, punctuated with yellowish orange stalagmites and crusty columns, stretched into darkness in every direction. Dillon began pointing to different locations around the room.

"You saw pool on way in," he said. "Is good water to drink, but nowhere else. If need relief, go over there." He pointed to another area where the wall of stone recessed to form a hollow pocket hidden from the rest of the cavern.

Daniel noticed a small, cantilevered break in the floor off in the distance. Dillon paused, noticing what Daniel was staring at.

"There is tabuli," he said. "You stay from there, understand?"

"No, not really …"

"You stay from there. Is tabuli!"

"Okay, I'll stay away." He squinted to get a clear look at the shadowy scar in the cavern floor, but couldn't. Then he wondered what the heck a *tabuli* was.

The village lay beneath them, fully exposing its jumbled pattern of development around the lodge of the May'r. A hundred small plumes of smoke rose above the dwellings like skinny fingers that pushed to support the jagged ceiling only a few meters above Daniel's head. From this vantage point he realized the chaotic arrangement of dwellings had a pattern of concentric rings. The assorted colors of the tents, some made of synthetic animal hides and others of metallic cloth, resembled colored beads strung around the Elder's Circle.

Dillon stood up on the narrow ledge. "We go down now. Show you where food is kept. Got no wo'am to fix meals, so you need t'know."

Daniel followed along the ledge, trying to make a mental map of the locations Dillon had pointed out. He noticed a slight breeze on his face. The air was sweet and clean, much better than the dirty feet and stale smoke of the lower level. The ledge terminated at the lip of a steep ramp whose moist, polished limestone traversed the main wall all the way to the floor.

"Way down easier than way up," Dillon said with a grin. He sat on the damp slippery rock and slid down twenty meters to the floor.

Daniel paused to study the narrow ramp. Dillon was waiting at the bottom, his hands raised impatiently. "Well?"

"I'm coming," he answered, convincing himself that since Dillon hadn't fallen off, neither would he. Maybe.

As he walked around the cavern he noticed more and more young men had returned. They arrived in groups, scattered an hour or so apart. Probably the interval between airbuses. It was impossible to tell when day changed to night inside the Cave and Daniel wondered if the Clan even made a distinction between night and day.

He wandered through the tangle of dwellings to the back portion of the cavern where the flat, relatively smooth cavern floor transformed into a rough, rock-strewn wasteland punctuated by scores of limestone columns. He climbed one of the shorter columns and sat down beside a cluster of delicate calcite flowers, clear formations that had squeezed out of the yellow rock in brittle curls of pure calcite. He watched the village as, one by one, the lighting panels were concealed, gradually and almost imperceptibly reducing the cavern's glow to a soft, artificial twilight peppered by the stars of flickering campfires. Okay, he thought, so they have nighttime.

He reflected about being the first time pilot. He had mastered time itself. Sort of. But he hadn't mastered this future world, yet, with its unexplained dominance by Blacks. He also realized that he hadn't noticed one, single Caucasian other than himself in the last two days. That bothered him. He'd also failed to uncover any answers, only questions and unsolved riddles. Not much of a scientific investigator, he decided.

He picked out some dried meat, he couldn't tell what kind, and parched corn from the communal food locker, then made his way to one of the local communal fires where the unsupported widows and social outcasts gathered for a minimum of comfort and fellowship.

This was the welfare block. Although the Clan was living at the poverty level as a whole, they did not neglect the even less fortunate. Those with no family. Daniel ate his meal, listening to the crackling of the flames. The others didn't talk much, just squatted and stared into the fire.

After the tasteless meal, he drifted toward the clearing around the Lodge of the May'r. The ring of painted rocks which marked the boundary for the Circle of Elders had been empty all evening, but now a large fire had been started and clansmen had begun gathering around the tribal fire. He recognized Allon standing in the front row of people across the clearing and made his way through the crowd to reach him.

"Where's your brothers?"

"With family," Allon answered, pointing vaguely. "Council start soon, much to talk about. Large crowd here 'cause tonight be challenge."

"Challenge?"

"Only of honor," Allon replied, "not vengeance. But Clan enjoys good fight."

"I don't understand."

"You see, later." Allon resumed his quiet stance looking over the fire.

"You don't have a family of your own?"

"Not yet."

"Me neither. Not exactly ready to settle down."

"I am. Blanket empty when sleep alone."

Daniel grinned. "Well, there are ways around that."

Allon stared blankly for a moment, then shook his head. "Not in Clan."

"Oh, of course. Skip it."

"Maybe tonight find gr'il presented to council." Allon studied the growing crowd for possible candidates. "If like her, take her for wo'am."

Daniel found himself sympathetically drawn into searching the faces in the crowd for a single maiden. He wasn't searching for a mate, just looking. The waves of heat rose above the flickering fire to blur his view. He strained to focus on an image walking along the other side, a stark contrast of beauty against the dirty faces and fat cheeks around her. He nudged his companion.

"Allon, over there. Who's that?"

"Where?"

"There, in the tight black leather. See?" He pointed to his intriguing mirage. "With the long black hair. Braided, with a red feather or something."

"Feather? Oh ..." Allon seemed suddenly disinterested. "Must be Lauriel."

Daniel repeated the name softly while attempting to follow her weaving through the crowd. He wondered how good she looked up close. He'd have to find out, he thought, as he returned his attention to the men gathering around the fire.

One by one, the elderly representatives chose their seats and sat down stiffly. Soon they were all perched on their worn swatches of carpet that encircled the sacred fire.

A hush had fallen over the crowd before the elders completed forming their circle. A flicker of movement came from the corner of his eye, and Daniel turned to investigate, feeling the attention of the crowd turn with him.

May'r Nathon, trusted leader of the Lowman Clan, emerged from his lodge dressed in black leather breeches. The tight fitting black vest revealed superbly developed chest muscles that had only recently begun to lose their sinewy tone. Draped majestically over his broad shoulders, he wore the faded shawl, tasseled with beads and feathers to commemorate deeds of bravery and manhood. As the leader of the seven tribes approached the Council with the graceful strides of an experienced hunter, Daniel noticed another mark of the hunter—a dagger strapped to one leg.

Nathon lifted his arms up into the air calling the Council to order, but they were already quiet. "We have visitor from, from afar," he said with a rich bass voice. "He is welcome to stay with Clan." Nathon looked around. "Where is Visitor Danon?"

After a prodding nudge from Allon, the newly renamed Danon stumbled forward to stand before the crowd where he could be seen and recognized. Hundreds of faces peered at him, swaying to get a better look. Their expressions betrayed no emotion other than curiosity.

The May'r turned his attention to the circle of elders. "What has Council to say?"

Murmurs arose from the Council. Several had the desire to speak, but graciously urged their neighbor to take the initiative. Daniel took advantage of the distraction to withdraw back into the crowd. After each elder had offered a token display of humility to the next oldest, the one sitting closest to the May'r finally stood.

"First request of Council is that our May'r live long and guide Clan with wisdom."

The age-old greeting brought echoes of agreement from the crowd. The elder waited a moment, then resumed. "But there is 'nother shortage of biotics to tend our children. Many are sick again from the coughing sickness and cannot be healed without Perf's biotics."

The man returned to his swatch as Nathon nodded acknowledgment. His simple statement had held more intent than Daniel was able to grasp. Another elder rose to speak.

"The Choc tribe has two who have reached age of mano. They seek to become warrior."

It was a formal introduction of the two young men who boldly stepped out of the crowd. The May'r knew the boys. He knew their fathers. Brave men. Brave sons. They would make good warriors, if they survived their test.

"If you send raiding party for biotics," the elder continued, "they will prove their courage to Clan."

Again Nathon nodded his understanding of what was being proposed. A third elder rose seeking audience. "I offer three gr'ils from tribe of Okee. Let the Clan know they are of age now."

Three teen-age maidens, dressed in brightly decorated ankle-length skirts and almost clean faces, walked timidly into the clearing. They stood with heads bowed as May'r Nathon spoke an inaudible blessing. As he dismissed them, the crowd whispered approval for the addition of the young "wo'ams" These women of childbearing age who would continue the lineage of the Clan. Allon was watching intently, approving also.

"See one you like, Allon?" Daniel asked.

"Maybe, need closer look."

"I know what you mean." Daniel grinned. "They never look quite as good up close. But they don't look too bad from here, though."

Allon motioned to hush. Another elder was already speaking.

"… is matter of honor. They come for you to witness this matter between them."

"What's going on?" Daniel asked.

"Is Rite of Challenge," came the answer. "Clansmen not fight each other unless come before May'r."

Two bare-chested men entered the circle behind the May'r. Each wore black leather pants similar to May'r Nathon's. Both wore the black dagger strapped low on one leg. May'r Nathon stood to acknowledge them.

"Warriors," Allon whispered. He pointed. "That one, Devon, will win. Is not wise to challenge him."

The two warriors bowed stiffly toward the May'r, then jumped apart with knives drawn. The one identified as Devon looked like a veteran of many such conflicts. His face bore two scars, and one arm had a long scar running down to the elbow. The scar writhed and twisted as he tossed his knife from one hand to the other. He circled his opponent stealthily as he approached. The other man clenched his knife with white knuckles, slowly pivoting to face his attacker.

Devon feinted to one side and then lunged with surprising swiftness. He jabbed, ducked, and snapped back with the blurring motion of a cobra that now stood coiled and ready to strike again. A wild slash of his opponent's knife had passed harmlessly over head. Devon again lurched forward, ducking low. He swept his victim's feet out from under him, sending him crashing backwards to the hard earthen floor. Devon somersaulted forward and plunged his knife downward. His dazed opponent struggled to roll over just in time to save his chest as the foot-long blade sank into the dirt. Both struggled frantically to their feet, knowing the first one up might be the only one up.

Devon ignored the trickle of blood where his knife had missed and only grazed his opponent. He crouched low, preparing for another attack.

"Stop!"

May'r Nathon rose to his feet with surprising agility, his fist tightly clenched. "It is over! Honor is satisfied by blood."

Devon still crouched, the sinews of his calves taught like compressed springs. He stared at the minuscule red trickle as if unsatisfied.

"I have spoken." Nathon said.

Devon slowly relaxed to stand erect and wipe his knife before returning it to its sheath. As his vanquished opponent shuffled off into the crowd, he brushed the cave dust off his arms, gave a cursory bow to May'r Nathon, then strutted back to his companions for a victor's welcome. Only one turned away in apparent unconcern, a woman also dressed in black like the other warriors, but with braided black hair that glistened as combed coal.

"It's her," Daniel whispered, poking his companion, "It's Lauriel." He strained to get a better look at her face, but she was too far away in the darkness.

"… wise May'r!" came another voice from the circle. Another elder stood, almost shouting to be heard over the boisterous crowd.

"Give us your wisdom!" the elder insisted. "The biotics?"

Nathon raised a hand of silent authority, and the crowd quickly hushed to hear his answer.

Nathon had decided. There seemed to be a unanimous desire for a raiding party, but the Counsel could not dispute his decision. He took a deep breath before making his announcement; it was never an easy one for him to make.

"We must hunt to survive."

His decree drew another energetic approval from the crowd, most of whom did not notice the lone figure entering the circle. Lauriel marched straight up to the clan leader and stood confidently, her shoulders erect and chin set. Her voice was firm and demanding, but not loud enough for most of the spectators to hear clearly.

"This one will lead raid, May'r. As clan warrior, this one is able and experienced from many quests."

Daniel found himself riveted to her face, impressed by her confidence, and attracted to her rugged athletic body. He wished he could see more of it and hear what was going on.

The warrior Devon ran into the circle, giving only a cursory bow to the May'r. "Only proven warrior can lead!" he said with a voice loud enough for all to hear. "This not time for testing."

Lauriel pushed her way in front of her intruder. "This one is proven!"

Nathon spoke with a finality that could have subdued a storm. "No! Warrior Devon will lead."

Lauriel stomped the dusty cavern floor as if wanting to argue.

"I have spoken." He waved dismissal to both warriors and nodded to the Elders before turning to leave. The council was over.

CHAPTER 11

The assembly had dispersed quickly as clansmen disappeared to their individual dwellings. Left by himself and unable to question Allon about the proposed raid, Daniel had wandered back to the communal lodge. There he had asked the old woman in charge for a quiet place to rest and a soft bed. Neither was available.

A few hours later, the sounds of bickering awoke him.

Two boys scuffled in the corner, tugging over custody of a stiff sheepskin, their bare feet polishing the dirt floor. He rolled away and pulled the synthetic buffalo skin robe over his head.

It didn't help. The floor was hard and the robe, which by its smell could pass as authentic, was too coarse to help. When he couldn't stand the smell any longer, he poked his head out for some fresh air.

Across the earthen floor he saw another pair of dirty feet approaching. Crooked toes with thick calluses like a dog's paw stopped directly in front of his nose. They didn't smell any better than the robe.

"You Danon?" the wrinkled woman asked.

"Who? Oh, yeah …" He twisted his neck to look upward with a groan. The snapping of joints grown stiff during the night. "I'm Danon, why?"

The woman stooped over, supporting her arthritic back. "Some'n waits for you," she said.

He tossed the robe aside to get up. He was dressed only in his underwear, but the old woman seemed unimpressed as she turned without even a smile and shuffled away.

The texture of the stony floor had left a numbing impression on his hip and shoulder. He rubbed a gritty hand over his chin, feeling its stubbly growth. His face smelled like dirt and his hands smelled like a dead buffalo, or maybe the other way around. He couldn't tell. Outside the boys waited impatiently start the new work day.

# # #

The elevator doors slid open to the penthouse garden. "Miss Lillian? Miss Lillian," Allon called. "We're here."

Daniel headed for the dayroom and found a crisp new one-piece jumper under the cabinet. As he was pulling off his dirty clothes, Miss Lillian walked by the open dayroom.

"Danielle!" she said with a shrill voice. "You are a filthy mess."

He held his breath to remove the ripe tunic. "Can't argue with that."

"Get out of those, those disgusting clothes."

"That's what I'm trying to do."

"No, not in here. Into the bath, at once." She pinched her nose and jerked him into the hall. "You smell almost as bad as one of those nasty little dirt workers. Go on. Get!"

She prodded him to the guestroom.

"And find some cologne when you're through. Don't you dare come out smelling anything less than a flower garden," she said as she carried his clothes away like a bundle of toxic waste.

# # #

The hot, soapy water felt extremely good. Steam drifted lazily off the water. His muscles began to relax and lose some of their soreness from the hard cavern floor.

He melted into the frothing bath. Perfumed bubbles floated around his face, the first pleasant smell he had had since following the brothers home to the Clan. It would almost be worth it, he thought, the comfort of a soft bed and hot baths, to remain a houseboy. No, it wouldn't. Not for Miss Lillian.

He remembered her strange behavior: how she had reached between his legs after hearing his name, like searching for a cluster of grapes. He recalled May'r Nathon's explanation of gender names and grinned. No wonder she was confused by what she found. He remembered her reaction upon entering her bath area nude, before "Danielle" had been able to leave. He wondered. What would have happened to <u>Dan-on</u>?

He lay back in the warm, bubbling water of the ultrasonic tub and closed his eyes. Maybe he'd tell her his new name. He lingered on the edge of euphoria for only a moment and then the wristlet buzzed.

"Danielle! I'm waiting for you." Even under the water it told him what to do. "That is a business bath. Quit playing with yourself and get back to work."

He choked off a reply and reached for a towel. There were none. The others were in the linen closet next to his dayroom, and she had taken all his clothes.

He peeked through the door. Miss Lillian stood on the veranda overlooking the garden. She seemed engrossed by a cutting of miniature roses which she toyed with in her palm.

She would have to be standing there, he thought. Well, he didn't owe her a peek. He made a dash for it, trying to cover as much as possible, run as fast as possible, and yet do it as quietly as possible.

Miss Lillian glanced up from the miniature rose buds and smiled casually. He heard a snicker behind his exposed backside.

"Pretty little things, aren't they?"

# # #

He set the silver tray on the marble table and backed away to admire his handiwork. Fruit cups, fried meat, and poached eggs decorated around the edges with herbal cuttings and small rose petals.

"I think this will start your day out properly."

She took one of the poached eggs and cracked it. "It looks adequate."

She leaned over to him and sniffed. "I would think that cologne you're wearing, a trifle robust. A little macho for one with your, let's say, preferences?"

<u>I got your macho hanging, lady</u>, he wanted to say. But he didn't. He felt obligated. He had to keep working to earn the payment he had promised the Clan, but he was gaining nothing for his investment. He still knew nothing about this culture of dirt workers, Bios, and Perfs. What he knew was that this obligation to the Clan was quickly becoming an entrapment to servitude. He quietly walked away to the dayroom. He still had to dust the sculptures.

# # #

Miss Lillian kept to herself most of the day, and that was fine with Daniel. She still came out periodically to give additional instructions, usually one or two at a time. Whenever she came near, the smell of her perfume made his heart race and he wanted her more than he would admit. But as soon as she would leave, the resentment returned.

He went into the empty living room and found the telecom center unlocked. He looked around. He'd seen her use the computer once or twice, enough to figure out the procedure. He queried ACCESS and gave the personal code for her credit voucher. It worked. He looked around again and made his selection—PERSONAL HISTORY. He'd get some answers one way or the other.

What he found stunned him.

Banion was working on the base of a rose bush by the patio. Daniel walked over to question him.

"Tell me, do you know what a mulatto is?"

"Naw ..." Banion snipped a withered branch and paused to inspect his job of pruning. "Don't care 'bout status of Lizers."

"Technically, it's not exactly a status." Daniel glanced around. "Miss Lillian doesn't have many visitors, does she?"

"Not in day."

"What do you mean?"

"They come at night most times."

"I wasn't talking about social gatherings."

"Not gatherings, visitors. Mano visitors, late at night. Sometime my brothers work late during planting season. We see them come and go."

"What are you talking about?"

Banion looked disgusted over Daniel's ignorance. "What is to tell? She pleases them and they bring her gifts. Is what Socializer does."

Daniel's mouth dropped. "Well I'll be damn! All this time I've been taking her upper-class, socialite crap and she's just a high priced prostitute?"

The wristlet interrupted him. "Danielle!"

He glared at the intercom around his fist, and knew where he'd like to shove it. And it'd probably fit.

Banion caught his arm. "What you do? Upset her and will lose job, maybe for us all. What you tell May'r then?"

Daniel pulled away and tramped through the freshly planted gardenias. He approached Miss Lillian from behind, catching a whiff of her sensual perfume. Just the smell aroused him. He found himself wanting her again. He shook it off. Pheromones, he realized, designed to enhance the male's urges. He couldn't resist its effect, but he tried hard to ignore his growing reaction.

"I shall probably be up late tonight, so I don't wish to be awakened before brunch."

"I'm sure you'll need your rest, after a busy night's work." He left before she could question his statement. *What she needed was a swift kick in the—*

He made a field goal attempt with a dwarf chrysanthemum, but it never reached the imaginary goal, exploding into a yellow cloud. Banion's warning returned to sink in, penetrating his anger. Daniel didn't need this job, but Danon did. The Clan needed it.

Another Chrysanthemum turned to powder.

Chapter 12

Returning to the Grotto, Daniel worked his way down the twisting passageway, brushing shoulders with a stream of clansmen hurrying in the opposite direction. They were all warriors, he realized, wearing the characteristic black vests and short leather breeches and large knives.

"Watch where you're going!" someone yelled, and then pushed him out of the way.

He spun around to find a darkly tanned face staring at him. Her lips were thin and tight. Squinting green eyes burned with determination. Her leather vest was drawn over her breasts and held loosely by two leather thongs.

He gave his best smile. "Sorry, my fault. My name is Daniel, I mean Danon, and I've been wanting to …"

She sidestepped him with a frown and resumed her beleaguered attempt to follow the others.

"Hey! Lauriel, where are you going?"

She kept going, her tight breeches bouncing up the steps. As she had disappeared, he slapped himself in the head.

Danon! His name was Danon, now. Why couldn't he remember that? Daniel was a girl's name. That would never impress her. From now on, his name was Danon.

Clansmen squeezed past, pausing to give strange looks at the white skinned visitor abusing himself. He tried to smile, but they didn't seem charmed.

He continued on all the way to the poolroom before stopping again, where the air was moist and cool. And clean. Old women and children trudged up and down a narrow walkway several meters below the rim to gather water. Since the pool was a crater surrounded by fragile formations, someone had constructed a fulcrum device to reach out into the water. A water soaked wooden bucket leaned over the pool like a one legged pelican and gulped another mouthful of water. Rivulets trickled through the gaps in its staves to fall back into the pool. He wished the Clan could smell that good.

"Too bad there's not another pool somewhere," he said.

"Is another," said a small voice.

He looked down in surprise, realizing he had been talking to himself again.

The young girl struggled to fill her plastic jar. "But is tabuli," she said. "Bad medicine."

He kneeled in front of her. "Bad medicine?"

"Is cursed!" She had the confident voice of a five-year old. "Ever one knows that. Go there, and die."

He smiled and turned away. He didn't have time to listen to ghost stories.

Descending the ramp, he entered the main room and realized he had nowhere to go. The communal lodge didn't sound inviting, and he'd explored very little of the cavern so far. He tried to recall the short tour he had been given. As he scanned the vastness of the cavern he noticed the cantilevered floor in the distance, the one Dillon had warned him to stay away from.

Is another, echoed the girl's remark. Bad medicine.

# # #

He approached the general area he had spotted from the ridge. The wall recessed to the left, forming a dark pocket of rock. He noticed sounds, female voices from around the corner. He also noticed a foul smell. He skirted around it to avoid intruding on them. He didn't know the local customs regarding communal toilets, but it would draw more attention than he desired at the moment.

The floor became more rugged as he ventured farther. Through the fading light, ageless stalagmites appeared. As he climbed around them, their brittle surface crumbled beneath his grasp. The air grew fresher, cooler. Somewhere back there, he realized, must be another entrance to the cavern.

He squeezed between two limestone formations and emerged into a brightly-lit chamber. He froze in the flat openness. A large shadow, its menacing arms outstretched, hovered in front of him.

He held his breath, waiting for the shadow to move. His pulse pounded in his ears. Had someone caught him poking around in the one area that he'd been warned to stay away from? His gaze darted from side to side searching for movement. Nothing. Neither he nor the shadow flinched as the seconds crept by. His own shadow? He turned around and grinned embarrassingly at the lighting panel, recessed into the rock formation behind him, which had captured him backlit on the stony wall. He turned around in relief, then stopped again. Between him and the dark crevice of the cantilevered floor stood a line of skulls impaled upon short sticks. They were neatly arranged in a line as if to form a barricade. Obviously a warning of tabuli.

They did their job well, even if they were only animal skulls. Nice touch, he thought. He passed the warning boundary, thinking about the child's comment: "... bad medicine."

He cautiously peered into the crevice but it was too dark. The soft glow of the panel was too weak to catch any reflection, only the shadowy image of a long, winding ramp descending into the murky depths.

# # #

Devon was standing guard, rigid as a monolith. As Danon approached, he cleared his throat. "I'd like to talk to the May'r."

"'Bout what?" There was something strongly intimidating about him, besides the arrogance. He had the look of a seasoned predator who knew no fear.

Danon started to repeat himself with a more defiant tone when Nathon's voice beckoned from inside the Lodge.

"Send the Visitor in."

Danon entered the hazy Lodge to find Nathon reclining against the far wall. Spirals of gray smoke rose from a glowing pit of embers, gathering into a bittersweet cloud that hung over the room.

"This one is approached on matters affecting Clan," he said. "Does Visitor Danon have such a matter?"

He nodded and sat down on the carpeted floor. It felt greasy. "Yes, May'r. To benefit the Clan, I have come seeking your council."

Nathon took another puff before lowering the long pipe to his lap. He stared intently, like a great cat studying its prey.

Danon cleared his throat. "I'm here to learn of me the mystery of the pool that is called Tabuli."

"Is no mystery. Is tabuli, you must stay away. Is bad medicine to Clan."

"Why? What happened?"

Nathon took another puff from his calumet before answering, as if recalling an old legend. "Many yars ago, when Clan first came here to live, we found water and shelter. Shelter from cold, from rain, from Perfs. Clan drank from up there." He pointed. "Some drank from other pool also. Many grew sick, some died. Medicine Man say back pool was bad water. No more may drink or will die like others. Their May'r placed tabuli on pool to keep Clan safe."

"How long ago did this happen?"

"May'r who placed tabuli on pool," he said slowly, "was father of this one's father."

"You mean you've never tested it since? Fifty or sixty years, I mean yars, is a long time. The natural replenishment should've purified any contamination by now."

"Pool is tabuli," Nathon repeated. "And no one breaks tabuli."

"Not even if it would help the Clan?"

Nathon leaned forward, his eyes hard and questioning. "How could this help Clan?"

"Come on, May'r, you know what I'm talking about. Even though you're constantly surrounded by it, you must be aware of the stench. Your people live here in filth."

Nathon's countenance hardened. "You do not enjoy our hospitality?"

"That's not what I'm saying. I'm deeply in your debt. And I offer my assistance because of my concern, with you, for the Clan's well being."

"What assistance can Visitor Danon offer?"

"We could all stand a good bath, right?"

Nathon said nothing.

"Wouldn't the Clan enjoy a cleaner village? A better smelling home? A healthier place to raise its children?"

"You can make the children healthier?"

"Absolutely!"

Nathon stood and faced the buffalo robe hanging on the wall, staring at the smoke darkened pictures.

"This one must choose what is best for Clan. But cannot endanger Clan to save Clan."

"You can let me investigate," Danon suggested. "Let me find out if the pool's still bad. With just a few medical supplies, I can take samples."

Nathon spun around. "You know powerful medicine of the Perfs?"

"Well, sure, why not?"

"Perfs' medicine is strong magic. Even Medicine Man does not understand all."

Danon grinned. "Believe me, I've worked much stronger medicine than this."

Nathon's face wrinkled in puzzlement. He seemed reluctant to break tradition, especially one which offered protection. His face revealed hints of indecision. Finally he nodded.

"You will talk to my daughter," he said. "When she returns from raid, she will have biotics, maybe is what you need."

"Your daughter?"

Nathon nodded sternly as if he were admitting to a serious offense. "She wears leathers of a warrior and is called Lauriel."

"She's your daughter?"

Nathon gave a puzzled look at the visitor who seemed slow to catch on.

It hadn't seemed important before, but now it was. Lauriel was a princess, or something equally important. Just his luck. The only good looking girl around here and she's the daughter of a May'r.

"They not return till late," Nathon said. "You can see her tomorrow." He resumed his position on the floor and reached for his pipe. "Come back and we talk again, but pool is tabuli for now."

Danon didn't like waiting, but he was thankful for an excuse to approach Lauriel again. As he stepped out of the Lodge, he almost bumped into Devon who stood stiffly with his arms folded like a cigar store figure. His intense gaze projected a statement of certainty. Maybe his shorts were too tight, Daniel thought. Or maybe his parents were first cousins.

# # #

Danon wandered around the village, exchanging greetings with the elderly men who sat in scattered circles. Some sat glassy eyed, passing a ceremonial pipe of boredom releasing cannabis, while others passed the day trading stories from their forgotten youth. Danon wondered if any of the stories were true. He appeared to mingle socially, but he was scavenging for tools and a light to take back to the pool.

Since the raiding party had been leaving as he had arrived, the distance to town and back, if they traveled on foot, would mean a very late return. Although he was ready now, he'd have to wait another twenty four hours. He would be asleep when they came in, and they would still be sleeping when he left for work at Miss Lillian's.

That slut.

He found a scratched, dented lantern lying in the dirt beside one of the tents. He glanced around before picking it up. He looked around again and then examined it closely. It looked like a lantern, like one of the antique railroad lanterns he had seen in the museum. But how did it work?

There was only the slender bail for carrying and a small lever located at its base. He put his thumb on the lever, and pushed. A shutter on the side of the square frame rose partially, releasing a thin beam of yellow light that rushed out into the darkness. He let the squeaky shutter fall back down, glancing around nervously.

He was still alone.

He pushed the shutter fully open and looked inside at the curious yellow rock that glowed with a soft intensity. He wondered how it worked. Geoluminescence? Phosphorescent isotope? Magic?

He started back for the crevice to stash the lantern for his trip tomorrow night. He took the shortest route, through the middle of the densely packed dwellings. He carried the isotope lamp loosely by his side, trying to look at ease and not attract attention from the scattered clansmen he passed on his way. He smiled back at an old woman with a prunish face. She had a warm, revealing smile, he thought. It revealed three missing teeth.

CHAPTER 13

Danon returned to Grotto Cave shortly after dark. He had spent the entire day dodging Miss Lillian, avoiding her as much as possible. Still undecided as to how to deal with her occupation, he just ignored her. He had also spent the day in anticipation. He wanted to meet this she-warrior Lauriel, and investigate the mystery surrounding the pool. One of the prospects aroused more than just his professional curiosity.

Below him lay the village. Most of the men had returned to join their families and relax after a long day dealing with the Perfs' society, welcomed with squeals by their excited children. The sounds of hundreds of reunions flittered up like scattered birdsong as he made his way down the ramp. The smell of the crowded cavern with its smoldering fires, unwashed bodies, and open latrine also greeted him.

A large bat-like shadow swept over him, causing him to pause and look up. High above an elderly woman swayed on a rope ladder. She wrestled to tug the heavy cloth over one of the lighting panels embedded in the wall. She spit a brown streamer of tobacco juice through determined lips and then started again. Danon hurried passed under her, and made his way to the village. Searching the crowd for Lauriel, he noticed his accelerated heartbeat. Something about her excited him, something wild and untamed.

But he couldn't find her anywhere. He turned toward the Lodge. Nathon would know, if he could just get past old Tight Shorts. When he neared the entrance he was relieved to find a different warrior standing guard. He bent down to duck under the door flap, but heard a challenging shout.

"Hey!"

He spun around, expecting Devon.

"Father said you were looking for me," said a clean face hiding beneath a few smudges of dirt. Her coal black hair hung down her chest in a single braid. At its tip a delicate, crimson feather dangled just below her breast. Nice breast too, he thought, from what he could see. She wore no perfume, yet she smelled good. Like a woman should, nothing added to her scent, and nothing missing. He liked everything about her: the pale green eyes, thin bottom lip, and velvety-smooth brown skin which seemed to peek out everywhere.

"Hi," he said. Not his best line. "I thought you were someone else, but yes, I've been looking for you. My name's—"

"You are visitor who asks for biotics," she said. "Nothing you can do going to help, but if you want'em, follow me." As she walked away, the tight leathers seemed to caress her slender physique—a waist that could be encircled with one arm, round hips that were two hands wide, and slender thighs that refused to wiggle.

"Oh, yes," he said. "I definitely wanted them."

# # #

They approached another lodge, similar to the one May'r Nathon lived in, only smaller and not as elegant. Still, it stood in contrast to the shacks around it. She slapped the flap out of her way and ducked inside. Danon followed her into the darkened interior.

"Where are you?" he asked, groping blindly. A hand, slightly callused, caught him and pulled.

"Over here, can't you see?"

The touch of her hand wasn't as soft as he'd expected, but he liked it.

"Sit down here," she said, pushing him back. Then she reached over his head for something, her hand pressing gently on his shoulder. "The lamp is shuttered."

"That's allright; I like the dark. With you here." He placed a hand on her bare waist. Her skin was cool and soft. He glided slowly up her side, wondering what her face would reveal if he could see it.

She leaned closer, close enough for him to pick up a faint musky scent.

"What d'you think you're doing?" she whispered.

"Falling under your spell," he said with a grin she couldn't see.

Something sharp pricked him in the ribs.

"Raise your hand any further, and you be needing more than just biotics." The sharp point of her dagger nudged deeper, dissipating any amorous intentions.

"Maybe I should apologize. I didn't mean—"

"Enough," she said.

The lamp's shutter flew open to flood the room with soft, sodium yellow light. The floor, he could now see, was covered with a patchwork of carpet pieces and a pile of folded blankets rested against the far wall beside two plastic crates.

"Here's some we brought back from the pharmacon last night." She pointed to one of the crates. "Sometimes we grab wrong bottles, biotics that cause strange sickness to Clan. Only Medicine Man knows all the pills. He keeps them for later if they're good. Is it what you need to remove tabuli?"

He leaned forward slowly to ensure the knife really was strapped in its sheath. "I try to show a little affection and you pull a frigging sword on me? Are you crazy or what?"

She smiled and raised the lid of one crate. "This one is not hungry squaw to be fondled. You are here to examine these, not me. Now ..." She raised the lid higher. "D'you want any of this?"

He eased over to sift through the contents of the box, which contained a black leather pouch filled with bottles of vitamins, pain suppressants, and stimulants.

"Is this all?"

"We did good to grab this before catchers came!" She slammed the lid, almost catching his fingers. "Think you could do better?"

"I mean is there any more? You know, the other stuff?"

"Medicine Man keeps some, to study or something. Mostly he throws away what is not good."

"Can you take me to this medicine man?"

She tilted her head as if studying his motives. Then she grabbed the pouch and extinguished the lamp. "Alright, let's go. Give me your hand."

The room was black again.

"Well?" she repeated.

"Promise you won't cut it off?"

\# # #

Benon was the Clan's medicine man, a solitary position inherited from his father, and his father. He ignored the intrusion as he carefully poured a red mixture into the vial. His hands shook more than they used to, and he didn't like being watched when he made medicine. He didn't look up as he sealed the vial because he already knew who was waiting at his door.

"Come in, little princess. What you bring me this time?"

Lauriel placed the leather pouch on his table, a wobbly board laid across two adobe bricks.

"Biotics," she answered, "for children's fevers. And I brought the Visitor. He wants to see Perf's medicine, some of the old bottles." She turned to introduce her godfather and friend, the only other clan member besides her father who was born into his position.

Danon offered a handshake, but the thin, wrinkled man seemed suspicious. "We meet b'fore?"

"Yes, maybe. On the airbus, I think, a couple of days ago."

"Why you want look? You not medicine man."

"Me? No, not exactly. I can help do some healing, I suppose, but—"

"I do all healing in Clan." Ben-on straightening as much as possible, squaring his rounded shoulders.

"Don't worry, old-timer, I'm not here to compete. I just want to test the water in the pool."

"Water has gone bad?"

Lauriel placed a hand on the old man's shoulder. "No, is alright. The Visitor means water in other Pool."

"Other pool is bad. You, you not go there," he said, shaking a knobby finger.

"Yeah, I know. Tabuli. I think I've heard that somewhere before."

"Is alright," Lauriel said. "He works for Father, but is secret. He may be able to remove curse from the pool."

Ben-on seemed unimpressed. "Need powerful medicine to do that," the old man said, studying the new visitor. "Strong magic."

Danon grinned. "Maybe I have some strong magic."

The old man seemed startled. "This one must go now. Need to grind herbs." He left the room.

Lauriel flashed a cold look. "Be careful what you say to him. That one is old and believes the lore, the legends and superstitions."

"What about you? You don't believe in magic?"

She tossed her long braid behind her back. "Don't believe anything I can't see with own eyes, or feel with hands."

She led him to an old crate stuffed with vials and bottles: an assortment of white pills, green and purple capsules, greasy creams, and bitter smelling elixirs.

"That's a very practical philosophy, almost scientific. I'll bet you're difficult to argue with, but can you accept new beliefs."

"What do you mean?"

Danon pushed aside bottles of old vitamins. "Suppose I showed you something to see or feel, something you hadn't accepted as true before. Would you believe?"

She shrugged.

He inspected and discarded several more bottles. "You're quite a contrast to most of your people. Not like the others, I mean."

"Father has often said that. He thinks I am rebellious."

"You, too? I guess some things never change between parents and children, or Chiefs and May'rs."

"This one is not child! I am warrior, regardless of what my father thinks."

"Relax, I don't know what your father thinks." He gave his best sincere look. "But I think you're kind of special." He leaned closer, noticing the salty sweet smell of her leather vest. "Even your language is different, better than most of the Bios'."

She rose abruptly, resting her hand on her dagger. "I am not—We are not Bios, houseboy!"

Danon moved back, eyeing her dagger. "What'd I say now?"

"We are Lowmans, without guilt of Holocaust."

"Calm down, okay? I didn't mean anything. What are the Lowmans, if not Bios?"

She cocked her head as if confused. "Where did you come from to be so …"

"Uninformed?"

"I was thinking ignorant?"

"You wouldn't believe me. Until you could see and feel, remember? And we don't have time for that right now. Tell me about the Bios and the Perfs."

Lauriel shook her head. "Everyone knows," she said. "Everyone." She paused, noticing Ben-on poking his head around the corner.

"S'cuse me, princess, but Devon is outside. He demands to see you."

"Oh, he does? No one demands me."

Ben-on shrank back out of sight.

She turned to Danon. "Keep looking. I'll be back."

He covered his grin and returned to the jumble of old medicines. They were useless. He needed more, much more. And the growling voices outside shack sounded much more interesting than the cluttered room. He eased over to the door to investigate.

The two warriors were speaking low but harshly to each other. Devon flailed the air with his arms, denying whatever she had accused him of. She repeated herself and poked his chest. Then she shoved him backwards before he could disagree.

"Excuse me," Danon said, thinking someone needed to step in and calm them down. A bad idea.

A knife whistled through the air to materialize in front of his face.

"If I want somethin' from houseboy, I send wo'am to fetch you." Devon's voice was low and bitter. "You best learn your place. And quick!"

Danon's fist hardened into an iron knot before he had time to think. He was getting tired of having knives pulled on him today. "If you're planning on using that frog sticker, do it. If not, put it back before it gets you into trouble."

Devon's beady eyes widened. With a mocking grin, he lowered his knife and turned to Lauriel. "That one is not worthy to stain my blade. But tame your pet if you want him to stay around."

Lauriel considered Danon's clenched fists and balanced fighting stance. "You might find him more difficult hunting than you think, brother."

Devon gave a smug grunt. "There is only warrior … and prey. Even you should understand."

Lauriel tensed as if insulted, but didn't respond. Instead, she spun around quickly, flinging her braided hair like a whip in his face.

"Where you going? We're not finished."

She strutted off, leaving the two men alone. Their mutual stare shared a common thought, the white-skinned intruder would not enjoy the protected status of visitor forever. One day Danon would have to prove himself with old Tight Breeches. But not now.

Danon tried to catch up to Lauriel. "Hey, wait up! I'm not through talking to you yet."

"I don't feel like talking anymore."

"Okay, just answer one question for me about the pool."

"What." She kept going, taking long strides.

"On your raids for medicine, have you ever noticed a microscope?"

"Don't know."

"Please, it's important. It looks like this." He stopped to draw a hasty sketch in the dirt. "Does this look familiar?"

She paused to look at the crude picture for only a second. "Yes, maybe. Why?"

"I need one to test the water for bad medicine."

"Don't believe in bad medicine. Can't see it, can't feel it." They turned off the winding path and started down another trail, rougher and unlit.

Danon followed, tripping on the scattered rocks that hid in the shadows. "Lauriel, you don't understand. Ouch, damn!" He rubbed his ankle. "You don't understand. If the water's bad because of microorganisms, the microscope will let you see them. Ouch, will you slow down? These rocks are killing me."

"You are clumsy. Walk like duck."

"You walk like a man."

She stopped and spun around. “What does that mean?”

“They’re too small to feel, but I promise you can see them. Plain as day.”

“What?”

“The microbes.”

“Have never seen your crobes. And pool is not bad. I know it isn’t, because I—” She stopped, her expression seemed disturbed for just an instant before she recovered. “Can you prove this to my father if I bring you this, this scope?”

Danon reached out to hold her still. He was tired of trying to keep up with her, but the look she gave caused him to let go.

“Without it, I can do nothing. But just maybe I can prove your breaking taboo, I mean tabuli, was actually beneficial to the Clan.”

“Who accuses me of breaking tabuli? That is challenge of honor.”

“Just a guess, okay a wild guess. But you smell too nice, too clean compared to the other women. And how would you know that pool was safe, unless you had already tested it?”

She looked past him, far past, and glanced all about, no longer masking her innocence. They were alone. Danon realized their suddenly tenuous arrangement as options raced across her mind. What would she do? If she were exposed to the Clan as having broken a sacred law, she could become an outcast from her family and stripped of her warrior status. Even her father could not protect her from the law and customs of her people.

She was going to make a decision, and soon. She didn’t seem the type to offer him a bribe, but she appeared fully capable of silencing him permanently. As her fingers crept down her leg toward the hilt of her dagger, Danon noticed the subtle movement and took a step back.

“Where are you going to hide the body?” he asked.

His question threw her off guard.

“Relax, Lauriel. I’m not a threat. It might be a big deal with your people, but not to me. It’s none of my business where you take a bath.”

Her face of stone softened a little, but her green cat-like eyes continued to study him as fingers tightened around the dagger’s hilt.

“I swear, Lauriel! You have nothing to fear.”

“This one is afraid of nothing,” she said softly, “but the word of houseboy means little.”

“Then what if I told you that I have broken tabuli, too? What if I said I’ve already been to the pool? Do you think I’d expose myself?” She couldn’t know that he hadn’t actually been there, yet. He hoped.

She looked around the darkened path again. When she spoke her voice was low. “And what do you ask in trade for silence?

"Why do you find it so hard to trust me?"

"Trust?" She almost smiled. "Trust is earned, not given."

"All I'm asking is to help bring a little hygiene to this place."

She stared at him inquisitively.

"Less dirt. Less stink. It's obvious you want to live cleaner than most of your clan. What about the rest of your people?"

After an awkward moment of considering her options, she released a sigh. And the dagger. "In Medicine Man's tent are some relics I did not show you. They are *magic* items passed from father to son and not talked about outside of Medicine Man's lodge. Their purpose is long forgotten, but maybe you find what you seek among them."

She turned and bounced back up the trail with the spring of a young gazelle. Danon trudged up behind her, groping his way along the rugged trail. Once they were back on smoother ground, he caught up to her.

"You weren't really going to use that on me, were you?"

"Does not matter now."

"It does to me!" Danon matched her stride. "You know, killing me would be a lousy way to start off our relationship."

"Maybe you are right. Maybe you should explain to Devon also."

He smiled at her first display of humor, then realized that she was serious. "He seemed upset about something. Of course, he always seems upset. What did the grouch want with you?"

"Is not your concern."

"Okay, didn't mean to pry, just trying to start a dialogue that doesn't involve me and daggers." He offered a friendly smile which she did not return. "Are you two very close? You called him brother."

"You talk too much," she said without slowing down.

Chapter 14

The dark interior of Benon's lodge gave no hint of relics stored beneath the layer of musty grit, but Lauriel knew right where to go. She evicted a pile of worn carpet pieces to reveal a dented metal container with a sunken top that had remained unopened for a long time. Beneath its stubborn lid, Danon found a packet of brittle yellow documents that smelled older than last night's buffalo hide. Beneath them he found numerous containers, some cylindrical, some square, all entombed in the layers of brown, crumbling paper.

Danon began unwrapping them. "Tell me about the Perfs," he said.

"What about 'em?"

"How did they come to control everything?"

"Smallest child knows that," she said. "Blacks rose to power after the Hol'caust."

He examined a set of rusted dental tools. "What holocaust?"

"Biowar, what else?"

"What did the whites do? Just stand around and let them take over?"

"What whites? Not many survived. And they hid or ran away."

"You mean to tell me everyone else died? A whole race?"

She cocked her head. "Everyone knows this!"

Danon fought the growing knot in his stomach and rummaged through the bottom layer of paper wrappings. "What happened then?"

"Perfect Ones said they's chosen by God to survive. So it was their destiny to purify the land. And then the bigots blamed us for all the death." She couldn't sit still any longer.

"Caucs, Spanics, Urpeans, and even Lowmans was all blamed as Bios. Them Perf buzzards still blame us! Maybe some clans, like Du Ponts, deserved it. I don't know. But not my people! We're just like all other ethnos. We had no part."

Danon collected a few more pieces of equipment while Lauriel settled in a corner, seeming to relax a little.

"During Great Purge, when became against the law to live in Perf's cities, they came here," she said. "Sioux and Manchees with others like the Okees to live as one clan. Other clans made home in other places. Anywhere they could." She leaned back and took a long steady breath. "But Hol'caust not our fault."

Danon found something large and heavy beneath the shredded paper and held it up. "This is it, the frame at least! And here's the lenses."

He soon found the missing items and tossed them into his collection of rumpled packages, ready to leave. But Lauriel carefully repacked the box and closed the lid. Then she arranged the carpet just as she had found it. When they finally turned to leave, they discovered the artifact's curious owner standing in silent observation.

"What you want with forgotten magic of grandfathers?"

Lauriel approached the man she knew as both Shaman and godfather. "My old friend, I'd not take anything without asking you. The Visitor needs this to remove curse from pool. He says he knows their purpose and how to use them."

She held the items up for his approval. "You will allow us to borrow what your grandfathers once understood? My word, as warrior, it will be returned."

The old man's frown softened. "The word of my daughter is good. Remember my honor and go."

# # #

Danon juggled the items as he hurried to keep up with Lauriel's long strides. "Hey, wait a minute. Don't you want to help? This is a lot of equipment."

"You can carry it fine."

"But I need a place to put all this."

"So?"

"So you have plenty of room in your lodge."

"Is more room in communal lodge," she answered.

"Yes, but the communal lodge isn't exactly the most private place in the cave. I'm sure I could set up my equipment and still stay out of your way. I might even promise to behave."

Lauriel stopped. "You are like feather wandering in the wind."

"What does that mean?"

"You are trying to ask for something. Say it. What do you want?"

He took a second to regain his composure. He used his best hurt-puppy look. That one always worked. "Can I move in with you? Just so that I could help the Clan."

She studied him, as if trying to judge the integrity beneath his perfectly honest expression. Maybe she wasn't buying it.

"If it's going to cause any problems between you and Devon, I'll understand. I don't think Devon likes me. I don't know why, but if you don't think he'd approve …"

"That one does not own me. And I ask no one's advice to make decision." She turned away. "Yes, is good if you are close where I can keep an eye on you. But only to remove curse."

"Of course." He followed her on the narrow path, grinning to himself. "So, what did Benon mean before about his honor?"

"Is concerned with saving face as Clan's healer. He is afraid."

"Of what?"

She paused to face him with a demanding stare. "You claim to possess great magic, magic that could endanger his status with Clan. Whatever you find or prove, you must give him credit." Her expression almost softened for the first time he could remember. "Is important to me."

"No problem. All I'm looking for is a little fresh air."

She studied his eyes for only a second, then took off again.

"And I'm sure we'll get along just fine." Maybe he still had a chance, he thought, admiring her firm waist.

# # #

Back in Lauriel's lodge, Danon stared at the silk-screen painting. In the foreground, timid deer grazed in a shallow depression of a grassy meadow while towering pines arched their backs against the sky blue of the background. The forest scenes seemed to sway on the opaque backing of the room dividers that sectioned off the large room into small compartments. Their delicate beauty seemed out of place, he thought. They were too clean to exist down here, and too feminine to belong to Lauriel.

She pointed to a small patch of floor behind the one of the screens. "You can sleep and work there," she said. "But is all. Don't get lost in dark and stumble into my room."

"Don't worry. I figure you probably sleep with your knife."

She didn't answer, but her dry lips wrinkled into a smile. "You are hungry?" she asked.

"Yeah, I am. What's for supper?"

"A warrior does not cook meals. The Brotherhood shares its game in Warrior's Den. Is where this one always eats," she informed him. "If anything is left over, I can bring some back for you."

"Oh."

Some unknown law of physics was at work here, he was sure of it. Somehow the Timeslip event had screwed up his charm. She'd come around soon, though; she just needed to get to know him better.

# # #

The Warrior's Den sat in a natural rock alcove at the far edge of the village, out of sight from the rest of the Clan. Unmated warriors gathered there regularly in the evening to share the camaraderie of fresh meat and strong drink. Many of the pair-bonded warriors also gathered, leaving their wo'am and noisy children behind. They ate venison and drank brien, an alcoholic mixture brewed from vegetable peelings and fruit scraps. Mostly they drank and challenged each other to games of bravery. Lauriel walked in, as always, with her defiant stride.

Two "brothers," who did not consider themselves related to this she-warrior, watched from across the room. One stood in front of a ragged target board that hung on the wall. Before she came in, they had been taking turns throwing their dagger at the board. One would stand so close to the target that his opponent's dagger missed by only inches. If the challenger flinched, he lost a token. If he managed to catch the dagger, he won two. Tokens were important in the Den. Not only were they a measure of status, they would buy more beakers of brien.

When she walked past, they continued to stare. Everyone did. Most of the warriors did not accept her as one of them, but they no longer tried to keep her out. Her skill with the knife had left a cutting memory with more than one impetuous brother.

Lauriel ignored the hushed room and walked over to the spit of roasting game. She jerked her dagger free and held its tip in the air—the sign of challenge for anyone who cared to accept.

As everyone returned to their warm brien, she covered a satisfied smile and sliced off two chunks of meat. On her way out, she stabbed a half-eaten loaf of squaw bread and rescued it from a startled brothers' table. Although the brown squaw bread's texture resembled a dry bath sponge, she enjoyed its flavor. For many of the Clan's families, the chewy loaf was too often a substitute for meat. She glanced behind her to see who was still watching before ducking through the door flap.

# # #

Danon carefully removed the microscope's frame from its storage tube. It didn't look that different, he thought. In fact, it almost looked like the one he'd used just a few days ago. He stopped. Just a century ago, he remembered. It'd probably been abandoned for at least half that time.

"Here!" came an unexpected shout.

He looked up just in time to catch the still warm venison. "Thanks. Smells good. It's been over a hundred years since I had barbecue."

"You mean hundred yars?" She shook her head as she tore off some of the squaw bread and tossed it. "Don't think so."

He was surprised by the good flavor, once he finally got it chewed. "I wasn't expecting you back so soon," he said. "Not that I mind the company, but I thought you always eat with the others."

"I decide to eat here. I s'ppose you are guest of sorts."

The soft glow of the isotope lamp sparkled in her ebony hair, inducing an iridescent rainbow. Where the cool shadows fell across her face, they only enhanced the alluring quality he found so difficult to resist.

His attention drifted down the shiny black leather encasing her muscled thighs to focus on her unusual footwear.

"Tell me. With the choice of so many modern boots, why do you wear something as ancient as moccasins?"

"They let me run swiftly and silently," she said, "to pass unnoticed in the shadows, and feel presence of Earth Mother beneath my feet. And strike like viper from the grass."

"Does everything about you revolve around war and fighting?"

"Is not matter of war," she answered. "Is matter of survival."

"Excuse me, since I am a guest, of sorts, is there anything to drink?"

She tossed a green bottle. He held it up to the light to read the label—2120. "Was it a good vintage yar?"

"It should've been," she said softly, "Was when my Madera returned to Earth Mother."

"Returned?" he asked, tipping the bottle.

"When one dies, they return to Earth Mother."

Danon almost choked on the wine. "Sorry, I didn't realize."

"Is no sorrow. Is where we come from, and where we go home to rest. Someday."

He looked for a hint of remorse or sadness in her face, but saw none. "I guess you still miss her, though."

"Sometimes," she said. "She was good to talk to."

Danon nodded as if he understood. "Well, there's still your father."

She shook her head. "We are close, I suppose. But he does not understand how I feel. Seems we disagree on everything."

"Some things never change, I guess. I take it you wanting to be a warrior would be an example of your disagreement."

She looked at him suspiciously. "How'd you know?"

"That elder's thing, the council meeting or whatever," he said, looking for a place to wipe his hands. "He didn't seem to think much about your request to lead the raid."

"He thinks cause I am not mano, I should not be warrior. Has never presented me to Clan as one worthy of leathers. Is why I asked in front of Council to lead raid. But he refused and even this one cannot argue in front of Council."

She walked over to the to the door flap. "Does not matter what he thinks, what anyone thinks. This one walks the warrior path! Have been on many raids and have fought both catchers and bounties."

"Bounties?"

"Yes, Bounties." She rolled her eyes at the need to explain another well-known topic. "They lie in wait at night to catch warriors when they're careless. Then they sell them to the Catchers for a reward. Blood money," she said, and spit out the door. "What more must one do to be accepted?"

"Is being a warrior that important?"

Her look was again cold and callused. "How could you understand, you are mano. A wo'am is no more than property of her mano, with life of raising children, mending clothes, preparing meals. What greatness can she make? Maybe as daughter of May'r, a princess." She laughed. "Maybe I hope for something I shouldn't, something better than my sisters have found." She lifted the flap, tying it to the doorpost, and stared out into the dark expanse of glowing tents.

"I think a wife, I mean wo'am, is more than, well, you know. Actually I think this wine is a little stronger than I thought." He took another sip. "But I kind of understand how you feel, you know, about not becoming what people expect you to be." He took another, longer drink. "I'm not ready for that either."

"Is not that. Maybe am trying to be someone else. I know Father cares for me. But when he looks at me he is reminded of no son to follow him as May'r. With no prince, and a princess who refuses to pair-bond, there is none chosen to wear the shawl."

She walked back into the room and sat on the cushions. "That means challenge of combat for some warrior to prove his worth. That one must fight to lead our Clan. If I chose to bond, my husband would be accepted as next may'r."

Danon nodded as if he understood and tossed the bottle of wine back to her. All this talk about bonding made him uncomfortable.

"Maybe I should," she said, taking a drink. "But only if find someone who could become the leader I know I would be."

"You want to become May'r?" He quickly covered his smile. "I mean that's a lot of responsibility."

"Why not?" She tossed the bottle with force. "Is time for change. Someone must lead my people out of this dirty tomb. We should live free in the open, as it once was."

"I don't know about all that, but maybe we can break one tradition." He held the bottle of wine up to propose a toast. "Make this place a little cleaner?"

She wiped off the top and drank long and hard. "Why do I tell you all this? You are just visitor. Have never told anyone else."

"I'm kind of glad you did. I'd really like to know you better. I mean—"

"I think I know what you mean. You desire what you cannot have."

Her thin smile made him uneasy. Not many people could see through him as well as this she-warrior. "Since the May'r, I mean your father, hasn't given permission to visit the pool, it's still considered off limits by the Clan. What if we're caught breaking tabuli?"

"You would be banished," she answered. "Could no longer to stay in cavern."

"And what about you?"

Her gaze swept the floor as she again considered the consequences. She'd face the loss of more than shelter. The Clan was everything. Her family. Her status as warrior, even if it was unofficial, was all she had.

Danon finished his meal and got up to leave. "I'll be back in a minute."

"Where you going?"

"To see your father. He's giving me one more try to convince him. If that doesn't work …"

"Then you probably go to pool anyway." She said, releasing a friendly smile. "This one thinks you are rebellious, too."

The lighting panels had been covered, blanketing the edges of the giant domed room with darkness. Only the scattered fires that speckled the cavern floor helped illuminate the path to Nathon's lodge. As Danon stepped from Lauriel's doorway, the pungent smell of mesquite campfires sagged heavily on the air, graciously masking the other odors present.

In the shadows, a figure dressed in black silently observed Danon's departure. The Visitor's appearance in the doorway of Lauriel's lodge had been a surprise and halted his approach. He watched the intruder leave and felt an unexplained sense of danger. As a hunter he knew when he was being threatened, and he knew how to deal with it. He started to follow his prey, but heard other footsteps approaching from behind. Muffled voices getting closer. He lowered the dagger into its sheath and faded away into the concealing darkness. He would choose another time.

CHAPTER 15

The path to the pool was dark and he often stumbled over hidden rocks as he wondered where Lauriel had gone. He had run all the way from Nathon's lodge eager to tell her about her father's permission, but she had disappeared again.

With the pharmaceutical supplies he had obtained from the medicine man, he could perform a few tests. They would be crude by laboratory standards, but at least he could analyze for toxic chemicals. He needed more sophisticated equipment to identify any complex organics: residuals from pesticides, or industrial waste, but the old man's microscope would be able to find any microbes that might be causing the "curse."

He passed the limestone formation holding the lighting panel. He unshuttered the lantern and tiptoed across the row of skulls. The ramp sloped down beneath an overhanging ledge to dissolve into the darkness below the cavern floor.

He took a deep breath and started down, almost losing his balance immediately as his feet skidded across a slimy floor. He lowered the lamp to investigate. Thousands of tiny, brown fungal stems sprouted along the damp surface of the wall. Even the floor was covered with the delicate fungal carpet that squished beneath his feet, leaving juicy shadows of his boots.

He slowly descended the damp tunnel, each step bringing new features to view in front as the blackness swallowed the curved path behind. Calcite flowers glowed purple in the lantern's beam, their slender thread-like petals squeezing out of the rock. Clusters of brilliant white gypsum needles sparkled when plucked out of the eternal night. Only the squishing of his boots disturbed the foreboding silence.

He wasn't scared of the dark; he just didn't like it. Besides, science had never proven that there wasn't something really hiding under the bed at night.

The air cooled noticeably as he continued. Abruptly, the ramp flared and he stood in a large room almost twenty meters wide. Stalactites and stalagmites riddled the room, some having joined into glistening columns of lime carbonate. A trickling stream bisected the cavern floor and disappeared into a man-sized opening in the left wall.

He followed the stream to the edge and stopped. Through the opening the stream cascaded over twenty meters of limestone nodules and glittering quartz before it splashed into a subterranean pool of glowing blue-green water. What caused him to stop was another light at the edge of the pool.

He shuttered his lamp, squinting to make out the image below. In the soft yellow glow of the other isotope lamp, he watched the water ripple as the nude figure of a woman surfaced in the pool. He quickly recognized the slim athletic body.

Lauriel was as beautiful as he had imagined. He wanted to sit quietly and enjoy the view, but his conscience overruled. It seldom did. But he decided to make his way loudly down to the pool and allow her some warning. He'd pretend he had not seen her bathing. Besides, he couldn't see very much in the distance anyway.

His valiant effort at stumbling and rock kicking was in vain. He was halfway to the pool before she noticed and covered her lamp.

"Stay there!" she shouted, tugging her pants and vest over wet skin.

"Who's there? Is that you, Lauriel?"

"Of course it's me! Who else d'you expect to be down here breaking tabuli?" She sounded more irritated than embarrassed.

"I didn't expect to find anyone," he said, advancing slowly. "If you'd told me you planned to take a bath after supper, I would've—"

"You would what, been here sooner?"

"No! I'm not a voyeur. I came to take some samples. And if you don't mind, that's all I'm going to do. I hope you didn't piss in it and screw up the bacterial count."

He tried to walk passed her, but she moved to block him. "What is voyeur?"

"What? Oh, well that's someone watches someone else taking off their clothes, or taking a bath without them knowing."

She just looked at him with raised eyebrows.

"No! Not like this, I mean. I'm not a skulking voyeur. And, by the way, you might want to finish getting dressed."

She glanced down to realize her vest was still invitingly open. As she finished tying the thongs on her vest, she studied his expression. "So, you did not watch me come out of pool?"

Danon fumbled with the bottles, attempting to complete his water samples. There was no good answer, so he just ignored the question.

"Why? You do not find me appealing."

He turned in confusion. "What? Now you're insulted because I didn't stare longer at your firm, round butt?"

She released a justified smile. "So, you did watch me!"

"No, well maybe a little. Look, I don't know if you're upset because I did look, or didn't watch longer. I could've stayed up there and gotten an eyeful, but I didn't." He packed up the samples and turned to leave. "I give. You're so mixed up, you don't know what you want from a man. If and when you make up your mind, let me know. I might still be interested."

She grabbed his arm and spun him around. "You might be interested?" She struck him.

He'd been slapped enough before to understand the subtle nuances of a slap. Some said "absolutely not, but thanks for asking" others were feminine attempts meant as an insult. Most slaps never really hurt, but this one nearly jarred his eyes loose. He gritted back the pain and forced a painful grin.

Her eyes narrowed and she swung again, this time with a balled fist that never reached him. He caught her by the wrist and held on firmly, even when she tried to pull away.

She struggled briefly before realizing she couldn't pull free. Then she relaxed, her look softening as she stepped closer, placing her other hand gently on his chest. She rubbed his shirt with a tempting smile.

Danon smiled back. He had seen this look before, too. Who could resist his winning smile?

"You are most strong," she admitted in a whisper, pressing against him. Then she shoved him backwards, while sweeping his knees with an unexpected back kick.

Danon crumpled and landed hard on the cavern floor, but he refused to release his hold on her. She tumbled down on top of him, quickly wrestling to gain the advantage. When he proved too adept for her to pin down, she struggled savagely, even biting to break free of his determined grip. As they rolled around on the damp cavern floor, her hair brushed his face, along with the hastily bundled firmness of her breast as her body writhed grinding against his. Her strength was impressive, with no sign of weakness or vulnerability, only a growing rage that seemed to fill her eyes with fire.

Her wild look was exciting, and a little scary. She fought with the desperation of a wild animal suddenly caged, and he knew that if he lost control this little wildcat would tear him to shreds, especially if she reached her dagger.

She struggled for several more minutes to free herself. Eventually, she conceded and lay still beneath him.

"Enough," she said, pausing for deep breaths. "You win, now let me up."

"You're pretty strong for a woman," he admitted. "But, I don't know. You didn't say, 'please.'" He shifted his weight to a more comfortable position, still on top of her. "Now that you're ready to listen, let me explain why I came down here."

Her lips tightened. "Dishonor me and I'll gut you when I get loose."

"What? You think this is my idea of a mating ritual? Please, get real."

She didn't smile back.

"I tried to find you. I thought you were going to help me investigate the pool. But when I got back from speaking to Nathon, you were gone. How was I to know you were here and not at the Warrior's Den? Or out prowling for Bounties on the surface?"

"Did not know what Father would say. So I came for your precious samples. They're over there." She pointed to a leather pouch propped against a column. "Took bath afterwards. And this one does not piss in water."

He moved to let her sit up. "How was I supposed to know?" He examined the vials and put them back inside the pouch. She had done a good job.

"I don't know what to say."

"Don't say anything." She straightened her vest that had come untied again. "Did not do it to help you. I do it for Clan."

"Well, thanks anyway." He offered a hand to pull her to her feet. "You ready to leave?"

She paused to contemplate something, then reached for his hand, looking into his eyes. "You defeated me in combat."

"I wouldn't exactly call rolling around on the ground and grinding hips combat. Besides, I kind of enjoyed it."

The momentary softness of her voice almost revealed whether or not she had also enjoyed it. "Is first time being defeated."

"Skip it." He started up the path back to the ramp.

"Where you going?"

"Up there, of course. To the entrance."

She shook her head and pointed to a dark fissure in the wall. "Is too dangerous. This way better."

As she guided him through her secret passage, she shared its story for the first time. "Discovered pool when only young gr'll," she explained as she led him into the narrow, snaking passage. "Was exploring corridor one day and found pool of clean water. Only after climbing the ramp that leads to main floor did this one realize it was tabuli pool. This one still believed in many superstitions back then," she said with almost a smile. "Just knew I was going to die, but was too scared to shame Father by telling anyone. So I waited. When several days passed and was still alive, not even sick, this one knew curse was gone. But still could not tell anyone."

They emerged on the main floor of the cavern, through an exit concealed by a large column. Danon squeezed around the column and saw the village sitting off to the left.

"Nice hiding place," he said.

"Is good to make sure I am not followed," she said, looking directly at him. "Do not like surprises during my bath."

Chapter 16

Danon followed the three brothers as they returned to the cavern.

It had been a good day for the houseboy and the dirtworkers. Miss Lillian had left for a convention or something, Danon wasn't sure and didn't care. She had left him in charge with a complete list of "things to do" recorded on her communications terminal. She seemed to place a great deal of trust in him. Very little had been accomplished.

Danon had persuaded the brothers to try a new experience while she was away. A bath. They had been hesitant at first, afraid that somehow she would know, somehow they would get caught. But once inside the bubbling, perfumed water they refused to get out, spending most of the day stewing in the hot tub. Danon served wine and snacks from the pantry while they soaked away layers of accumulated dirt and grime. Even Banion had smiled occasionally when he thought no one was watching.

When Danon finally dragged the trio of brown prunes from the water, each brother found a freshly washed jumpsuit waiting for him, although Allon had insisted that none were his. His was brown, not blue.

During their day of leisure, the four had become much better acquainted. Not only did Dillon know how to smile, Allon had disclosed a stinging sense of humor, taunting Danon repeatedly about his moving in with Lauriel. Although Danon had tried to explain their innocent relationship, Allon remained unconvinced and had reminded him of the danger of getting caught with a princess.

As Danon crossed the cavern floor, he noticed Allon had stopped to talk to someone, one of the maidens who had been presented at the last council.

"Hello," he said, stepping between them. "I don't believe we've been introduced. Say, this isn't the same gr'il you were with yesterday."

"Go 'way." Allon tried unsuccessfully to shield her from Danon's interference.

"Not until I meet her. She's much cuter than the other one."

Allon frowned, and seeing no easier choice, decided to introduce them. "Alright. Gabrielle, this is Dum-on."

"He means Danon."

"Is only visitor with Clan, you can ignore him," Allon said. "We do."

Gabrielle smiled shyly as she moved around her guardian for a closer look at the fair skinned visitor with the mischievous grin.

"That's enough," Allon said with a threatening swing of his hand. "You can leave now."

Danon dodged the mock attack and left, convinced his suggestive remarks would keep his new friend busy for a while trying to explain things to Gabrielle.

# # #

He entered the empty lodge and went straight to work. He placed a small sample of water under the microscope. He found nothing in the first sample. The second and third samples also appeared pure. He switched to a higher magnification, and two single-celled euglena swam past.

Although there were some life forms present, he saw nothing that seemed dangerous. A clear mountain stream would contain this many protozoa, probably more. He rotated the lens to a higher magnification and the thin sample of water became a vast ocean hundreds of feet deep and miles wide. A lone bacterium floated by, riding on thermally driven currents. Behind it a paramecium swam in pursuit, its tiny cilia flicking back and forth like tiny oars propelling it forward, steering it closer and closer until it could scoop up the bacterium in its long oral groove.

"Everything so far is harmless ..." He was talking to himself again, a habit acquired through hours of boring research. In deep concentration, he identified several more species of protozoa, but none of any consequence. These could all be destroyed with a simple disinfectant. "But why bother?" he wondered aloud. "Some of them are actually beneficial."

"What is beneficial?" asked a curious voice.

He glanced up to find Lauriel staring at him. "Hi, I didn't hear you come in."

"You never will." She pointed to her moccasins. "What were you looking at?"

"Go ahead," he said, moving to give her room, "Take a look."

She bent over for a hesitant peek, then jumped back. She examined the bottom of the microscope.

"Where'd it go?"

"It's still there," he said, trying not to laugh. "I told you they were too small to be seen or felt, but they're still there. Some of those creatures are called beneficial because they are helpful to us."

She didn't seem convinced.

"This magnifies them, makes them appear much bigger. That's what this magic relic was made for, studying the microscopic world that surrounds us."

She took another look. "How can that, that thing in water be good for me?"

He grinned. "That's a little difficult to explain. You see, these animals are obviously very small. In fact, if you swallowed them with a drink of water, you'd never know it. But some of them might attack your body from the inside. Two or three at a time can't do much damage, but if they stayed around long enough to multiply, they'd attack by the thousands and you'd get sick. Maybe even die."

"This is curse?"

"Well, not really. These particular species don't cause the sickness. If you drank them, nothing would happen."

"If nothing happens, what is good about them?"

"The beneficial part is that they eat the harmful ones."

Lauriel nodded. "As long as good ones live in the pool, we are safe."

"Yeah, it's like …"

"This one understands," she said. "I take hunting dog to protect me from wild packs. Is important to Clan that we keep them healthy and strong."

Something in her simple comparison bothered him, but she didn't give him time to think about it.

"Where'd you learn secrets of relic?" she asked.

"Huh? Oh, I've used one of these for a long time, almost since I was a kid."

She gave a strange look. "You said you was not medicine man for your clan."

"Well, no. Not exactly."

He tried to think of something that wasn't a lie. As much as he wanted to explain everything, but he knew he couldn't. "We had med-techs, I mean doctors, who practiced the art of healing. But their medicine was very advanced compared to yours."

"We used to know more," she said. "Benon has told me how the first medicine man worked great magic, but could not pass everything to his son. This one thinks he has forgotten much of the ancient knowledge … knowledge you somehow remember."

She studied him for a moment. "For one pretending to be houseboy, is powerful aura to your spirit."

"Aura? I thought you didn't believe in all that magic stuff."

"Is not magic, is spirit. Everything has spirit." She tilted her head slightly. "Even you."

"But you can't see a spirit."

"Of course not, but you feel it. If you try. You talk of secrets lost by the ancient ones, then act so dumb about simplest things. Where can you come from that is so different?"

He ignored her question and focused on the samples under the microscope. Her curiosity was becoming too tempting. Maybe someday, he thought.

# # #

He stood outside Ben-on's shack. He had some questions for the old medicine man. He hoped Ben-on had some answers.

A wrinkled hand folded away the heavy cloth flap. "Come in, Visitor Danon," he said. "Your magic is welcome in my dwelling."

Danon gave an exaggerated bow of respect. His success hinged on the old man's cooperation, and a show of courtesy wouldn't hurt.

"I need your help, Ben-on."

The old man's eyes widened. "The spirit of great magic is within you, secrets of relics, mysteries lost by many grandfathers. Is much more than you've chosen to reveal. How can simple medicine man help you?"

# # #

In the shadows a silent figure waited with stalking patience. He did not trust this intruder. Why had he come? Where was he really from? And what was he doing in Lauriel's lodge? Surely this visitor would not dare to be his rival. Lauriel was his, or soon would be. Everyone knew that.

His instincts told him to do away with the white-skinned visitor with a single thrust of his dagger, but the stranger provided two kilo credits. And that payment was needed by his clan. It would feed a family for two weeks, longer if meat could be provided by the hunters. Yet, he still sensed a greater danger, a desire to change the old ways. A warrior preserved the old ways. A warrior protected the Clan. A warrior did what must be done, and this outsider was not to be trusted.

# # #

Danon already had a theory based on what he'd gained from researching the pool and talking with the medicine man, but he decided to test his samples for toxicity. He wanted to eliminate all the other possibilities before he spoke to the May'r. He didn't want to be embarrassed in front of Lauriel by being wrong. He was checking the last sample, which also indicated zero trace of heavy metals, when Lauriel stormed into the lodge, slinging her hunting pack across the room.

"Not my fault!" she growled. "Perf's medicine always worked before. How is warrior supposed to know which bottle to grab?"

He peeked around the divider before venturing into her sight. She might have something left to throw.

"Something wrong?"

She seemed surprised to see him, but quickly recovered. "Leave me alone!"

"If you want to talk, maybe I can help. Lying on that cushion and sulking isn't going to solve anything."

Her sullen look would have sent a more sensible man scurrying.

"Well?"

"You don't understand. Is the children, the coughing fever. Should be cured by now, but they only get worse. This one brought Perf's medicine back from pharmacon. This one gave it to Medicine Man to heal them. Now he says I didn't bring right stuff. This one is warrior. We grab what we can and run before the catchers show."

"If Medicine Man knows which drug he needs, why don't you have him write it down and—"

"And then what! Is this one going to hand paper to pharmatech and ask to steal everything on list?"

He felt embarrassed for not realizing it earlier. "You can't read, can you?"

"Of course not, since is against the law for a Bios to read."

"Sorry. So why not take Ben-on? He probably knows what he needs."

"That one is too old. He'd only slow us down, then we'd all be caught by the catchers, or a bounty." She kicked off a moccasin, slinging it across the room.

He waited a moment for her to calm down. She didn't look calm, but she was quiet.

"Then take me."

"Go stare at your water. You are not warrior to understand."

"I can read. And I know the difference between antibiotics and vitamins."

She paused as if studying the muscles under his tight shirt. "This one doubts you can keep up with raiding party."

"I can handle myself. I beat you, remember?" His teasing smile wasn't returned.

"This is different. Is very dangerous."

"Is very necessary," he said, mimicking her accent.

Finally she nodded agreement, but pointed a warning finger. "But if you are caught, you will be left. They won't risk party for one member."

"I won't be caught." He wondered what happened to raiders who got captured, then decided he didn't need to know.

"I talk to others. If they agree, then Brotherhood will ask for another raid when Father sits at council of elders tomorrow."

"The Council! I almost forgot. I have to give an answer to your father about the pool."

"Well?"

"Huh? Oh, the curse is gone, of course. It's perfectly safe. The Clan can start taking regular baths. And you and I can enjoy a little clean air for a change."

"You can prove this?"

"With a little thanks to you, yeah."

"Me?"

"It was what you said about the hunting dogs. That started me thinking, so I talked to Ben-on. He told me about the tradition of blessing a pool before the Clan can use it. I think it was originally practiced for sanitation, probably some kind of a chlorine or ammonia compound added to the water to kill all the microbes."

"Microbes?"

"Germs. Anyway, later I think the original intent was lost. It became just a ceremony, blindly followed as some sacred, mystical tradition. Ben-on showed me his cleansing potion, a very mild disinfectant, too mild to destroy any bacteria. But it could be strong enough to destroy the beneficial protozoa. You know, the ones that guard—"

She shook her head impatiently.

"Well anyway, when the last medicine man poured his concoction into that pool, yars ago, it probably destroyed most of the good germs, allowing the others to grow and multiply. And that eventually led to the sickness and death of some of your people."

Lauriel wrinkled her nose. "Is that what you wish to tell my father?"

"I guess not. Maybe I should just tell him that with your help we have removed the curse and the pool is safe to use again."

"And you will remember Ben-on's status with Clan, and his honor."

"Don't worry. I'll give him plenty of credit. And this time when he performs the purification ritual, he'll only be pouring water from his sacred jar. I have to finish a few more tests to make sure I haven't overlooked anything. You know, rule out the long shots. It'd be embarrassing to give the May'r my guarantee, and later have people start dying on me."

She put her moccasins back on and walked over to the door, her voice suddenly cold and hard. "Would be more than just embarrassing."

# # #

Lauriel pushed back the entrance flap to the Warrior's Den and quickly scanned the smoke filled room with austere furnishings. She found the mixed aroma of narcotic tobacco, roasting venison, fresh squaw bread, and warm brien almost soothing. As usual, the sounds of manly banter faded quickly as she entered.

Opposite the entrance was a long, flat stone shelf. The bar. Behind it she could always find Gregon, a once formidable and still proud warrior who refused to count his yars. When he managed to walk, he did so with a severe limp, the result of an old encounter with a bounty. Gregon had recovered from his wounds. The bounty had not. Gregon still took great pride in that fact. Although no longer able to run with the pack on nightly raids, he was too proud to join those old men who sat idly around a fire and smoked their pipes while waiting to die. Gregon had dutifully remained at the Den, tending the bar and trading adventures with any warrior who would listen. He also ensured the Den never became boring.

Lauriel ignored the hushed resentment of the crowd and walked over to his inviting grin.

"Beaker o'brien?" Gregon asked, nudging the thick mug toward her.

She reached for the beaker, but Gregon held fast, his bushy eyebrows raised with anticipation.

She pulled a polished agate token from her vest and dropped it into his hand to satisfy him. Then she hoisted the squatty mug to her lips and forced down a gulp of the bittersweet brew. The biting liquid foamed like acid in her stomach. She almost smiled as the warmth spread. She didn't realize how much she had needed that drink. It felt good, but not good enough.

"Bad luck 'bout the raid," Gregon said, his scarred face giving a crooked smile. "Wrong biotics, I mean."

She clenched the handle of the heavy beaker like a war club.

"Say what you mean, grey-hair! This one crawled through the pharmacon. This one made the grab." She paused to empty the sour nectar and drop the beaker to the bar. "And this one took wrong stuff."

Gregon wiped up the spill with his sleeve. "I s'ppose any warrior brother could'a done the same."

"But it wasn't a warrior brother," she said. "Was me."

Gregon's expression hardened. "A warrior don't lick his wounds." He studied her for a moment with the same hard look, then nodded. "You need a good fight to burn your angers."

He reached into his worn vest and fished out five tokens, which he dropped inside a small-mouthed plastic bottle then he shook it. The room fell silent as everyone stretched to the sound of rattling tokens inside the challenge beaker.

Lauriel tried to grab the bottle. She had watched the often bloody game before. Whenever Gregon got bored, he'd put a handful of tokens into the challenge beaker, toss it to the middle of the floor, and watch the younger warriors fight over the prized agates like hungry dogs. The last one standing with the bottle won.

Rattling the bottle again, Gregon goaded the partially drunken fraternity. "There's five token in here! And Lauriel here, says they ain't a brother here good enough to fetch 'em!"

Some grumbled, but no one moved.

"Well?" Gregon shook the bottle harder. "Is she right?"

Lauriel snatched the bottle out of his hand and started dumping the tokens out. She'd return them to Gregon and stop this nonsense.

A harsh, angry voice sounded behind her. "Wo'am or not, I ain't taking that kind o'talk." The swaggering warrior was huge, at least three times her size. He was also smelly drunk as he reached for the bottle. "I'll tan yore overstuffed breeches."

"No!" She tried to pull away. "I make no challenge. Just give it back before—"

The unexpected backhand blinded her with stinging suddenness. The salty taste of her lip refocused her attention just as the second backhand landed. The smelly warrior ripped the jar from her fingers, and leaned against the bar to count his easy reward amid the laughter of his approving brothers.

She could have walked away. They weren't her tokens and it wasn't her challenge. But they were laughing at her. She grabbed his arm and turned him into striking position. He started to swing again, but she put an angry knee between his legs, stopping him cold. He bent over like a broken tree branch and toppled to the ground, wondering where his testicles had gone.

She bent over with a smug grin to pick up the scattered tokens when a sharp blow between the shoulders sent her stumbling across the floor.

"I'm not as drunk as Grogon," the new challenger boasted. "And I'm more than enough for the likes of you!" Honon was named for the Hopi term for bear, and it suited him well. He wasn't tall, but he was broad and solid with his feet firmly rooted to the floor. He didn't sway and his speech wasn't slurred.

She wiped the bitter dust from her face, smiling coyly as she walked to within arm's reach.

"You want it? Here …"

She tossed the bottle over his head. When he reached for the flying prize, she planted a moccasin squarely in his groin. He grimaced and slumped over, but he didn't go down. He straightened slowly and forced a bearish grin.

She took a step back and glanced around for a weapon.

"You're a sly kitten, Lauriel. But you met your match with me. This one's gonna peel those leathers and give'm to a real warrior. Does that sound like fun, kitten?"

Her eyes burned as she drew her dagger. "I'll peel more than leather, you nutless scavenger!"

Gregon grabbed a lance from the wall and swung it down over the counter, barring her way. "You put that away in here, gr'll. This is a friendly fight."

She gave a threatening stare, but Gregon stood firm. Her arrogant challenger waited, still grinning. When she reluctantly reached down to sheath her dagger, he attacked, rolling her over and pinning her to the ground. Before she could recover, he grabbed her by the hair and breeches and tossed her completely out of the Den.

He strutted over to the beaker and dumped its contents on the counter. "Was not serious 'bout taking off her leathers. But these ought to buy everyone another beaker." Boorish laughter flooded the Den.

Honon stood with his back to the entrance as he admired his booty, and didn't hear Lauriel's moccasins swiftly crossing the room. With the stealth of a panther she charged, aiming for the small of his back, just below the kidney.

The big warrior toppled face first into the dirt with a deflated groan. He tried to catch his breath, while spitting the orange mud from his mouth. Then he looked up to his devious attacker.

"If you're thinking of gett'n up," she warned, "Better think again." She stood rigid, one foot drawn like a crossbow aimed at his face.

He blinked just before he moved to dodge her foot. He did not realize that he had signaled his intentions until later, much later.

Another warrior closed in to take his turn.

"Enough!" she shouted. "It is finished."

Gregon was slamming his fist on the bar in uncontrollable laughter. "S'down, boys. The fun's over. Them's my tokens you all is fighting over. Lauriel here didn't insult nobody. I started this here carnival." He stopped to wipe a tear from his good eye. "So pick your brothers off the floor and have another beaker, my treat."

Lauriel dusted herself off and headed for the door. She paused to glance back at Gregon and slowly smile.

The old warrior nodded understandingly. She felt better now.

Chapter 17

Allon and his brothers stepped out of the elevator and quietly went to work. As they melted into the garden, picking up their tools and resuming where they had left off the day before, Danon went to his day room to wash, shave, and change into a "more presentable" tunic. After that the drudgery started.

He entered her bedroom, carrying the silver tray of fresh fruit and poached eggs. He refused to admire the partially covered body lying in the tangled sheets, her dark body bare from the waist up. She had not worn her negligee and the silken sheets crept lower and lower. An overpowering smell of perfume hung in the room, but it didn't cover the lingering telltale odor. She had had a busy night again.

"Your breakfast is ready."

She stirred, her curly hair matted against her neck. "I need a bath first."

"I can believe that."

"What? Did you say something, Danielle?"

"Draw my bath first," she yawned. "And then I shall need a good massage."

"Yes, Ma'am." He'd sooner massage a bucket of spit.

He sat the tray and started to leave when she arose from her tangled sheets and strolled to the bathroom with total disregard of her nudity in front of her house servant.

He was in the pantry, taking inventory of the food supply, compiling a shopping list, and trying to put her nude image out of his mind when his wristlet buzzed.

"Danielle, darling, I'm ready for my massage."

He threw the list on the counter.

She was sprawled atop the padded table. Her once tempting buttocks glistened with lingering beads of moisture. He tossed a towel over her, and began the massage.

She moaned softly beneath his rough touch. "Mmm yes, just what I needed."

She had just taken a bath, but still didn't feel clean. She felt used. He tried to think of the Clan as he massaged her oily skin.

"Oh yes, that's it."

He squeezed harder. "Does that hurt?" *Slut!*

"Just a trifle," she moaned.

"Good."

She cooed softly as she writhed under his touch. "A little lower."

He moved down to the small of her waist.

"Oh, good … good. Now lower …"

He paused. "I'd rather not."

"I said lower."

He gritted his teeth and put his hands over the towel. He started to rub, but she reached behind and threw the towel on the floor. "I want to feel the touch of your hands."

"Look, this isn't my idea of fun."

"You will do whatever I say," she ordered. She rolled over, grabbing his hand and placing it on her inner thigh. "And wherever I say. Understand?"

"You may be a frigging whore, but I'm not!"

Her shock lasted only a moment before she responded with stinging slap to his cheek. "Learn your place, boy!"

Slap her, his gut screamed. Just slap the racist crap out of her. But he couldn't. He might wind up in jail. He'd lose his job for sure, and the support he'd promised the May'r. He swallowed hard, and continued the massage."

# # #

The long airbus ride home was completed in silence. Danon said nothing to Banion or the others. He just stared out the dusty window, searching for a way out. But he had found none.

He didn't stop to admire the calmness of the pool or the water bucket. He didn't pause to return greetings to the few clan members who recognized him and welcomed his return. He headed straight for the solitude of his room.

# # #

Lauriel sat in the middle of the floor, her legs folded in lotus position. She had emptied her mind of the petty things that pestered her confidence. It was time for prayer.

Most of the clan maidens prayed to the spirit of fertility and youth. Her father often prayed to Sophist, spirit of wisdom, and sometimes to the Pawnee spirit of the hunt. All warriors prayed to the Spirit of the Hunt—for courage and bravery, or swiftness of foot—but she did not.

Too many spirits, too much mystical stuff she could neither see nor feel. The only spirit allowed in her pragmatic world was that of the sacred Earth Mother, the one who nurtures all living things. Known as Nokomis in the old Algonquin stories, the Pawnee in the Clan called her Atira.

She listened in meditation. To the chirping of the cave crickets outside her lodge. To the slow beating of her heart. To that part of her which was somehow connected to the Earth Mother, the part that defined her existence and explained her purpose. Whatever it was. Become the wife of a May'r? Was that all? No other destiny, no better calling?

"Watch over me," she whispered, "Grandmother of all living things. Guide my moccasins. Guide my dagger—"

Danon stumbled into the room. He looked surprised to see her, but said nothing. She would not appear eager to see him, but she awaited his cheerful greeting—a greeting which she had come to expect even if she pretended to ignore it.

But he gave no greeting. He didn't even acknowledge her as he recovered from his surprise and ducked behind the silken divider.

She could have forgiven the intrusion on her prayer, she was almost through anyway. And although she tended to overlook his casual comments, for he was always talking about something, she didn't like being ignored.

"What is wrong?" she asked, stepping around the silk-screen.

Danon rolled over on the bed cushion, turning his back. "Skip it, you wouldn't understand."

She bit her lip to keep from grinning at the young coyote pup who looked freshly weaned.

"Have bad day with your mistress?"

"I don't need this, not tonight. So just leave me alone."

"We talk and you will feel better. Or maybe a good fight is what you need."

"Just skip it," he repeated, "okay?"

"You are visitor with Clan and guest in lodge." She bent down, putting a hand on his shoulder to feel the tightness of his muscles. "Have obligation, I s'ppose, to help."

"Leave me the hell alone!" He knocked her hand away with surprising swiftness.

He had no right, she thought. She reached to get his attention and remind him of her status, but he brushed her off again. She reached to grab his face, but he moved causing her hand to land harder than intended. The unintentional slap landed on the same cheek Miss Lillian had struck earlier, and his eyes burned in anger.

Before she could apologize, a strong backhand sent her reeling backward over the silk-screen. She sat up shocked, but not as shocked as Danon.

"I'm, I'm sorry. I mean, I didn't mean to—"

"Is alright." She rubbed her cheek. She would have been mad had he not looked so ashamed. She almost felt sorry for him. "Is my fault. Did not mean to challenge."

"No, it's not." Danon wanted to hold her, to touch her softly, but she moved away. "I've never lost control like that. Well, almost never. Lauriel, I am so ..."

"I know, sorry." She repositioned the screen divider. "This one was wrong," she said on her way out. "Will respect your privacy now."

"No, wait ..." He followed into her bedroom. "Let me explain." He grabbed her with pleading eyes. His touch was gentle, but unsettling.

"I was wrong, very wrong for hitting you."

"You hit a warrior. You are not afraid of combat."

"But you're not just a warrior. You're a woman." He gently palmed the red mark on her cheek. "A beautiful woman."

Her cheek flushed even more with his touch. Then she recoiled as if startled. She was skilled in the art of self-defense, but seemed unnerved by his soft touch.

"Is nothing," she whispered, turning away. "Give me a moment, then we talk."

When Lauriel came out, she once again appeared confident and in control. "Council will be starting soon," she said. "If you are through with research, you should talk to Father before they meet."

"The Council!" He jumped up. "I nearly forgot. I'd better see him right now. I may have some convincing to do." He stopped at the door flap. "We still need to talk later. You are going to the Council, right?"

She gave an eager nod. "This one will be there."

# # #

The Circle of Elders had filled early and they were waiting with the crowd in hushed anticipation. They knew something big was going to be announced, but could get no details in spite of their political negotiations. Danon had left moments earlier and tried to make his way through the knot of warriors to stand with Lauriel. They had been hesitant to let the houseboy join them.

"Look," one of the leather-clad figures had sneered, "Lauriel brings her pet. Is he lodge-trained?"

Muffled snickers echoed around them, but quickly hushed as May'r Nathon exited the Lodge toward his seat of honor.

"What has Council to say?"

Again each member urged the other to take the honor of initiating the night's business. When the traditional diplomacies were dispensed, the eldest rose to speak.

"Honored May'r, it is Council's wish as always you live long and prosper. Continue to guide us with your wisdom, for tonight we bring matters for your judgment." Finished with his opening statement, the white-haired elder sat down as a cue for the others to speak.

Danon waited impatiently for the Council to get around to his business. He had hoped it would be first. One elder discussed the urgent need for more food, then another stood to be recognized. He wore the striped fawn of the Choctaw.

"One of my tribe has chosen a mate. He waits your blessing."

Danon was amazed to see Allon step out of the crowd and awkwardly approach the Circle. May'r Nathon motioned him closer.

"Who are you?" he asked. He knew the young man well, but the formality was expected by the crowd.

"Pr—Provider Allon," he said. "Of Choc tribe."

Nathon smiled and motioned for the young man to sit. "Tell me of this wo'am who has captured your heart."

"Is the gr'll Gabrielle," Allon answered, "from tribe of Manchee."

"You work in town?"

"Yes."

Nathon waited, expecting Allon to say more as proof of his ability to take a wife. "You are able to support a mate?"

"There is room in family dwelling, and food. We will give Clan many children."

Nathon pointed toward the crowd, pretending not to know exactly where the young maiden was standing. "Then call her to you."

Allon rose to make the traditional choosing. If she accepted and came before the Council, the May'r would bless them as being pair-bonded. Simple but permanent.

Gabrielle waited at the edge of the clearing, held by the arms of her father. When her name was called, she tiptoed quickly into the Circle with her head bowed and fingers clenched. But as she entered, another figure also stepped out of the crowd. He followed to stand with her before the Council.

The silent figure spread his arms, shedding his long antelope robe from his massive shoulders and chest to reveal the black leathers of a clan warrior.

"I claim the rite," he announced. "This gr'll is mine."

Danon tugged on Lauriel's arm. "What's going on?"

"Is rite of challenge," she answered. "Grogon is claiming Gabrielle. Since she is betrothed, is challenge of blood."

"What does that mean?"

"Only dishonor or death can stop pair-bonding."

"If he wanted her, why hasn't he come forward to claim her before now?"

"He knew she would not answer, then his claim would be gone. Cannot challenge for gr'll if scorned before Council.

"He looks big. Does Allon have a chance?"

Lauriel shrugged. "When sober he is strong warrior, but mind is slow. Maybe if Allon looks for his weakness ..."

May'r Nathon stood tall and imposing, an oak tree who had never bent with the wind. He spoke to Allon, but addressed the assembled Clan. "This one is warrior trained, but is his right to challenge you. You must accept or forfeit."

Allon took a deep breath as the crowd waited for his answer, wondering whether or not they see blood tonight. Gabrielle also waited, with trembling hands as she watched her betrothed trapped in a game he could not win. He must freely give her away, or die proving his love for her. She saw him agree to something and then hold out an empty hand.

Grogon pulled a spare dagger and flung it skillfully between his victim's feet. He had doubted that Allon would be foolish enough to face a clan warrior.

"Char Hemos begins!" Nathon shouted. The stern warning rang out like a peal of thunder for all to understand. No one was allowed to interfere with the challenge of blood. Then he backed away to observe, with the rest of the Clan, one of the more savage facets of their judicial system. This system of harsh justice ensured the survival of the Clan, purging it of weakness and preventing the incubation of troublesome jealousies. And this system had no court of appeals.

Allon fidgeted with the awkward knife and tried to steady himself. He studied his opponent closely. Grogon lumbered into striking range and waited, his feet spread and knees flexed. He swayed slowly back and forth, like a cobra toying with its meal. He held his knife firmly, its tip pointing at his intended victim. Back and forth he swayed, almost too rhythmically. Allon saw his chance. When the warrior rocked forward again, Allon lashed out.

Caught off balance, Grogon could not move back in time and the tip of the blade bit through his vest, carving a shallow gash across the sun-bleached leather. The veteran of many knife wounds laughed at Allon's feeble attempt. "Is best you do?"

"It's good enough, you dumb ox." He pointed at Grogon's chest. "You're too stupid to see how bad you're bleeding."

Grogon glanced down at the superficial cut for only an instant, but Allon had already lunged forward. Knife extended. Arms locked rigid. The grisly blade disappeared into the warrior's chest with little resistance. The veteran's confident smile faded; his expression of surprise turned to disbelief as he crumpled to his knees.

The crowd was stunned. The challenge had barely begun before Grogon lay dying on the floor. Allon had dispatched the battle-proven fighter too quickly to believe. Their fatal conversation had not been overheard, giving the impression that Allon's attack had been lightning quick—a story which, after being retold a few times, would assume heroic proportions.

Nathon motioned Medicine Man over to examine the motionless warrior as Gabrielle dashed across the clearing to embrace her champion, staining his cheek with tears. With assurance that Grogon was in fact dead, Nathon waved for the brothers to remove the body.

"It is finished!" he said with no hint of sadness. Then he pointed to Allon and Gabrielle as he faced the still silent crowd. "Allon has chosen Gabrielle as his mate and she has accepted. He has proven himself worthy. The Clan rejoices at their pair-bonding!"

Allon escorted his new wo'am out of the Circle. They would formalize the bonding later with a small group of family and friends. The echoing murmurs of astonishment continued long after Nathon had taken his seat and signaled for the Elders to continue.

Danon waited. The background noises of the crowd and the Council's proceedings blended into a monotonous drone. He waited, nervously rehearsing what he would say. Through the drone and haze came a sharp elbow. Someone had mentioned his name.

May'r Nathon was reminding the Council of the tabuli placed on the cursed pool. He pointed again to Danon and motioned for him to enter. With a nudge from Lauriel, the hesitant visitor stumbled forward as the other warriors showed their surprise to hear the houseboy requested before the May'r.

"Visitor Danon came to us only a half moon ago," the May'r announced. "A stranger offering two kilos for shelter. Tonight he offers more than simple payment. At my request, Visitor Danon has braved the curse of Tabuli Pool. Using secrets of our grandfathers, he has brought powerful magic to protect Clan. I have listened. I have considered. And I have decided. Tabuli is to be lifted."

Murmurs rippled through the crowd again. None were old enough to remember the sickness caused by the curse, but many had heard the stories.

"Medicine Man will purify pool spirit tomorrow. No one is to gather water from there, but all are allowed, and encouraged to bathe. The curse is no more, I have spoken."

The crowd was too overwhelmed to react immediately, stunned this time by the lifting of a tabuli. Then, the excitement swept through the crowd as everyone realized the importance of what Danon had accomplished. The murmurs grew into a roar of approval.

Danon waited to address the Council, but they could not hear him above the crowd. May'r Nathon raised an arm for silence, then threw both arms into the air to quiet the assembly. Then he pointed to Danon.

"Wise elders, do not make the mistake of giving me credit for what has been done." Danon struggled to control his shaky voice. "The truth is, I could not have succeeded without help from one of your servants, one whose life is dedicated to protecting this clan. That one is Medicine Man Ben-on."

The old healer shuffled slowly into view, straightening his shoulders as he entered the Circle. Nathon greeted him with a strong embrace, then escorted him to the Council where he was offered a seat. The old man sat down with a glow of pride as whooping cheers erupted from the crowd again. Tonight he shared status with the elders; for the first time in his life he sat in council to the May'r.

Danon thought he detected a glistening in Lauriel's eyes, too. He bowed to the Elders and the May'r, and walked over to rejoin her. She quickly wiped a hand over her face.

"You have made an old friend happy."

A strong hand slapped him on the back. Danon turned to find a warrior with an almost friendly smile.

"Maybe you are no longer just houseboy," the warrior said.

Through the waning noise of the crowd Danon heard arguments coming from the Circle. One elder was standing shouting to be heard.

"… we can ask for Perf doctor!" he tried to explain.

"Perfs don't give spit 'bout us," replied another elder. "Why should one o'them bring medicine? We can treat the childrens ourselves."

A third elder rose. "You would shame your tribe by asking their help?"

"Is better than dying!"

Another elder stood without waiting for the first two to finish. "No! Send our warriors and overpower them. Take all biotics in the pharmacon. Bring it all back!"

The Council was splitting into rival factions when Medicine Man rose shakily to his feet. He waited patiently until the Elders were hushed by his audacity to stand in their presence.

"Honored May'r, this one is bold to speak; forgive, but you gave me seat on tonight's council. Hear me and judge wisdom of this old one's thoughts. Another raid is called for, I agree. But not one that brings danger to us all. A small party with proven leader can reach pharmacon easy enough, but our warriors not trained in ways of healing. The children need special herbs and potions, but one untrained cannot tell one biotic from another. This healer is too old and slow, but there is another. One who is strong and brave as warrior. One who understands the healing magic almost as medicine man. He could find the one biotic needed to cure coughing fever. If you asked, this one thinks he would go."

Everyone, including the May'r, waited for Ben-on to name his mysterious person.

"Well? Send him before me!"

Ben-on pointed to Danon. "The visitor can do this."

Whispers rippled across the astonished crowd. What else could this visitor do, they wondered. What magic did he possess that rivaled even that of even their medicine man?

Danon walked awkwardly into the Circle for the second time, slightly embarrassed as everyone expected another miraculous deliverance, watching his entrance like some revered folk hero—everyone except Devon.

Nathon gave Danon a look of caution. "You know of the danger?"

"Yes …" He swallowed hard. "Yes, sir, I am. I mean I do."

In a quiet voice that only Danon could hear, Nathon continued. "You have done much already while only a visitor among us. Why would you take this challenge?"

Danon shrugged. "It needs to be done."

Nathon nodded understanding, but his frown did not show approval. "Is not good for clan to ask this from an outsider." He glanced around at the anticipating crowd, knowing many had children who were sick and were willing to try anything.

He walked over to the Council and spoke softly. The elders still appeared divided, shaking their heads in objection as they discussed the consequences that defied tradition. Finally, Nathon returned to give the crowd his answer.

"This is not the path for one who is not Clan," he said with a tone of finality.

Danon started to object, but Nathon raised a hand to silence him.

"Only a Clan member may face this danger," he continued while addressing Danon. "Do you still say yes?"

Danon nodded.

Nathon faced the Elders, but spoke more to the crowd. "It is decided. One who has worked so hard for Clan and asked nothing in return, now volunteers to save our children. His spirit is one with us. He lives among us. He should be one of us."

Nathon paused to see many of his clansmen nodding agreement to what seemed to be destiny unfolding. "The visitor is accepted into Clan as Provider Danon. I have spoken!"

The Council meeting collapsed amid the following chaos. May'r Nathon adjourned the Elders when the throng swept up their new clansman in its frenzy and carried him festively off into a night of celebration that would continue into the early morning. He sampled his first taste of brien, kindly offered by an old man with only three teeth. Something floated on top of the cloudy mixture, but he decided not to ask. The brew tasted surprisingly good, even though it stung his tongue, burned his throat, and settled in his stomach like a puddle of fire.

Soon, beakers of brien were everywhere as clansmen celebrated. They celebrated the demise of their traditional smell. They celebrated their new brother. They celebrated the biotics that would heal the children. And Danon celebrated with them.

He did not notice Lauriel leaving when the other warriors withdrew to the Den for the customary wake in honor of their fallen brother. There they held a private celebration of his honorable death in combat. Each took a turn recalling bold and daring exploits that would qualify Grogon's entry, and the carving of his name, into the roster of warriors who now served and protected the Earth Mother.

Chapter 18

Provider Danon held his eyes tightly shut and tried to convince himself that he was in control. If he didn't the room would start spinning again. He didn't even know where he was, if he had managed to stumble back to Lauriel's lodge, or had spent the night somewhere else. He started to stand, but the pounding in his head returned like a giant gong. Surely he had been poisoned. He was sick and he was going to die. No, first he was going to puke.

"You don't look so good," said a voice unfamiliar to him.

He choked back the acid in his throat and tried to focus.

"This one thinks you're not 'customed to much brien," she said.

"Who, who are you?"

"This one is called Aleshanee," she said. "In O'kee, it means likes-to-play." She bowed timidly and started folding his blanket.

"Okay, one more question. Where am I?"

"On the floor," she answered with a grin. "Lauriel is gone hunting so I clean lodge, not work for warrior to do."

Aleshanee leaned over for a closer look at her new clansman. "You want me come back later?"

"No, it's …" He sat against the wall and waited for the room to stop spinning. "It's alright, I need to go to work." He stared at his fuzzy watch.

"You be walking if go to city," Aleshanee said. "Airbus not come again till evening."

Danon didn't feel like standing, much less walking. "You know what I need?" he said.

"Yes, wash." She pinched her nose playfully. "You enjoy, pool is good. Many people there now."

A pool party wasn't what he had in mind. The previous night's celebration was enough social interaction to last him for a while. But the overly cheerful maiden was correct about needing a bath. And some aspirin.

# # #

Constantly alert for any signs of danger, the nervous coyote paused to sniff the wind. Natural instinct made it cautious, but two days of hunting had made it very hungry. The nearby cry of the dying rabbit drew it further down the embankment. It crouched cautiously as it crawled toward the clump of brush.

Lauriel drew back slowly, taking aim along the carbon-fiber shaft as the bowstring creased her fingertips. Her arm refused to quiver as she held her breath and waited. Only the beating of her heart was uncontrolled as the target crept into view. She released the arrow, letting it scream across the clearing, and the coyote fell dead.

She stood, proud of her aim but still disappointed. She had been unable to track the much needed larger game. She cocked her head against the wind and sniffed. She listened for a sign of distant game: a ripple in the high plain's gentle whisper, or a crow raving over the horizon, or rock quail chattering on the wing. Whitetail deer sometimes migrated through this area, even though it was late in the season. She had spent all morning searching the winds for the faint odor of musk.

She also searched for signs of another predator, the bounty. He was more cunning than any coyote, and much more dangerous. She knew that from experience. The Perfs offered a lucrative reward for poachers, and the bounty—usually a Slant or Spanic—patrolled the game preserve as a professional traitor.

She had learned a great deal about surviving in the open. In the beginning, she had followed the other warriors, against their wishes, when they went on raids across the moonless plain. She had learned how the party of trained hunters used the shrubs and weeds for concealment. She had watched them always scatter before crossing an open area, crossing in ones or twos. Once, after following them through a depression of waist-high buffalo grass, she realized one of the warriors had not made it. No sounds, no warning, just missing. The bounty was a worthy adversary who was always hunting the Brotherhood. So he was always hunting her.

She freed her broad head from the limp coyote with a silent oath. Not if she saw him first. Someday he'd end up the same as this varmint.

She field dressed the carcass and tied it off with her carrying strap, a stiff coil of untreated leather she kept in her vest pocket. Its ends were hard and crusty from use. With the load positioned on her shoulder, she started back along the winding ravine. She had a long walk ahead of her.

Her supple moccasins moved quickly like hushed whispers over the loose rocks and dried twigs that sprinkled the bottom of the gorge. As the top of the ravine dropped, she crouched lower to stay below the horizon. When the path grew too shallow to continue confidently, she stopped, lowered her game to the ground, and peered cautiously over the bank.

The midday sun felt good on her darkly tanned face. She weakly scanned the horizon to her right. Only the viper could conceal itself in that flat wasteland. She looked with greater respect to her left toward the breaks where shrubs, thorn bushes, and small trees mingled to form a thicket of concealing growth. She studied it closely. That would be a good place for game to hide—

She froze.

From the thicket came the sound of a snapping twig. She raced over to the other side, knife drawn. Twenty meters away, she saw movement within the stubby trees. More sounds of scattering brush and pebbles. She sheathed her knife and readied her bow, then waited. The bowstring bit into her fingers, demanding release.

The thorny branches of two mesquite trees parted across the clearing and a figure stepped into view.

Stupid oaf!

She glanced around for any more unwanted visitors as the figure disappeared back into the brush. She slung her bow, grabbed her game, and exited the ravine into the nearby cover.

# # #

Daniel licked his dry lips, unaccustomed to the noonday heat. Salty beads trickled off his forehead ran down the corner of his mouth. He moved around another clump of thornless cactus that hid like Easter eggs in the short prairie grass. They weren't really thornless, but covered with hundreds of tiny bristles.

He walked on, enjoying the pleasing smell. Wild hyacinth? He tried to remember, but a sneeze interrupted him. Or maybe blooming sagebrush. Although he enjoyed the country air and fresh breeze, but he did not enjoy the pollen that swept along with it. It made his nose run and his throat itch, but worse it made him sneeze. Again.

Damn! He had forgotten to renew his vaccine before he left. It should've lasted longer. One month, maybe two at the most since his last vaccination. It had been several years since he had suffered an allergy attack. He had almost forgotten how miserable the symptoms were. He lumbered on, past the dense thicket of mesquites.

"You walk like pregnant ox!"

Danon almost swallowed a sneeze and his heart with the same gulp. "Jeeezus! You nearly scared me to death."

Lauriel looked around quickly. "Is not safe place to walk. Come on."

"Where?"

"Away from here."

"Why? It's nice out here."

"Even blind bounty could track you! Now hurry, before you get me captured, too."

She led him out of the thicket and back toward the cave's entrance. Occasionally she paused to sniff or listen, but did not speak until they were inside the cavern. As they approached the entrance to the Warriors' Den, she turned and placed a restraining hand against him.

"We will talk, but you must wait out here. Den is for warriors only."

He nodded and waited reluctantly as she carried the meat in the Den. As he waited, Devon seemed to materialize out of nowhere. His face seemed as sour as always.

"Lauriel says you can keep up. Hope she is right."

"I didn't know you cared enough to worry about me."

"Not worried 'bout you. If can't keep up, you be left behind. But Clan needs them biotics."

"Look, we're in the same family now, remember? And tonight we'll be a team. Working together to help the Clan."

"We not the same, houseboy. You live each day how you feel. Never know, never care 'bout tomorrow." His black eyes focused with a calculating intensity. "You do not live by code, you can not understand."

"I hate to agree with you, but you're right; I don't understand. What are you talking about?"

"Is code of honor. What was done before … what must be done again." Devon shook his head and turned to leave. "You will never understand."

"What'd Devon want?" Lauriel had come out of the Den to stand silently behind Danon.

"Would you stop sneaking up like that, you two make me nervous!"

"What did he want?"

"Nothing, he just stopped by to share some riddles."

She regarded him curiously, as if to say Devon did not usually waste time with senseless words. "Come with me," she said.

She led him to steep wall across the cavern and climbed it to a small ledge high above the floor. Another mountain goat, he thought, once again sitting precariously on the edge. There was just enough room to sit touching each other, which wasn't bad.

Several hundred square meters of cavern floor lay beneath him to view, too far beneath him. He was too busy hugging the wall with his butt to enjoy the touch of her thigh against his.

"We must talk of plans for raid," she said. "I prefer corner in Warrior's Den, but no outers is allowed inside." She looked around. "This will do."

"I'm not an outer, remember? I am part of the Clan now."

"Is not same as warrior."

"So I've heard. But why all the way up here? Don't you trust even your own people?"

"I trust no one with my safety or success of party." She leaned closer. "Now, 'bout the raid …"

"If you're concerned about whether or not I can keep up, don't bother. Devon's already covered that."

"Maybe you can, I don't know. Pace will be steady there and back. But you need more than strength to survive."

"I don't understand." He was tired of saying that.

"You do not have warrior's instinct. You have dulled sense of cavern dweller, not taught to survive on surface where predators lurk in shadows."

"Predators? You mean wild animals?"

"No, greedy bountys. This one is concerned."

"I knew it. You really do care," he said, placing a hand on her thigh.

She brushed it off indifferently. "You know what I mean. There is danger, it is real, and our clan depends on you. Up there, I heard you stomping through brush over thirty meters away. Then, I walked right up to you completely unnoticed."

"Well, I wasn't really trying. Tonight'll be different."

"Yes. It will," she said. "Won't be me who comes sneaking up to you with snare net and stun gun! You should stay close to me."

"I think you're a little over protective."

Lauriel's look hardened. "I was one who promised you'd find biotics. The Brothers risk much going back so soon. And if you don't deliver, it is my honor you break. This one will not allow that to happen. So stick close where I can keep an eye on you. Understand?"

Danon smiled. "I look forward to a night of being close with you."

"You must leave those clumsy boots here. I have other pair of moccasins you can use. And whatever you do, remember. Must be quiet as possible."

Danon nodded. "Okay, I'll be quiet. When do we leave?"

"Soon. Devon makes plans with others now."

"Yeah, I'll bet he's just thrilled. About taking me I mean."

"He is good leader and will do what must be done. You should try and get along with him."

"Me?" He almost laughed. "I don't think I'm the thorn in his side as much as you are."

She started to argue, then moved to climb down. "Is not your concern."

They made their way back to the Den where Danon again waited outside as the others gathered for final instruction. Finally the troupe of warriors came out and headed for the surface. Lauriel was the last to exit.

"Devon wants you inside," she said as she passed by.

He walked in hesitantly to find Devon sitting in the far corner, holding a bundle.

"Is for tonight," he said, and tossed a set of leathers. "They will cloak you in shadows. Maybe even get you back alive."

The breeches would be tight, but they looked flexible. The vest was obviously Devon's, by the size, and would fit a little baggy even with the thongs cinched tight.

"Thanks, I really appreciate this."

"Was not my idea." He pointed outside. "Lauriel insisted."

He studied the sour warrior for a moment. "Somehow I just don't believe that, Devon. I think you'd do just about anything for the sake of the Clan. Except be friendly. That's what you meant before, about what must be done, isn't it?"

Devon stood. "Is time to go. Put those on if you go with us."

# # #

The evening sun melted into the horizon, casting ever-lengthening shadows as the party trotted off into the semiarid prairie. Danon found the pace easier than he'd expected, slightly less than the five-kilometer pace he had run regularly back home. Well, almost regularly.

They crossed the open prairie, passing an old caliche pit. Danon remembered that the pit lay just outside one of the emergency exits of the S-RAY complex. Seeing the scarred pit took him back to the friends he had left behind in the past present.

He wondered what they're doing right now, or back then. Nothing, he realized, since everything they had ever done had been history for over a century. He suddenly felt very far from home. How much longer before he went home? How would he know when it was time to go back? He'd really hate to miss the boarding call. It was the only one.

Although the "easy" pace remained constant, they had soon traveled over ten kilometers and he was gasping for air, but they showed no signs of slowing. Lauriel was directly in front, trotting happily along like some gazelle, her bow swinging rhythmically across her back. She wore the same open style vest as the other warriors, only hers had a trio of leather thongs tied to the front that prevented the flaps from fully opening. He had already noticed their rhythmic bounce, but he was too tired to care. He noticed her cinch the vest tighter against her breast. Too bad, he thought.

They would be stopping soon, he hoped, looking ahead to Devon. But the veteran seemed ready to break into a full sprint at any moment. No, they weren't stopping. He tried to discipline his deep breaths and match them to every third step. He noticed the bouncing hips in front of him, following their fluid motion from side to side. He worked on his breathing as he followed the slender, black form and ignored the growing ache of his legs. No jiggle, he noticed.

Chapter 19

The last traces of twilight were gone from the starry sky when Danon realized that the group was slowing. Devon sprinted ahead to scout over a short ridge, the black stain of his leathers disappearing in the night. Although Danon's lungs felt as if they were going to burst, he couldn't afford to stop; he'd never get his feet moving again.

Lauriel offered a couple of salt pills. They tasted good as he rolled them over his dry tongue and tried to swallow. How long had it been? He squinted at his watch. An hour and fifteen minutes of running.

"The next time … someone asks me … if I can keep up," he panted, "I'll say no!"

"Shhh."

They stopped at the edge of a grassy hollow and Lauriel pointed ahead where the lights of the city were visible. He could just make out Devon's silhouette on the horizon, signaling to stay low. The dense cover of the waist-high buffalo grass would make it easy for them to hide in. Or anyone else, he realized.

With only a few gestures, Devon split up the party before starting to cross. No one had to explain to Danon that a loose, thinly spread party would have a better chance of survival. He remembered the story of the dreaded bounty.

Lauriel pulled Danon's arm to go with her as everyone disappeared in the darkness. He tried to mimic her silent movement and low crouch, crawling when the tall grass thinned out.

He scanned the dimly moonlit scene with each step, listening for the faintest sound. It was almost too quiet and he wondered if Lauriel could hear the pounding beat of his heart. From out of nowhere, a quail skittered across his hand. He jumped back and the rest of the covey exploded into flight with a heart-choking chatter.

He swallowed a shout and stood to run, then fell back to the ground, holding his breath and listening. Within moments the deathly quiet of the night returned. He couldn't even hear Lauriel ahead of him. Maybe she was no longer ahead of him. Remembering what happened to those who got left behind. He hurried to catch up.

He was the last to reach the other side. Devon said nothing, but gave Lauriel a told-you-so look before taking off again. Within minutes they were in town. Sometimes they walked, sometimes they crawled. They curled up in the shadow of buildings. They crept single file along dark streets and scattered into any available corner when a roving police vehicle cruised by. Always, Devon scouted the way and decided which path to take. Eventually they entered a drainage tunnel and followed its slimy underground conduit for several meters until it opened into along a dark roadway. Finally they stopped.

"This is it," Lauriel whispered.

Danon peeked over the sides of the damp culvert to find a darkly lit warehouse. A faded sign hung over the stucco facade.

# # #

PHARMATEC INC
Medico Supplies
Security Provided by Com-Sec Exec

# # #

Devon pointed twice and two designated warriors scurried out to inspect the building's perimeter. They checked both ends of the alley, the blind corners, and the dark rooftops, closely examining each shuttered window and barred door. Satisfied that it was safe to continue, Devon nodded. Lauriel and Danon ran to the back of the building. Dazjon was waiting as sentry and directed them to the roof.

Danon paused at the ladder expecting Lauriel to lead the way, but she made him go first, probably to scrutinize his silent agility, he thought. Then let her. He'd show her just how stealthy he could be.

He rolled over the brick levee onto the roof without disturbing a single pebble of the graveled roof.

"Not bad, huh?"

"Shhh." She pointed to a rusty ventilator and whispered. "Is way inside. And be quiet."

He followed her through a maze of creaky ventilation ducts wondering if she really knew where she was going. Finally, she stopped at an exhaust grate.

To Danon it looked like a dozen others they had passed, but she seemed confident. She laid her lamp aside and peeked through the metal slats.

"Is room we want," she said.

The grate popped free with the first kick and Danon almost dropped it. When Lauriel started to slip through the hole, he grabbed her arm.

"You wait here," he said. "It's my turn now."

He squirmed backwards through the small opening, stretching for something solid to stand on, but found nothing. He dropped a short distance to the floor, but landed hard enough to echo across the room. He held his breath and looked around. He was alone. So far. Something soft hit his shoulder and he spun around, swinging a fist at the empty air.

"Well? What're you waiting for?" Lauriel pointed to the leather pouch on the floor. "Fill it up."

Rows of shelves, each filled with cases of bottles, stood lined up across the floor, most were vitamins and analgesics. Two aisles over, he found what they had come for. Antibiotics. He raked a dozen bottles of sulfates and polymycins into the pouch, fighting the urge to constantly quick glance over his shoulder. Since dropping into the room, he had heard a myriad of unexplained noises that convinced him he'd been there long enough. He sealed the pouch and pitched it up to his skeptic partner.

"Are you sure?"

"Trust me, okay? I'm ready to get out of here."

Using a rolling stepladder, he climbed up to duck into the open shaft when he saw something that stopped his racing heart—two strips of metallic tape. Their broken ends led away from the dirty shadow where the grate had sat.

"Electrical contacts!" he whispered, pulling himself up.

"What?"

"Burglar alarm. The police are probably on their way, hurry!"

"Catchers?"

"Yes, catchers. Get going!" She reached down to help him up when they heard a shout.

"Hold it, right there!" the voice commanded. "Or I'll, I'll shoot."

Danon turned around to find an old black man standing behind him, gripping a shaky pistol. He was too far away to reach with a leg kick. Danon's foot was fast, but not faster than a speeding bullet, especially when standing on a rickety ladder.

"What, what are you doing in here?" the man stuttered. "Don't move, I'll shoot. Swear I will."

"Easy, friend. I was just trying to get some—"

"You were stealing drugs again, weren't you? Damned narc addicts!"

"No, not drugs. Biotics."

"What?"

"Antibiotics," Danon repeated. "It's for some sick children."

"Don't give me that. You can get all you need at the Free Clinic. You don't have to break in here for that."

"No we can't. We're not allowed in the clinics."

The young man slid nervously over to the wall and found the light switch. "What do you mean—Oh, you're a Bios!" He looked shocked as he surveyed the room and noticed the undisturbed narcotics locker.

"No, I guess you're not a narc, are you." He lowered his gun. "You better hurry, police are on the way."

"What?"

"Did you get what you need? The right kind?"

"Yeah, I think so."

"Then get. Go take care of your kids. God knows Apartheid won't. Only next time save me a heart attack and let me know what you need, like the others do. I usually set it outside in the culvert."

Danon gave a confused nod. He wasn't sure why the geezer was helping him, but he didn't have time to stick around and find out. Maybe some Perfs weren't all bad after all.

He hurried toward the roof and met Lauriel on her way back, her deadly bow in hand.

"What happened, thought he caught you."

The sound of approaching sirens wailed in the distance. "I'll explain later."

Devon stood at the base of the building, waving frantically for them to come down. He held the bag of medicine that Lauriel had tossed over the edge before going back to rescue Danon.

"Go ahead!" she yelled. "Will meet you at the berm."

Danon's heart pounded as he scrambled down the skinny ladder. It was more of a controlled fall, his toes just touching every third rung. Lauriel's moccasins chased his ear all the way down and somehow she beat him to the ground. Then to his surprise, she took off running in the opposite direction of the party.

He had no choice but to follow, and it wasn't easy to keep up. They ran down a narrow alley so dark an entire police force could have hidden easily and had shadows to spare. Suddenly she skidded to a halt. A high wall blocked the way. He turned to run back the way they had come, but heard shouts approaching. Angry voices and clomping footsteps echoed up the alley.

"Up there!" Lauriel said, pointing to a nearby ladder.

Danon stared down the dark alley trying to make out shapes, but she gave him a rough shove.

"Get your butt up there! And don't look back!" She darted behind a trash collector and readied her bow.

Three uniforms—black, trimmed in red—emerged from the darkness. They waved their stun guns anxiously side to side as the they trotted forward in unison, their shielded faces searching the shadows. Then they noticed a dark figure halfway up the fire escape and together swung their weapons to bear, but the night exploded with a brilliant flash of white.

Danon nearly fell off the ladder, but managed to stumble blindly onto the roof.

Lauriel fired a second fire arrow, then flew up the ladder as the dazed catchers stumbled around in the darkness.

"What the hell was that?" Danon asked, still rubbing his eyes.

She pulled him away from the edge. "Told you not to look."

"You could've done something a little less drastic. Every cop in town must have seen that blast."

"Good, they will follow us now. Must hurry."

She took off again, leading him across one rooftop after another. He couldn't remember how many. At first the buildings had been joined together, then they drifted farther and farther apart, forcing them to leap across ever widening gaps. Down below, the moonlit catwalks and passageways carved a dizzying pace between the darkened structures. Danon ignored the intimidating height, intent on finishing this deadly version of follow-the-leader. If she could make it, he knew he could too. He hoped he hadn't underestimated her ability.

Eventually, they came to the end of the string of buildings. Lauriel stopped to listen. Danon stopped to puke. He could hear sirens in the distance, but nothing moving their direction.

"We go down," she said. "Street is safe now."

He glanced up from the splattered rooftop to see her disappear over the edge. He was too tired to be embarrassed.

She chose the most dimly lit streets, moving quickly from one shadow to the next. She would pause to listen or sniff the breeze, then run to the next shadow.

Danon constantly looked behind. He couldn't stop seeing ghostly images of red and black uniforms hiding in each dark corner. Every time they ran across an open street, he expected to hear a shout of capture. They had to be careful, but they had to hurry. They had intentionally gone in the wrong direction to lead the catchers away from the others. Now they had a lot of time and distance to make up if they were going to reach them before Devon was forced to leave.

Lauriel stopped in a damp walk-through and peered around a rotting wood crate. Several more containers were tumbled about, discarded between the two old buildings that smelled of urine and decaying grout. He was surprised that he could detect the subtle aromas over the odor of his own sweat-drenched leathers. Lauriel was upwind. She waved him forward.

In front of them lay a field of welcomed darkness, but the street was well lighted. Lauriel cocked her head and listened for a moment.

"You must hurry now," she whispered.

The approaching whine of another siren pierced the night. It was too close to guess the direction. They ran into the field and beyond, ignoring the rocks and thorny mesquite bushes until they finally reached the caliche bank where they could stop to catch their breath. Lauriel scanned the darkened landscape.

"Almost there," she said between deep breaths. "'Bout a klick where this berm joins other. That is where we find others."

"You sound thirsty," he said between gasps. "Got anything to drink?"

She muffled a laugh and handed him a soft pouch that resembled the remains of some unfortunate animal.

"What's this?"

"Is canteen," she replied. She extended a wrinkled nipple from one end and demonstrated how to squeeze out a drink.

He was thirsty enough to try anything. He swallowed a gulp of what should have been water, then choked. Some unknown fluid oozed down his throat. It was sweet and tasted old, very old.

"Did something die in there, or what?"

"S'pposed to taste like that," she said. "Has essence of Earth Mother to give us strength for trip back."

"It tastes like essence of skunk," he said, licking his parched lips. "And don't even tell me what it's made out of."

She took a long drink.

"So we were the decoy, right? I figured that out about two miles ago. And you gave the biotics to Devon in case we didn't make it."

She nodded agreement. "Is what must be done."

"He's got everything he needs; are you sure he'll wait for us?"

"Not for long," she said, then took another squirt. "Want some more?"

"No."

# # #

Although the other warriors seemed relieved to see them, Devon said nothing. He was anxious to leave and instantly took off in a steady trot.

"Great," Danon grumbled, "here we go again."

Twenty minutes later they reached the shallow, grassy depression. They split up onto separate trails and again Danon followed Lauriel. Halfway across the hollow, they heard something, a muffled groan. He looked out over the swaying buffalo grass, but could see nothing in the darkness. Lauriel did not stop.

"Wait," Danon whispered. "What are you going to do?"

The night exploded with brilliant flashes of light. One passed just over his head. He dove blindly to the ground, waiting for the spots in front of his eyes to fade, wondering what had happened. He listened desperately for clues, but heard only the pounding of blood rushing through his head. He couldn't even hear Lauriel moving in front of him, because she was already gone. They were all gone by now, he realized, but unfortunately he wasn't alone. Someone was out there, waiting. A bounty.

Danon jumped up and ran as fast as he could. He reached the end of the grass and scaled the soft, crumbling embankment. He tumbled down the other side and landed next to Devon, who didn't even bother to frown.

"Sorry. I made it as fast as I could. I know you don't like to wait."

Devon did not respond as he continued to stare out into the darkness of the hollow. Lauriel was also watching silently with the others. He sat up to catch his breath. "Not that I don't need the rest, but why haven't we left yet?"

"Dazjon is missing," she said.

They waited in silence for several minutes. Devon searched the empty field of grass, giving his brother ample time to make an escape. Finally he gave up his vigil and returned to the group.

"Is time to leave."

"What about Dazjon?" Danon asked.

Devon mumbled a short prayer to Thebes, then turned to leave. "We will miss him."

"Aren't you going to wait for him?" Danon asked. "What about the old rule of no one gets left behind."

"Is over for that one. Cannot risk party for one member. Clan needs biotics."

"You heard him," Lauriel said. She tugged for him to follow her. "Is over."

"Not for me, it isn't!" He pulled away. "You can head on back with the medicine, I understand. But I'm going to find Dazjon."

"You?" Lauriel almost laughed, but he slid over the dirt bank and disappeared into the darkness before she could catch him.

She turned to Devon and stared. "Well? You just going to stand there? He is only young pup with the heart of a wolf."

Devon looked again to the darkness. The houseboy was out there doing what he wished to do himself. But he could not leave the others.

"Your pup makes his own choice," Devon said. "Maybe he is brave."

Lauriel readied her bow. "You and the brothers can buy the first beaker of brien when we meet tonight in the Den."

Devon grabbed her arm. "You make the claim of leather. You know our code."

Her expression was not defiant, as he'd expected. She even nodded agreement.

"Is why I must go help him. He is guest in my lodge."

"What does this one tell you father?"

"Tell him I do what must be done." She almost smiled. "He will understand."

Danon crept along the grass, thankful for the constant chirping of the night crickets. He crawled in the direction of the scuffle he had heard, placing each step carefully before shifting his weight, moving as silently as he could.

A dull glow appeared ahead of him, not like a lamp, just a soft radiance. He held his breath, focusing on the sounds and smells of the surrounding night. A faint sound, one that did not belong to the grassy plain, drifted through the damp air.

A groan.

He knew its direction, but was uncertain of the distance. He took a slow breath and tried to concentrate. Footsteps approaching, somewhere off to the right. They were coming closer. He waited.

Suddenly a streak of orange ripped through the night. The angry bolt of energy disappeared over the waist-high grass as quickly as it had come. The returning wave of darkness swept over his stunned eyes. Along with the returning night came a chilling sound, a cry of pain. It was Lauriel's.

He fought the urge to run to her, knowing she was hurt. But he couldn't lose track of the gunman. To do so would be the end of them both. He had only one chance of helping her now.

His eyes were re-adjusting. Just ahead of him the weapon's muzzle glowed a dull red, still warm from firing. The glow was coming closer. He gathered his feet under him like a tightly coiled spring and lunged at the dark shape.

The surprised Asian fell with a groan as the air was squeezed from his lungs. Danon scrambled to grab the dropped gun. As soon as he reached it, something whistled through the air and wrapped around him. A snare net of sticky filaments.

He struggled against the invisible mesh, but only became entangled worse. His anger burned within him. He was mad at the lowlife who earned his living as traitor to his own people. Mad that his impulsive actions had gotten Lauriel hurt. Mad at himself for not expecting more than one bounty. And furious for being caught so damned easily. If he was going down, he was taking someone with him.

He fired the stun gun recklessly. At everything, at nothing. A scattered array of dazzling flashes sliced through the blackness in every direction. He repeatedly fired the stun gun until its energy charge was completely spent and lifeless in his trembling hands. The bounty had run away during the barrage, so the only thing he hit was the scorched net that had disintegrated away from him.

He heard another moan and followed it to find Dazjon stunned and bound in the back of a land rover.

Danon used the warrior's dagger to severe the restraints, but the wounded warrior was too groggy and too large to drag out of the vehicle. Suddenly, the area was ablaze with light as an angry voice shouted.

"Freeze, Bios!"

Danon turned around holding the dagger low to his side. He could see nothing behind the blinding searchlight.

"Drop it, boy! Face down in the dirt!"

He had come so close to rescuing Dazjon, he thought. Too close. He whispered to Dazjon, "When I throw this dagger, you take off."

"No, can't move my legs. We both caught now."

Danon realized he was right, and dropped the knife.

"Smart decision, Boy," the satisfied voice said. "Now, face down in the d—!"

The searchlight wavered, then tumbled to the ground, leaving them both night blind again. Danon waited, then he heard a chiding voice from the darkness.

"Well, you two going to stand there all night, or what?"

"Lauriel? I heard you scream and thought ..."

"You thought wrong," she said, appearing in front of them with bow in hand. "Is impressive attack you make," she said with a smile. "Foolish, but impressive."

Danon grinned sheepishly. "At the time it seemed the only thing to do."

"Is same thing I said." She replied. He wondered if her comment expressed admiration. Perhaps, even respect? It was too dark to tell.

# # #

Beakers of stale brien lined the bar. The smoke of Gregon's nervous pipe hang heavily in the Warrior's Den as everyone solemnly waited the dawn. They would drink in honor of a brother departed, or they would toast his return. But they would not drink until they knew. Danon and Lauriel stumbled into the room carrying Dazjon.

"Finally!" Gregon shouted. "Now, maybe I can sell some brien. You're bad for business, girl." He winked as he slid a beaker her way. "First one is on me."

"No, first one is on Devon," she corrected.

Danon collapsed into one of the short chairs, surrounded by curious warriors. "I'll be leaving now," he said softly. "Soon as I can get up."

"Aren't you gonna stay?" she asked.

"No, better not. I know how fraternities are. Besides, I'm too tired to party." Daniel stumbled out of the Den in search of a much needed rest.

Devon watched the visitor leave, then offered a compliment. "Maybe the houseboy earned status of Provider this night."

Lauriel suddenly found herself face to face with the surprised Devon, poking his chest. "He has earned more than that. Who has more right? Who else had badger's heart to run the bounty's trap? Who dared to rescue our brother? That one wears the leathers tonight. And has earned it. He fought without weapons, and attacked the bountys with bare hands. Even snare net couldn't hold him."

Her poignant outburst had everyone's attention riveted to her storytelling. Even Gregon leaned over the bar for more. But in her heart she realized it was futile. The rule would stand as it always had. Only those tested and found worthy were accepted.

Devon did not respond to her outburst. He turned to the bar and grabbed one of the warm beakers. He raised it in salute to her with a weak smile. "Have him return my leathers tomorrow."

She wasted a perfectly good burning stare. He was too experienced at ignoring her. Then she reached for a badly needed drink and drained it.

Lauriel had seen the visitor's courage. She had glimpsed a rare quality in his aura and knew he was due some respect, only she was too tired to care. Her strength was spent and so was her anger. She reached for another beaker, but Gregon placed a friendly hand on hers.

"Devon's right, and you know it. Den is for brothers. Many of 'em still don't cotton you being here."

"But he has done much for us and earned much respect?"

Gregon shrugged. "Provider Danon walks his own path. Does not wait to seek respect of your brothers."

"Maybe not, but has earned much respect with me," she said with a long, revealing look.

Dazjon hobbled over to join the others at the bar beside Devon. "I understand 'bout leading others home. You done right thing. But I seen him fight and Lauriel's right. He has much courage. With training, he would make good warrior."

Devon gritted his teeth. "That one is outsider. He does not understand our ways. And to become one of us, he must beat this one in combat. That will never happen, my former brother."

Dazjon looked confused.

"You was caught by bounty. You know what must be done."

Dazjon slowly nodded his understanding and turned to leave.

Chapter 20

As the airbus slowed to pick him up, Danon once more considered not going. But if he didn't show for work today, he might not have a job at all. Big deal. He could stay in the cave and go back to bed. No, then he'd have to tell May'r Nathon of losing the two kilos payment which he had faithfully promised.

Just climbing the steps into the airbus stretched sore muscles all the way to his chin. His muscles ached and dark red abrasions ran over most of his body, a reminder of every rock and thorn bush between the cave and town. He was glad he had taken the trouble to bathe before falling into bed.

The ride into town seemed shorter than usual, and all too soon he entered the penthouse garden. The Miss Lillian was waiting when he arrived. Danon had figured he was in for a reprimand, but the look on her face was chilling. I'm in charge here, it said. And I'm going to prove it.

"It's time you learned a little more respect, boy." She pointed to the day room. "Get in there! You too, Allon."

Danon looked to Allon for a clue, but he only shrugged.

"It's my fault," she said. "I've been too easy on you, but I'll make a proper houseboy of you, yet." She unlocked a cabinet and removed a velvet-handled whip, trailing a dozen short thongs.

"Are you crazy, slut? You're not using that on me!"

"What did you call me? You will learn your place, Boy!"

"I think you're the one who needs to learn your Black place in this society. Or should I say mulatto? You know what that means, don't you?"

She stepped back. "Where did you—I don't know what you're talking about."

"Sure you do. You just don't know how I found out. Is it supposed to be a deep pale secret? I guess your computer didn't know that. It spilled the beans, and in this case they're not all black beans, are they? They're a mixed bag, black and brown. Reddish-brown, I believe."

She lunged to strike his face, but he caught her wrist and held it.

"I won't hit a lady," he warned. "But you'd better think twice, you half-breed whore."

Her shocked face flushed with rage.

He forced her backwards, twisting her arm. "Your mother was a middle class prostitute who made one mistake. And you're the result. But that's not the best part, is it? Tell me about your father."

"I don't, I don't have a father."

He twisted harder.

"Please stop. You're hurting me." Emerging tears washed away her rough. "Yes, my father was a Bios. And a heartless bastard. Are you satisfied? My mother got pregnant by some dirtworker on payday who forgot he was married."

Danon had finally broken her arrogance, but wasn't proud with himself. He released her.

"Why all the racial pretense? You of all people should understand. You can see the hate on both sides."

She rose with dignity, ignoring Danon's offered hand. "You think you know the truth? You arrogant little white boy. Yes, I've seen more of it than you could ever imagine. That filthy dirtworker you call my father? Yes, I knew him. When my mother gave up trying to raise me, she dropped me off on him, and his surprised wife. That was her biggest mistake, because your wonderful little clan people have their own inbred ideas about the society they've hated for so long. And I was very convenient. I was right there to abuse." She wiped her eyes and straightened the pleats of her skirt.

"But, didn't your father protect you?"

"My Father? Where do you think I learned about sex without love? Oh yes, I learned a lot from your people before they kicked me out."

Danon's anger evaporated, replaced by remorse. "I'm sorry. I didn't know."

"I don't need your sympathy!"

She walked over to the dresser and keyed the small control device that released the manacle to fall on the floor. "And I don't want you in my house anymore."

"You still owe me for a week."

She almost smiled at his trivial plea as she wiped the last vestige of a tear from her face. From her pocket she pulled a five-kilo note, wadded it, and tossed it at him.

"Here. This is more than enough for your back pay and severance. It's nothing to me. I'll make twice that in one night."

"Yes, you probably can. But you'll never enjoy it, will you?"

He could tell from her expression that one hurt, and he immediately regretted saying it. He suddenly regretted a lot of things as he went to the elevator. And he'd have plenty of time to consider their significance, during a very long walk home.

# # #

He stumbled into the lodge and collapsed on the soft cushions, exhausted by the four-hour trip from town on foot. He would have fallen into the pool and tried a quiet drowning, but it was full of giggling maidens enjoying their turn of the day.

As tired as he was, he found it impossible to fall asleep. He knew how much the lost income was needed by the Clan. He had tried to find another job at the unemployment office. The social worker had been very sympathetic and very kind. She had also been unable to help. It seemed the demand for houseboys lacking references was at an all time low. Being unemployed was a new feeling, especially with so many depending upon his earnings. He didn't like it. He was just about to give up on sleep when Lauriel ran into the room and started shaking him excitedly.

"Father wants to see you."

He sat up and nodded. "Bad news travels fast, doesn't it? I think I know what he has to say."

"What are you talking about?"

He held up his arm with the missing wristlet. "That half-breed actually tried to whip me."

"Is not important, now. Get up."

"I lost my temper. I guess I lost control, too. Told her where she could shove her job. I said some things I'm not proud of."

"This one is very proud of you, now must hurry."

"I almost feel sorry for her."

Lauriel shook her head. "Hurry, he is waiting for very important talk. You talk too much, and say nothing."

"I'm unemployed, Lauriel. Broke!"

She leaned over close to his face. "You talk too much." Her eyes sparkled with excitement. "You are being chosen …" She stopped as if about to reveal a secret.

"Chosen? For what?"

She smiled. "Must let Father tell you." She placed a quick kiss on his cheek. "You stink. Wash face before you come."

Her smile seemed real, he thought. What was he being chosen for? And did she just kiss him? Sometimes she made no sense at all.

# # #

Inside the Lodge, incense coals glowed dimly in the center of the room, filling the room with a sweet, earthy aroma that most found calming. Danon didn't notice. Lauriel sat on the carpet beside her father, concealing her pride rather well. Devon sat opposite Nathon in front of the coals. His frown was missing.

"Devon has informed me of raid's success," Nathon said. "I am pleased. And Lauriel has told of your courage to rescue of Dazjon." His weathered face cracked with a smile. "It might be wise to carry weapon next time you decide to attack such a serious opponent."

"That's probably good advice. But that's not why you wanted to see me, is it?"

Nathon seemed amused. "You are also impatient?"

"I just don't like waiting for bad news to fall. Let's get it over with and I'll find some other place to stay."

Nathon glanced to Devon with a confused look, then continued. "You have given Clan great service. You offered two kilos in support of those not your own. You returned the badly needed biotics. And you returned fallen warrior to the Clan. My daughter thinks you'd be worth more to Clan as warrior than provider. Is this true? Two kilos is of great value."

"I ..." Danon's throat was suddenly very dry. "I can no longer offer two kilos. I lost my job today."

Nathon reacted with mock surprise, as if he didn't already know. It seemed that little was beyond his cognizance. "So, question of value is settled. Tonight, then you will be chosen at Council."

"Chosen?"

"As one seeking warrior status," Lauriel said.

Danon looked at Devon for the punch line, but the senior warrior sat stoically, still without a frown. "Warrior, me? I mean, are you sure?"

Nathon shrugged and reached for his pipe. "Will find out tonight. To wear the leathers, one must prove himself, defeat one of the brotherhood in combat."

"Combat?"

"It is tradition," she added, ignoring her father's scolding look.

"You mean kill someone?"

Lauriel started to answer again, but stopped to glance at Nathon, who rolled his eyes in surrender. "No. Is only challenge of honor. First blood, or last one standing. And you are honored to have a worthy challenger."

Danon looked suspiciously at Devon and understood as the silent warrior nodded with a smug grin, the kind of expression seen on a cat who's just realized how to open the birdcage.

Nathon picked up the calumet from his lap and lit it with a glowing ember. After taking a long draw, he passed it to Danon and recited the warrior's prayer.

"A warrior protects the Clan and Earth Mother. He enjoys all her blessings. His heart fears nothing, for in the end he finds honor of joining her forever."

Danon took a mouthful from the ceremonial pipe and tried to hold his composure from the stinging effects of it pungent smoke as he passed it back.

Nathon took another long draw. "Tonight will be large crowd. You are well known, and many will watch your sacrament."

Again Danon studied the silent warrior rigidly staring through the haze. He seemed confident in the night's outcome. Too confident.

"We will talk later." Nathon stood. "There is much to do, you have game to hunt and I have other things to attend."

"Game?"

Lauriel jumped to her feet and tugged on his arm. "Is another custom, for your celebration. Come and I explain." She led him out of the Lodge, worming their way past the crowded dwellings. Even though she had her bow, as usual, strapped to her back, she wanted to stop by her lodge for something before going out to hunt. She held up the leathers, freshly cleaned and oiled.

"Would be alright to wear these to challenge tonight."

"Oh yeah, I was supposed to take them back to Devon. So you think it'd piss him off good if I wore them? Okay."

She held out a pair of moccasins. "No, I meant you can wear these. Is good luck for you."

Danon smiled. "I thought you didn't believe in luck."

"I don't, but you do. The Earth Mother smiles on you. Father was not sure about your becoming warrior. With Devon as your challenger, he knows it will take much strength and cunning to defeat him. And maybe the spirit of my moccasins will keep you alive."

"Great. Am I supposed to feel honored, facing the best? Just how good is he?"

Her smile faded. "This one must speak truth. He is best at art of challenge. Has never been defeated. If you succeed, you gain great honor."

"And if I don't?"

She turned away and started up the trail to the surface. He figured out that there was no second place in this game of status and challenge. He quietly considered the alternatives till they were alone on the surface.

"Tell me, who did you fight when you became a warrior?"

She swung her head arrogantly, tossing the braided hair over her shoulder. The fire in her eyes overcame the softness of her voice.

"No one would honor me with challenge. They was afraid of a wo'am in their brotherhood. But they could not keep me away. I followed them on raids. They tried to lose me but I was a shadow everywhere they went. Then one day I walked into that den of jackal pups, wearing the leathers for all to see. I raised my dagger and dared them to throw me out. Two of them made feeble attempt." She bent over to examine a faded track crossing.

"Well, what happened?"

She smiled to herself. "They failed."

Chapter 21

News of the challenge spread quickly and the entire Clan had gathered to crowd around the Elder's Circle. Danon was now known by all, having gained instant popularity for removing the curse at the pool. He had been accepted by the Council as a new clansman. And rumors of his encounter with the bountys had propagated a mythos of ferocious courage with some of his new clansmen. But Devon was still the undefeated warrior, and therefore invincible.

Wagering was more than a tradition to the native peoples, practiced for generations before the White Man appeared. And this night's event demanded its observance. Every clansman brought something of value as tokens, pipes, and blankets were dropped into two separate piles. Devon's pile was the largest.

As the time grew near, the clansmen squeezed forward, leaving the women and children in the back, toward the center for the best advantage to observe the ceremony. Hundreds of voices babbled with excitement, nudging their neighbor, debating the outcome, and anticipating the celebration that would follow. Within the Circle of Elders, the scene was repeated, only slightly more dignified. Some doubted, and still debated the wisdom of choosing an outsider. Only the earlier announcement that the Visitor had some fraction of Okee blood had silenced the last outspoken opponents. Glimpsing movement from the Lodge, they hushed to an almost reverent silence.

Two figures, dressed in black, made their way across the clearing. They entered the ring of sitting Elders and stood side by side, looking back to the Lodge as if waiting.

Devon's scowl deepened. He had said nothing while waiting inside, as a predator biding his time. "You got no right to wear leathers," he said. "You understand nothing of what they mean."

"I will after tonight," Danon answered. "I think this is what you call, what must be done, remember?"

Obviously Devon did not agree.

Nathon entered the center of the Circle with noble dignity. If he still had doubts over his decision, he would not show it. He had left his royal shawl in the Lodge and wore only the snug black vest and breeches of Clan warrior. He understood, all too well, the status of ultimate protector of his clan. He faced the two contenders and studied them. In their eyes he saw the determination and he understood each one's motivation. They were both ready. He turned to his people to formally announce what everyone knew.

"Provider Danon is chosen to enter the brotherhood of warriors! Devon is his challenger."

He held an open hand to them and demanded their daggers. Devon surrendered his and then gave a smirk to the houseboy who did not yet have one to surrender. With a nod of restrained encouragement, Nathon took his seat with the Elders.

"Let challenge begin!"

Danon bowed in respect to his opponent, but Devon did not waste time with subtleties. He felt the ground knock the wind out of him. Then he saw a fist plummeting toward his face. The cavern dimmed. His lips spread with fire as he tasted the warm saltiness of his own blood.

Somehow he twisted free. He backed away to clear his blurry vision, but Devon rushed in. With a reflex action, he ducked down and threw his shoulder against the charging knees and then tossed them upward.

Devon flew an awkward cartwheel and landed with a grunt, but he sprang to his feet instantly in a low crouch. He moved closer, more cautiously this time. Then with a snarl he lunged again.

Danon landed a sweeping roundhouse kick that landed solidly on Devon's jaw and sent him sprawling to the ground again.

Devon rose slowly. He rubbed his jaw and moved in a wide arc, stalling as if waiting for his head to clear. He continued to circle, keeping a watchful eye on Danon's feet. The feet had surprised him, he had never seen anyone fight in such a manner. He would be more careful.

He no longer lunged with arrogant confidence, but darted in and out with wild swings with his fist, but never close enough as Danon dodged each attack. With a cry of rage, he ran forward, a flying body slam that knocked Danon on his back. He moved quickly, pinning Danon's arms to the floor then pelted his face with rapid, bloodying punches.

Danon struggled to free his arms and block the storm of painful blows. He was weakening. He was losing. He tried again and again to buck the suffocating weight off his chest, but each time Devon held his balance. Finally a hand slipped free and Danon grabbed the dust-covered warrior and rolled him over. He returned a half-dozen blows of his own. Devon's nose twisted under one and blood trickled down his lip, but Danon kept hitting. He had to win. He had to finish him. He landed two more before being tossed aside.

They both staggered to their feet, breathing heavily. Red, damp dirt clung to their faces. When Danon tried to wipe the sweat from his eyes, Devon landed a fist of stony knuckles. Danon stumbled back. The floor reeled dizzily. The room dimmed again and he felt himself slipping into unconsciousness. He struggled to hold on, forcing the cobwebs away. Suddenly, a fuzzy image appeared—Devon rushing toward him again. He was tired. He was hurting. He was losing.

He concentrated what little strength he had remaining into one final kick. It landed, catching Devon's chin with the heel of his foot. Both warriors felt bone meeting bone before they collapsed together. Danon didn't hear the squish of moccasin against skin, or the dull thud of Devon's body landing on the rock beside him.

He staggered to his feet and waited for Devon again to come charging through the fuzzy darkness. He fought back the pain, the throbbing in his cheek, the ringing in his ears. Then as his sight gradually cleared, he saw Devon lying unconscious at his feet.

Through the haze of pain and fatigue, he heard muffled cheers from the crowd, then came the voice of Nathon making his official declaration.

"It is finished!" Nathon said. "Provider Danon is worthy to be chosen as Warrior, protector of Clan. I have spoken!"

Lauriel raced across the clearing and embraced him enthusiastically. Before he could appreciate the significance of her display, she quickly turned loose and backed away.

"Not bad, huh?"

"You were lucky," she answered.

The other warriors also came out. They surrounded him with approving slaps and astonished faces. Then, they picked up the semi-conscious Devon and carried him away to the Den where he could be revived with a beaker of brien. Danon started to follow.

"Where you going?" Lauriel asked. "Don't worry about Devon. Will be his ornery old self soon enough. Besides, you are new warrior. Must go to Elders to receive honor. Father must recite Clan's heritage, it is expected."

He watched as the group of warriors carted Devon away.

"They'll be back," she said. "Come, Council is waiting for you."

The Elder's Circle buzzed with private conversations as Danon limped by.

"Is as prophesy foretells," one elder whispered to his neighbor, "... he shall defeat the undefeated."

"Your years have grown too many, old friend. Who believes that superstition anymore?"

"You do not respect the legend?"

"Hush," said the younger man. "The May'r is starting to speak."

A young boy ran from the Lodge to drape the ceremonial shawl over Nathon's shoulders. It would not be right to recite the Clan's heritage without wearing it. May'r Nathon rose and began to recite. He spoke smoothly, faithfully repeating the words as his father had instructed him, as had his father before him.

"Was eighty yars ago, in summer of 2050, when the Hol'caust began. Two moons passed with none but a few of the great Whites aware of its arrival. The bios plague did not come across the great waters, as was first told, but caused when Caucs launched their great flaming arrows into the sky. When hand of the Great Spirit caught and crushed a flaming arrow, spilling its poison back on those who launched it. When the Wind Spirit caught some of the poison and swept it far across the land to punish all Caucs.

"The plague had little effect on Spanics, Slants, and Blacks, or the tribes of True People. The winds of death passed over us, bringing only the stench and 'tamination that followed the death of millions of Caucs.

"Before we learned who had called up the terrible sickness, the once proud White race who had caused it were no more. The survivors, minorities of pure bloodline, joined what few Caucs had survived. We, too, helped in burying the dead. When the cemeteries had filled with multiple graves, the fires began. They blazed through the night as piles of bodies increased.

"The land was shocked by what had happened. But when that shock wore off, the Blacks realized they were no longer one of the minorities. They were the largest surviving ethnos."

Someone handed Danon a cloth to wipe his face as he listened intently to the events following the war: the period of confused reconstruction which had culminated in the Black's supremacy, how the National Apartheid Party came into control and manipulated the national shock. He learned how anguish became outrage, then racial hysteria. Their vicious desire for retribution had hungered for vengeance, war trials to convict the guilty. The pathetic handful of Caucs who had lived through the holocaust were forced to bear the blame for a multitude of real and imagined atrocities relating to the War. Some, like the Du Pont family, were sought out around the world and hunted down to be punished for being the 'Angel of Death.' But all this was not enough. Still the Apartheid party was not satisfied. They wanted more, and whatever they wanted became the "will of God." They were the Perfect Ones, chosen by their God to continue a purge He had started to free them from centuries of bondage. They proved their supremacy.

Any non blacks were distant relatives to the Great White race, they believed, and therefore were also Bios, and collectively responsible for the Biowar. A core of fanatics controlled the country's legislature, confiscating property and barring all minorities from living in the cities. A perfect society could not have ghettos or unkept slums, so they would prevent their breeding. All non black were relegated to the legal status of servants and laborers, outcasts of a Perfect Society.

"Into this cave some came," Nathon continued. "A mixture of tribes seeking refuge. Slants and Spanics assembled where they could, in abandoned buildings far from town, in sewers beneath city they formed their own clans.

"Here, in Grotto Cave, the tribes of Chocs, Manchees, Okees, and Lakota have lived for many yars. We raise our children. We wait for the prophecy."

Nathon lifted his arms outstretched to finish. "And we summon the spirit of Supreme May'r to come from afar."

It was over. Several elders struggled to their feet to stretch their stiff legs. Some placed a congratulatory hand on Danon's shoulder before leaving. Others hurried to catch Nathon before he reached the Lodge. Soon the Circle was abandoned. The dispersing crowd cast occasional glances, but seemed unwilling to approach, as if suddenly distanced by his new status. Only Lauriel approached from the edge of the clearing.

"Your brothers wait for you." She pointed to the waiting cluster of black leathers. "They will take you to Den. Is much to learn tonight."

"What about you?"

She glanced back to the waiting warriors as if making a choice, then smiled. "This one will teach you later."

Her offer sounded vague, but intriguing. Unfortunately, before he could question her, she walked off and the warriors approached to drag him away.

His indoctrination—a sacred ceremony—lasted far into the night. There was much for the new warrior to learn, and Devon ensured every step of the ceremony was followed meticulously. He was presented with his own set of leathers and a dagger, the symbol of both death and survival. Tucked inside the knife's hollow handle was a curl of parchment, the prophesy.

# # #

The visitor comes from afar … to defeat the undefeated
… to lead his people to freedom
… with great magic, the warrior sacrifices himself for those not his own
emissary to the future … leader of clans … the Supreme May'r.

# # #

Without any explanation, he was charged to keep it safe and protected. He learned that the members of the Brotherhood had all died, a ritual death that severed their ties as clan members. In their new life, they served apart from, and watched over, the other clansmen. Some of the original Grotto warriors could trace their lineage back to the Cherokee guardians, called Mankiller, who watched over villagers well into the Nineteenth century, till removal by the encroaching Europeans. Like their Samurai and medieval knight counterparts, their path of sworn duty was to protect the Clan from any threat and ensure its survival. He learned the simple, yet sacrosanct code that would guide his steps on that path.

Loyalty to May'r and Clan above all.
One warrior was expendable; the Brotherhood must continue.
What needs to be done, must be done.
Hunt with courage, and die with honor.

The concepts of courage, honor, and commitment were reinforced with blood oaths. As each warrior had done before him, Danon took his blade and drew enough blood to smear over his face. His symbolic death to a former way of life. Then each new brother embraced him with a solemn pledge to live and die by the code.

When Danon finally returned to Lauriel's lodge, his head was spinning with symbology, codes, and several beakers of Brien. He tried to pass through the darkened room with a warrior's stealth, but bumped into the screen divider. He managed to catch it before it fell, making even more noise.

"You still walk like pregnant ox."

He spun around and peered into the darkness. Finding the lamp, he lit the room and revealed Lauriel sitting against the wall, sharpening her dagger.

"I expected for you to be sleeping." He leaned on the table to keep from swaying. "Were you waiting up for me?"

"Of course not." She inspected her knife, then sheathed it and picked up a sponge from the basin of water. "Come here."

"What are you doing?"

"Your face, bend over." She wiped the dried blood off his face and lightly sponged his purpled mouth.

"Ouch! Take it easy."

"Be still. A warrior does not fear pain."

"This one does not fear pain," he said, mimicking her accent. "But you could still do it a little softer. What's this prophesy thing about a Supreme May'r?"

"Is old myth from before the Hol'caust. An old riddle that makes no sense." She stood up to examine the cuts on his chest, ensuring they were shallow and would heal quickly. "One of many legends that some, including my father, put too much faith in."

Danon gritted his teeth as the sponge raked across his chest. "I think you're enjoying this. So just what exactly is he supposed to do?"

"The old story tellers add stuff 'bout uniting the separate clans into one tribe. Some kind of revolt, I don't know. If went out there and asked ten different elders, would hear eleven different answers."

"So what do you think?"

She dropped the dark red sponge back in the basin. "Is no one coming, I think. And if our life ever improves, it'll be cause we make it. We must work for it. And it won't ever happen sitting on our butts waiting for some mythical spirit to appear!"

"Profound wisdom," he said with a mocking smile, "coming from a wo'am."

"Careful, young warrior. I'm more than enough wo'am for you."

He leaned closer, smelling the day's sunlight lingering in her hair. She was right about one thing. He reached around her waist.

She pushed him away, but not forcefully, her callused hand was almost gentle. "That's not what I meant."

Danon pulled her close to stare into her eyes, pale green pools of fire that never quenched. Her confident expression waivered under his penetrating gaze. What was she thinking? How did she really feel about him? Was he stirring similar emotions deep within her? Was she reaching for her dagger again? He gently embraced her, bringing her lips close.

"No, Danon. I don't …"

"Thank you," he said.

"For what?"

"For talking to your father, about becoming a warrior." He felt her shallow breathing.

"Was not my choice. Was what must be done. Now, must get rest for tomorrow."

He pulled her closer, willing to risk the feel of her dagger to taste her lips. They almost touched when he felt something on his chest, but it wasn't steel. It was her trembling hand, pushing him away.

Chapter 22

Danon crawled out of bed and leaned against the wall, his legs stiff and stomach cramped. The swollen lip reminded him of winning last night's fight, but his ribs didn't agree. And the pink cuts on his chest itched.

He called for Lauriel, but got no response. She was definitely not a late sleeper. He hobbled over to the wash basin and noticed everything was fuzzy. His disposalens had been worn out by all the dust and sweat during the fight. At least they hadn't given out during the fight; that could have made a difference in the outcome. A big difference.

He retrieved the last set of contacts from his old jumpsuit and applied them by feel. The basin of water had no mirror above it. Just as well, he didn't want to know how bad he looked. His cheek was still tender beneath the scraggly beard and his whole head felt puffy. He splashed some water on his face and stumbled outside toward the Den.

The cavern was fully lit, indicating late morning. He could see people walking about, children playing. An old woman gummed a smile as she passed by carrying a load of laundry.

"Morn, Warrior Danon," she said.

He smiled back even though it hurt. He liked the sound of her greeting, much better than "houseboy."

Inside the Den Gregon was wiping a cluster of beakers behind the long stone bar. He wasn't cleaning, just wiping. None of the warriors would know or care.

"Well, lad, how is newest member of brotherhood?"

"Sore."

"Was some fight last night. Ain't never seen fancy foot slaps before, not from clansman. Where'd you learn to fight like that?"

"Just part of my physical training back at the …" He stopped. "I mean back home."

Gregon eyed him suspiciously. "Where is home, son?"

"That's a little hard to explain, let's just say far away. Very far away."

The gray-haired veteran seemed a little uncomfortable about the answer. "Then why'd you leave home clan?"

"That's a little hard to explain, too. I thought it was a noble idea that compelled to come here and explore, discover a new life."

The old warrior squinted hard. "Hmm, maybe, but my gut tells me you was running away from something. You planning on staying, or running again?"

"You ask a lot of questions for a bartender." Danon surveyed the empty room. "So where is Devon and Lauriel?"

"Devon's still sulking over his defeat. Won't see him for a while, since he made a few boasts 'bout putting a certain houseboy in his place."

"It was just a challenge to prove myself. Nothing to get upset over."

"Don't bet on it, son. Being top dog is everything with Devon. And he ain't never tasted defeat before last night. I reckon for sure that ain't the last tangle for you two." Gregon went back to wiping. "As for Lauriel, who knows. I hear game's been spotted at far end of reservation."

"Thanks," Danon turned to leave.

"You say you come from afar, do you?" Gregon asked as the young warrior walked away. "Reckon that 'splains why some folks talking like they is. Not that I listen much to rumors. Or legends."

# # #

The whitetail deer stood motionless, tail pointed to the sky, revealing the white tuft underneath. Even with its keen eyesight, it could detect no movement. It snorted the early morning breeze. Something in the air disturbed it. The doe perked her ears and listened for a clue for which way to run. It paused for only a moment in indecision, then bolted away too late.

The arrow had already struck, destroying its heart. The animal skittered only a few dozen yards then fell to the ground.

Lauriel also sniffed the breeze before venturing into the open. She had been hiding in the scratchy brush for over two hours, waiting. She ignored the stiffness in her legs as she sprinted across the grassy plain to claim her kill.

Although a small species of deer, the whitetail still weighed over sixty kilos, too much to carry the entire distance home. She scanned the horizon quickly before drawing her dagger. Within minutes she had field dressed the carcass and sectioned the shoulders, rounds, and loin. She tied the still warm sections over her shoulder and started home.

The fresh kill of the carcass masked any other scent which she might have detected. And the heavy load impaired her stealth abilities. She could only pause occasionally to listen. She kept to the low ground, avoiding the open, unprotected clearings.

While her moccasins stepped as quietly as they could under the added weight, they often rustled the dry high plains grass, sometimes even snapping a heavier twig. She paused at the edge of a small clearing to looked and listen. Nothing. She went on, slipping between two mesquites.

"Hi, need some help?"

Her heart lurched at Danon's unexpected voice.

"Don't do that!" She quickly glanced around. "If I hadn't been carrying this, I might've killed you!"

Danon laughed. "If you hadn't been carrying all that meat, I would've wrestled that beautiful, firm body to the ground. But I didn't want to get supper dirty."

She flashed a scolding frown. "How'd you find me?"

"Just followed your tracks. It wasn't too hard."

"Don't lie to me, houseboy."

"Brother," he corrected. "Remember?"

"I may leave an occasional track, but not any you could follow."

"Okay, I was tracking a deer. The same one you nailed with your bow."

"Is what I thought," she said, handing him two hind sections. "I knew something had spooked it. It almost got away." She looked him up and down, then nodded approvingly. "At least you look like a warrior."

He nodded back. "I do look good, don't I. Nice shot. That must've been almost forty yards."

She shrugged. "Closer to forty-five. But why'd you come all way out here?"

Danon cleared his throat. "I just wanted to spend some time with you today. You know, soak up some sun."

"Why?"

"Look at my skin. It's whiter than … than …"

"Than sidewinder's belly?"

"Yeah. I guess. Besides …" He looked out over the prairie. "I think I'm falling for you."

She moved closer to investigate his eyes. Her thin lips almost curled into a smile. "Yes. You are." She turned to walk away.

"Well?"

"Well what?"

"What about you?"

Her eyes almost softened. "I feel something. Don't know. You make me feel … strange."

"Strange?"

"Have never felt this before. Am getting sick or something."

He reached for her, but she backed away.

"We must get this meat back," she said. "Then we can go for a walk, or something."

"Okay," he said reluctantly. "I know the perfect place we can go."

# # #

They approached the oasis, or what was left of it. Only three trees remained, thick trunks with tired limbs reaching for the sun. A gang of thorny mesquites had moved in and surrounded the old fruit trees. The apple blossom and other surface plants were gone, along with the grass which had withered away decades earlier.

Danon sighed with disappointment. "Well, this is it. Or at least it was. It used to look a lot better. I guess the leaky water pipe's been fixed or turned off a long time ago."

Lauriel shook her head. "Has always been like this." She walked over to sit on the bone white remains of a concrete bench.

He joined her on the leaning bench, sitting close enough to enjoy the smell of her hair. He wanted to hold her, not passionately, just touch her. He leaned close to her salty cheek.

She flinched instinctively and scooted away with an insincere scowl. "You take too much for granted."

"Do I? I don't think so." He leaned back on the weathered slab to stare off into the distance, beyond the drab green of the neglected garden, beyond the brown whirling dust devil, beyond the moment. He tried to remember the garden as it used to be. The thick carpet of grass. The fragrant patch of wildflowers that always sprouted along the edge of the grass. He could almost smell their delicate aroma, reminding him of the one friend that he shared that memory with. How was his friend, Thomas, doing? When would he see him again?

Lauriel leaned against him, hesitantly at first. The touch of her shoulder pressed lightly against him, adding the warmth of her body to the afternoon's sun.

Not too soon, he hoped.

They sat on the crooked bench, without speaking, for quite a while. The warm afternoon breeze turned cool. Across the parched plains they watched the sky darken as a prairie thunderstorm swept in front them. In its wake, the afternoon sun broke through to paint a palette of colors stretching over the dampened earth.

"Is hand of Earth Mother," Lauriel said.

"Only if you like rainbows."

She looked at him strangely. "You do not like?"

"Let's just say I've have enough rainbows to last a lifetime. Like the fresh rain stopping, rainbows always seem to come at the end of something good."

"This one does not understand," she said. "Earth Mother brings bow of colors not to announce end of rain. Is her promise that sunshine will return. Only sunshine can bring new life from moist ground."

"I guess that's one way of looking at it." He tried to shake off the painful memory that had returned.

"You are sad when alone with me?"

Finally he smiled. "No, being here with you has been very nice."

She searched his eyes. "Perhaps this rainbow brings you more joy later."

He didn't like her penetrating gaze, but he did like how close her face came to his. He reached one arm around her, but she quickly stood up.

"Is getting late, should start back now."

As they made their way back to the cave, Danon tried again for an answer that had eluded him since he arrived.

"Lauriel, I still can't understand why your people allow the Perfs to treat them the way they do. They violate every civil right you have."

"This one lives free!" she said with defiance, then lowered her voice. "What is civil right?"

He couldn't hide his grin. "Civil rights are, you know, life, liberty, the traditional pursuit of happiness."

"Liberty? You have many strange words."

"Liberty means being able to live, act, and think according to your own choice."

"I live as I choose."

Danon gave a sincere smile. "I think that's first attribute that attracted me. Well, maybe not the first, but certainly the strongest."

She turned and cocked her head.

"You chose to be more than a daughter of the May'r. You refused the tradition of your fathers and demanded to be part of the Brotherhood. You made the claim and dared anyone to deny it. Why can't your clansmen be more like you?"

"They talk of a better life, but most are weak and take the easy path. Many feel they have little choice."

"But you do, they do!" Danon's voice grew with a passion she had never seen. "If everyone stood together, society would have to change."

She stopped to stare at him. "You have seen Perf's society. You have worked as houseboy. You know how little they care for us. They are too many and we are outnumbered."

He took a deep breath. "I know they have the advantage of wealth and being the majority, but that doesn't make it right. Or permanent. Someone needs to take a stand for equality."

Lauriel placed a hand on his shoulder. "You talk words of power. Do these words come from mouth, or heart? As warrior, you know the code."

"What?"

"What needs to be done, must be done. This one would fight by your side, but we are few, our clan only one of many. Is no way could kill them all."

He appreciated the intent of her offer, even though he flinched at her reference to the code. "No, I'm not talking about fighting the Perfs. I meant we could fight the injustices."

Danon paused to stare out over the sagebrush. "But you are right about something. We are one of many clans. We have to become organized somehow." He tried to recall a theorem from an old Political Science class. "Social change must come from within. No matter how much the Apartheid party has corrupted it, the fundamental concept of freedom and equality still exists. It must. The nation's original Declaration and Constitution are based on these ideals."

"Again you speak of strange things, of declarations and institutions."

"Constitutions, and there's only one."

She shrugged. "How do you remind an entire nation of these things forgotten?"

"Well, the last time was done by demonstrations. And boycotts. Maybe a rally, or a march."

"This one does not understand."

"Maybe that's the real problem," he said. "Nobody understands. We need to get a copy of those ancient documents. Let everyone know. Make them understand."

"What documents?"

He stared at the ground for a moment. "Miss Lillian's! Her computer terminal has access to the central library. When does the next airbus come by, going to town?"

Lauriel glanced at the sun, then down at her shadow. "'Bout an hour, maybe hour and a half. But we can't ride it; they'd take us straight to jail. Brotherhood is outlaw."

"If we hurry, we can make it back to the cave in time to change and still catch the ride. Come on! And try to keep up."

Lauriel jumped to her feet and released a giggle, as if she would ever have to worry about keeping up with the houseboy warrior.

# # #

They stood on the cracked pavement in their sweat soaked coveralls. To any outsiders, they were just another pair of grubby dirtworkers waiting for the airbus.

"Maybe we're too late," he suggested between quick breaths.

"I don't think so." She looked down the road into the distant heat waves. "But if so, we could always run. Is only an hour or so across open ground."

He glanced over the dry plains, still breathing hard. "I'd rather not."

Lauriel held up a hand of silence, peering down the distant road. "There it is," she said, pointing a finger.

He strained to make out the shimmering mirage floating over the distant blacktop.

Several minutes later, the scratched and dusty airbus hovered to a stop. They climbed aboard. Danon paused in the aisle, spying two empty seats near the front. Lauriel grabbed his hand and pulled him to the back.

"Save your revolution till later. We have a raid to finish."

He followed quietly to the back.

Lauriel asked, "When we get there, what are you going to say to her? You said you left her under, well, not so good conditions."

"She'll never know we've been there. Every day, late in the afternoon, she takes a long bath. To prepare for her night's work. While she's locked safely away in the tub, I'll access her computer for the information we need. You'll be my lookout to make sure there are no surprises."

# # #

The monorail rumbled past overhead. Aircars hummed through the air like giant bees searching for a hive, casting their reflections in the gold mirrored buildings that rose to the sky on both sides of the street.

"City looks different in daylight," she said, admiring the tall buildings.

"Over there." Danon pointed to get her attention. They crossed the busy street and headed toward the double glass doors. "I hope the doorman remembers me."

The large Asian was primping his golden tassels and picking off nonexistent flecks of lint. His brow furrowed deeper as they approached in their wrinkled overalls.

"Hold up, brother. You can't go in there. Oh, it's you, Miss Lillian's houseboy." He crinkled his nose. "Haven't seen you for a while."

"Yeah, uh, I've been busy. Miss Lillian wants to interview for a new gardener."

He grabbed hold of Lauriel's arm and hurried through the door toward the elevator before anyone else noticed. He hoped he was correct and his former mistress wouldn't decide to take an inopportune stroll through her garden. If she were outside, she'd spot them the instant the elevator opened. His pulse quickened as the elevator halted with a bump and the twin doors backed away to expose them.

Danon dashed through the clearing to one of the nearby shrubs. He turned to motion for Lauriel to follow, but she was already crouched beside him. The elevator closed with a distinct metallic click. It was the loudest click he had ever heard.

He looked around. Allon was off to the left at the end of a row of bushes, too busy pruning to notice their arrival.

"This way," Danon whispered.

He crawled along the damp black soil toward the covered patio of the main house. They reached the white stucco wall fencing the edge of the patio, and peeked over. No sign of Miss Lillian.

"You wait here," he said. "I'll check the living room."

He hoisted himself over the low wall and crawled over the patio tiles into the living room. After looking around to ensure it was empty, he signaled for her to join him.

"The door to her bath is closed," he whispered. "I'll make sure she's in there."

He tiptoed across the thick carpet and leaned against the door long enough to hear water running. He pointed for Lauriel to meet him in the next room.

"You stay here," he said. "If the water stops, or that door opens, get over and tell me."

Her computer terminal was fashionably nestled inside the entertainment wall. Turning everything on, he typed in Miss Lillian's personal access code and waited for mainline approval. It took him less than two minutes to locate and download a copy of CONSTITUTION and DECLARATION OF INDEPENDENCE. He quickly logged off and sent the file to the printer. The cryogenic printer Miss Lillian had purchased might have been considered stylish, but it was slow. And though it barely whispered as it released each page into the holding tray, he waited anxiously for it to finish, constantly glancing over his shoulder.

Lauriel appeared silently by his side. “Water’s stopped. I think she’s coming!”

Danon glanced at the few sheets in the paper tray. “It’s not through. I need more time.”

The bathroom opened, releasing a cloud of steam. Lauriel disappeared as he grabbed the printouts. He tried to leap behind the nearby sofa while fumbling with his papers, but tripped, scattering them across the carpet.

He heard noises from Miss Lillian’s bedroom. He scrambled across the carpet, scooping up the sheets, while Lauriel exited in a noiseless run across the carpet. She gracefully bounded over the patio floor, vaulted over the garden wall, and landed without a sound in the soft garden dirt. He rose to follow her lead, but froze when a voice called from behind.

“Well, look who’s here. I would recognize that derriere anywhere, but it seems my little houseboy has become a dirtworker.”

He turned slowly, expecting her to be carrying a weapon or alarm key. She held only her bath towel.

“Actually I’m a clan warrior now.”

“Did you come to peek through the door again?”

“No, and I never did peek. Well, just that once.”

“So, they made *you* a warrior? Impressive. Times must be hard at the old home cave. I suppose you’re here to steal food and liquor. Sorry, I have no narcotics. Or did you come back to show me more of your brute strength.”

Danon held up the papers. “I didn’t come to steal. And I don’t want to hurt you. I needed your computer to print these.”

She gave the papers a cursory inspection. “What would a houseboy, or even a warrior, need with such ancient documents?”

“These are the precepts this country was originally founded on. It seems they’re still active, just ignored. And unless your people change—”

“Let’s get something straight about my people. Not everyone hires a bounty hunter.” She adjusted her towel for modesty. “Some prominent members of the Perfect Society actually sympathize with your predicament and talk privately of social reform.”

“And you? What have you done to stop the exploitation?”

She adjusted her towel. “I’m just a socialite, although that isn’t the term you used. What can I do about it?”

“I’m sorry for what I said, it was wrong. Not because of some social status boundary, but just ethically wrong. And maybe there is something you can do. You have some powerful friends with a lot of influence. You probably know which one of your *friends* should talk to which politician to encourage some of that reform. And for starters, I could use your help getting the rest of these documents."

"And why would I want to help you? What's in it for me?"

He stepped closer and for the first time regarded her with no condemnation. "I'm offering you a chance to make a difference. Maybe you can help the next little girl born to mixed parents, give her a better start in life. Everyone deserves that, don't they?"

Her scowl slowly softened. "Do you really think you can change anything?"

"Not by myself, no. But like you said, not everyone supports this Apartheid policy."

She shrugged and handed the papers back. "I'll think about it."

# # #

It was late in the evening and the city's transit system only took them to the edge of town where they had to complete their journey home on foot. Lauriel seemed able to run endlessly with little effort. Danon, seeing no urgency, couldn't force himself to continue the pace for more than a few kilometers before slowing to a walk.

"Some warrior you are," Lauriel said with a scolding tone.

"I'm a warrior, not a gazelle. If the Earth Mother had intended humans to prance across the countryside, She wouldn't have invented busses."

"Go as slow as you like," she said. "But when I get back, am going straight to pool for nice cool bath. With, or without you." She gave a teasing smile and took off again, disappearing before her words registered.

Danon broke into a run.

When he finally reached the cave entrance, cramping for breath, his dirt-worker coveralls were drenched and his eyes stinging with crusty salt. Still he had lost sight of Lauriel long ago. He staggered down the path to the pool for a satisfying drink.

"You stink!" cried a small child's voice.

He looked down to the young girl dressed in a clean jumpsuit, pinching her nose.

"Thanks, munchkin. I hadn't noticed."

He hurried to the bathing pool. Since it was late, the ramp from the upper waiting area was long deserted. He shed his shirt and trousers along the way, eyes still burning with sweat. Stopping at the edge of the pool just long enough to drop his moccasins, he dove in.

The chilly spring water felt like ice. He surfaced with a shout, teeth shivering. "Brrr, that feels good!"

"Yes, I know," said a feminine voice.

He brushed the wet hair out of his face and turned around.

"Lauriel! I'm sorry, didn't see you."

"But I saw you," she said with a faint blush. "I was hoping you'd get here in time." She swam over, hesitated, then put her arms around him, letting him pull her tightly against his shivering body.

"I wasn't sure I understood you correctly." He kissed her most lips. "But I guess I did."

She kissed back, her firm body conforming to his, her heart beating tightly against his chest.

He couldn't remember how many women he had held before her. Too many, but Lauriel was different. She had something special, a warmth unlike any other. He didn't want to stop, didn't want to break her clinging embrace and end his dream, but they were beneath the surface of the pool and sinking.

They came up, splashing and laughing at each other, then swam to the rock ledge. Lauriel climbed out and began wiggling into her leathers. As he admired her dripping beauty, her expression changed.

"My instinct tells me to run away, but my heart …" She bit her lip. "Is old maiden's poem that says:

The one who carries you above your dreams on wings of pleasure,

Is one you offer heart and soul."

She looked deeply into his eyes, as if searching for something. For the first time since he had met her, she looked vulnerable.

"This one has never surrendered to any mano. Do you really care for me?"

He rubbed his hand along her chin and touched a finger to her lips. "Lauriel, you have touched my heart, in a way no woman ever has. And even though you have no idea how much this really means, I have no desire to look into any other eyes than yours. I think what I mean is I …"

"You would pair bond with someone like me?"

"Is that forever?"

"Yes."

He didn't know if he could answer. He didn't know if he could stay forever. When would he go home? Home. Where was home, S RAY? Or was this home now? Could it be? He looked again into her waiting eyes. He could be happy with her. Somehow he knew that. And wherever he could be happy, he would be home. But pair bonding? Commitment to just one woman? Maybe she was right about the rainbows. In the soft emerald sea of her eyes he found his answer.

"I insist on nothing less," he said.

She giggled—a soft, girlish giggle he'd never heard before—and wrapped her arms around him. The room, the pool, and the evening disappeared in another embrace.

# # #

Looking down from the waiting area, stood a silent figure. He stared through unblinking eyes at the couple below, clenching his fists as the fire burned within him. The intruder still knew nothing of Clan ways. He wanted to change things, destroy their heritage. And now he dishonored Lauriel.

She was his and everyone knew it! The shawl was his, too. His fists clenched tighter as he watched them step out of the pool and leave through the hidden passage. This intruder had become a dangerous predator and could not be ignored any more. When two hunters went out after the same game, only one returned.

He knew what must be done.

CHAPTER 23

The night before seemed like a dream, until he rolled over to face the long braid of hair tousled against his face. The dream was still in his bed. They had made love tenderly and gently during the night, the first time for her. It was his first time, too. He'd had sex before, but he had never made love.

He draped an arm gently around her waist. Lauriel turned to face him, her sun ripened cheeks wrinkling in a smile.

"Is morning?"

"I think so." He didn't bother to look. For the first time he could remember, he was content; the search was over. He could remain with this unusual woman, in the present future, forever. He knew that. He felt no desire to return home. He was home.

"Out of my bed, you poacher!" Lauriel gave a hard push that landed him on the floor.

"What's the matter? I love you," he said. It wasn't as difficult as he had thought.

"You've slept with me," she said. "If really love me, you'd go now!"

"Where?"

"Talk to Father, ask to call me in pair bonding."

"I was planning on it." He jumped back on the bedroll, pinning her down. "Are you going to turn into a nagging wo'am, or do I have to straighten you out right now?"

She wrestled him aside and quickly ended up on top, holding his arms pinned. Her long hair dangled in his face.

"Do not want to be your wo'am," she said. "This one wants to be your, your equal."

"My what?" He gave an insincere frown. "I knew I was making a mistake educating you. Next, you'll be talking about Women's Lib."

"What is wo'am slib?"

"Skip it. You don't want to know."

She got out of bed, taking the cover and draping it around her nude body.

"Hiding from me, after last night?"

"You were staring at me."

"Maybe I like what I see." He jumped up and pulled her close, returning her fragile smile.

"Am not 'customed to being seen. You are first ..."

"And I'm the last," he said as a hasty promise, once more pulling her tight.

# # #

Danon entered the hazy focum of the Lodge and waited to be acknowledged. For centuries a focum like this one had been the meeting place for Nathon's ancestors when they would discuss important choices, or make decisions that might determine the outcome of an entire clan. Danon had come to discuss two topics; civil rights and equality, and marrying this leader's only daughter. Nathon sat against the far wall, stuffing the bowl of his calumet with a grassy mixture of tobacco and cannabis. He knew Danon was waiting, but seemed to take his time as if collecting his thoughts. He finished the ritual of lighting the long pipe and took a long puff.

"Sit, Brother, and join me."

He lifted the pipe as an offer to share, but Danon declined.

"Each time you come to visit, you bring another new idea to complicate this one's life." He took another long puff. "What is this you speak of, that which concerns freedom of clan?"

Danon wasn't surprised that Nathon already knew about one of his topics. He was just unsure if the leader knew of both and only chose the simpler topic first.

"Nathon, are you satisfied? Are you content to see your people live down here? Shunned from the surface, unable to live, work, or play wherever they wish? Do you really see a future for the Clan in this, this dimly lit grave?"

The May'r was taken aback.

"This discrimination and treatment under the Perf's domination must cease! Their behavior toward us and other minority groups is intolerable."

He handed Nathon a bundle of paper. "This is a copy of two, very old and very important documents."

Nathon studied the papers a moment, holding them upside down. "What are they?"

"They were written a long time ago, before the holocaust," he explained, "even before tribal memory."

Nathon regarded the freshly printed pages with skepticism. They were no older than the growing ache in his forehead. He took a deep draw on his medicine pipe.

"These are the concepts on which this nation was founded." Danon tried to quote excerpts from the wrinkled pages, how all men were created equal … and were endowed with certain inalienable rights … shall not be denied on account of race, color, or previous servitude … the right of people to peaceably assemble … securing the blessings of liberty …

"This is the Law!" Danon said with growing enthusiasm. "Regardless of what local ordinances might have been passed, these basic truths remain."

Danon leaned forward, his voice gaining authority. "We do not have to submit. We must not submit to such flagrant violations of our rights. We have the right to live free and equal among the brotherhood of Man!"

Nathon had sat passively through Danon discourse. Finally he laid down the calumet and spoke softly. "Are you through?"

"Yes, sir."

"You have gained much boldness I see."

"Sorry."

Nathon shook his head. "No. Trust in what your spirit feels." He rubbed his chin. "But you speak strange words and new ideas. Some are uncomfortable with change, and fear the dangers that may come. These words you speak do not fit in Perfs' society."

"They're not my ideas."

"They contradict the Apartheid Party," Nathon said. "Perfs will not accept such change. Besides, Clan is comfortable. Do we not have all that is needed for life? Look farther down the path you are choosing, can you not see that change would bring upheaval to the Clan?"

"They're not my ideas!" Danon lowered his voice. "Sorry. This isn't change, it's the way it was in the beginning. It is we who must not accept. We must not accept the denial of our fundamental rights. And we must take a stand for what we believe."

Nathon rubbed his temples, but it didn't seem to help. "How would you change a nation?"

"Well, first we need to spread the word to the other clans. Teach them the lost ways of freedom, convince them to join us in a peaceful, organized confrontation of these injustices."

"Others?" Nathon shook his head. "Clans not mix with other clans."

"Why, is that another tabuli?"

"In learning to survive, trust becomes closely guarded gift. There is little outside one's clan."

"That lack of trust has weakened us and given the Perfs the advantage. Once the clans get to know each other, trust can be gained and friendships formed."

Nathon looked away, staring at the wall covered with painted animal skins. "As clan warrior, this one has learned to hunt with courage. But as May'r, this one sees many risks of traveling the path you suggest."

"What's the risk of staying down here? What will be the consequences, a generation from now? Who knows what restrictions they'll place on our children if we sit back and do nothing."

"But we have lived in peace for over a generation."

"No you haven't. You've lived in surrender."

Nathon's eyes hardened and his posture stiffened.

"Believe me, May'r, I can assure you that history never remains static. It's always changing, for better or worse, it's changing. Times of peace bring times of war. Times of slavery bring times of freedom. And times of indifference will bring times of regret."

Nathon picked up his pipe and relit it, mulling over the young warrior's words.

"There are others who can help," Danon said to break the silence. "Not every black agrees with the Apartheid party. I've discovered that some of them care, too."

Nathon gave a sigh, the burden of leadership showing in his eyes. "Sometimes, this one wonders if acted wisely letting you stay with us, becoming one of us." He stood and walked over to the painted hide, tracing some of the glyphs as if they held an answer. "But if this is common destiny woven by the Earth Mother, then is what must be done."

Nathon studied the visitor, provider, warrior as if he was looking at a stranger. "Who are you, Danon?"

"Excuse me?"

"You come from afar. You bring knowledge of time before the Hol'caust, and speak of leading Clan to freedom. You can work magic long forgotten by our medicine men. This one senses something in your aura, a force that molds our lives to your destiny."

"Then you will help me?" He decided to skip the discussion on predetermined futures.

"I will not stop you. But I do not seek war."

"Neither do I. This path will take a warrior's courage, but not for battle. Our goal is to walk into the enemy's camp and sit down as friends."

Nathon smiled at his illustration and picked up his calumet. He then looked surprised when Danon sat back down on the cushion. "There is more?"

Danon suddenly felt intimidated. "Yes. Now I ask for something else, something over which you have the final word. Can I …" He took a nervous breath. "I'm asking your permission to call Lauriel?"

Nathon almost dropped his pipe. "Pair bonding?"

Danon nodded.

"You ask for Lauriel to be your wo'am?"

"Yes, no. She's much too special to become just some warrior's wo'am. I want her to be my mate, my partner.

Nathon leaned over and stared incredulously.

"I think I honestly love her."

Nathon laughed. "You must, my son. Not even clan warrior holds the young wildcat by courage alone." His smile died. "But there is matter of custom to be considered. She is my daughter, but was never presented to Council as gr'll of age."

"Or as a warrior," Danon added before thinking. He had overstepped his limits and knew it.

"Was not easy decision to make." Nathon's tone seemed remorseful. "As May'r, could not approve of path she has chosen. But as father, she has made me very proud."

Nathon rose, seeming suddenly troubled, and crossed the darkened floor. "Is importance of status which cannot be ignored."

"My feelings for Lauriel have nothing to do with her status."

"She holds status of Princess. You know what this means?"

"Yes, sort of. You have no son to succeed you."

"And do you reach for this status, in the tradition of my grandfathers?"

"What?" Lauriel hadn't warned him about this.

"Does Danon, the warrior, now seek to be son of May'r?"

Holy crap! Son of the May'r. Danon could feel the beads of sweat popping out of his forehead. He knew the answer Nathon wanted. Just give it. Just give the correct answer.

"No, sir, not really."

Nathon looked confused by the answer. He wasn't alone. "You turn from this one's status? Is May'r not worth your choosing!"

"It's not that, it's just that …"

He tried to find the words to explain. He didn't know if he could ever live up to such a responsibility? He realized that he'd just screwed up the biggest interview of his life. But if he couldn't handle the job of Chief Administrator, how in the world could he ever consider becoming a clan May'r? He wanted her but, damn it, but he hadn't anticipated the legacy of her heritage.

Nathon waited for an explanation. He deserved the truth, so Danon gave it.

"I want your daughter. But I don't want her status. This one will never be worthy of such honor or responsibility." He turned to leave.

The leader reached out to rest a hand on Danon's shoulder.

"You have answered truthfully. And wisely. No mano worthy of position would be eager to seek such burden." He gave an assuring look. "You are worthy to be my son."

"I, I don't understand."

Nathon's leathery countenance almost revealed a smile. "You have permission. Her father will present her to council as wo'am of age. And her May'r will recognize her claim as warrior." Nathon cleared his eyes as if there was too much smoke in the room.

"You will enter Circle and call for her. If she accepts ..." He took a deep breath. "Then both will have my blessing before the assembly."

"But I told you, I'm not—"

"Go now, and do not argue. Will be much time later to train you in path of leadership."

He returned to his seat cushion and retrieved his smoldering calumet. He didn't hear Danon's heavy feet running from the lodge as he drew a deep puff and again studied the faded glyphs. The past and future were all circles within larger circles. He couldn't tell whether the prophecy was in the past or the future. In his heart, he knew he had made the right choice. But in the glyphs he saw a path that led to danger and uncertainty. And death. He might have exaggerated the amount of time left for training his new son.

# # #

Danon ran into the Warrior's Den and looked around eagerly. He couldn't wait to tell Lauriel about being presented, but first he had to find her. He was surprised to discover the Den already had a few customers sharing a drink. Although it was too early for Danon to consider a beaker of brien, some of his brothers had been up before dawn hunting fresh meat. They were now ready for their reward.

He spied three brothers gathered at the end of the bar having a lively discussion. Behind them stood Lauriel.

"There he is," she said almost accusingly as Danon approached. "Ask him yourself."

"Ask me what?"

One of them poked a finger to his chest. “What’s all this ’bout Perfs being equal?”

“Yeah!” added another.

Danon tried to step back, but the inquisitive trio encircled him. “All I said was, we’re all equal under the Law. It doesn’t matter if you’re born black or brown or red. You’re born with certain rights. And no attempts of bigotry can change that.”

Gregon hobbled around the back of the counter. “You needs to learn way of life here, son. Perfs don’t give us no rights, except the right to work for ’em for almost nothing.”

“With all respect, my friend, you have much to learn. Before the holocaust, did your people not live free?”

Gregon managed a slight nod of agreement, without actually committing himself. “Was long time ago.”

“Did you know they were guaranteed that freedom by law?”

Gregon shrugged.

“They were,” Danon said with authority. “And the very law that ensured their liberty still guarantees yours, if you’ll only make use of it.”

Gregon didn’t look truly convinced, but hobbled back around the bar as a new voice came from behind.

“What law? Ain’t never heard any such law before.”

Danon turned to address the new brother. “Two and a half centuries before the Holocaust, our ancestors …” He paused to consider the implications. “Those who came before the Perfs. The ones who were welcomed by the ancestors of Chocks, O’kees, Pawnee, and others. Those common ancestors preserved the principles of liberty, freedom, and equality with two basic documents. And every law, passed in this country since then, has been required to conform to their tradition and guidance.”

As Danon continued to speak, additional warriors wandered in looking for something to do. They curiously joined the band of listeners. Each statement Danon made about civil rights or equality spurred another round of discussion. Some made blatant denials; others seemed sincerely interested, asking more questions. As the audience grew larger, some clustered tightly around Danon, while others broke off into smaller groups to argue with each other.

When Danon got the chance to look around for Lauriel, she was gone. “Where’d she go?” he asked Gregon.

“Who, Lauriel?” The aged warrior grinned. “She’s only smart one. Left while you was blabbing. Ain’t never seen a warrior talk so much in my life.”

# # #

Lauriel stood with a circle of older men gathered around a glowing fire pot. As Danon approached, he quickly recognized the content of their talk.

"What are you doing?"

"You said people need to know, need to be educated."

"May I talk to you, privately?" He pulled her aside. "Aren't you interested enough to ask what your father said?"

She shook her head. "This one already knows his answer."

"How?"

"Cause I know my father. And I know how he feels about you, superstitious. He believes in the legend, remember? His own daughter cannot pry a favor from his iron fist, but you have power to ask for almost anything."

"Maybe not anything ..."

"He senses your aura. I think he is afraid."

"Your Father? Of what?"

"He is afraid to stand in way of your destiny."

Danon winced. "What destiny? All I want to do is motivate your people enough to desire a little better living condition. And bond with you of course. I don't see that as any great destiny."

She placed a finger on his lips. "Easy, any louder and the whole Clan will hear us."

Danon glanced over his shoulder to the elderly men who were listening intently with toothless grins. He turned his back on them to continue, but Lauriel started first.

"Will talk 'bout this later," she whispered. She pointed to the group of men. "They have some questions for you about quality and liberty."

Acting on her cue, the men instantly began questioning him about the new concepts she had mentioned. An inquisitive crowd again captured Danon. He tried to satisfy their curiosity quickly so he could get back to Lauriel, but as soon as he answered one question, more were asked. When he paused to notice, Lauriel was gone again. He politely excused himself to search for her once more.

Walking along the twisted path that wound between the staggered columns of limestone, he looked right and left trying to catch a glimpse of her. He turned to walk past another group of men, but they recognized him and called out inquisitively. They, too, had listened to Lauriel and had many, many questions.

# # #

He fell on his bed cushion, exhausted. He'd never realized the cave was so big. He had spent most of the day talking to one group, searching for Lauriel, and pausing to answer questions again and again.

"Busy day?" Lauriel asked, coming in from her bedroom to sit down beside him.

He gave her a vicious glare. "Not as busy as yours. Everywhere I went, I found clansmen loaded with endless questions. Seems someone's been busy stirring up the Clan."

Lauriel gave an innocent shrug. "You said we need to spread the word." She leaned over him and began massaging his shoulders.

"I didn't say do it all at once! Mmm, don't stop. That feels good."

"Why have you never told me 'bout yourself?"

"What do you mean?"

"You know what I mean," she said, slapping him on the butt. "Like where'd you come from?"

"I told you, from a place very far away."

"Where?"

"It's a little hard to explain."

"Try hard then," she said. "What'd you do before you became a houseboy?"

"Research."

"Research? What is that?"

"I studied things."

"What things?"

"Physics. Math. Time anomalies"

"You speak words, but you tell me nothing."

"It's sort of like … like the mysteries of Mother Earth herself."

Her hands stopped as she considered his words. "Is why you know about healing and Benon's relics. Did you use one of those, those scopes to study Earth Mother?"

"Yes, sometimes. We used many tools." He thought back to the complex and Thomas. "But that was a long time ago."

"Not so long. You been with Clan less than two moons."

"Maybe so, but my past life seems so far away now. I think I like this life better."

"Sounds like you left good clan. You don't want to return?"

Danon remembered the Chief and Thomas, standing by the system console as he had crawled into the capsule. He lay in silence for a minute, thinking, then he rolled over to take her in his arms.

"I couldn't ever take you there, Lauriel. If I went back, I'd have to go alone, and I don't ever want to leave you. No," he said with finality. "I don't want to go back. Ever."

He wondered how he could be so content in such a primitive world. How could Lauriel affect him so strongly? What would Thomas do when he didn't return in the capsule?

The capsule!

It was the mode of travel through time to his past present. Would it activate without him? Did he have to be inside it, or would it somehow snatch him away from this future present when it went? He didn't know. As the project manager, he hadn't actually designed it; that had been accomplished by the team who had worked under him. He realized that he truly didn't know how it worked. And he didn't know what it would do, or when. He shuddered as realized some of the implications, and decided that he couldn't take chances.

# # #

As they walked into the haze of the Warrior's Den, they were greeted with tempting smells of roasting venison and warm brien. They walked over to a hide covered table and sat down with two other warriors. The sounds of the crowded room had not changed upon their arrival. Ever since Lauriel had helped rescue Dazjon, a subtle change in their attitude had become apparent as if maybe they had finally accepted her.

"Well?" Gregon hollered from behind the bar, "You drink'n or not?" Lauriel held up two fingers.

Danon said went over to the fire pit to examine the remains of an over-cooked deer loin. He drew his dagger to saw through the crust of charred meat. Juices flowed from the pink cut and danced on the hissing coals.

"That looks good," Lauriel said as he dropped the steaming hunks of meat on the table. "But did't you want some, too?"

Gregon limped over to their table and deposited two beakers of brien. "Been hearing lots a talk lately. Most the Clan's gossiping 'bout it like a bunch of idle water maidens. You responsible, ain't ya?"

Danon glanced suspiciously over to Lauriel. "In a way, yes."

"Perfs won't never hold to such a notion," Gregon said, as he grumbled back to the bar. "Not withouts a fight."

Another voice shot across the room. "Then a fight is what we give them!"

Danon turned to see who had made the comment, but couldn't decide since many of his fellow warriors were shaking their heads in agreement.

"No!" he said, standing up from the table. "Fighting won't get us what we want. Not this time."

"Why not?" someone asked.

"Violence will get us noticed, sure. It'll gain their attention, but not their sympathy."

"My dagger'll spill their sympathy just fine!"

He recognized Devon's voice without turning to look. "And can you hold your dagger to the throats of every Perf in this country?"

"Is good idea to me," Devon answered with a smile.

Rowdy shouts and laughter followed. Danon had to raise his voice to be heard.

"Don't you understand? This battle of civil rights has been fought many times before, not just in this country's history but in other lands as well. Violence has never worked, only a well organized and peaceful confrontation."

"What kind of warrior speaks of peace?"

"A warrior who's concerned about the welfare of not just his clan, but his brothers everywhere. A warrior who knows when to fight and when to wait."

Devon grumbled an incoherent retort and went back to his brien.

"Then what can we do?" asked a curious brother.

"For now, I guess start by refusing to bow into submission. Refuse to sit in the back of the bus. Drink from any fountain, not just the designated ones."

"I have to warn ya," Gregon said, "can't see no good that'll do."

"It's little things I admit, but until we get organized ..."

"Organized?" Devon interrupted. "Who's gonna organize?"

"The clans, all the clans. Soon, we'll spread the word to all our people, wherever they are. We can all meet in the city to stage a demonstration, maybe a march."

"Demonstration?" Devon repeated with a mocking laugh. "What is there to demonstrate?"

"We will demonstrate publicly that we will no longer hide while our rights are abused. Prove that we are united in our belief, and that we demand the respect due every human being."

More shouts of approval filled the air, but not unanimously. Devon and others sat at their tables, shaking their heads.

"It won't be easy," he shouted. He knew that more than he wanted to admit. "It may not even happen in our lifetime, but the day will come when Perfs and Bios will live side by side in the city. The different ethnic groups must be reunited. Maybe not in perfection, but at least in peace."

# # #

Danon didn't know if he had accomplished anything or not, other than letting his meal get cold. The debates were still going strong when Lauriel had dragged him away. Although she had refrained from displaying any affection publicly, she lifted inviting arms to him the instant they entered the privacy of her lodge.

"You were impressive."

"I didn't intend to lead a crusade. I just can't forget how it felt to be treated like dirty laundry. Nobody should have to take that kind of treatment."

She held him close, her firm breasts pushing against him. "Is late and I am tired." She smiled and started for the bedroom, but Danon didn't follow.

"What's wrong?"

"I don't know. It's just, well I've been thinking. About us I mean." He would have stuffed his hands in his pockets, but the leather breeches had none. "This is hard for me to say. You're very special to me, Lauriel."

Her inviting eyes and luring smile did not make it any easier. "You see you're not, well, you're not the first woman that I've been with."

"So?"

He gently kissed her tanned cheek while soft green eyes waited for an explanation.

"I want you to be different. Understand? I'm talking about something that was always missing before."

He couldn't even find the words to describe his fear. He had avoided this kind of intimacy for as long as he could remember. But now he realized it was more than that. He had been trying to run away from the rainbows of pain and disappointment. As he looked into those trusting eyes, he knew in his heart that she was worth the gamble.

She caressed his face. "Your heart is speaking, but I cannot hear its words."

"I wish you could understand what's in my heart. This would be a lot easier. I want you go to your bed, alone. I'm going to wait for our wedding night."

"Our what?"

"Our pair bonding."

"But we have already …"

"I know. I hope you can understand."

She kissed him. "I can. But you'd better be ready for our bonding night. This one has waited long for you to come along. And I don't like to wait."

"It won't be long," he promised. "Abstinence is a new virtue for me. And I don't think it suits me well."

# # #

Danon was almost there.

Several kilometers down the seldomly traveled road, he found what he was searching for, a turn-off barely recognizable as a road, or what used to be a road. He paused to look around once more. Dawn was approaching and he could see for miles in the flat, West Texas twilight. He was still alone, except for the long-eared jackrabbit that skittered nervously away in the distance.

Dawn was too early to be doing anything, but he had business to take care of, without Lauriel. Another reason not to sleep with her, though not quite as noble. He left the paved road and followed the faint remnants of tire tracks till he reached the abandoned office building that was once S-Ray Inc.

He entered the empty structure and wondered why none of the clans had moved in. It was a lot nicer than the cave, with plenty of rooms. When he thought about the capsule still waiting and functional, a shiver of anticipation raced up his spine. If Thomas were here to question the sanity of his plans, he wouldn't have been able to explain anything, except maybe it was what must be done. He grabbed a fire axe from the glass encased fire hose and descended the dimly lit stairs.

Finally he stood in front of the dust covered acceleration tube. Inside, the empty capsule waited for him. He felt separated from the memories of the launch room, as if they were too far away, part of another life. He didn't know how it was supposed to return home to the past present; there was no longer any facility power for the tachyon drive. It didn't matter. He was there to ensure that it went nowhere. Thomas would never understand his disappearance, but he would understand this if he was here.

He raised the heavy axe to guarantee no return, and no future time pilots.

# # #

As he stepped outside, a dark figure stood before him, silhouetted in the bright sunlight with hands perched on hips.

"Where you've been!" her tone was frustrated and impatient.

"Lauriel? What are you doing here?"

"This one followed to find out what you are hiding." She glanced behind him for a better look, but Danon moved casually to stay in her way.

Danon tried to think of something believable. "I, uh …"

"Well?"

"That's a little hard to explain."

"You always say that! Try, I've got time."

"How did you follow me?"

"Answer my question. Why'd you come here and what were you doing?" She tiptoed to look over his shoulder. "This place is 'nother tabuli. Have never been inside. Even the Perfs stay away."

"There's no mystery in here," he said, opening the door. "See for yourself."

She peeked in hesitantly. "Has something to do with your past, doesn't it?"

"You could say that."

She stepped in, looking around the disheveled office foyer. "You said come from far away, but you'd been to that garden before. What does this have to do with your past?"

"Okay," he sighed, "You really want to know? This is where I came from, a long time ago. Before you were born, before you father was even born. I used to work in there, spent most of my adult life down there."

"You lived with another clan down there?"

"No, I lived in the city."

"Only Perfs live in city."

"Maybe now, but not then." He wanted to explain, but how could he? She'd think he was crazy. "Everyone lived in the city, if they wanted to."

Laurel shook her head.

"I'm talking about a time before the holocaust."

Her expression of curiosity died. She turned and walked past him to the door.

"Where are you going?"

She spun around angrily. "You don't want to tell of your past, fine. Maybe there is secret you are afraid of sharing. But don't make up wild stories. Whatever it is, when you tell me, I will listen. But this one is too old for child's tale."

"Lauriel! Wait. It's true, I'm trying to explain."

She did not stop to listen.

Chapter 24

Once again, Danon sat in front of May'r Nathon. The haze of incense hanging lazily in the air seemed not as intense. Perhaps less was needed to cover the smell since everyone was taking regular baths. New background odors of the Lodge almost peeked through: old leather, leftovers from breakfast and freshly ground cornmeal. Danon wondered why he had been called.

Finally Nathon laid the calumet across his lap and gave a somber look. "There is much talk," he said. "I hear of brothers arguing. Many Elders are disturbed by these new ideas. Do you know what spreads from campfire to campfire, what words are disputed?"

Danon started to answer, but Nathon continued, "This idea of liberty spreads quickly, like prairie fire. Young and old argue need for action, or restraint. Already, this one has heard of bold actions by some brothers. Clansmen have broken tradition, refused to sit in proper place on bus. Some have demanded respect from their masters in city. It is ..." He took a deep breath. "Too much and too quick."

Danon chose his words carefully. "Change never comes easy. It's never been eagerly accepted by society. Any society. It was never easy to gain liberty in the past, and it won't be easy this time. But it will happen."

"You have a great faith in this."

"I think I understand the will of our people. They're not content to be outcasts. They feel the need to be recognized as human beings. With some they might need that desire awakened, but it's there. I don't know how long it will take, but we will eventually succeed. It's not a matter of faith. This is something that I know."

Nathon seemed taken aback. "You can see the future, also?"

"No, but I understand the past." Danon felt a sudden chill of memory. History was replete with social reformers. All were opposed with open hostility. Most were beaten.

"Some may die," he said softly to himself.

A worried frown creased Nathon's face. "How many?"

"I don't know, but we will win if we stand firm. We can't allow any violence on our part. Peaceful confrontation is the only way."

Nathon rubbed his chin. The tone of his voice held a fatherly warning. "You challenge their ways. And path of challenge is not gently walked."

Danon nodded full agreement, thinking of the riots of the Sixties and the over-zealous riot police. "It will be a long struggle. And our actions will be futile unless the other clans join us. It's time for you to act, Nathon."

Nathon sat back. "This one? How?"

"We have to spread the word. Go with me to the other clans. Introduce me. They respect your authority. They'll trust a May'r from another clan."

Nathon shook his head. "Never has May'r of one clan visited another."

"Then it will definitely get their attention," Danon said with a confident grin.

Nathon leaned back in deep thought. He was not a man who made rash decisions, since everything he did affected the Clan. He glanced at the glyphs and gave a resolute nod.

"Is what must be done." He stood and pointed outside. "Gather two warriors. Tell them to dress as commons, we travel by bus."

# # #

By the time the un-airconditioned bus arrived, Danon was grateful just to sit. At least it would provide some shade. The late morning sun was already spawning dust devils, and the dry, dusty air made the wait seem even longer for the disguised warriors.

Juston boarded first, ahead of May'r Nathon. The warrior did not appear eager for the expedition, but it was his day as personal guard to the May'r. Under his arm, he carried Nathon's shawl, concealed in a worn swatch of linen. Devon had also chosen go along, apparently deciding that any mission which took the May'r outside the cave was much too important to be excluded from. Each wore jumpsuits usually worn by workers traveling to the city. They also wore regular work boots, except for Devon who had retained his moccasins. Danon followed them up the steps, but stopped partway down the aisle and sat down.

"What're you doing?" Devon asked.

"Sit down," Danon answered.

"Is not place …"

Nathon turned to investigate. He motioned to Juston who had already taken a seat in the back, then he walked up to sit behind Danon. Devon and Juston were still standing with indecision when the anxious driver shouted at them.

"Sit down!"

They fell into a seat across the isle from Danon and Nathon. The driver turned around. "Hey! Not there!" He waved them back like cattle. "Get back where you belong."

Devon leaned forward, reaching for his calf and the dagger concealed beneath the loose trousers. Danon calmly stared back to the irate driver.

"Why?"

The driver hesitated. "Because. It's not right."

"If that's all, then I think I'll sit here anyway." He watched the driver closely, wondering how far he would go to enforce the traditional segregation.

One of the passengers, a large man with stocky shoulders, rose from the front of the bus and lumbered toward them. His black eyes narrowed with determination.

"Mind your place, boy!"

Juston rose to answer the challenge with Danon, while Devon remained seated, his hand resting on his leg.

"My place?" Danon echoed. "I have the right to sit anywhere I choose. And don't call me 'boy'. Or my place is going to be stuffing my size ten boot up your fat backside. Now why don't you carry your little pea brain back up there and mind your own business!"

The man gritted his teeth, looking around for support. He found none. The other passengers sitting safely at the front only stared indifferently. He would have to back down or stand alone.

"What's matter, Perf?" Juston said as the man's face reddened. "You deaf, or just dumb? He told you to get!"

An older gentleman with a kinder face offered some advice to the lone challenger. "Oh, just leave him alone. They aren't worth the trouble."

Seizing the opportunity to save a little dignity, the self-appointed enforcer turned away, mumbling a racial obscenity as the driver reluctantly resumed his journey. The older gentleman covertly nodded his approval before turning around.

Nathon leaned over to Danon with a confused frown. "Is peaceful confrontation?"

# # #

The airbus glided along, stopping only to pick up an occasional passenger along the almost barren highway. Each new arrival would stop abruptly upon noticing where the "out of place" minority sat, glance around, and finally take a seat. A flurry of whispers and curious stares always followed.

Eventually, they approached an intersection May'r Nathon recognized. He stood and led the others to the exit, waiting for the bus to stop.

The driver seemed anxious to open the door and get rid of them. He muttered something under his breath, and slammed the hatch the instant they had disembarked.

"That felt good!" Juston shouted, watching the airbus speed away. "To challenge stupid rule and win."

Danon couldn't keep from smiling. It did feel good, but Nathon's look of displeasure restrained him. The leader walked across the cracked pavement, with Juston scampering quickly behind, to sit on a bench under a drooping shade screen. He squinted at the sun and then glanced down at their shadows.

"Must do better at next peaceful confrontation."

# # #

The second airbus pulled up and they boarded. Choosing again to sit near the middle row of seats caused a similar reaction as the first. Everyone was quick to notice, but none seemed willing to engage with the determined looking group.

After another lengthy ride, they walked across an open field.

"Are we getting close?" Danon asked, walking at Nathon's side over the plowed furrows of maize. "I'm getting tired of sitting on my butt."

"Almost there," Nathon said. "Then you have more to do than sit on butt."

They broke out of the field's soft sandy soil and crossed over firmer, weed ridden ground. "There is Data Clan," Nathon said, pointing to a pair of deteriorated flattop buildings. Danon recognized the structure, the former office building of Data Life, Incorporated.

# # #

The beige stucco walls of the underground parking lot were faded. Sand filled cracks meandered along the walls, revealing weathered cinder blocks. Its large, square opening, darkly recessed from the noonday sun, revealed few signs of life within. The constant stream of people that flowed in and out of their own entrance was missing here.

Nathon walked up to the opening and stopped abruptly, causing Danon to bump clumsily into his back. He glanced behind to see who all had noticed.

"Ya t'hay!" Nathon called in his native tongue to the dark interior. "This one wishes to speak with Council. We are from Grotto Clan."

A moment of silence followed before they heard sounds of scurrying feet and whispers.

"Grotto Clan?" came a delayed echo.

"That's right," Danon answered. "The May'r from the Grotto Clan. How long are you going to make him wait for a proper reception?"

More whispers and hurried commands. Echoes of footsteps running away. "Not long," came a nervous reply. "You wait. Rezon Sen comes."

Danon was tired of waiting. The sun was hot. He was about to go on in regardless when two guards jumped into the daylight. They wore leather breeches similar to his, but no vests. Multiple tattoos decorated their chest. Each sour-faced guard sported an earring and a javelin, whose wooden shafts were decorated with owl feathers and colored ribbons that fluttered gently in the breeze.

A tall figure stepped out, wearing two earrings and a large chest tattoo. He wore a shawl similar to Nathon's, only smaller. It signified his status as prince, and heir apparent. As he stepped forward between the two guards, Danon noticed that his eyes had a pronounced slant at the corners.

"I am Rezon Sen, prince of Data Clan. I take you to Fu Quin, my father." He bowed slightly and disappeared into the darkness.

Inside, the shadows faded to reveal a dirt floor and walls covered with countless layers of graffiti, some almost worthy of being classified as art. Hanging on the far wall, beneath layers of smeared paint, hid a large plastic sign. In spite of some missing pieces and generations of vandalism, Danon could make out the words:

# # #

DATA LIFE INC.
VERBATIM DISCS
MEMORY CUBES
COMPUTER LOGIC DEVICES

# # #

The aroma of cooking food hit Danon as he walked into the large room. It was mingled with the odors of sweaty bodies and something reminiscent of week old garbage.

Even with everyone in the Grotto clan taking regular baths, the Grotto Cave still held an indigenous aroma, but it smelled like home. This was different, Danon realized. A foreign smell. People he had never met, customs he had not learned. Throughout the room, heavy columns supported the concrete roof, reminding him of the formations in the cavern, only these were man made and lacking the natural beauty of living limestone.

They descended a wide, winding ramp passing one level after another, the sound of their footsteps slapping against the bare concrete walls as they passed the ever-present support columns that punctuated each floor. He saw families gathered around small campfires, performing tasks of smoking and curing. Women squatted together in quiet gossip as they quilted patches of fabric, or mended clothing. The shabby dwellings were no better or worse than the ones back home, except they were arranged more orderly, in rows along the walls.

As the visitors passed by, curious faces observed the strangers. On the bottom level of the abandoned parking lot, the young prince led them to a square dwelling, a simple wooden frame draped with yellowing sheets of plastic. He raised a hand to halt, and ducked inside. After a few moments, he reappeared and bowed stiffly.

"FuQuin will see you now."

# # #

The dank Lodge had the smell of damp carpet and a green film of algae clung to the plastic. In the center of the room sat a white haired man wearing a dirty shawl that hung limply over withered shoulders. Nathon unfolded his and draped it over his arm as a gesture of deference.

"I am Rezon of Data Clan," the old man said with a cold formality; his wrinkled face seemed curious, but distrustful. "Who is this who carries cloth of May'r?"

Nathon peeled the jumpsuit off his broad shoulders to reveal the black leathers hidden underneath. "This one is Nathon. May'r of Grotto Clan."

Danon, Devon and Juston also removed their jumpsuits.

Everyone's eyes widened, and hushed whispers rushed from the back of the dark room: "Warriors!"

"And this is Warrior Danon."

Curious eyes stared at the still pale visitor who now sported a full beard. They had never seen a "pasty" before.

"He has come from afar to become one of us," Nathon explained. "He brings knowledge of the time before Holocaust. He wishes to speak to you and your council."

"Council?" The old man's voice was shrill and irritating. "Council? To speak of what?"

"Liberty," Danon answered. He was tired of formal introductions. It was time to get to business.

# # #

The late night trip back to Grotto Cave was long and tiring. They had arrived at the second bus stop too late, and walked the remainder. Danon entered the lodge quietly, trying not to wake her.

"Danon? Is that you?"

"Go back to sleep," he whispered.

She came out of her bedroom with a light blanket tightly wrapped around her. "Where were you? Gregon said you left with Father and some others. Where'd you go?"

"To see the Data Clan."

"My father went to 'nother clan?"

"Sure, why not?"

"The May'r of one clan visiting another?" She could not hide her disbelief. "Has never been done!"

"Well, it has now." He stretched out on his bedroll. "We spoke to their council."

"About civil rights?" She fell down beside him. "Tell me all about it."

"Darling, it's late. I'm too tired and sore from the fight."

"Fight? What fight?"

Danon groaned. He had been unprepared for his encounter with the militant clan. "They're even more warrioristic than we are!" He stretched out with a groan.

"You fought with them? I thought you went to talk."

"I did. But to be worthy of Council honor, I had to prove myself and challenge their best warrior. Mean little sonuva—"

"Danon!"

"Well, he was. He knew some effective self defense tactics of his own." He rubbed his side. "He really enjoyed jabbing my kidneys."

"You defeated him, of course."

"Let's call it a draw, but I gained enough respect so he could introduce me before the Council."

"Well? What'd they say?"

"I don't know. They seemed to have trouble grasping the concept of a peaceful confrontation. They were more than willing to join a fight, but seemed to balk at the idea of a simple march."

"March, what march?"

"I still not sure about them. They might be trouble." He rolled away from her, holding his side. "Please, let me sleep."

"What march?" she repeated, shaking him.

"A march downtown. To demonstrate. But only if the other clans agree to come, too. Now please … go to sleep … leaving early."

"Where are you going? With my father again?"

"Yes," he moaned. "To the next clan, and do it all over again."

She shook him again, but he only groaned. She gave up trying to keep him awake and lay down beside him, watching the rising and falling of his chest. She placed a tender kiss on his neck as she snuggled against him.

# # #

He stirred slowly to a tinny buzzing sound somewhere in the distance. He held his watch close to his face and squinted to read it. It couldn't possibly be time, yet. He'd barely lain down. He turned it off and rolled over on the soft, inviting blanket.

"You better get ready, Father don't like t'be kept waiting."

He sat up slowly and opened his heavy eyes wider. "Lauriel, what are you doing up so early?"

"Getting ready for trip, this one is going with you."

"I don't know if that's such a good idea."

She walked over and jerked his bed cover away. "This one is going."

"Fine. Whatever." The determined look in her eye told him that her mind was made up and he didn't feel like arguing with her. Not this early. He didn't feel like doing anything, except going back to sleep. He stumbled to the table and splashed his face with the cold water. Pointing to her leathers, he said, "You'd better cover up those with a jumpsuit or something if you're really planning on going with us."

When he finished washing up, she was already changed and waiting.

As they approached the Lodge he noticed Juston was again standing as Nathon's guard alongside Devon.

"Juston, I thought it was someone else's turn to stand personal guard for the day."

"This one volunteered," he said with a smile. "Is exciting to watch you fight. I'd only sit around Den and drink too many beakers."

Danon rubbed his tender side. "I really hope I don't have to fight anyone today."

Devon stared as Lauriel approach, wearing a baggy jumpsuit. He stepped in front of her.

"You are not allowed."

She pushed him aside and continued toward her father. "I go where I please! Only May'r can order this warrior around."

Juston backed away to give the May'r and his daughter some privacy. As he moved near, Devon flashed a stern warning look to the first warrior who grinned. They all knew that although he and Lauriel frequently argued, their relationship had at one time been much closer. The recent rumors about a pair bonding had not helped his demeanor.

"This house boy warrior is dangerous," he said to Juston.

"Is no longer house boy," Juston said. "Is one of us, now."

Devon shook his head slowly. "He does not respect the old ways. And does not understand the code our brothers have lived and died by for generations."

Juston gave an incredulous look. "You were there. He passed the ritual of blood oath. He knows our code."

Devon continued to stare at his adversary, and then smiled. "Is one custom he cannot ignore."

Nathon had observed his daughter's tart dismissal of Devon and tried to stifle his amusement. As she neared, he struggled to retain his serious countenance.

"Why?" he asked.

"Am concerned 'bout future as anyone else. This one wants to be part of it."

Nathon nodded. "You never were one to sit for long, even when you were little gr'll. You had to be doing something, going somewhere. But this one knows you do not come to follow your May'r. You come to follow him." His eyes seemed to sparkle. "This one expected you here."

"You did?"

His stern countenance softened. "This one is proud of little princess who would be warrior. You have chosen good mano who will someday become strong May'r. And you will stand tall by his side."

Lauriel started to reach out to give her father a hug, but stopped. Nathon shared a rare smile, then returned to the hardened leader she had grown up with. He turned away with a shout to the others.

"We go!"

She wiped the dust from her eyes before following them.

Chapter 25

Lauriel leaned on the stone bar, absently sipping her brien. She paid no attention to the warrior games around her even though someone had actually invited her to join in. Her thoughts were on Danon.

He was gone again, like so many times before in the past two moons, speaking to other clans about rights and freedoms. She hadn't seen him in almost a full moon now. She had accompanied him on the shorter trips and enjoyed watching the charismatic effect he had on others, but she had duties at home that could not be neglected. She was still the best hunter in the Clan and meat was always needed, more so with so many clansmen losing their jobs over this civil rights question. Still she'd rather be by his side than left behind.

She remembered the confidence he had displayed at the march, a confidence he had claimed he didn't feel. But she had seen it as did the others. He had the spirit that commanded people's attention, the spirit of destiny. The march had been relatively successful even though it was much smaller than he had hoped for. There were some from the Mex and Oahou clans who had joined them for the demonstration. And even though a few rowdies from the Data clan had gotten slightly over-zealous, the march had gained national attention. The Perf's newspapers and news viewers had carried the story to millions of homes. Then the longer trips had begun.

Messengers from clans far away had come to Grotto Cave and asked to speak to Danon. They brought many questions from their leaders about equality and the ancient freedoms. They had been impressed by his insight and had invited him to visit their councils. An invitation that Danon had been reluctant to take until her father had insisted.

"You have chosen this path," he had said. "You must walk it to the end."

Danon had been worried that things were moving too fast. And he still did not share her idea of destiny.

Suddenly she was aware of someone staring at her. Devon stood beside her at the bar.

"You drink alone?"

She shook her head. "Was only thinking."

"You are too silent for one full of panther's spirit," he said, smiling. "Maybe I put you in barrel again."

During the month of Danon's absence, Devon had relaxed somewhat. His frowns were less frequent and occasionally he joked again as he had done when they were younger, playing in the hundreds of hiding places afforded by the giant cavern. The water barrel had been one of the few times he had ever bested her in a struggle. She had started the fight, of course, but he had finished it by dumping her in her father's supply of drinking water.

She smiled back. "Would be easier to drown a mountain cat. This one is much wiser now."

"And much older," he agreed. "You are no longer gr'll. You are young wo'am."

"Not yet, but Father plans to present me before next Council, as gr'll of age and daughter of the shawl."

Devon seemed surprised. "Then it is time for us to talk."

"No, my friend, it has nothing to do with you. The presentation has been postponed because I wanted Danon to be here for it.

Devon frowned. "He is bad medicine to Clan, can you not see it? He changes the old ways and ignores our customs."

Lauriel finished her brien. "What good is custom when have no rights?"

"As may'r things will be protected. We will fight for what rights we need."

Lauriel acted surprise. "You plan on wearing the shawl?"

"Has always been so and you know it. We talked of it often as children."

"That was long time ago, Devon. Things are changed now."

"Yes, you are gr'll of age. Soon you will be proclaimed. And I am lead warrior."

She started to leave, then turned her hard green eyes at Devon. "Do not call me to Circle. I will not answer my childhood friend."

# # #

The Council members had taken their seats.

The crowd that had gathered around them was the largest ever assembled. Every man, woman, and child of the Grotto Clan waited around the council fire, their multiple conversations filling the cavern with a drone of excitement.

The Elders were only a little more restrained as they waited for the May'r; they leaned one way and then the other, whispering and speculating over the latest news. Everyone had heard the camp fire rumors.

Their May'r no longer accompanied Danon on his journeys, because he was no longer needed to introduce the "One Who Comes From Afar" as he was known outside the Clan. Danon's status had risen even about that of Nathon's. At home he was a warrior, but outside he had become their emissary. From Texhoma to the territory of Utazona he had converted many followers, a core of dedicated believers who eagerly spread his ideas. Already there was talk of a great rally to be staged in the capitol. Tonight they anticipated an announcement.

Finally, Nathon emerged from the Lodge, sending a hush over the cavernous room. He strolled into center and took his seat.

Lauriel stood next to Danon. Her long black hair glistened under the glow of the lighting panels, accenting the clean new feather she had added. She watched as the elders rushed through their formalities of conducting tribal business. When they were through, Nathon stood to make an announcement.

"Lauriel, of Okee tribe," he shouted, "Come forward!"

She was stunned to hear herself summoned in such a manner. She bolted into the Circle to stand before her father.

He smiled to reassure her. "I had foolishly hoped you would tire of the warrior's leathers and accept your destiny," he whispered. "This one was wrong. Is time to proclaim your true status." He turned to address the elders.

"There is no son to offer as heir to shawl."

The elders were noticeably disturbed. Although they were painfully aware of this fact, they avoided the unthinkable outcome of open challenge to determine the next successor. At his death, any warrior could step forward to claim the shawl. If more than one stepped into the Circle, one would die.

"Lauriel is no longer gr'll, but wo'am of age. Her status is princess and heir to the shawl."

Lauriel tried not to blush as everyone looked on. At first the council said nothing in reply. They whispered among themselves. How could she be an heir to the shawl, they wondered. Only a son, and a warrior, could wear the mantle of leadership. They feared another break with tradition about to threaten them, but they did not wish to openly challenge the May'r. Hesitantly, the eldest stood to give reply.

"Is council's wish that May'r live long and guide our tribes for many yars to come, but we will embrace your daughter as princess, and her sons as ours."

The crowded cavern echoed the elder's acceptance and Lauriel struggled to retain her stoic facade. Then, before Nathon could finish and grant her the status of warrior, the elder dismissed her.

Lauriel was caught off guard. She started to object, but with the political slyness gained by years of sitting on the Council, the elder smoothly cut her off and refocused the Clan's attention back on the anticipated announcement.

"Our Princess may leave council's presence," he said. "Our May'r has other news to give us."

Nathon's frown betrayed his awareness of the elder's manipulation. After a stubborn pause he yielded and turned to the assembly.

"Warrior Danon has traveled to many clans since Council last met. He has taken his words of civil rights to them and his plan to win back our liberty. Many of the other may'rs agree. But not all of our brothers are willing. The Data and Mex clans do not like our plan. But even though they parley for stronger actions, they will not sit and watch. They seek an end to yars of oppression and have agreed to join with us for a time.

"Messenger have been sent and returned. Tomorrow we meet in city, to go downtown as one people. We will gain attention of Perf society. We will show them our honor and our pride. We no longer accept unlawful discrimination. We did not cause Holocaust and will not bear its blame. We are Lowmani, 'the people.' We have rights, and we demand them as nation of many clans!"

The cavern exploded with war cries of approval. Everyone accepted the need for action and knew the timing was right. Danon was called to stand before the Council. He entered the clearing, greeted by boisterous cheers, and waited for the May'r to silence the crowd. But Nathon stepped away to leave Danon alone to control the crowd.

"My brothers and sisters," he said, raising his hand for silence. "Tomorrow will be a big step toward liberty. It will not be easy. The catchers will be there to prevent us from gathering and will attempt to intimidate us by brute force, perhaps even arrest. But we must be strong.

"We must remain peaceful. Let them be guilty of any violence, not us! The entire nation will witness what happens on their news viewers. If we are innocent, the nation's sympathy will be ours. If we turn violent, the nation will scorn us as deserving punishment!

"We face a challenge greater than any one clansman, more important than any one clan. We must all show strength, for only through peaceful confrontation can we ever regain our liberty. Each one must possess the courage of a clan warrior and be willing to die rather than fight. This is the true test of courage and strength."

Danon remembered the words of another civil rights leader long ago, a man with a dream. He repeated that plea to see Perfs and Bios living side by side in peace, brown and black working together to prevent another holocaust, working together to enrich each other's condition. He emphasized that only they could make this dream come true.

# # #

Lauriel listened with a deep sense of pride in her chosen one. Even though she had heard the words before, she again felt the crowd's enthusiasm. She had seen the other clans respond to his call for liberty and equality. She had seen some dare to challenge his peaceful tactics. And she had witnessed his scathing replies.

He no longer tolerated the weak-hearted. He held in his mind some plan. She had heard him discuss that plan and the outcome of the social revolution. He often referred to the struggle as though it had already happened and he somehow knew the inevitable outcome. She knew what the crowd was feeling because she felt it too. A sense of destiny. What they were beginning could not be stopped, not by anyone or anything, not even Danon's secret doubts about himself.

Danon had finished his speech and was rejoined by Nathon as the cavern slowly quieted. He spoke with her father who nodded approval of something. Then the warrior who had become emissary called the crowd to silence once more. With the same confidence he had displayed to the crowd, he called Lauriel's name, inviting her to him.

Lauriel blushed. She couldn't help it. Hundreds of eyes had turned to her, wondering, examining, doubting. She caught a glimpse of Devon, standing stone-fisted. His face also burned, but not with embarrassment.

Danon was calling her as his mate! This time, if she stepped out of the group of warriors and into the Circle, it would be to show her acceptance. Soon she would become his wo'am. As Lauriel approached Danon, she expected a warm smile. What she saw was a look of surprise that turned to anger.

Devon had followed her into the Circle. He continued past her to stand before Danon and Nathon.

"I claim right of challenge!" he shouted.

Lauriel lunged out and jerked him around. "What is this! You are on wrong hunt. I said would not answer if you called. You are no longer …"

"Is my right," he answered coldly with a tone of determination.

Danon shook his head. "This is crazy. I've already proven I can beat you."

"I claim what was mine before."

"Yours?"

Lauriel swung the veteran around to face the green fire of her eyes. "You can't claim me. I am warrior, too. Leave now, or it is my dagger that will remove your heart in Char Vulga!"

Devon ignored her empty threat and returned his attention to Danon. "Challenge of vengeance is for warrior to claim. She is only gr'll, never presented to Council as one proven."

"But I fought!" She looked to Nathon for reassurance. Her father looked at her for a moment as if to apologize, then the clan leader turned away.

Devon nodded. "This no game, houseboy. Challenge of Char Hemos is with knife, till finished."

Danon glanced to Lauriel. Then to Nathon. Then back to Devon. "I don't want to kill you. I can't"

"Then you will forfeit claim, or die."

Nathon raised a hand to silence everyone. Then he rubbed his forehead in contemplation as if considering all the consequences of Devon's challenge.

Lauriel reached back for her long braided hair. She knew what her father's answer would be. Everyone knew. There was only one way to end the Char Hemos once it started. She removed the delicate red feather and handed it to Danon.

"The victor will return this," she whispered, "to claim me."

He drew his dagger, unscrewed the cap, and tucked the feather into its handle. "I don't like this."

She looked up, courage glowing in her face. He wondered if it was real, or only for his benefit. "Devon is right," she said. Is no other way. If refuse his challenge, I am his. Go now, and do what must be done."

When Nathon finally called the two warriors together, his forehead was beaded with perspiration. He kept his voice low. "Is your right, but your claim will not be granted tonight."

Devon's face reddened. "Even you cannot interfere with custom!"

Nathon's eyes were cold and sad. "Only one will survive this time. I do not know which one; you have proven nearly equal. And I must consider welfare of Clan. Too much depends on Danon tomorrow. Was not me who persuaded other clans to join. They follow his path. Even in our own clan he is risen to status of almost legend. If you kill him tonight, they could tear you to shreds in anger, or loose heart in the struggle for rights. Or both. If he kills you, it destroys his words for peace. He would lose both ways. A killer of manen does not lead a nation to peace." Nathon took a deep breath. "This one cannot allow such a thing to happen."

"This challenge must be done," Devon said.

"Not tonight." Nathon's eyes again hardened as he raised his voice for everyone to hear. "Both the choosing and the challenge is postponed till after the rally. I have spoken!"

Devon bowed stiffly in an outward show of respect, and approached Lauriel.

"This time tomorrow he will be dead. And you will be mine, as it should be."

"This one believes his destiny is already decided," she answered. "And his spirit is strong to defeat you. But if something should happen …" She lowered her voice to make sure no one else could hear. "Before I lose him, I'll send you to Earth Mother myself."

"I do what must be done, wo'am."

"So do I, my brother. You have lost the hunt, understand? One way or 'nother, you are dead to me." She spoke coldly, as if telling a fact already done.

# # #

Devon paused to look around before entering the Warrior's Den. Business was good for Gregon; the room was packed and everyone held a beaker of the bittersweet nectar. The large crowd caught him off guard. Their mundane duties to the clan normally kept most of them occupied. Two or three would always be out hunting for game. A party of five or six would be on one raid or another to steal supplies of grain or medicine, or some tool that was too difficult to make. For the first time in a dozen moons, every member of the Brotherhood was present. Some stood in clusters along the wall; others sat on the rock floor, all babbling excitedly over the night's unusual council meeting and tomorrow's rally.

The Council meeting had ended strangely, leaving most of the audience confused about Devon's presence in the Circle. His entrance had at first seemed like a challenge, but they had all left together without incident. Only Devon knew the truth.

He shoved his way to the bar, drained a beaker, and then studied the room with a look of disgust.

"I thought this was Warrior's Den!"

The sounds of camaraderie faded and Gregon leaned over the bar. "What's with you, lad?"

"A warrior enjoys the hunt," Devon grumbled. "Have you forgot? All of you? Perfs are our sworn enemy! Only way to end their suffocation is 'liminate them, one by one if necessary."

Murmurs drifted through the room. His words had kindled mixed emotions. One brother spoke up timidly.

"But we never been able to strike hard enough, to really hurt them."

"We strike fear in their black hearts. They are afraid to meet us one on one. We have honor. Where is honor in begging for privilege?"

More murmurs. Some agreeing, some not.

"Brother Danon offers new hope …"

"Danon is weak! He hides behind other clans for strength. We never asked their help before. Why should we now? And now that we become united, adding their strength to ours, does he use that to conquer? No! He asks us to hide our leathers and go unarmed as defenseless commoners. To do what? Be arrested and beaten by the catchers?"

Juston staggered closer, shifting from one foot to the other. "Our new brother is weak? This one is little drunk, but can still remember. He was not too weak to defeat you."

Devon's stare hardened like the stone bar beneath his hand as he stiffened and squared his stance. "Maybe you want to try?"

Juston stepped back in surprise, his casual swaying suddenly gone as the still room waited for his answer. He shook his head slowly.

"This one is not that drunk."

Devon raised his dagger at Juston, then pointed to everyone in the room. "Think hard 'bouts this unproven leader, this houseboy you follow. Where does he take you? To victory, or dishonor?" He gave each brother a penetrating stare before leaving.

# # #

Devon folded his leathers and tossed them on the rough wooden table in his private quarters. The table was mesquite trunks laced together with rawhide. Simple and functional. Lauriel's words echoed over and over as Devon paced back and forth inside his cramped dwelling. He was still the mightiest warrior in the Clan. He could defeat anyone, especially the pasty visitor, whose crazy ideas were deceiving so many clansmen. His followers were forgetting the old ways, and that was dangerous. Devon wondered why he was the only one who could see it.

And Lauriel. How dare that pretender threaten him! She had no status. She could do nothing to interfere. Or could she? Would she dishonor her father? When the time was right for battle with Danon, if he quenched his dagger's thirst, would she break the sacred customs and interfere with Char Hemos? Actually attack him to protect her houseboy?

They had grown up together, learned to hunt together. He probably knew her better than anyone in the clan. She was unpredictable and rebellious, but she did not make idle threats. She possessed what few outside the Brotherhood understood—the will to kill.

But what could he do? He couldn't back down from his challenge. He refused to lose any more respect with the Clan. Already he had fallen in status from his only defeat. He did not fear Danon's ability with the knife, but Lauriel never failed a promise. If he defeated Danon, he might still die by the hand of the wo'am he fought for.

He wanted her. He'd always wanted her, always tried hard to impress her, not just for the shawl, couldn't she see that? But the status and title she carried to her mate was too important for the Clan. She must bond with him!

The crude table collapsed to the floor.

It was the warriors who protected the Clan; it was the reason they had survived for countless generations. The houseboy would end all that. He could never be May'r!

There must be a way to get rid of him without Lauriel knowing. If only he could find someone else to do it for him.

He thought for a moment then nodded to himself. Slowly, he smiled. It might work, he thought. And no one would know. The Brotherhood would not like the solution. There was no honor, and no challenge, but it must be done to save the clan. He slipped out of his lodge, making sure the way was clear before slipping into the shadows on his way to the surface.

He had a long trip to make.

Chapter 26

Unable to get much sleep, Danon approached the Lodge shortly after dawn. Volunteers from over a hundred clans were to assemble downtown that afternoon. For the Grotto clan the journey was to be on foot, because the airbuses came by too infrequently and had only a fraction of the capacity needed to transport an entire clan.

He expected to find Devon standing as honor guard, but instead he found Allon standing by the entrance.

"Where's Devon? Isn't it his turn today?

"Came in late, just before dawn," Allon answered. "Asked me take watch for him, been hunting or something."

It didn't sound like Devon to shirk his duty, but at least the two adversaries didn't have to meet this morning. He entered the Lodge.

"Come in, my son," Nathon said in greeting. "Scouts have returned from outskirts of city. They find many camps, many people. They also invited other may'rs to join in our celebration. And in mourning."

"About tonight ..."

"Am sure Data clan will not pass up chance to watch good fight," he added with a forced smile.

"There's nothing good about it."

Nathon nodded. "Regardless of outcome, my daughter will be bonded and I will lose a good warrior."

Nathon faced the wall as if studying the symbols and drawings that marked the major historical events on the great clan calendar. "Much is happening, so many changes. Have restless feeling of being only observer, events not under my control. Destiny races toward us. For better or worse, it races."

He turned around, showing the wrinkled lines and creases that come from constant worrying. "And everything centers around you."

"Nathon, I wish you wouldn't use that word so much."

"You still deny the magic?"

"I have no magic."

Nathon shrugged. "Is still there. For my daughter's happiness, I wish you strength. My heart fears the path your spirit takes, but we both can sense your destiny. So she makes plans for the bonding and I invite guests."

"About the challenge ..."

Nathon retrieved his smoldering calumet. "Yes?"

"This challenge is, well, it's stupid!"

Nathon smiled condescendingly. "You do not understand its purpose."

"Lauriel and I have chosen each other as mates. Devon knew it would be useless to call her in front of the Council because she'd reject him. But a stupid custom now lets him claim something not due him. I want your daughter more than anything else in the world, believe me I do, but I don't feel this is justification to kill one of my brothers."

Nathon lowered his pipe as if it had lost its flavor today. "Is reason for our customs," he said. "They have guided us for many generations. Is never good thing to kill a brother, I agree. But a leader must always think of the Clan, my son. Survival of strongest means survival of Clan."

"How is killing Devon going to help the Clan survive?"

"When you are older, you will understand."

"That's sounds like something my father would've said."

Nathon grinned. "Then he is most wise. You should listen to him more."

"I should have, but he died a long time ago."

"Then listen to your new father. Come, there is gift for you." Nathon unfolded a square of woven linen, revealing a small replica of his own shawl. "Is shawl of prince. Is time you wear it."

"But I'm not a prince, not yet. And what happens if Devon wins?"

"Then it would become his."

# # #

Outside, at the edge of the clearing, where Lauriel's lodge was situated, came the excited chatter of feminine. Lauriel was also receiving a gift. Aleshanee held up a white silk and suede knee-length skirt for her to inspect.

"You like?"

The geometric patches of bone bleached suede highlighted the shimmering skirt with colorful patterns of beads and appliqué.

"Is beautiful," she said. "But you shouldn't have, is too valuable."

"Was Madera's bonding dress. We had it cleaned in town and now looks good as new."

Lauriel tried to hand it back. "You should keep it for your own bonding."

"No, is too fancy for me. Is for princess to wear. Please, is my gift."

"Is perfect," Lauriel said, giving Aleshanee a strong hug.

"You are sure you will wear it tonight, after the relay?"

"Is called rally. And after the challenge," she said. She went silent for a moment, then nodded with more confidence than she felt. "Yes, this one will wear bonding dress tonight."

"Must try it on. See if it fits."

Lauriel slipped out of her breeches and vest and let them fall to the floor as Aleshanee helped her into the bridal skirt.

"I hear special guests are coming. From other clans."

"Yes, Father invited the other may'rs. I wish he hadn't. I didn't want a big crowd, It makes me nervous."

"Lauriel, the grass viper, nervous?" Aleshanee said with a teasing smile. She got a stern frown in reply.

# # #

Danon needed a quiet place to think. Outside in the cool morning air, he climbed to the top of Grotto Hill. The mound was hardly a hill, barely ten meters to the summit, but it was the highest lump of ground for miles in any direction. Staring out from the limestone outcropping, he could see for miles in every direction. Miles of sandy prairie where the scrub brush and tumbleweed competed for survival in the arid caliche soil. This far from the irrigation of the suburbs, only the spring weeds and determined mesquite maintained a splash of green against the landscape.

A dozen thoughts raced around his head. He thought of the rally and wondered about its success or failure. The senseless duel with Devon that he could neither win nor lose. He thought of Lauriel and her rugged beauty. The flickering image of her standing across the council fire. The delicate red feather that had dangled from her braided hair was now tucked away in his dagger. He tried to imagine their life together and what surprises the future held for them.

The future. He was living in his own future, but this was where he belonged; his past was another lifetime. Another person. Although Daniel had been prone to arrogance and self-centered pleasure, Danon's life seemed consumed by the needs of others. Nathon's irritating comments about "destiny racing toward them" returned to haunt him. What destiny? He couldn't see past this evening.

He remembered something Chief Todd had said, like a two-bit prediction, about his destiny being "more rewarding than most men." He had moved up quickly in the Clan, from a visitor and provider to clan member. Before he realized it, he wore the leathers of the Brotherhood, the elite status of warrior. And now he was claiming the hand of a princess. Was this destiny? Or was it his destiny to repeat history by leading another civil rights movement? Civil rights leaders had the bad tendency of dying.

# # #

Lauriel walked softly into the smoke filled room of her father's lodge. Nathon's back was to her as he watched Medicine Man Benon carefully adding another symbol to the buffalo calendar.

She quietly watched them for a moment, remembering images of her childhood. Sitting impatiently in his lap. Sneaking a smoke from his ceremonial pipe. Saying good bye to her Madera.

"Father?"

He turned quickly and smiled. "Daughter, am pleased you could come. I know you are busy."

"Never too busy for you."

"I remember when cornering you long enough for a talk was like holding the wind."

"Must've been when I was much younger, only a gr'll." She lifted her arms and turned around for him to see her bonding dress. "This one is wo'am now."

Nathon nodded his agreement. "And so beautiful. Your Madera would be very proud."

She glanced down to her stained moccasins and noticed how out of place they looked. She also noticed she was biting her lip, something that only happened around her father.

"This one has not been the best of daughters. Seems we always argue 'bout something."

"You was always different from the others, never content with traditions of ancestors. Did not know how to handle such a free spirit. I suppose I drove you from Lodge."

"No, Father." She stood on tiptoes and kissed him on the cheek. "Was something I had to do. To be more than daughter of May'r, and then some warrior's wo'am who'd clean his lodge and bear his children and wait patiently at cooking pot while he went hunting game or on raiding parties. This one wanted to do more."

Nathon's dark eyes were compassionate, but still searching hers as he listened.

"You still do not understand?" she asked. "Just believe my respect for you. Have always wanted to make you proud."

Nathon wrapped his arms around her in a warm embrace. "This one understands, Little Butterfly."

She couldn't suppress a laugh. Only her father ever called her by that name.

"Should have honored you in front of Council long ago. You have given me honor many times and, yet, stood outside the Circle because of my stubbornness. Believe my pride in you, my daughter." His arms squeezed her close.

"Then honor me!" she said.

"In front of Council? As warrior?"

"No. I don't care about that, not anymore. In Brotherhood of Leather there is one token of status that few warriors can boast of." She beamed a mischievous smile. "Hunt with me."

"What?" He was obviously surprised by her request.

"Please?"

"You want to accompany the May'r on a hunt?"

"No," she said softly. "This one wants to hunt with father … as your son would have."

Nathon gave a sigh of remorse.

Lauriel sensed his reluctance and again dropped her gaze to the floor. She understood that he still had work to do and didn't have much time before they were to leave for city. It had been a rash request. But the great oak that had never bent with the wind slowly leaned over and whispered.

"I hear your bow is quite good. Is time I find out for self."

# # #

Danon stepped off the airbus with Lauriel at his side. May'r Nathon was several steps ahead, escorted through the growing throng by three nervous warriors. A crowd of ethnic diversity filled the sidewalks, spilling onto the street. The conventional jumpsuits of the Okees mingled with the multicolored folk dress of the Manchee and tribal shawls of the Choc tribes. Down the crowded street he noticed the layered serapes of the Mexs and bare, tattooed chests of the Slants. The city had never seen so many tribes together.

Bewildered Perfs gawked at the entourage swelling before them as more and more clansmen poured into the downtown area, flowing down the street toward the old square.

Lauriel's grip tightened on Danon's arm. Black and red uniforms also speckled the crowd. The riot police were already there, and in force. They seemed to be cocked and waiting for an excuse to attack the crowd of insolent Bios. Any excuse.

# # #

The amphitheater was a memorial of the great Biowar, constructed decades earlier to remind the Perfs of the arrogance that had almost exterminated an entire race. Nathon had suggested this place to begin the "great struggle," as he called it. He stood in the center of the amphitheater on a large podium. Around him stood other may'rs from each of the gathered clans. Danon and Lauriel joined them.

Looking out over the assembly, he couldn't begin to estimate the number of people. A thousand faces bobbed up and down, swaying back and forth like a field of wheat rippled by the wind. Young and old, they had traveled great distances, some for days. They were here to show their solidarity. He also noticed several Blacks in the crowd who seemed willing to show their support.

He knew they were all willing. They were hungry for freedom, but they were still unorganized. Danon was here to give them that focus. In spite of his better judgment, he had agreed to be their leader. He swallowed hard, then stepped up to the microphone and raised his hands for their attention.

"I welcome all my brothers here today. Though we come from many clans, our hearts are one. We share the same desire, freedom! But freedom has its price. Liberty has its toll. Society has never accepted change easily. As a Madera brings a new child into the world, so too we will feel the pains as we struggle to bring our liberty to life. Liberty to live where we choose. Liberty to educate our children. The freedom to do as we wish, whenever we wish."

As Danon addressed the crowd, no one paid much attention to the pairs of red and black uniforms gathering together, forming a cordon around them. Across the square, looking out from an upper story window, sat the figure of another uniform poised in lethal silence.

# # #

"Are you sure you can get a clean shot from here? We're not supposed to hurt anyone else."

"Don't worry about me," the man answered as he leaned further out the window. "Just help me figure out which one of them bastards is the leader. I'll stop this insurrection before it starts."

"The Commissioner said he will be easy to spot. Whiter skinned than the rest. Some say he might even be a Pasty."

"No way. Those Pasties killed themselves off a long time ago."

"Must be a pretty dangerous renegade, his own people turning him in."

"Yeah, said he wants to start a bloody revolution and take over our society. Can you believe that?"

His partner shrugged. "Still don't seem quite right, though. In cold blood?"

"What's the matter, you some kind of Bios lover?"

"No, it just doesn't seem right. Killing him I mean."

"Shhh. I think I got him spotted. Just hold still a second, whitey ..." The officer held his breath as his fingers tightened around the trigger.

# # #

Lauriel looked up with pride to the man she had chosen. He spoke with authority and strength. He spoke of rights, equality, and the Brotherhood of Man. He explained the path of peaceful confrontation. He shared his dream for liberty. He shared his excitement. And the crowd absorbed it all.

As the crowd echoed his call of, "we shall overcome," Lauriel's gaze swept over the thousands of heads. Her eyes drifted upward along the silvery buildings that mirrored a reflection of the thundering crowd. Something caught her eye.

At first, the dark figure didn't make sense. She saw what resembled a sniper's rifle protruding from a window. She blinked several times. It was a rifle! And it pointed at Danon.

She screamed out to warn him, but the enthusiastic chanting blanketed her warning. She began pushing her way forward, trying to reach him in time.

She looked back to the gunman and froze as she saw the intense flash. A blue bolt of energy leaped through the air to find its target in a sizzling microsecond. She screamed again, a tight throated squeal of a mortally wounded animal.

Those of the crowd closest to the podium gasped in alarm. The assembly of may'rs glimpsed the movement of someone crumpling to the floor like a wilted branch. A ripple of shocked silence spread over the crowd.

Lauriel bounded up the steps of the podium, then stopped. She wanted to scream again, but couldn't. Her throat tightened and nausea swelled inside her as she reached down to touch him. His body lay limp and unmoving. A small charred spot on his back oozed an expanding stain of crimson onto the podium floor.

Chapter 27

A swarm of warriors leaped onto the stage to surround their respective May'rs. Led by the protective instinct bred by generations of survival, they stood shoulder to shoulder forming a human shield.

Inside the knot of crowded dignitaries, Lauriel knelt beside her father. She tried to conceal the tears as she embraced his lifeless form, but couldn't.

"Why?" she asked. "Why?"

"I don't know," Danon answered.

In the crowd, accusing fingers pointed through toward the open window. Rumors spread through the crowd, igniting tempers in a violent wave of emotion. Cries for vengeance shattered the stunned silence.

A strong hand grabbed his shoulder. It was Rezin, leader of the Data clan. "We will avenge our brother!" he said. The other May'rs nodded their agreement and war cries erupted from the warriors. An army had been born.

"No!" Danon shouted over the confusion. "Take your people and leave. Get out of here!"

"No Perf gets away with murdering clan May'r."

"Listen to me, you don't understand! The riot police, they're already in position. Compared to them you're unarmed, it'd be a slaughter. Your first responsibility is the survival of your clan, not to start a massacre. Take them safely away from here. Grotto Cave isn't far. You can spend the night there. Now!"

Resin shook his head stubbornly and turned away. He summoned his warriors and gave the order they were eagerly awaiting.

"Blood vengeance!"

The rally disintegrated in confusion. Family members became separated and mingled in the hysteria that followed. As Grotto clansmen had pressed to the center of the mob trying to learn the truth about their leader, the black and red uniforms had also tried to penetrate the mass of clansmen to investigate, but their actions were mistaken as an assault. Zealous warriors lashed out in retaliation.

In the center of the turmoil a solemn procession formed, led by Danon and Lauriel. They escorted Nathon's body out of the square and took him home.

The journey back to Grotto Cave took most of the night. Several clan may'rs and council leaders accompanied them into the cavern. Sleeping arrangements were made hurriedly with as many as possible being located in the communal lodges. Individual families took in the remainder, but throughout the night remnants continued to stumble into the cavern and fall exhausted wherever they found room. Lauriel maintained her composure as she welcomed the other may'rs and prominent elders into the Lodge. Her forced composure supported her long enough to fulfill her formal duties to her guests, then she withdrew to be with her father.

# # #

Nathon's body lay on a cushion of artificial furs blanketed in a haze of incense from the smoldering censers. Lauriel knelt beside her silent guardian's deathbed, her hands caressing the faded shawl.

Danon stood in the doorway, unsure of what to say. When he approached, he had heard sounds of soft crying, but now Lauriel was silent, her back toward him.

"It's late. Maybe you should …"

"Leave me alone!" she snapped. "You have done enough."

The truth behind her words stung even more than her tone as he remembered the moments just before the assassin had struck. She had waved frantically at him as she pushed through the crowd, pointing to an open window. He remembered stepping back to look, when a bright blue flash had passed within inches of his head. Then Nathon had collapsed behind him. In her attempt to save his life, Lauriel had unwillingly sacrificed her father's.

"I'm sorry …" That was all he could say. It should've been him and they both knew it. He turned to leave, but Lauriel jumped up and raced across the room to stop him, her arms wrapped tightly around him.

"Wait!"

Her eyes were red and burning, and her dusty face streaked with tearstains. She buried her face against him, clinging to one she had chosen.

"I hurt. But do not blame you."

"Why not? Nathon would still be alive and …"

"You think spirit of my love so weak? Had I known this part of our destiny ..." She ignored the shiver that ran down her and held him tighter. "This one would have done the same. If must choose, I choose you."

He held her close without speaking and let her cry.

# # #

An old woman shuffled closer to the fire pit to perform an old custom of mourning. Even before the first lighting panels were unveiled, Medicine Man Benon had arranged the sacred fire of offerings and called on the Great Spirit to observe their tribute. The old woman finished reciting her chant and went on. Next a small boy advanced to the burning coals and, with his mother's guiding hand, sprinkled the contents of his medicine pouch. He seemed captivated as the tongues of flame leaped upward, danced with bursting warmth, and then died out. Behind the boy waited a long line of clansmen. They encircled the hearth, waiting to pay honor to their fallen May'r. The line of tribute would continue throughout the day in preparation for the night's ceremony.

Inside the Lodge, elderly women with crooked fingers prepared the body for burial. They came from the communal lodge. Having no husband or surviving son to care for them, they had become another burden on the Clan. But today they performed a service. They had brought with them a roll of burial cloth, the traditional Sikh, woven by hand from deer and antelope hair, using ancient techniques passed from mother to daughter. As they wrapped the body and stitched the decorative hem, they sang the chant of mourning that was also passed down through generations.

The brotherhood of warriors had passed the hearth earlier, before retiring to the Den for their own peculiar type of ceremony, a ceremony honoring a departed brother, a fellow warrior.

# # #

"Grab another, lads." Gregon stood behind the bar, slinging beakers of brien up and down the worn counter top. "I've another story to tell."

"Yars ago, when I was young an' sprite enough to embarrass any one of ya in bare handed combat, warrior Nathon went on his first raid. He was nervous a little, as was we all first time out, but did his darndest to hide it. Any ways, we went to this food warehouse and ..."

Devon entered the crowded room scanning it quickly. He made for the bar to join the wake and listen to one of Gregon's stories. Any warrior who was old enough to remember would be reciting personal anecdotes about the brother's glorious past. They would all drink a toast to each tale of adventure. They would boast and toast until they felt assured of securing a proper status for the fallen warrior with the Earth Mother, or until they passed out.

When Gregon finished his story, Devon joined the others in rowdy approval and offered one of his own.

"When this one was young, warrior for only short time, we was out hunting game just after sun up when we spot a bounty. He was sitting upwind with his back to us, just waiting to snare a poacher." Devon grimaced to incriminate himself as one such poacher.

"This one was scared and admits it. Was ready to leave and circle wide around, but Nathon says if we leave him, he'll only catch one of our brothers sooner or later.

"He drops his bow and pack and takes only his dagger as he crawls over rock and scrub as silent as a copperhead." Devon whispered to emphasize his story. "That bounty collected his final reward and never heard it coming!"

The image of one of the most detested clan enemies meeting justice brought a round of cheers as everyone stood and hoisted their beakers in salute.

"I can just imagine what Danon woulda done," he added. "Can you see him wanting to stroll down in front of that bounty, to peacefully demonstrate his right to hunt there?"

An explosion of laughter followed to Devon's satisfaction. He had pressed his point without making a direct attack on Danon's honor.

"How about another, Devon?"

"Yeah, tells us another story."

Devon took the opportunity to recite another feat portraying Nathon's bravery and courage in the face of danger. At the end of the story, he again drew a sharp, if imprecise, distinction between the former May'r and Danon.

"Is true, Devon," one of the warriors agreed, "I doubt Danon would handled that same as Nathon."

"There's not a brother here who doubts the ability of our last may'r."

Murmurs of hallowed agreement echoed through the room.

"Is important," Devon suggested, "that next May'r has same quality."

"Maybe you should be May'r," someone suggested.

Devon shrugged and said nothing.

"I don't know," Gregon said. "Danon has some fine merit of his own."

Devon slammed his beaker hard on the counter, shattering the mug and splattering its contents. "What kind of honor did we bring back from town? Was our May'r who got murdered by the Perfs, and only Data Clan had courage to strike back!"

"Did they?" Gregon's crooked jaw dropped in surprise.

"Saw them before I left. They was raiding stores, burning buildings, airbuses, and attacking every black and red uniform who tried to run away."

Devon voice climbed over the noise of the room. "I say it's time we stop hiding behind fancy words and lead raid of vengeance on Perf society. Our brothers from Data Clan beg to join us in restoring honor. Teach our enemy to fear every dark shadow for the danger that might lurk within. A warrior's dagger!"

"Then we needs a strong May'r!" someone shouted. "You must claim the shawl!"

Opposition grew silent as other warriors joined in, urging him to accept. Devon stepped to the door.

"Then no more brien for me, must wait to honor warrior Nathon's memory. Must have clear head to make challenge."

# # #

The remains of the memorial fire glowed feebly, the last offering having flickered away hours before. Around the dying embers waited a conclave of silent tribesmen. Visiting may'rs sat with elders inside the Circle. Many of their clansmen, who had postponed the long trip home the night before, stood reverently in the crowd also waiting for the ceremony to begin.

Devon stepped out from the warriors and silently entered the circle. He said nothing as he moved over to the ring of dignitaries and sat down, generating a wave of whispers that rippled through the crowd both inside and outside the Circle.

# # #

Inside the Lodge, Lauriel displayed her impatience with a frown. "Is time for ceremony," she said, holding the great shawl in front of her. "Here ..."

"I can't take that."

"Already have one like it." She referred to the smaller replica draped over his arm. "Father gave it to show his acceptance you as son."

Danon handled the material, stiff as if woven many years ago, but its colors were still bright and clean. It had never been worn, awaiting the arrival of a successor, one who was worthy. He didn't feel worthy.

"As prince, you would be heir," she said.

"But I'm not a prince. Not yet, remember?"

"So you must claim it!"

"I don't want to be May'r. I never did."

"I know," she said softly. A rare trace of compassion shown in her eyes, as if she understood his reluctance.

But she couldn't. No one could. He didn't want the responsibility. Against his better judgment, he had led the clans in open defiance of segregation, manipulated by Lauriel to find himself rallying them together. And now, because of that, Nathon lay in the next room.

"You are only choice," she said. "Clan follows your leadership already. Wearing the shawl tonight in front of Council is only right."

She draped the heavy weave over his shoulders and stepped back to inspect. She gave a nod of approval, and placed an encouraging kiss on his cheek.

"We go now." She stepped out of the Lodge and walked across the clearing.

Danon hesitated. He watched Lauriel walk into the circle, her gait sure and quick as she crossed the stone floor and stopped beside the swatch of carpet reserved for the May'r. He studied the waiting crowd, a wall of faces that stretched around the entire clearing. There were so many of them, he thought, so many faces: young and old, weak and strong.

Dammit, he didn't want it! He didn't want the burden of accountability for each one of those dirty, confused, questioning faces. But he couldn't turn it away. He had started something and now he had to finish it. *What must be done.*

His appearance from the Lodge immediately grabbed everyone's attention. What they noticed first was the shawl. He was wearing the shawl of clan leader, their leader. He forced a slow dignified walk as he crossed the clearing, passing the seated elders and visiting may'rs whose hushed whispers echoed his own feelings of doubt. Finally he reached Lauriel and sat down before the hushed assembly.

"Is there any business that must be settled before we honor the memory of May'r Nathon?" As he waited, he tried to swallow the lump in his throat. The elders would either confirm or deny his right to sit in the seat of the May'r.

Heads turned and more whispers passed along the ring of aged leaders, but none rose to speak in the tense silence that followed. Finally the eldest stood.

"Is wish of council that ..."

"No!" Devon shouted, rising to his feet. "You have no right. You are not chosen!"

"Sit down," Danon said with authority. "You and I have unfinished business, but it will wait till after the ceremony. We pay our respects first."

"Will not wait!" Devon responded. "This no longer Char Hemos for my wo'am. This one claims the shawl." He drew his dagger and threw it between Danon's feet, then turned to the elders.

"Char Matra!"

The solemn dignity of the Circle disintegrated; elders and may'rs stumbled backwards, scrambling to clear the area between the two defiant warriors. Within seconds, they stood alone before the stunned crowd.

The dagger's black pommel still quivered in dying tremors between Danon's feet. He jerked his own dagger free by the coarse handle, squeezing its unforgiving nature, and hurled it between Devon's moccasins. It did not stick.

"I deny your claim."

"What must be done," Devon said. He bent over to retrieve the dagger, then hurled it upward in a lightning quick motion at Danon's chest.

Danon swatted at the dagger to deflect it, but almost missed. The blade's jagged edge cut into his wrist, and landed flat against his chest.

His challenger lunged forward but stopped short, cautiously regarding Danon's peculiar stance, one he recognized from their previous encounter. He began to circle, easing in closer and closer like a patient shark. Danon had prayed for another way to solve this, but now realized there was none. He waited for the shark to come in just a little closer, his clenched fist at his side.

Devon continued, glancing at his weapon waiting in the dirt behind Danon. He obviously did not intend to accept a barehanded conflict, since his undeniable advantage was with the knife.

He dashed forward and feigned a leap at Danon who easily dodged out of the way. Devon landed hard on the earthen floor, raising a puff of brown dust, but with a grunt of triumph. Rolling over, he snatched the dagger and came up quickly. The confidence in his eyes spoke his thoughts. The inexperience contender should have stood firm and blocked his charge. That mistake had allowed him to regain his knife. Now the houseboy would pay for his mistake.

Danon looked around for his own knife, which was too far behind him, as Devon advanced like the grim reaper at harvest with a confident grin on his face.

He misjudged the distance and Danon spun around with a hasty roundhouse kick that sent Devon's dagger spinning harmlessly through the air to land with a metallic ring. His aggressor stopped, glowering at the weapon that again lay out of his reach.

"What's the matter?" Danon said. "Afraid to fight without it? And you want to be May'r?"

Devon unleashed a blood cry and charged forward. This time Danon planted both feet to meet his aggressor head on.

Lauriel watched intensely from the edge of the crowd, her fingers tightly gripping her bow. She studied the two warriors closely as they battled. They struggled fiercely for several minutes, neither significantly gaining ground nor losing.

Soon both held their daggers again and were using them savagely. Each attack, each thrust made her flinch as if aimed at her. Danon fought with the courage of a true warrior, but she could see that he was tiring.

Danon's wrist throbbed. He struggled to hold his dagger, the handle wet and slippery with blood. His blood. Shallow cuts trailed up his arm and over his back. Bitter dust clung to his mouth and salty perspiration stung his eyes, blurring his vision. His contacts were giving out again. He kept moving, trying to focus on the fuzzy image of Devon's ever sweeping blade. He felt his heart pounding, his breathing deep, and the knot of doubt tightening in his stomach. He could not defeat an opponent he could not see. He felt his confidence slipping as the cavern blurred more.

"Maybe is better this way," Devon said softly. "Nathon was like father to me and you made shooter miss. Now you will pay."

He lunged forward, but Danon dodged and parried.

"You blame me for Nathon's death?" He slashed outward repeatedly, keeping Devon at a safe distance. "Wait, how do you know the shooter missed?"

"Was you they wanted. This one knows." Devon's voice quivered as if with remorse. "Now good warrior is gone, but now I free Clan of your danger."

"What are you talking about?"

"He should not have stood so close to you. But he looked on you as future son! If they'd done job right …" His knife came within millimeters of Danon's stomach in a blurring slash.

"Your jealousy has blinded you, Brother."

"Do not call this one brother, houseboy!" Devon lunged again, but Danon blocked the attack and managed to graze his arm, drawing another trickle of blood.

Danon maneuvered himself back in front of the watching warriors. A chilling thought came to him that no one would believe. He didn't want to believe it himself.

"You knew the assassin was after me?"

Devon slashed and feinted, looking for an opening in Danon's defense.

"You knew before it even happened."

Devon hesitated just a moment with a puzzled look, but gave no sign of denial. It was enough to confirm the growing knot in Danon's stomach.

"How would you know someone would try to kill me at the rally?"

Devon lunged again and Danon jerked back just in time as the razor sharp edge narrowly missed his throat. He pushed in close to see better, forcing them together in deadly embrace.

Devon's face revealed the pain of his guilt as he shoved back, blade to blade. "Once you are out of way, this one will restore old ways. This may'r will teach Perfs lesson in honor."

Danon glanced over to the listening warriors. He had maneuvered close enough for them to hear each word, but had lost advantage to Devon. And he could feel the blade tip prick his ribs. He pushed back desperately against Devon's hand, but couldn't stop it. It was biting deeper and deeper. There was no other way out, he realized.

"So you are behind Nathon's death!" he shouted, then collapsed backwards. Devon was caught off guard and toppled over as Danon yanked him to the hard floor. With a painful twist, he sat astride the surprised veteran and locked his hands rigidly beneath his knees.

"You betrayed the Clan!"

"Only did what must be done," he shouted back, struggling to free himself. "This one protects Clan. You bring end to our path. You destroy things you do not understand."

Danon held the point of his knife into the soft depression in Devon's neck. "So you planned for me to die at the rally, not Nathon?"

"Yes!"

Danon pressed the blade deeper and glanced up to the stunned warriors.

"Look at your brothers, Devon! What are they thinking?"

Devon struggled to free his hands, but couldn't. He glanced over, but couldn't look them in the eyes. He knew from their expressions they blamed him for the accidental death of their May'r. They did not understand the importance of keeping the old ways.

"Tell them. Tell them why you betrayed the Clan!"

"No. Was not my fault. Tried to save Clan. Warned catchers 'bout you, told them you was dangerous. Is best for Clan, for everyone, if you ... but Nathon was accident."

"Nathon's death was no accident," Danon clarified, pressing the knife deeper. "It was murder."

Devon sensed defeat to his plan. The brothers did not understand. He relaxed the grip on his knife. "Then finish it, houseboy; am not afraid to die."

"I don't have to," he said hoarsely. "No one will ever follow you again. You have broken the very code of honor itself. Because of you, a May'r is dead."

He rocked back to stand up. When he did, a sudden rush of pain stabbed his leg and the hard floor rushed up to slam his face.

With intuitive reflex, he rolled as he landed. He heard a dull thud behind his ear, and felt the wind brush his neck from Devon's blade biting into the cavern floor.

He staggered to his feet and launched a series of kicks before the blurry figure in front of him could stand. One missed the knife; the second didn't, jarring it loose; one landed on the side of Devon's face, splitting his lip; the next twisted his nose like putty.

Devon tried to crawl away, stumbling to his feet, but Danon pursued with a punishing kick landed in his ribs. He managed to grab his tormentor's foot and put them both on the ground.

For only a moment both lay still, drenched with perspiration and weeping cuts and gasping for air. Slowly they rose, limping as they faced each other, waiting. Devon teetered forward a shaky step and Danon reacted, focusing the last of what little energy he had left into one more kick.

For a split second the stiff moccasin conformed to the side of Devon's face before it violently snapped his head aside. Then the veteran's knees collapsed.

Danon looked down at the gleaming dagger still in his hand. He felt the ancient blood lust burning to viciously thrust it in and terminate the challenge.

He grabbed a handful of his enemy's coarse, black hair to yank bank and bring his dagger against the exposed neck. The knife-edge was still sharp enough to bring another rivulet of blood. This time it would be over.

"You caused Nathon's death!" Danon screamed in rage, finally releasing his own guilt.

Devon could see the brothers' doubt and suspicion was now spreading to the elders' faces. He wanted to make them understand, but it was too late now. They would soon learn how wrong the houseboy was. He waited to die. He had been defeated. He could accept that; to die a warrior's death would restore his honor.

But Danon released his hold. He stepped back, and threw down his dagger. He staggered back, gulping for air as he spoke.

"You have no right to challenge my leadership. You broke the code. You are no longer my brother. You do not deserve to die with honor as one."

Devon seemed shocked that the intruder dared to pass judgment on him.

"You have betrayed the Clan, so you no longer have one. You are banished from this Clan. Forever."

He faced the council members who had maneuvered close enough to hear the battling warriors' last discourse.

"I, May'r Danon, have spoken." He turned away from his former opponent and staggered toward his seat of office. He needed to sit down; he had earned it.

Devon looked to his brothers for support, then to the crowd around him, but found only looks of shock and disgust. He stared back to the intruder who had refused to honor him. He had taken Lauriel, the shawl of May'r, his status, and even his standing as a warrior. By refusing to kill him, the houseboy was now taking his honor.

A warrior must die in combat, not as commoner. He reached for the dagger lying beside him. The hunt was not over. He clenched it tightly. As he slowly rose to his feet, he glanced at the wo'am that had refused to accept him. In her eyes he saw that she understood. He would not die a commoner. As he readied himself to throw the dagger, he concentrated. *What must be done …*

Lauriel winced as if feeling the sharp pain herself.

Danon heard the sharp whistling noise from behind and spun around, but he was too late. He didn't have time to react, only to realize what had happened.

Devon had an anguished smile on his face. He faltered forward a step as the hurt drained from his eyes and the heavy knife tumbled from his hand. He slumped to his knees, examining the slender, feathered shaft that protruded from his side. A perfect shot, he realized, the broadhead point was buried deep in his heart.

Lauriel stood at the edge of the crowd, still gripping her bow with white knuckles. She stared at the childhood friend who had taught her many of her warrior skills: how to sniff the wind and track game, how to avoid the bounty's traps, and how to use the bow. She would miss that friend. And she would miss the great warrior that he became. She knew that he understood, but she still felt the pain.

"He killed one May'r," she said, mostly to herself. "He would not kill another."

Danon shivered as he realized how close he had come to death.

The crowd waited in stunned silence. Rarely, perhaps once every third generation, could they observe the Char Matra to become May'r. Never in the collective memory of all the elders had a clan warrior brought shame or dishonor. The elite few who wore the black leather walked a path dedicated to service, and were never questioned. No one in the cavern stirred, except for Lauriel.

She walked into the clearing and stood over Devon's crumpled body, showing no sign of remorse. He had killed her father, and she had sent him to the Earth Mother with honor.

"Give him proper burial," she said.

The huddle of warriors hesitated, unsure whether or not to follow her instructions. Some had been close to the fallen comrade and still harbored doubts about this she warrior.

Danon faced the reluctant group, struggling to maintain composure. "I … have … spoken!"

Several warriors scurried in to carry away the body. One of them crossed the clearing to stand in front of Danon. He bowed his head and held out his hand, returning Danon's dagger. May'r Danon acknowledged the act of obeisance and returned to his place before the fire.

"There is a ceremony to attend," he reminded the shaken Council.

The dignitaries filtered back into the Circle to retake their places that they had so unceremoniously departed. Lauriel came up behind him and draped the shawl over his shoulders. He had earned that, too. She paused to examine the scattered cuts and streaks of red, then knelt beside him.

"Get up," he said with a voice of command. "That is not the proper place for one who mourns her father."

She looked up showing confusion.

"You are a princess," he said. "Today you sit on the Council."

She walked hesitantly toward the group. The oldest and most respected elder stood when she approached. She recognized him as the one who had interrupted Nathon when he was about to introduce her as warrior.

He gave an arthritic bow, but ignored the obvious pain. "I am honored, my Princess. This thing has never before happened."

"What? A brother lost to the darkness?"

He shook his head and smiled. "No, have never seen a she-warrior sat at council. Take my seat and let us honor you."

Lauriel choked the tightness down. She could only nod in reply to the elder's formal acceptance of her status. Now all the council knew that she was now truly a clan warrior.

Danon shuffled to the center, still weak in the knees. He held up the lesser shawl to the crowd and they understood. He had called Lauriel in front of the Council and she had accepted. Nathon had shown his approval and blessed his new son-in-law with the shawl of prince.

"I would have worn this with pride to be his son," he said. "I will, instead, wear the great shawl of Grotto Clan."

He made a sacred pledge never to forget its heritage or the tradition that lies behind it. He understood the responsibility that rested on the shoulders of the man who wore it. He drew a deep, unsteady breath. He was ready to accept that burden.

"What has the council to say?"

Everyone in the crowd turned to the venerable elder and waited for his response. The gray haired elder knew the consensus of the others. He patted Lauriel's hand as he rose to give the council's response.

"Great and honored May'r, is Council's wish you live long and prosper. Continue to lead our clan with wisdom. We know it was your father's wish that you bless Clan with many strong and healthy children." He looked around to his contemporaries. "We wish the same."

The crowd could remain silent no longer. The cavern shook with a shout of celebration and reverberated the acclaim as they began to shout the name of their new May'r over and over.

Danon tried to acknowledge their allegiance, but the chant continued. He had wished with all his heart that he could only give the responsibility to someone else, anyone else. He knew, however, that he no longer had a choice. It was simply what must be done.

He lifted his arms, but the crowd continued to chant. He stretched to amplify his silent command, feeling all of his cuts stretch with him. Gradually, the assembly yielded to let him speak.

"There will be time for celebration later," he said. "First, we honor the memory of May'r Nathon. And send him to the arms of the Earth Mother."

He gestured toward the Lodge where the funeral procession still waited. They were caught unprepared, watching the drama like everyone else. They scrambled to regain their assigned places and assume a more reverent composure.

A dozen maidens in bleached calfskin gowns led the procession like a string of pearls. Each maiden carried a smoldering taper of incense as they stepped gracefully over the cavern floor. Behind them followed six warriors who bore the royal Sikh on their shoulders. The mourners that followed were dressed in traditional, tan buckskin skirts decorated with beads and feathers. From somewhere in the domed room came the slow beating of drums. The procession walked slowly, to the rhythm of the solemn drums.

Danon stood in silent reverence with the elders and visiting may'rs as Nathon's shroud passed by. Its appliqué of decorations commemorated his life and accomplishments with dozens of beaded mosaics. The pictures denoted his deliverance from the Earth Mother, his passing into manhood, his entrance into the brotherhood of warriors with feats of courage, his coronation as leader of the clan, and his final return welcomed by the Earth Mother. The sweet scent of the maidens' tapers drifted over them, the smell of sunny spring day with freshly cut grass and blossoming flowers.

Tight lipped youths held stern countenances as the funeral march proceeded. Aged men with cheeks of leather bowed to hide their eyes while bitter wails erupted from gray haired women with sagging breasts. Clansmen from other tribes also paid homage to the great leader who had been first to visit other clans. Throughout the cavern flowed the sorrow of hundreds as they mourned the loss of their leader. Through it all, the visage of Lauriel remained resolute, a stoic warrior who showed no pain.

The procession rounded the Elders' Circle and headed into the crowd, scribing a long, weaving course through the mixture of clansmen before finally leaving the main cavern for the dark recesses of the distant chambers. Danon watched the flickering candles disappear like fireflies in the night.

Lauriel took his arm. Her fingers tightened. "We go now to Chamber of May'rs," she said, maintaining her rigid composure.

He looked into her eyes and sought to comfort her, but she looked away.

"Take me to burial chamber."

# # #

The Chamber of May'rs was situated deep in the caverns far away from the main room. It held the remains of all the past may'rs who had ruled since the holocaust. Through the dark chasm of the main cavern and along a low, narrow corridor the entourage traveled in whispered silence. The dignitaries followed behind Danon and Lauriel, strung out according to rank as they observed some vague form of protocol. The band of warriors brought up the rear guard.

Danon noticed a gentle breeze against his face as they entered a tunnel he had never seen before. The glow stones of the lanterns induced phosphorescence in the stone's matrix; the walls of the naturally formed tunnel glittered with tiny flecks, mineral formations that reflected the lanterns' glow with a prismatic burst of color.

The tunnel ended in a small, debris filled room. Sheets of shale rock hung precariously from the ceiling like chunks of peeling plaster. Overhead, a large boulder seemed to balance itself against another, which in turn leaned for support on a third. They reminded him of an old circus scene of three elephants standing in a row, perched on their hind legs while resting on one another. Detouring around the pile of rocks they filed into another narrow corridor, rougher hewn than the first. This corridor opened up into a large, oval room. The burial chamber.

Around the undecorated room ran a wide natural shelf about a meter above the floor. On top of the shelf lay five human sized bundles. Their yellowed coverings and hand-stitched decorations matched the shroud surrounding Nathon.

"My grandfathers," Lauriel said, as if answering an unspoken question. "All may'rs of Clan."

"I suppose I'll wind up here someday." It sounded flippant, but he didn't mean it that way. He didn't like to think about the inevitable.

"Is great honor."

"I know, but I'd just as soon not have that honor bestowed for a very long time."

She nodded understandingly.

"What's that?" He pointed to the middle of the room where lips of stone protruded from the floor like a gaping mouth.

"Is Sipapu, the Well of Souls," she answered. "Where the spirit enters to find Earth Mother."

"You really believe that?"

She stared at the well a moment before answering. "Does not matter."

He leaned over the dark pit and a cool, damp breeze caressed his face. "There's fresh air blowing up," he said, peering down the black shaft. "Where does it come from?"

"Legend says …"

The procession entered the crowded chamber. Nathon's body was laid on the shelf next to his father. Benon, the medicine man, squeezed in front of the assembly and faced the shroud. He reached into his decorated bag and withdrew a small glass vial. He cupped it between wrinkled hands, holding it reverently up to the ceiling as he muttered some forgotten incantation or prayer. Danon couldn't understand its meaning and wondered whether or not Benon actually understood the significance of his own words. The medicine man opened the vial and sprinkled white powder around the shelf, lightly dusting some of its closer inhabitants. Another mournful chant and the ceremony was over.

After everyone filed out of the chamber, Danon stood in the doorway, waiting for Lauriel. She stood beside the shroud.

"Good bye father," she whispered, her voice almost trembling. "Will miss you." She turned to Danon to be escorted out.

"If you'd rather postpone the bonding, I'd understand."

She shook her head. "His journey is over. We must go on with ours." She looked up to him, her callous mask now transparent. "Take me as your wo'am tonight. Hold me to your side when soul of father soars away, and I am alone."

He tried to think of something to say, something to ease her pain, but couldn't. He could only nod.

Chapter 28

By the time Danon and Lauriel returned to the main cavern, most of the crowd had dispersed. Preparations had to be made for the pair bonding, plus a feast and celebration to commemorate the new May'r. The young women had scampered off to change out of their mourning attire into more cheerful dress while the older women gathered at the far end of the village, preparing the reception meal. The children, finally free from the restraints of the long afternoon, played freely around them.

Only the men of the Clan still waited. They waited for the pale warrior who spoke of things from long ago. They waited for the new May'r who promised a better future. At first glimpse of Danon, the cavern walls again reverberated with shouts of his name.

It seemed each one wanted to pat his back or shoulder, or touch him in some way. Sincere words of encouragement and congratulations came from all sides as clansmen affirmed their undying allegiance. He endured their adulation with forced dignity as he wormed through the enthusiastic crowd. When he finally reached the Lodge, he recognized a solemn figure waiting awkwardly near the door flap.

"Dazjon! It's good to see you, brother. Where've you been?"

"Am no longer warrior, lost status to join raiding party. Am hunter now, find food and game to feed communal lodges."

"What do you mean, can't join raiding party?"

"Was captured by bounty and rescued at great risk to party."

"That's crazy! Lauriel and I chose to go back for you while the rest made it safely back with the biotics."

"Does not matter; restore status with important news for May'r. For you."

"We'll talk about it later. I have to go now." Most of Danon's body was numb, except the parts that still throbbed with pain. He needed to rest. He needed to fall down and die.

"Do not think will wait," Dazjon said gravely. "Is something May'r must hear."

Danon nodded reluctantly and led him into the Lodge. Inside, he discovered the focum filled with visiting leaders and elders. They all stood at his arrival and bowed with deference. He returned a stiff bow before taking his seat.

Dazjon seemed only slightly intimidated by the collection of leaders. He stepped to the center to deliver his news about the riot that had followed in the aftermath of the tragic rally.

Danon had already heard the rumors from the Den. He leaned forward. "You saw the riot?"

"Yes, many attacks. Much burning. Many catchers injured when they tried to stop Data clan. Was not enough of them to stop so many warriors."

"I didn't know it got that bad."

"Is not worst part," Dazjon continued. "Catchers see it as matter of honor. They want, how you say …"

"Justice?"

"No, revenge."

Danon couldn't believe the grim faced ex-warrior. The police wouldn't. They're supposed to uphold the law, not break it. He noticed the growing whispers and understood their concern. The riot police attacking the Data clan, catching them unsuspectingly in the underground parking complex. It had only one entrance; there would be no way to escape.

Dazjon shook his head insistently. "Travel far in my hunting and have found many ways to move through city. I know this is true. Do not know how, but will be soon I think."

Danon grabbed the hunter's solid forearms. "I need you to make a trip for me as soon as possible."

"Can leave now," he said eagerly. "Where does May'r send?"

"Go to the Data clan and warn them. Explain that they should leave for another place for a while. They can come here. Do your best to convince them not to stay and fight. It won't help the struggle. Tell them."

"As my May'r wishes."

"No, as your brother wishes."

Dazjon looked surprised, then almost smiled with understanding of his restored status. He bowed quickly and left.

One of the Manchee elders stood to address Danon.

"Today has been filled with much sorrow. Many events to record on history panel. Many stories to tell at future campfires. Is true that new leader of Grotto Clan speaks with wisdom and shows concern for other clans' safety."

Danon shook his head. "I am concerned about another police clan confrontation. I'm afraid that the leaders of Data Clan are too proud and too warrioristic."

"You have done all that is possible. They must choose their own path." The Manchee elder bowed and turned to leave, taking the assembly with him.

When Danon was alone, he rubbed his temples in frustration. He knew they wouldn't run. He prayed that Dazjon would succeed. He prayed the Data clan would listen. When he was through, he realized he had prayed to the Earth Mother.

From outside, he noticed the sounds of the cavern penetrating his lodge: singing, laughing, children playing, and women chattering as they prepared the food. He could smell some of it already. It would be a large meal for the celebration. His celebration. He wondered what he was supposed to wear to a clan wedding.

Even after living with the Clan for three months, he owned very little clothing. His original jumpsuit had deteriorated away. The pair of dirtworker's coveralls weren't appropriate, neither were his warrior leathers. He knew Lauriel would be wearing something special, even though he didn't know exactly what, and he wanted to look good for her. He realized he needed a bath. Then he was going to lie down and die.

# # #

The large cushion had looked more comfortable than it had felt. The layers of blankets covered with antelope hide still had an antelope hiding beneath it somewhere. When he finally gave up his attempt at sleep he realized he was no longer alone. In the middle of the floor, knelt a young maiden dressed in white buckskin.

"Aleshannee, what are you doing here?"

"Princess Lauriel sent me. Asked me to help you dress."

"How long have you been here? You should've said something. Did you say help me dress?"

"Yes, must show you special mufti."

"Mufti?"

With her head bowed to hide her smile, she pointed to a pair of buckskin pants hanging on the far wall. Hanging with them was an open jacket and flat vest plate of beadwork. Danon admired the fine craftsmanship. Each piece of the hand-softened suit was made of purest white suede. Long fringe dangled from both arms and legs. The breastplate was magnificent, a matrix of tiny beads forming a red and white mosaic, trimmed in indigo.

He fingered the beadwork as he slipped into his mufti. It felt like one continuous piece, fused into the soft, bluish white leather. It was hard to imagine the individual beads being sewn on separately.

The soft chamois texture caressed his skin as he slipped his bare feet into the leggings. The jacket covered only the top of his shoulders, back, and arms; leaving his chest exposed to show off the ornate beadwork of the breastplate. A matching pair of beaded moccasins lay on the floor.

"Does it fit?" Aleshanee asked. "Was not sure how much to modify." She held a tarnished mirror for him to see.

Danon was astonished by his reflection. The image before him was impressive, all the dignity and splendor of a clan May'r. He didn't feel like a true May'r yet, but he did look like one. Aleshanee attached the shawl to his jacket to hang like a regal cape.

"Now you are ready?" she asked, kneeling again. "Elders wait to escort you."

"Already?" He removed the red feather from his dagger's handle, and tucked it into his vest pocket. At the ceremony he would tie it back where it belonged.

# # #

Flickering shadows danced on the walls of the great domed room. In addition to the lighting panels, some of the visiting clansmen had erected traditional torches. The melancholy notes of Medicine Man's flute, called a "hollow reed," echoed off the cavern walls. As Danon stepped outside, a channel of warriors, lined up shoulder to shoulder, guided the procession path into the Circle.

He followed the elders through the narrow channel. Children tossed wildflowers and mesquite needles in front of him at his feet, as they had been taught, signifying both the blessings and obstacles that lay ahead on his journey. The procession entered the clearing and fanned out to encircle the unlit fire pit. Nathon's memorial had been removed, and fresh wood and kindling had been and arranged. Its lighting would be delayed as the final symbolic act of their bonding. Danon reached his appointed place beside the medicine man and waited for Lauriel.

A change in the rhythm of drum beats signaled her arrival. Across the clearing, a double file of young maidens broke through the crowd. They separated like a flower blossom to let Lauriel pass between them. She wore her gown of silken white suede to match Danon's buckskin. He squinted to see her clearly. The quick bath had helped his deteriorated contacts some, but he still saw a fuzzy halo around her. It didn't quite fit, he thought with a grin. But she was beautiful, especially in the flickering light of the torches. Her hair, no longer confined in a hunter's braid, cascaded in ebony filaments over her shoulders to spill over her covered breasts.

She stopped beside him and the drums stopped.

The chief elder came into the Circle and stood beside the warrior-princess. In place of her father, he presented her to Danon in front of the Clan. Medicine Man Benon straightened his drawn shoulders and waited. The cavern was visited with dancing shadows as the lighting panels were covered, leaving only the flickering torches. After a whispered prodding from the old medicine man, Danon spoke with a strong, if not nervous, voice.

"I, May'r Danon, have called Lauriel to be my mate! My wo'am."

It was the last chance for anyone to object, but everyone in the crowd knew none would dare challenge this newly proven May'r or his princess-warrior.

Danon felt Lauriel's hand tighten as the flickering silence was torn by a startling shout that echoed through the cavern.

"They're here! May'r Danon, the catchers. They attack!"

CHAPTER 29

The light of the panels once again flooded the room. A gasp of unbelief swelled from the crowd, most of whom stood unmoving, unsure of what to do. Perfs in the cavern? No one from ever bothered to travel this far from the city. No Perf had ever set foot down here before. They couldn't attack. This was clan sanctuary.

But they were here now. Dozens of red and black uniforms poured through the narrow opening, charging down the ramp. Their fearsome weapons belched tongues of orange fire. Some spewed pellets of tear gas in lazy white arcs that landed with a pop to spread their noxious fumes.

Teary eyed children scattered in blubbery fear, their mothers racing to snatch them up. Some huddled over their infants to protect them, others stumbled over each other searching for escape as more red and black uniforms advanced into the main cavern. Streaks of blue light flashed everywhere, multiplying the confusion and panic.

Danon had to do something, he had to protect them. People were suffering. His people. He raised a fist and shouted.

"Warriors, attack!"

Lauriel released her grip and spun around to leave. He grabbed her arm.

"Where do you think you're going?"

"To get my bow, of course."

"No. Take the women and children and the elders. Go to the back, to the burial chamber. We can't hold them back long, there's too many of them."

Lauriel hesitated.

"Go on, I'll join you later."

She placed a momentary hand to his cheek and disappeared.

He turned to run toward the Lodge, but bumped into Dazjon who had suddenly appeared at his side.

"Tried to get here sooner," he said, gasping for breath. "To warn you."

"It's all right. Go with Lauriel, help her lead the others to the back."

Dazjon started to leave and then stopped as if confused by his sense of duty. "Is no guard for you."

"Is now, Lad!" came a husky shout. Gregon held his ceremonial lance with determined hands. He could no longer make the trek to find a battle, but this time the battle had come to him.

Danon nodded approval to the ancient veteran, then turned to Dazjon. "Take a rope ladder from the lighting panels. And find more if you can, but hurry, Brother. Take them down the Well of Souls."

He was hoping the unexplored shaft would lead them to safety, and praying that he was right. The doubt in Dazjon's eyes didn't concur.

Gregon gave the hesitant warrior a shove. "Go quickly. Your clan needs you again. This young May'r has me to look after him."

The fumes drifted closer, burning their eyes. Danon could see other warriors already returning from their dwellings, weapons in hand. He needed a weapon, too. He raced to the Lodge with Gregon shortly behind.

# # #

Angry flashes of orange and blue streaked across the cavern to dozens of running targets. The cries of pain were brief as clansmen crumpled to the ground when they found their mark. A few red and black uniforms fell, pierced by a silent arrow or hurled spear, but the advancing wave of catchers continued forward.

As the renegade police encroached further into the cavern, they met the first organized resistance as a barrage of rocks rained down from the upper ledges. Skilled Choc warriors used their ancient slings with lethal accuracy. Others heaved heavier rocks over the side of the tall ledge, occasionally squashing one of their enemies below.

The attack slowed, like an expanding puddle of lava. The warriors fought valiantly, but knew they were seriously outnumbered.

By the time Danon had retrieved Lauriel's bow and quiver, the attackers were already at the far edge of dwellings, suppressing the counter attack warrior by warrior. Shacks and tents were riddled with gun blasts to eliminate any hidden attackers. There were none. Most of the Clan had fled, leaving only a few stragglers who crisscrossed the smoky floor from one shack to another searching for friends or relatives. Danon caught a glimpse of his clansmen, or at least most of them, disappearing into the dark recess that led toward the burial chamber.

Gregon got his attention and pointed up the cavern. Through the smoke and flames of burning lodges, came more blurry figures.

He raised the bow to take aim but hesitated. He had never killed a man. Fate had even spared him the task of taking Devon's life. He drew back and stared down the aimpoint. What would a real civil right's leader do, he wondered? What would his clan think? He hadn't even practiced the ancient art of archery in a long time.

An intense blue flash sizzled in front of him, narrowly missing his head. He recognized the high-energy plasma that had killed Nathon!

He spun around, centered the aimpoint in the chest of the red and black uniform, and released. The barbed shaft sliced through the air with a high pitched whistle that lasted only a heart beat before sinking into its target.

Danon's heart pounded, pumping too much adrenaline through his body to let him get sick over killing a man. He notched another arrow and swept the aimpoint across the attackers. He chose another victim and watched him fall. He fired quickly and accurately. More uniforms fell. The knot in his stomach grew tighter with each one, but he couldn't stop.

What must be done.

A searing bolt of plasma flew by just inches from his shoulder. Another exploded near his feet, kicking pebbles and dirt into the air. He eliminated the attacker and ran for a safer position in the rocky wall.

Orange stun flashes and blue plasma bolts flashed in front and behind him as he ran. To stumble was to die. He tried to keep low, dodging left and right, as he made his way across the exposed openness. Gregon followed like a stubborn shadow.

"Was close," the old warrior said, hugging the safety of the rock. "Perf's not aim good as you."

Danon readied another arrow and leaned out from the wall just far enough to get off a shot before jumping back behind the rocky crag. His victim fell with a silent gasp, clutching the shaft that had suddenly sprouted from his throat.

The two warriors were suddenly illuminated with reflections of orange and blue flashes. Salty rock fragments sprayed their faces as the energy bolts blasted small craters in the limestone, and left a bittersweet smell of ozone.

He ducked behind a rocky crag and groped for another arrow, his last. "Where did they all go?" he asked. "I had a full quiver."

Gregon pointed toward the Lodge and he saw them, lying like scattered toothpicks along the ground to mark their trail across the clearing.

"Damn!" How could he have been so stupid! He took the arrow and placed it on the nock point. When he fired this one, he would be out of ammunition, except for his warrior's knife and Gregon's lance.

He peeked around the crag. The invaders' attention was focused on the upper ledges, concentrating their fire upward where only a few warriors remained. Several bodies lay scattered on the cavern floor, mostly fallen warriors. As Danon watched, another defender was struck and tumbled to the floor. It was Allon.

He sent his last arrow in flying retribution and took another look behind. No more clansmen. They were on their way to the burial chamber. He had a good chance of making it to the exit; the police were still a ways off and, as Gregon had pointed out, not very good shots. But even if his lame escort could keep up and they did join the others, he had no weapon to defend their retreat.

He peeked around once more. He saw no more warriors, only the main body of police who huddled behind the smoking dwellings across the clearing, and a couple of scouts who were advancing slowly along each wall with their weapons poised.

Their weapons! Danon pointed with a silent curse.

Gregon leaned out to look. "What of 'em?"

"If I could get one of those ..." He glanced around to the rugged wall behind him. About five meters up, he saw a tempting shadow.

"It might be a ledge," he said. "If we can climb that far without getting shot."

Something heavy landed with a thud behind them. A cylindrical pellet the size of his thumb was burning, furiously spewing out white fumes of tear gas. Two more pellets landed and quickly formed a dense white cloud that rose up between them and the police. Soon it blocked them from view.

"Come on, we don't have much time," he said, his eyes already burning. "We have to try for it."

"I gives you the time, Lad." Gregon readied his lance. "Be a surprise wait'n for first Perf through that smoke."

"I can't leave you here, you wouldn't have a chance."

"Gots no choice, lad. You must think of Clan. You knows what need be done. Hunt with courage, young May'r."

Danon nodded reluctantly. "Die with honor, old warrior."

He pulled himself up the wall, stretching for handholds. He climbed as far as he could, and then crabbed sideways to find another handhold. He had to be careful; one wrong move would send him tumbling down below. But he had to hurry. The scouts would be coming through the curtain of smoke any moment.

Finally he reached the tempting shadow. It was a ledge, but not wide enough to stand on. Forget about crawling or hiding, he was stuck. The scouts were behind him and closing in. Soon they would come through the smoke to investigate. When they did, he'd still be clinging to the wall like a fly waiting to be swatted.

Maybe he could jump. He looked down. No, bad idea.

He strained to see upward, easing outward from his precarious hold, but couldn't tell. Higher up, he spotted what might be another ledge or change in strata, or maybe just a discoloration in the rock.

He clawed his way upward, higher above the cavern floor. He heard a groan from below, but couldn't stop to look. His arms were giving out.

He felt something above, a deep recess in the wall just over his head. He pulled his tired body over the ledge rested for a moment. The ledge was just wide enough to hide on. It extended for several meters as it gradually descended the escarpment. He moved as silently as he could; each hand, each knee carefully placed.

He heard the tumbling of loose rocks and froze. Someone was moving beneath the ledge. He eased over to look. The main group of police still remained at the clearing, fifty or sixty meters away. He leaned further out and saw one of the scouts directly beneath him. The second scout stood across the floor against the opposite wall. Neither seemed too eager to accomplish their mission as they inched cautiously forward.

Danon stared at the scout's weapon. A blaster!

Before he took the time to consider it, he had swung his feet over the side and dropped—another bad idea. The fall seemed to last forever.

When he landed on the unsuspecting scout, the man collapsed to the rocky floor like a discarded accordion. The other scout turned to investigate, but seemed confused. Danon picked up the rifle, squinting through his fuzzy contacts, and squeezed the trigger.

Nothing happened.

He stared at it with stupid amazement. The weapon didn't look damaged. The second scout started in Danon's direction, then raised his own weapon. Danon aimed again. He squeezed the trigger as hard as he could. Again nothing happened. The scout paused to take perfect aim. He was trained to be accurate. Awkwardly he staggered to one side, firing the blue bolt high and to the right. His next and final burst was aimed in another direction away from Danon.

Gregon's lance had entered the scout's back and protruded from his chest. After all these years, the old veteran still knew how to hurl a spear, but he no longer had the agility to dodge a counter attack.

Danon frantically examined the stolen rifle. The rear grip had a small indention just above the thumb rest that made a clicking sound when depressed. Of course! Again he felt stupid. Every weapon had a safety.

A close flash of blue woke him to his surroundings again. A single sniper shot that barely missed his head. He bolted for the dark exit at the back of the cave. Searing bolts of plasma raced him to the dark opening, as if they knew where he was headed.

He passed the crag and spotted Gregon, but he didn't need to slow down. Through the thinning smoke of the tear gas, he had a clear view. Both the scout and the veteran warrior were victims of the other's accuracy.

Danon swallowed hard. *Die with honor.*

He ran on, still more than twenty meters away when he saw a third scout exiting the pool entrance. The catcher saw him, also, and fired quickly. He missed.

Danon depressed the thumb safety and carefully squeezed off a blue flash that caught the scout squarely in the chest.

When the last scout fell, his comrades no longer needed caution. A barrage of energy bolts erupted all around the lone renegade warrior as he ran for the safety of the exit.

The dark opening loomed nearer. Just before he reached the breached wall, a bolt of angry plasma barely creased the white leather of his jacket, but delivered an intense spasm of white-hot pain that exploded in his head. The searing pain lasted only for an instant, and then it was gone, leaving his arm numb and paralyzed.

He stumbled but kept going, plunging into total darkness.

He ran by sound rather than sight, using the echoes of his footsteps to judge the proximity of the stone walls. The tunnel narrowed, then opened into a small room with several exits. Gradually the darkness began to dissolve. He could see each exit now as searchlights glowed behind him. The police were catching up. If he didn't slow them down, he'd rejoin the others just in time to warn them before it was too late.

He crouched in a dark corner and waited. Searchlight beams soon sparkled through the air, illuminating tiny dust particles. He lifted the rifle with one arm and fired down the passage. He heard angry shouts and gruff swearing as the lights went out. Satisfied that he had slowed them down a little, he started off again for the burial chamber.

The black passage tightened as it descended. Then a change in his footstep's echoes told him he had entered the last room, the one that held the balancing boulders. He crossed the rugged floor slowly, tripping over unseen obstacles, groping along the wall searching for the exit. Lauriel was just ahead, as were the others. They would all be waiting, depending on him to lead them to safety. He stepped on something soft that squeaked and scampered away. He kept moving. He didn't want to know.

# # #

Lauriel helped the older woman climb into the narrow shaft. The old woman offered no complaint, except a slight moan, as she climbed over the basin and clung to the rope ladder. Even though the room was full of people, Lauriel heard someone new enter the room behind her. She spun around, her dagger drawn and ready, then sighed with relief.

She ran over to embrace him with more zeal than his shoulder could take. "You're hurt," she said, noticing the patch of scorched leather. "Let me see …"

"I'm all right, I think." He hadn't taken time to look, but feeling was returning, a tingling of needles. And he could move his fingers again. "You didn't think a few catchers would stop me, did you?"

She smiled briefly, then returned to a more somber expression. "The others?"

He shook his head reluctantly. "I saw many of our brothers fall from the ledges. Allon was one of them. And Gregon." He swallowed hard. "Gregon is gone."

She looked down the silent passageway and nodded. "Was good warrior."

Danon noticed the crowded room. "You have to hurry. They're right behind me. I don't think I slowed them down very much and there are still too many people left in here." He kissed her and swung the rifle up to leave.

"Where you going?"

He gave a condescending glance. "To do what must be done."

# # #

Danon readied himself in the room that had been formed centuries before when the brittle layer of shale strata had collapsed into the void no longer supported by the water eroded limestone. Above his head, large fragments still hang loosely, some wedged in place or leaning on others as if too tired support themselves. He lay prone on the cluttered floor waiting in ambush. Soon the reflections of searchlights bounced along the twisting corridor.

He readied his rifle with a silent curse and waited. They wouldn't ever give up, he realized. They had to be stopped. A warrior was expendable, he reminded himself. The Clan must survive. If he held his fire until they stepped into the open, he could take out most of them. Maybe all of them. His finger tightened around the trigger. They deserved it.

It was self defense, he tried to tell himself; they started it. He cursed again. This insane plan contradicted everything he had been trying to teach the Clan. His finger cramped.

He was May'r now, the protector of the Clan. What would Nathon have done? All he had to do was stall long enough for the others to escape. He had killed enough. Too much, dammit!

He fired a volley of bursts into the opposite tunnel to warn them of his presence. Return fire flashed out of the far tunnel and riddled the room with blinding explosions that vibrated the very floor he lay on. Dust and rock rained from the ceiling. He caught glimpses of the balancing boulders, frozen by the brilliant strobes of energy. They seemed to teeter for a moment. He wondered.

He considered the possible consequences of a cave-in for a moment, then decided. He fired upward to the ceiling. He fired again. Answering shots from the advancing police added to the growing concussions.

Explosions shook the mountain, choking the room with dust. Larger pieces of rock toppled and crashed to the floor. He felt a deep shudder as one of the large boulders slipped from its precarious roost and crashed down in front of him, sealing the tunnel. He had done it. The cave-in would completely entomb the passage and keep the police from reaching them.

The thunder of the collapsing tunnel rumbled all around him. Choking dust filled his eyes and nose. An avalanche of dirt cascaded around him. It was a good idea, he thought. Maybe. He heard Lauriel scream his name from the end of the collapsing tunnel, but the sound was muffled and far away. Maybe too good, he realized. If he didn't move quickly, the mountain of dirt and rock would seal him along with the passageway.

# # #

Lauriel recognized the distant rumble of ground thunder and knew what had happened. She started to scream his name again, remembering the last time she had called out to him. Her words were choked off. Again she was helpless to save the one she loved.

She stared into the black tunnel, hoping to see something. A thick cloud of dust floated into the chamber. She held her lantern up vainly trying to penetrate the floating silt, and waited, but found only silence, the silence of a crypt.

He was gone.

Chapter 30

Lauariel helped the last straggler over the side. The stooped man with skin of parchment had no family members still living and had insisted on being last. As he slowly made his way down, Lauriel took a look around the room.

She was the last. All of the Clan waited below, beneath the Well of Souls. Only the bodies of her ancestors remained in the chamber, the former leaders of the Grotto clan. She was the last of their bloodline. She took one last look at Nathon's shrouded body. There was another may'r who belonged here, who had given his life for the Clan, but he would never rest with the others. He was buried somewhere else. She wiped the burning cave dust from her eyes and started down the well, but stopped.

She sensed something approaching from out of the darkness and spun around. Even before her heavy heart could release its mourning, the warrior stood in a crouch, her dagger already drawn.

Danon stumbled into the chamber, still coughing on the half-pound of dirt he had swallowed. He grabbed the stunned warrior and pulled her close.

"Miss me?"

She held him tightly, then remembered his burn. "Your face …" She pulled back in unbelief. "You're alive!"

He grinned weakly. "Yeah, I think so."

"But I thought, I thought you was dead."

"So did I."

Her clenching arms released him, and the firmness returned to her voice. "Is good to see you, but we must go. They wait for their may'r."

He followed her over the edge into the cleaner air rising up the shaft. The true depth of the Well of Souls lay hidden beneath murky shadows that retreated from the lantern's glow as they descended the swaying rope ladder, deeper into the quiet chasm.

Each step stretched the unhealed knife cuts and renewed the dull pain in his arm. He hadn't stopped to see how much damage the plasma blast had done. If it looked like a chunk of roasted meat, he'd rather not see it. He could still use it. Besides, he wasn't in a position to stop and receive medical attention. If the cave-in hadn't completely blocked the passageway, the police would be on their trail again. If it did, the Clan was trapped. They had no way out of the caverns unless he could find one.

Finally they reached the end of the shaft, a hollow stalactite column that descended from the ceiling like some strange, inverted smokestack. He gritted his teeth and worked his way down the last few meters of swinging rope ladder.

Most of the crowd huddled in the center of the room around a lonely pair of lanterns. Not much light for exploring, he thought. He was relieved to discover that few seemed injured, except for some stun blasts that would wear off quickly. He was probably the only one hit by plasma. Most victims of a plasma bolt didn't live to brag about it.

Lauriel had been drawn over to the side of the room, surrounded by several elders and may'rs in muffled conversation. She came back alone.

"I told them 'bout falling tunnel," she said. "They understand and wait for you to guide them." Uneasy murmurs grew from the huddle and rippled through the dark room like an unsettling breeze.

Lauriel squeezed his good arm. "You must be strong, my bonded one."

"What's wrong?"

"Is because we have passed beyond Well of Souls. Is land of Sipapu, only spirits pass this way." Her expression indicated she didn't believe such things herself, but she pointed to the others who did.

# # #

With only two lanterns to guide a thousand people, the journey began in darkness for most. Blind feet shuffled along obediently as the thin line of fugitives stretched into the subterranean night, each trusting the new May'r to lead them safely through, though clinging tightly to the hand of the person in front.

The trail through the dark passageways was sometimes smooth, worn down by centuries of erosion by underground streams; at other times it was jagged and torn, littered with rocks or choked with debris from prehistoric earthquakes. Most passages were too narrow to pass except in single file. The line of clansmen meandered blindly back and forth. They crawled under cramped passes. They squeezed through narrow fissures. They lowered each other, one by one, over narrow ledges and dizzying chasms. For hours they followed an incline deeper into the earth. Occasionally a path promised to start upward, but it always turned, taking them farther away from the surface.

# # #

Danon stood in a wide trough, his fists clenched as he looked around. The pot marked walls climbed to disappear above the reach of the lantern's glow. He saw a dozen possible exits to take. Two were large and inviting, a third would be a little cramped but still large enough to pass. The others were too difficult for the older ones, he decided. He turned to Lauriel.

"Wait here and I'll scout ahead."

"You can't check them all," she said. "I take one and meet you back here in few minutes."

"Can't, there's only two lights." He motioned at the blackness that already obscured the faces behind them.

She started to argue when Dazjon interrupted. "Am not afraid of dark." He nodded toward the tired group of followers. "We will sing of our past, of former May'rs and tribal heroes."

One of the may'rs walked up to join them. He nodded agreement. "You will be back soon enough."

Lauriel quickly darted into one of the openings before he could argue. Dazjon handed his lamp to Danon.

"Hunt with courage, May'r."

"Don't worry," he said with confidence. "We'll be out of here and back home in no time." He started toward the other opening. Home in no time. If only he believed it.

# # #

He followed the promising route for a half an hour before it ended with a sheer drop-off into darkness. With sullen disappointment, he turned around.

When he returned, Lauriel and Dazjon greeting him excitedly.

"What'd you find?"

"Nothing," he answered in a hushed voice. He didn't want the others to overhear, but even his whisper echoed across the room.

"Is all right. I think we can take the other one. It gets narrow, but it climbs! Maybe is way to surface."

"If it goes up, it has to be the right one. Is everyone ready?"

"The old ones are brave, they don't complain. If May'r is ready to leave, Clan is ready to follow."

Dazjon quickly gathered everyone and reestablished their marching order. The group was growing weary, but no one complained. Even the children seemed to understand the hushed urgency and followed the new May'r, unaware of his growing doubts.

The passage did take them up. For over an hour they trudged upward, growing wearier, but feeling their spirits rise with the incline. Pausing for short rests, Danon led them on, hoping silently that he was making the right choice.

The band stumbled to a stop and strained to get a look. Another dead-end. The path squeezed inward like a funnel and then terminated in a chimney formation. Danon stared up the shaft that rose for over ten meters above them.

"Damn, not again!"

"Is no problem," Lauriel said, studying the shaft for footings and handholds.

"Look at it. The old ones would never be able climb that. It's almost straight up."

Lauriel studied the stone face closely, then nodded. "The children climb walls like this for play. Can use our rope, lower it down and pull others up."

"I don't know …"

Her expression hardened. "Does May'r offer other choice?"

He glanced back to the waiting crowd and shook his head.

"Bring the children," Lauriel shouted to them. "We climb!"

Lauriel scaled the chimney first and assisted the smaller children. Danon and Dazjon stayed below, prepared to catch them if they slipped. But none did. The giggling children scurried up the cracks and fissures of the rock wall like a pack of hungry rats.

Then Danon and Dazjon switched places with Lauriel. She worked below, securing the hastily fashioned rope harness to the older ones. She got them started while Danon and Dazjon held the rope. Many refused assistance of any kind, struggling to make the climb on their own, then insisting to help hold the rope for the others. Soon enough men had lined up along the rope that neither warrior was needed.

The assembly continued on, ignoring their exhaustion. The incline was moderate and the surface smooth, easing their fatigue slightly. Many began to sense that they were close to the end of their journey. When the path rose more steeply, it bolstered their hopes more. At last, the path leveled out and emptied into a large, round room.

They hurried in, chatting excitedly. Danon crossed the rubble strewn floor to search the far wall. He found only solid stone. No tunnels, no openings. No exit. Overhead, the domed ceiling appeared solid, formed not by eroding water, but by a collapse long ago. He searched again for hidden exits, any break in the continuity of stone. But he found none. Lauriel stood on the opposite side of the domed room, shaking her head. She hadn't found anything either.

Under the hushed murmurs of the waiting clan, Danon sensed something. A vibration beneath his feet. He couldn't believe it, but he recognized the deep rumbling sound of the approaching timequake.

Lauriel, and then the others, heard it. They glanced around nervously. From everywhere, from nowhere, it came—an angry disturbance that seeped through the stone walls and fill the room. It grew menacingly, rising in pitch.

He suppressed the cold shudder up his spine and called to Lauriel. He had to explain before it was too late.

From clear across the room, Lauriel felt the foreboding shiver. It clawed up her moccasins and chilled her heart. She reached out.

"Danon?"

The invisible maelstrom swelled to a shrill, bone rattling resonance. She could barely hear Danon as he screamed and reached for her. She started toward him, jumping over the rubble. Something was wrong. Something she didn't understand. She could neither see nor touch the danger, but she sensed that she was losing him again.

Danon again called out to her.

"Lauriel, lead them out of here! Lead them to safety!"

His words seemed to fade away in the air.

"I'll be back …"

The cavern shuddered—raining pebbles and dirt on the crowd—rocked with vengeance by the angry spirits who had once shaped the cosmos.

Lauriel stumbled. Looking up in awe, she could only stare with disbelief at the fading aura of her chosen. The image of Danon, outstretched arms reaching for her, flickered and wavered like a mirage. Then, came silence. The chaos was gone as suddenly as it came.

And so was Danon.

Chapter 31

The control room shook violently. Acoustical tile tumbled through the air, exposing patches of bare ceiling. Spreading cracks raced along the over-stressed concrete walls as chunks of plaster bounced off electronic equipment and skittered across the floor.

Thomas tried to concentrate on the blurry instrument panel in front of him while clutching the mouse-ear attenuators against his head. The pain of a thousand needles jabbed his brain. The raging sound was so thick, he could almost taste it. It made his teeth hurt, worst than the dentist had ever been.

The pandemonium finally peaked and then vanished as the capsule began the controlled, preprogrammed braking action of re-entry to gradually reduce its tremendous velocity.

"It's over!" cried a grateful medtech, as if no one had noticed. The crowd of engineers and support technicians cheered elatedly, celebrating their success at accomplishing another historical first—sending a human beyond the space/time barrier. Everyone cheered, except Thomas.

"Something's wrong," he said, tapping on a broken indicator. "There's a power failure ..." His voice trailed off as he scanned the dying control panel. "It's onboard the capsule."

Chief Todd hobbled across the floor, kicking tiles out of his way till he stood over Thomas' shoulder.

"What's wrong?"

"I don't know. Something has caused complete thruster shutdown in the tachyon drive."

The Chief's face wrinkled. "I thought it didn't need the thrusters to slow down."

"It doesn't. The force field draws power from the tachyon drive unit. They compensate each other." Thomas tapped the stubborn dials of the control panel. "It's designed to balance out, but if one or the other is just slightly off ..."

"The pancake effect?"

Thomas looked up, but didn't answer.

Chief Todd shuffled away toward the thick alloy viewing window where most of the technicians had gathered to steal a first hand look at the almost certain disaster. They parted before him like Moses and the Red Sea. He peered anxiously through the thick amber viewing port.

"Is there anything you can do?"

"No. It's all automated, or supposed to be. As soon as the door-lock releases, get the medtechs in there. Fast."

# # #

The capsule had ground to a halt, trailing bits of wreckage around the tube. Deep lacerations in the canopy showed where it had chopped through the dislodged fragments of the drive unit. The rescue crew had dropped the access hatch and retrieved the battered capsule by the time Thomas arrived and fought his way to the ladder. They released the locking bolts and lifted the canopy. A medtech pushed his way through and climbed the crowded ladder to lean over the motionless body.

"Is he alright?"

The medtech stumbled back in shock, dropping his bio-monitor. He looked to the open-mouthed assist-tech beside him.

"Do you believe this?"

"Is he alright?" Thomas asked again, straining to see over them.

"He's alive. But look at his clothes. And that frigging beard!"

Thomas shoved his way passed the stunned medtech aside and froze at the sight of his battered friend. It wasn't Daniel; it was some fugitive from a western frontier town, a haggard fur trapper complete with buckskins and a full beard.

Chief Todd started barking orders to get awestruck team moving again. "Get moving. Take him out of there and down to medical! Notify intensive care to have full life support ready. Thomas, I want to know what the hell happened!"

# # #

He awoke to blinding light.

Where was he? And why did he have headache the size of Montana? He tried again, but the white glare welded his eyes shut. He tried to focus on the blurry angel-like figures standing around him, but couldn't. Cracked lips moved to speak. His mouth was dry and his tongue heavy. He heard a familiar voice penetrating his fuzzy consciousness.

"You gave us quite a scare," it said.

The voice belonged to an old friend, a friend from his past. Thomas? He heard another voice droning in the background. Nathon? No, it was Chief Todd. What was he saying? Where did he come from?

"Daniel? Daniel, what happened?"

"Not … Daniel," he said weakly. "This one is … Danon."

Chief Todd and Thomas looked at each other in surprise. The ICU nurse leaned over the gurney to adjust the I.V.

"It's all right," she said soothingly. "Calm down, you're back home."

He tried to focus on the creamy face before him. She looked familiar. Why was the room still spinning, blurring his thoughts? Past memories slowly returned. The violent re-entry. His return to the capsule. The timequake. The Clan. The burning image of Lauriel and the Clan disappearing.

He had to save them. He tried to kick off the sheets and sit up, but felt entangled by some giant spider's web. He tried to brush it away.

Again the nurse tried to calm her patient. She struggled to reattach the I.V. tube that had snapped from his arm, dripping fluid on the spattered floor. But he started tugging on the telemetry lines, ripping electrode patches off his chest.

"They need me," he said with a pleading voice.

He looked up to the frightened nurse and mistook her for someone else he had disappointed.

"Cristina? I'm sorry, Cristy. Please, must get back. They need me …"

His tortured body finally collapsed and surrendered to the sedatives.

Thomas nudged his way forward, staring at his friend.

"What was all that about?" the nurse asked.

"He must be in shock. He doesn't know what he's saying. Cristina has been gone for a while."

She adjusted the biomonitor and checked all the connections. "He just needs to sleep off the medication."

"He's lucky to be alive. He must have pulled close to twelve 'G's." Thomas stared at the full beard. "Next time he wakes up, maybe he'll be able to explain some things. Like where he found that two-hundred-year-old Indian buckskin."

She straightened the sheets and paused before returning to her observation chair. Even unconscious the inner conflict of some unknown agony showed through. She had never met Daniel, but she had heard plenty from her friends. She stared with wonder at the full beard everyone claimed had appeared on a clean shaven face only a few minutes ago.

She watched the troubled sleeper tossing on the damp pillow. He was different from what she had expected. Despite the beard she was amazed by so many wrinkles. This man looked much older than the one she had heard of. She wasn't cleared for any details of the secret experiment that had given her this patient, and she would have understood little of the physics involved, but she knew that the man on her critical care bed was wrestling with his destiny. And like any good nurse she felt the burning desire to hold and comfort him.

Chief Todd left explicit orders with the nurse to be called immediately when Daniel became lucid. Then he motioned Thomas into the hall.

"We have to talk," he said with a tone of urgency. "Plans have to be made."

Thomas nodded understandingly as he glanced back to Daniel and his guardian angel.

"What has he got that does that to women? Even semi-comatose, he still mesmerizes them."

# # #

Daniel awoke slowly, the sedatives gradually wearing off. The bright white walls were still there, but not as glaring as before. He realized that he was back in the past present. Although the sanitized white enamel and chrome looked only vaguely familiar, as if they were from a distant time or another life, it was the smell. He recognized the sweet trace of alcohol and bitter disinfectant that lingered in the carefully filtered air of the intensive care unit. He was back in the complex.

When he tried to sit up, a sharp pain knifed through his upper arm into his shoulder. The plasma bolt. He rolled his arm to look at the small bandage of adhesi-patch clinging to the back of his arm. The stuff used to cover burns. Pinkish skin surrounded the patch, puffy and slightly swollen.

At least it wasn't roast.

A large plastic curtain separated him and his IV bottle from the rest of the sterile ward. Only the chrome breakfast tray stood beside him for comfort, and it was empty. He stared at the plastic curtain, squinting to see through the opaque barrier. He listened intently, but heard no one. Only the faint, breezy whispers of the ventilator grate above his head and a growling from his stomach. He swung his heavy legs off the bed and onto the cold tile floor.

"Where's my clothes!"

"Oh, God!" came an exclamation in return, followed by the sound of clacking footsteps racing across the tile floor toward him. Unrecognizable voices shouted in the distance, no doubt announcing his return to consciousness. Moments later his guardian angel returned, skidding around the edge of the curtain as her hard soled white shoes slid across the polished floor.

"I was only gone for a moment, I swear!" Her face was flushed. "How are you feeling, Mr. Williams?"

"Mister? I'm not that old, darling. But I am a little hungry, no very hungry. How about a steak sandwich." He glanced down at the stylish hospital gown. "And some clothes."

"I don't think so. I'll send an orderly for some carbohydrate blend."

"Skip it. Just hand me by pants. I'll grab some real food on the way to the launch room. In fact, I need a whole sack of stuff back with me for the others. Call the cafeteria and have them start packing."

"Mr. Williams, if you don't calm down, I'll be forced to give you another sedative. We can't subject your body to any undue stress."

Daniel offered his most charming grin. "You're a very attractive medtech, but I've had a heck of a day."

"I'm a nurse," she said with a firm, correcting voice. "And a nurse can tell you what to do. Now get back in that bed."

"What's all the commotion?" Thomas poked his head around the curtain. "Did somebody return from the dead?"

The determined nurse tugged the wrinkles out of her smock. "I was just about to use physical force on our stubborn patient here."

"Tom! Tell this woman who I am and that if she doesn't get out of my way, she's fired."

"How about I get you a milkshake?" he suggested, stepping between them.

"A what? Well, it sounds better than a curdled protein supplement." The nurse pulled a syringe from her pocket and took a step toward the hanging IV bottle.

"Okay, okay." Daniel sat back down on the bed to wait for his milkshake.

"It's alright," Thomas said. "I'll watch him and you can send an orderly to the cafeteria. Now run along, aren't you supposed to give the Chief a call?"

She flashed warning glare. "If you let him get out of bed, I'll personally put you in traction."

"Yes, Ma'am." He waited till she disappeared around the curtain, then turned to Daniel. "You still look green around the edges."

"Just a little queasy, I'll be all right. Help me up."

"The heck I will. She sounded serious. Just take a look at yourself. Your eyes are beet red from busted capillaries, a sure sign of G-stress syndrome. Some soccer team used your face for practice. There's a third degree radiation burn on your shoulder. And I'm still dying to know how you grew a full beard in a microsecond?"

"It's plasma."

"What?"

"The burn, it's from a plasma rifle."

"There's no such thing as a plasma rifle." He looked around the empty room. "Except for the prototype in the Nuke shop."

"You mean not yet. How long has it been? How long was I out?"

Thomas glanced at his watch. "Nearly twenty-four hours."

"Damn! I gotta hurry, they need me."

"You're not going anywhere. In case Miss Nightingale didn't tell you, you almost died yesterday."

"Yeah, that's been happening a lot lately. How's the capsule? Is it ready for another trip?"

Thomas looked dumbfounded. "What kind of drugs was she giving you? You're not going anywhere, especially in the capsule, or what's left of it."

"Why, what happened?"

Thomas shrugged. "Who knows? The tachyon drive went to pieces. Then it screwed up the inertial balancer and that's when we almost lost you."

"So, how long will it take to put it back together?"

"Are you listening? It's gone, Danny. Nothing but pieces. A million-dollar bucket of junk. Your controlled re entry went to hell in a hand basket."

"No it didn't. I tried to prevent it. If you can't fix it then we'll have to build another one."

Thomas took a seat and shook his head. "Even if we could, the Chief wouldn't authorize another experiment. They're still picking up the pieces down in Special Projects. And there's something defective with the drive, it's too dangerous."

"No it isn't. The tachyon unit worked perfectly; at least it did until I modified it with a fire axe."

Thomas stared blankly. "You did what?"

"Hand me some clothes first," Daniel said, clutching the exposing gap behind him. "This gown is a little humiliating."

Thomas pulled a folded jumpsuit from the locker and tossed it on the bed. "I brought this by earlier. Didn't figure you would want to wear that ridiculous Indian costume."

Daniel choked down a stinging reply and let the surgical gown slip to the floor. "Where's the Chief? I sort of expected him to be here by now."

"Don't worry, he's on his way. He said he had some 'clean up' to do first." Thomas pulled the stained buckskins from the clothing locker and held them up. "By the way, where the heck did this come from? And what is it?"

"It's the ceremonial dress of a Clan May'r. Actually it's wedding attire."

Thomas gave a puzzled look. "You were wearing it when you returned. Why?"

"Because," he said in a slow, deliberate manner, "I'm a Clan May'r."

"I think you're losing it, Danny, right over the edge."

"How long was I gone?"

"Come on, you know as well as I do." He tossed the buckskins back into the locker. "Timeslip duration is less than a millionth of a microsecond."

"Maybe for here, but not there."

"Where?"

"The future."

"You made it? You actually made it?"

"Where do you think I changed my clothes? I spent over three months in the future, 2130 A.D. to be exact."

Thomas waited for a punch line that wouldn't come. He shook his head. "But I was there. The power up sequence, the double-spike energy burst, and then re entry. It was all over in less than a few minutes."

"Three micro-seconds here, three months there. You can figure out the math if you want, but I don't care. The bottom line is that I was there. And I thought I was going stay there, that's where the fire axe comes in."

"I can almost believe that part."

"Tom, I found something there worth fighting for."

Thomas grinned. "A woman?"

"No, something more important. Okay, yes there's a woman. But not just a woman, the woman."

"You're scaring me now, Dan. I know you better than a brother and you've never gotten that serious over any woman before. You disappear for an eye-blink and then tell me you've met Miss Wonderful?"

He smiled and nodded. "Yeah, I guess I did. Her name is Lauriel and she's my wife, sort of. The ceremony got cut short."

Thomas removed his glasses and sat on the bed.

"It's more than just her. It's where I belong. I'm the leader of a clan of post-holocaust refugees. Can you believe it, me a leader?"

Daniel tried to balance himself on one foot and slip the other into the jump-suit. He gave up and sat down.

"That's why I have to get back, they're depending on me."

Thomas stood up with a disturbed expression. "Maybe you stay in bed longer."

"What's wrong?"

"You really are scaring me now. I don't know if it's the drugs, or some mind-altering side-effect of tachyon radiation. But you're not the same Daniel that I strapped into that capsule two days ago."

"Actually, they called me Danon."

"Okay, that does it. I might be the only crazy parrot in the cage, but I can't handle all this right now."

"Are you saying you won't help me get back?"

"I've already told you. You can't. The Timeslip Project is history. It's been canceled."

"By whom? This is my project, my responsibility. What idiot thinks he cancel my project?"

"I did!"

The startling voice came from the doorway. Chief Todd clutched his crutches for support, but still managed to give his famous intimidating stare. He focused it on Thomas.

"Are you through welcoming our time pilot to the land of the conscious? I though you had a project to work on."

"Yessir." Thomas made a hasty lurch for the door.

"As for you," he said, facing Daniel. "I imagine you want to talk to me."

"You could say that."

"Good. If you're adequately recuperated, why don't you finish putting your pants on and we can begin your debriefing."

Daniel had started getting dressed; but between his dizziness and argument with Thomas, he hadn't finished.

"It's a long story, Chief. Too long for right now. The important thing is the need for one more trip."

Chief Todd leaned back, aiming himself as he collapsed into the solitary chair near the foot of the bed.

"As Thomas so aptly explained, that impossible."

"Chief, you don't understand."

"Then perhaps you could enlighten me. Exactly what happened?"

# # #

Chief Todd listened calmly, without so much as a raised eyebrow, as Daniel gave a quick recital of his adventure: global war, black supremacy, the Clan, and the police attack. When he finished his story, Chief Todd nodded sympathetically and pulled himself up to depart.

"You can see why it's imperative that I return immediately?"

Chief Todd placed a hand on Daniel's shoulder. "I'm sure it seems real at the moment. A near death experience can be most vivid, but after you've rested and regained your strength this fantasy will have faded quite a lot and you will soon realize what is truth and what isn't."

"You don't believe me? Then explain this!" he said, holding up the sued leather pants and jacket.

"I'm afraid those are still a mystery at the moment, and will probably remain so."

Daniel studied the aged face of the Chief Administrator. The man who questioned everything had not raised a single objection to his entire story.

"You know it's true, don't you?"

What I know is that machine of yours approached catastrophic failure. Fragments of tachyon drive were scattered everywhere, embedded in the capsule, and fused to the inner surface of the tube. The Complex as a whole sustained nearly a million dollars damage as the result of its violent energy discharge."

"You know I broke the time barrier, but you don't care."

Chief Todd made another effort to stand up, but said nothing.

You're shutting down a successful project and accepting a total financial loss. Why?"

"The outcome of your experiment was not important. Me allowing you to complete it was all that mattered. You needed the experience of heading a large-scale, joint project. The experience you gained was the completion of your training. Now you are ready."

"For what?"

Chief Todd fought to suppress a cough as he climbed atop his crutches and headed for the door. "You know the answer to that question."

"We had a deal!"

"Yes, and I kept my part of that deal. When you feel you have fully recuperated, I'll see you in my office. To take your position as acting Chief Administrator."

"They need me, somewhere out in the future."

"No, Daniel. You belong in the present. And you are needed here."

\# # #

Daniel looked both ways before he slipped out of the ICU ward and into the hall. He was quietly checking himself out of Bio-Med. It had taken Daniel another day to convince medical he wasn't crazy. He didn't say anymore about his "near death experience" so his nurse had stopped sedating him. During his needed bed rest, Daniel realized his return did not have to be immediate. He could control time itself. He would somehow repair the capsule and return to his Lauriel in what would become only moments following his departure. He had to appear restrained and recuperated. He had to be covert.

The smell of alcohol and antiseptic disappeared as soon as the mechanical door closed behind him. He darted into the corridor of people to look for Thomas. Just as before, the flow of traffic up and down the corridors of the fourth level continued. Night and day, people scurried along like blood through an artery keeping the research organization healthy and productive. As he watched workers carry their test tubes of colorless liquids and computer printouts, this life didn't seem as important as it once did. And after spending two months in a wide-open cavern, he felt strangely cramped by the narrow hallway and nameless faces that squeezed past him.

A shout startled him. "Hi, love, missed you at the pub. Maybe tonight?"

The passing face disappeared in the crowd before he could recognize it. The voice and perfume were familiar, but he couldn't put a name with them. He continued down the corridor to the sealed, double doors of Special Projects. He reached for his identicard, but it wasn't there.

He couldn't remember when he last had it. It had been in his jumpsuit when he went into the future, but he never needed it there. He searched further back—or forward—in his memory. When donning the warrior's leathers, he had left the dirty bundle of used boots and jumpsuit in Lauriel's lodge. He'd never thought about them or his card since.

He opened a small square panel to one side of the card slot beside the door, punched the numbered buttons to call Thomas, and waited. He heard the intercom buzz. It buzzed again, but no one answered.

He entered the guard shack's number, and a bored voice answered.

"Level Five—restricted access."

"This is Danon, I mean Daniel Williams. Let me in."

He heard an accusing chuckle. "What's the matter? Forget your I.D. again?"

"Yeah, whatever." He waited a few impatient moments. "Well?"

The heavy, reinforced doors opened and he stepped through to the guard desk.

"Sort of a late start, isn't it?" The guard pointed a thumb to the clock behind him. "Must be nice to sleep in and still get paid for a full day's work."

"How about a temp, okay?"

"Touchy, too. Must've been some party last night. Here, lean over." The security guard took one of the LEVEL FIVE—NO ESCORT REQUIRED badges and pinned it to Daniel's jumpsuit. "Be sure you turn that back in."

"Thanks."

Daniel scooted around the desk and passed on, straight to the end of the hall, past Thomas' office, to the launch room. It was locked. He went to the control room.

Workers in blue jumpsuits struggled to load a large box onto a short dolly. The main computer console was gone, leaving only a shelfless table extension near the wall. He looked anxiously for the junction box that connected the master power panel to the launch room. He was too late. A dozen large gauge wires protruded from the box, their ends cut short and sealed with insulation caps. An electrician was installing a cover panel to conceal the wires and prevent tampering.

He strained to look through the thick plastic viewport, then sighed with relief. He could see the tube, the power transformer, and all the interconnecting cables. Everything appeared functional as soon as he managed to repair the capsule's propulsion system. That shouldn't take too long. Then he noticed the capsule was missing.

"Can I do something for you, Danny?"

He turned to recognize one of the assist techs who had helped on the project. "Where's the capsule?"

"Didn't you know? It's down at the Nuke shop. Thomas wanted to find out what went wrong." He turned to pick up another box. "Yeah, I heard it shredded like a—Hey! Where you going?"

# # #

Thomas looked up with surprise from the stack of design drawings scattered in front of him. "Danny, you're out? I thought they'd hold you in Medical for a while. I guess you're even tougher than I thought."

"We need to talk." He didn't return Thomas' smile. Turning his back to the two assistants who huddled around the nearby table, he leaned closer and whispered, "Privately."

Thomas fumbled to rearrange his glasses. "Well, sure." He pointed to one of the glass-topped cubicles. "In there?"

As they stepped inside, Thomas struggled to maintain his nervous smile.

"Why so glum?"

Daniel looked around, making sure no one was listening. "Where's the capsule?"

"The capsule? I don't know. The Nukes got really upset about being blamed for the drive problem. They stripped it bare, looking for a failure mode. I guess it's still there, probably in a dozen different parts bins."

"Can it be put back together?"

"Back together? Did you talk to the Chief?"

"Stop repeating everything I say. I told you before, Tom. I'm going back."

Thomas leaned back in the Plexiglas chair. "I can't believe I'm hearing this. For a genius, you sure are dumb. Chief terminated the project, impounded the console, and even disconnected the power cables. There's no way we can …"

"Let me worry about the simple stuff. What I want to know is can you reassemble the drive unit?"

"No. It was destroyed, remember?"

"But you know everything about it. You designed it. You could build another one, right?"

Thomas fidgeted uneasily in his chair. "There are some pretty exotic materials required in the construction of one of those tachyon drives. It's not exactly like going down to Wal-Mart for supplies."

"Give me a straight answer, Tom. Are you going to help me or not?"

"Do you realize what you're asking? That's willful disobedience of an explicit directive. I mean we've done some things in the past, but never a flagrant disregard for the Chief's authority."

"Don't forget who's going to be the next Chief Administrator."

Thomas leaned back and raised a bushy eyebrow. "That sounds like a threat. Is it?"

Daniel kicked open the door of the cubicle. He thought Thomas was his friend. He was wrong. He turned back. "What about your drawings and design layouts?"

"Dan, try to understand."

"Sure …" Daniel walked to the door. "I know all about loyalty."

# # #

The office was empty. Two shiny, chrome framed chairs glistened under the harsh office light. The antique mahogany desk was still there, littered with notes and calculations left two days ago. He walked over to the desk and picked up some of the papers he had been working on just prior to his timeslip.

Two days, he thought. Such a long time. So much had happened since then. He dropped the papers back onto the jumbled pile when he noticed his buckskins folded neatly on the couch. Someone had given up trying to explain their existence by lab analysis and simply returned them to his office where their enigmatic appearance could be forgotten. They weren't quite as inspiring as the first time he had seen them. Their bone-bleached whiteness had turned dull beige with cave dust, and the trip through the caverns had left random smudge marks and a small tear in one trouser leg.

He ran his hand over the fine beadwork of the vest plate. He reached inside the jacket and pulled the ruffled crimson feather. He shuddered as he recalled her long ebony hair and defiant green eyes.

"I'll be back," he promised softly.

He closed his hand softly around the feather and the whispered promise. Somehow he would get back. What could he do? He could steal the plans for the propulsion unit from Thomas. But that didn't seem right. Thomas was his friend, just in his own way. He followed his own simple code of ethics. He didn't agree with his friend, but he had to respect him. He didn't want to do anything that would implicate Thomas, but he had to have those plans.

The capsule would have to be retrieved and returned to the launch room without arousing any attention. Easy enough, he thought, but the antimagnetic repulsion field required critical precision. He couldn't do it manually. He needed to find another computer that could carry out the tasks of the main control unit which the Chief had removed. Not so easy. There was so much to do and he was beginning to feel helpless. Once more he felt all alone, with only a rainbow of memories. The first time he had seen her through the flames of the tribal fire; her graceful stance when stalking prey; his stolen glimpse of her at the bathing pool; the first time she had smiled at him; the stunning beauty of her bonding dress, and that look of surprise when the timequake had separated them.

How had it managed to suck him back in time? Although there was much concerning Timeslip physics that he admittedly was uncertain of, he had been confident that a functional capsule was required in order to return. He had destroyed the propulsion unit and even left the capsule outside of the tube. Lastly, he was nowhere near the capsule when it was activated. So why did he come back? How did he return?

Had his entire time spent in the past future occurred in that fraction of an instant between chronotons? One moment he was spinning at max velocity and the next moment, he was ... still there, spinning around inside his damaged capsule. But he had spent over three months in the future.

He went over and over the possibilities, mumbling to himself as he searched for an answer. What determined the length of the trip? Why did he arrive in

2130, why not 2150 or 2230? Was it the amount of power? Rate of acceleration? What was it?

"What's the answer!" he shouted in frustration.

"Is that a direct question?"

"What?" He looked around, startled by the unexpected reply.

"Shall I repeat the question?" asked the speaker on the wall.

"Oh, it's you." He'd forgotten about the constant eavesdropping by the central computer system, and he wasn't in the mood for interruptions.

"Turn it off, VAL. I don't have the time to tell you my troubles and you couldn't understand anyway." He headed for the door. "What I really need is the design specs on the tachyon drive."

"Working," VAL responded. "Please wait while processing data."

But Daniel didn't wait.

CHAPTER 32

Daniel stood at the entrance of the Nuke shop, waiting for the door to open. He rang the buzzer again, an inconvenience which was beginning to annoy him. The next thing he had to do was stop by Admin for another identicard.

The door finally opened. The surprised face behind it was named Bill, according to the nametag on his blue smock. Bill had a boyish face with a bird's nest of frizzy red hair. "Danny! What are you buzzing for?"

"Lost my card somewhere."

"Again?"

Daniel frowned and walked in as Bill ran his fingers through his hair in an attempt to neaten it up. It didn't help.

"So, what do you need?"

"I was wondering. You think I could pick up the capsule? If you're through with it, I mean." He tensed, ready for the argument that would follow. Chief Todd had probably impounded everything, but Daniel was ready to fight, or steal, in order to get it.

"Mind? Heck no," Bill answered. "About time someone came to get it out of here."

"It is?"

"Sure, just taking up space, you know? We don't have room to store a bunch of useless parts. Just look at all these abandoned projects." Bill walked through the cluttered room, waiving to shelves of forgotten equipment. "I called Salvage over an hour ago, told them they were supposed to take all the garbage the first time. They said they'd take care of it, but you know how Salvage is."

"You called Salvage?" Daniel nervously looked for the capsule.

"Yeah. Like I said, maybe an hour ago. Didn't they send you?"

"Oh yeah, sure. So where is it? You have the failed drive unit, too?"

"Our unit didn't fail! We build good stuff. Why does everybody try to blame us when some schmuck's crappy design won't work? If you ask me, looks like some jerk tried to calibrate it with an axe."

Daniel did not reply.

# # #

He returned to his office with the loaded cart and hurriedly wheeled it inside. So far his plan was failing miserably. He had tried to hide the awkward load in the launch room, but had been unable to get inside. When he slid his brand new identicard through the slot, nothing had happened. The electronic lock indicator simply ignored his card. He had tried repeatedly, barely escaping notice when two assist-techs from Salvage had come whistling around the corner.

VAL's speaker terminal came alive with a flurry of questions and comments.

"I have made several attempts to locate you, Daniel. You requested information but failed to specify where I should deliver it. Chief Todd has left two messages, the second of which stated that the first should be considered 'urgent.' Thomas called once, but left no message." The computer paused for a brief moment. "Which item do you wish to address first?"

Daniel shoved the cart and the capsule inside the closet. Something wasn't right, he knew. The Chief's security access surpassed his only in respect to certain archive files locked away in VAL's memory cubes. And since he had full access to any space in the Complex, the Chief couldn't lock him out without changing the entire security program.

"Excuse me," VAL said with his mechanical persistence. "You have another urgent call from Chief Todd."

"Tell him, tell him I'm not here yet."

"That would be an inaccurate statement."

"Okay, hold on. Don't go video yet, just audio." He closed the door as Chief Todd's presence boomed into the room.

"Daniel Williams! My office, now."

# # #

CHIEF ADMINISTRATOR. The boldface sign above the door seemed especially intimidating today as he stood in front of the unsmiling receptionist. Anita Jenkins only had two expressions; one was unpleasant, the other reminded him tuck his shirt in and stand up straight.

"Afternoon, Ms. Jenkins, I'm here to …"

"It's evening," she said to correct him, her eyes never leaving the desk. "And the Chief is expecting you."

Of course he is, he thought, like a lion expects a dinner guest.

A short hall with highly polished stainless walls led to Chief Todd's office. As soon as Daniel stepped in, the pressure of his foot tripped a closure mechanism and a steel door slammed shut behind him. It only took a moment for the system to grant him access to the double-walled, insulated oval office, but not before it had taken a full-body x-ray and scanned for radio frequency emitters. He hated the cramped exclusion zone and he hated to think about what all those x-rays were doing to him. Most of the engineers never had to worry about the cumulative exposure, but then they followed orders like robots and were seldom summoned to the inner sanctuary.

A second door in front of him slid open to reveal the oval shaped office. Chief Todd sat behind his teak and chrome executive desk. The white fluffs of disappearing hair circled his balding head like little clouds over a pink sea.

"Sit down, Daniel," he said pleasantly, a little too pleasantly. "I take it you're feeling much better."

"Yeah, I guess."

"Especially since you decided not to stay in Medical under their supervision."

"They ran out of sedatives."

The Chief stifled a smile which would have ruined his demeanor. "I want you to start acting more responsibly. You are the next chief administrator of this place. Start acting like it."

Daniel said nothing as Chief Todd continued to explain the meaning of responsible. He already knew what it meant. He'd accepted complete responsibility for the Clan. And now he was responsible for a thousand clansmen being trapped somewhere inside a mountain of stone.

The Chief struggled to stand without his crutches.

"I can't even do this anymore!" His knees buckled, landing him heavily back into the padded chair. "In case you haven't noticed, I'm aging faster than ever."

Daniel nodded. He had noticed the signs of accelerated deterioration: creased wrinkles, cottony hair, and arthritic joints.

"Are you paying attention?"

"Yes, you don't have much time left. I realize that, sir …"

"Damn it, Daniel! I'm dying. And whether you think you're ready or not, you must take over. This is your office now."

"It needs redecorating."

"I want you to attend the Departmental meeting tomorrow morning."

"Yes, sir."

Chief Todd reached for another cigar, but didn't light it as he studied Daniel's response.

"Is that all?"

"No, as part of your indoc, I had Ms. Jenkins prepare a series of briefs on current projects, financial budgeting, and a few personnel moves." He pointed to a stack of folders that would gag a briefcase.

"Papers?"

"You will soon discover that Ms. Jenkins has a few quirks to contend with. But she is very good at her job."

Daniel scooped up the folders. "It's a little cramped in here. If you don't mind, I'll take these back to my office, my old office."

"Those should keep you busy for the rest of the day. I'll see you tomorrow at the meeting. It's only the beginning, but you need to understand the basic premise of every project."

"By the way, Thomas is working on the Crystaltronic Project," he added as if an afterthought. "As outlined in one of those briefs, he'll be devoting his full efforts to staying on schedule. So leave him alone."

Daniel nodded. "I think I have enough to keep me busy for a while."

# # #

Daniel returned to his office and tossed the heavy stack of papers on the couch.

"VAL, respond."

"Acknowledge and standing by, Mister Williams."

"Mister?"

"As the new acting Administrator, protocol requires a more formal epithet."

"Yeah, whatever. Room 602, is it a standard cipher lock?"

"Affirmative, a standard Yale cardkey series."

"Are there any combinations in excess of Level Five clearance?"

"Negative, Five is the highest physical security."

"Then why can't I open it? It didn't blink, it didn't change color, it didn't even flash access denied."

"One moment, please. The security log shows that lock to be currently non-functioning."

"What do you mean?"

"Cipher lock 602 has been temporarily disabled. I have been instructed to ignore it."

"By whom?"

"One moment please. The security log entry was made by Chief Administrator Todd."

Daniel stopped to think. "Did he place any restrictions?"

"Negative."

"Then, if I wanted you to reactivate it and install a new combination, you could do it?"

"That is a viable possibility should it become an executive directive."

Daniel wheeled the cart out of the closet. "It just did. Reactivate immediately, using the last five digits of my social for the combo."

"Affirmative. Now, Mr. Williams, if you would please specify the format for the information you requested?"

"What information?"

"The design specifications and blueprint drawings for the tachyon drive."

Daniel was confused. "You have them? I didn't think they were on file."

"The information was posted a few hours ago."

"Who posted it?"

"One moment please. Pre-archive file received from Special Electronics division, posted by Thomas Caudle."

"Tom? But why would he ..." He stopped in concentration. Thomas had filed all the data in a Level Five archive file. Unless directed otherwise, an abandoned project is placed on indefinite hold until all research information is dumped into an archive file. His friend had followed standard procedure, followed every rule to the letter, but had still managed to give him what he needed. That was another one he owed Tom.

# # #

He waited for the lock to activate. An occasional assist tech walked by, but they paid no attention to him or his covered cart. He hoped.

When the red light flickered on, he fumbled to insert his identicard. Heard the solid click and was pushing the door open when an unexpected voice came from behind.

"What are you doing?"

Daniel jumped and spun around. "Tom, don't sneak up on me like that."

"Sorry, I didn't know you were so jumpy. What are you up to?"

He glanced around. "Nothing."

"Danny?"

"It's better if you didn't know. Really."

Thomas examined the lumpy tarp for a moment. "We haven't been able to talk since ..."

"I know, since I stormed out."

"Since you screamed, kicked my door off, and then stormed out."

"Sorry."

Thomas shrugged as if it were dropped and over with. "The word is getting out, you know. Not about being crazy, but about being appointed as the next chief administrator. There are several pissed off department heads who think their seniority is being slighted."

"So let them have the job. Suits me just fine."

"I see. So ..." He patted the side of the wrinkled tarp. "What are you doing with the capsule?"

"What capsule? How did you know?"

He gave a satisfied smile. "Just a guess. I was hoping maybe you'd forget the crazy notion. The project really is over, you know."

"It is." He glanced down both ends of the corridor. "Officially."

"The Chief is going to skin you alive if he catches you. But if he doesn't, you'll be the new Chief and then who'll care?"

"Tom, you still don't get it. I have no intention of becoming an administrator. I didn't imagine anything. It was real, and I'm going back."

"I know."

"You do?"

"You told me to go do the math, right? Well I did and I think I found the missing equation. You do know that you'll have to adjust the settings to arrive later than the first time, don't you?"

"I thought you didn't want to get involved. There might be some trouble later. What am I saying, there'll be a lot of trouble."

Thomas placed a hand on his friend's shoulder. "I'm not exactly one of the social butterflies around here. If this lab mushroom didn't get involved in some of your crazy schemes, I wouldn't have any social life at all. Besides, you can't pull it off without me, and you know it."

# # #

The door was deactivated as arranged. Daniel stashed the capsule and plans inside the launch room. Having VAL remove power from the lock when they were not around prevented any accidental intrusions. It also helped to conceal the room's continued use. If anyone happened to check, the cipher lock would still appear dead and unused as the Chief had intended. The room would be ideally secluded for his purposes. He could work in privacy without fear of discovery.

The weeks passed slowly as they began to gather the parts and supplies needed for reconstruction. Spare parts were harder to come by than he had supposed. The cost in favors was high. Thomas joined him in the launch room every periodically, assisting in the reassembly of the capsule's components. They worked nights, early mornings, or whenever they could find the time and still remain inconspicuous to the daily routine of the Complex, which became increasingly more difficult. Daniel had to take more frequent tours with Chief Todd as he was prepped to assume control of the facility, forcing Thomas to assume even more of the burden. That was another one Daniel owed him.

CHAPTER 33

Daniel arrived for work early, his first cup of coffee still steaming in his hands, and went straight to Special Electronics lab. He didn't even pause to return the random greetings from the invisible people he passed in the corridor. He wanted to know how Thomas had made out with the alignment.

If anyone could get the drive unit working, it was Thomas. He had probably worked all night on it, Daniel thought as he entered the lab. He glanced at his watch to remind himself of the Department Head meeting in half an hour. The night crew had left early, as they did every chance they could, leaving a few comfortable minutes of secrecy. He would slip in and retrieve it before the regular crew reported for work.

Scanning the cluttered bench tops and storage shelves, he found the power unit near the back wall, plugged into one of the test benches. Then he heard a groan from the other side of the acrylic partition.

"Tom?"

Another groan followed. "Is it morning?"

Thomas was slumped over in his chair, half sprawled on the top of a stainless workbench. "I was only going to take a short nap."

"You've been here all night, haven't you?"

"I, uh. Yeah …" He stopped to yawn. "I got the generator coarse tuned, but needed a full power check for the fine stuff."

"Full power? We need special shielding, and the launch room is the only place around that has it. But I haven't been able to reconnect full power there, yet. I ran out of favors."

"It has now," Thomas said with another yawn.

"How?. The power leads were terminated in the control room and there's no computer to monitor the energy flow."

"There is now, I tapped directly into facility power. And reprogrammed VAL's priority vectors so he could monitor it."

"Are you crazy, VAL knows? What if the Chief asks him?"

"What am I, a computer idiot? I took care of that, too. Just rearranged some jump vectors, nothing major, but it should block any access by his random logic circuits. Any unwanted inquiries will get lost in an endless loop. I think."

"You think?"

"You got any better ideas?"

"You always were grouchy after waking up, but at least you didn't throw anything. Here ..." Daniel offered his coffee. "You need this more than I do. How soon before it can actually make a run?"

"Tonight," Thomas mumbled into the hot mug.

"Are you serious, tonight?"

"No, we could run it up right now if you want, but somebody might notice when the building starts to shake."

"I'll take your word for it. Thanks, Tom. You're great."

Thomas shrugged. "Wait till you get my bill. I'll clean up and then take it to the launch room. For your sake, I wish we could test it to make sure it works."

"It'll work, what could go wrong?"

Thomas sipped his coffee. "Do you really want me to answer that? I can think of at least six different catastrophic failure modes—"

"Never mind. I'd like to keep my positive outlook."

"Okay, but there is one thing I have to warn you about." He sat the cup down slowly. "You know that this trip can't be permanent."

Daniel shrugged. "It doesn't matter, I have to go."

"I reviewed the report on your last telemetry data, then ran some calculations with VAL. When you slipped out of the time continuum, you returned to the exact nano-instant you left."

"So? I don't get to stay; I already figured that part out."

"You won't be able to stay long at all. VAL's hypothesis is that the timeslip event causes a rift in the fabric of space/time which creates a vortex of instability. This vortex stays attached to you and is somehow anchored between the chronotons you slipped through."

"Like a giant cosmic rubber band? Okay, so that's why I came back. You haven't explained when I come back."

"I can't. But I'd bet the farm that it will much quicker this time."

Daniel noticed the flashing message on his watch. "I'd like to stay and discuss vortex elasticity, but I'm late for the meeting. Again!"

# # #

"Sit down, Daniel," Chief Todd said with a falsely polite tone. His unlit cigar squirmed like a helpless victim of a shark attack. "I assume we can start now. Now that everyone is here."

Daniel took his seat at the long table for the Monday morning meeting. Chief Todd cleared his throat to begin the meeting.

"This morning we will review each of your summaries regarding current research status. Then we have a couple of proposed new projects."

The Chief's voice droned in the background. Daniel was already lost in his own thoughts. He hated departmental meetings, and he hated having to endure one. He was well aware how each department contributed to the overall success of the Complex. Occasionally a salable product would be developed and refined, a product which would eventually be sold in secrecy to one of the major global companies for production and marketing. That revenue was the lifeblood of complex. He knew that. It funded their very existence. He knew all about the importance of continued development and marketing, but today it didn't seem important when compared to his impending trip. With a little luck, he hoped, later that night he would return to Lauriel.

"Daniel!" It was a harsh whisper.

"Yes, what is it?"

Chief Todd leaned over. "Are you listening? You seem preoccupied with something today."

"Oh, no. Not at all. I mean yes, of course I'm listening."

Chief Todd squinted, then turned his burning gaze to the tall, thin figure standing at the end of the table who was trying to explain the necessity of funding some new medical project that required buying a DNA Sequencer and one thousand immune-deficient, white mice. Daniel sat straighter in his chair and tried to appear interested.

# # #

As soon as the meeting adjourned, he went to the launch room, but found it empty. He checked the abandoned control room, but the drive unit wasn't there either. Then he went to Thomas' office.

Thomas sat at his desk, stacking papers into neat piles and arranging the piles at different locations. He moved a pile to the back and started on another, seemingly indifferent to Daniel's presence.

"What is it, now?"

"I'm ready to install it" Daniel said.

"That's good. So, why are standing here. Go install it."

Daniel leaned over the desk to get his friend's undivided attention. "You said you'd bring it to the launch room? You didn't leave it in my office, did you?"

Thomas gave an annoyed look. "What are you talking about?"

"The power unit."

Thomas lowered his glasses. "Didn't you take it?"

"Of course not. That's why it's still here in the lab."

Thomas' expression grew ashen. "No, it's not."

Chapter 34

Daniel sat in the cafeteria at the farthest table from the door.

With quitting time nearing for day shift, the cafeteria was almost deserted. Only a handful of early arrivals from the skeleton night crew had stopped in for a quick cup of coffee or juice and a sweet roll. He hadn't been there long when Thomas came in and sat down.

"Are you crazy? This is the most public place in the Complex."

"And the only place with no surveillance monitors," Daniel said as a reminder. "I'm not taking chances. Now, what happened to the power unit?"

"It's gone!"

Daniel frowned. "I know that. Where? You were supposed to finish and bring it later."

Thomas squinted in concentration. "I finished the cal, then locked up the lab and went for a quick shower. When I came back, it was gone. I'm sorry, Dan. Maybe Salvage …"

"No, it's not your fault. I underestimated that old codger."

Thomas' eyes widened. "You think the Chief's got it?"

"Who else?" He stood to leave.

"What are you going to do?"

"Whatever I have to."

"I don't like that look in your eyes. What does that mean?"

"It means, my non-warrior brother, that I'm going to get it back!"

"Be careful," Thomas said.

"Thanks, but I've heard that before."

# # #

Daniel closed the door to his office and locked it. "VAL, I need some answers."

"Certainly, Mister Williams. What is the question?"

"Skip the synthetic politeness, just give me straight answers or I'll personally rearrange your organic memory modules and superglue them in place! Have you had any inquiries concerning room 602?"

"Affirmative."

"Who?"

"You posed several questions regarding the deactivated cipher lock."

"Besides me, toaster head! Anyone else?"

"One moment, please." The computer was silent, and agonizingly slow.

"VAL, I'm warning you. Respond."

"Searching …"

"It's a simple question. Any other inquiries about 602?"

"You are correct. It seems a simple question; however, the answer is proving quite troublesome to find."

"Explain. A restrict code, maybe?"

"Negative, there are no active restrictions currently in effect on room 602; however, I am unable to answer confidently regarding that room."

"Cancel last instruction!" he said, remembering that Thomas had done something to alter VAL's access. "Does the Chief know about me using that room?"

"Unable to ascertain, searching …"

"Cancel! Review the last ten hours of remote terminal and video input. Correlate the coincidences of the tachyon power unit, Special Electronics division, and Chief Todd. Any common occurrences?"

"One moment, please …"

Damn, he hated that phrase. He was about to interrupt with another cancel order when the computer finally responded.

"The tachyon generator was inducted into the calibration lab of Special Electronics, sometime prior to this morning's shift. Chief Todd conducted an informal zone inspection to the area at 1023 hours. Is that the coincidence which you were looking for?"

"Could be. When the Chief left the area, what was the status of the tachyon generator?"

"Insufficient data. I can say, with high a reliability, that within one hour of the Chief's visit, the tachyon unit was no longer in the work center."

"Damn!" He slammed his fist on the mahogany desk, rattling the terminal speaker.

"Please refrain from such outbursts. They are harmful to my …"

"Skip it! New instruction. Search through the remainder of today's input. Typed files and reports. Video. Remote terminal sensing. Everything. Correlate for probable location, or possessor, of the power unit."

"Understood. One moment, please." The speaker went dead as VAL sorted vast amounts of data while handling the thousand other functions of the automated Complex.

"Mister Williams, I have a message for you from Chief Todd. He requests your *immediate* presence in his office."

"Screw the Chief."

"I shall put him on hold," VAL replied.

"Keep searching."

Where could it be? Daniel wondered. The Chief must have taken it. That's why he wanted to see him now. What if it was in his office?

"VAL, how many rooms or compartments on Level Five are presently unoccupied?"

"Exactly seven rooms, counting storage and …"

"How many of them have been entered during the last six hours?"

"My cipher lock log contains only two recorded entries, 612 and 615."

"Who opened them?"

"The log record shows Chief Todd's identicard was used in each lock."

"Can you tell me when—"

"Excuse me, Dan, there is a priority-override message coming for you."

The tonal quality of the speaker changed from the artificial voice of the computer to Chief Todd's raspy bellow.

"Daniel, get in my office. Stat!"

"Sure, Chief, I was just finishing up some minor business and on my way …"

"Don't act dumb. It doesn't become you." The speaker emitted an audible click as the connection broke off.

The Chief did know. Daniel was too close to let it slip away. If he went to the Chief now, it would all be over. If he didn't show up, his career would probably be over. He had no choice.

"VAL, the two rooms which the Chief entered, have either of the locks been deactivated?"

"Affirmative, room 615."

Daniel finally smiled. He'd found the Chief's hiding place. "Reactivate it."

"Negative."

"What?"

"Unable to comply with instruction."

"Why not?"

"Executive security restrictions are in effect. The cipher log requires personal authorization from Chief Administrator Todd before reactivating."

Daniel grabbed a fire axe off the wall. "Never mind, I have my own key." He tried to sound sure of himself, confident. But he wasn't. He started for the door, then turned back to the speaker. "VAL, notify Thomas in the Cal lab to meet me in 602."

"Understood. What about your appointment with Chief Todd?"

"Tell him, tell him I'm on my way."

"According to your pulse rate and papillary response, I do not ascertain that to be the truth."

"Remember what I said about reconfiguring your core?"

"If queried, I will assure him that you have left the office."

It was quitting time and the flow of traffic moved against him through the corridor as technicians and workers eagerly scurried out of the building. They quickly moved aside, however, for the axe swinging individual on his way to a fire, or a murder.

# # #

Thomas passed room 602. He wanted to stop, but continued slowly down the corridor until the two med techs had walked around the corner, then he ran back to the door and quickly unlocked it to slip inside.

He set the briefcase sized remote terminal on the table and made sure it was ready to tap into VAL's monitoring system. Then he went back to peek through the door and wonder what was taking Daniel so long. He jumped back and locked the door as Jake, the security guard, came running around the corner. That was the fastest he'd ever seen the retired cop move.

# # #

Daniel paused in his attack on the door to catch his breath and glance up and down the corridor. Curious workers had gathered to watch him, but kept their distance. He had obliterated the access panel on the face of the door. The destroyed lock mechanism was now splinters scattered across the floor. Still, the door wouldn't budge. He heaved the axe again, repeated blows. He was tired, swinging wildly. He leaned against the wall nearly exhausted, his heart pounding.

The crowd began edging closer to investigate. Time was running out and he knew it. He lunged toward the door. At first his shoulder was the only thing to give. Then a split second later, the battered door collapsed, and he was in.

The room was small and crammed with storage shelves draped with dark green tarps. Under each tarp rested enigmatic lumps.

He jerked the dusty tarps to the floor, revealing a collection of plastic shipping containers whose age and purpose had been forgotten long before their property stencils had faded away. Most of the stencils read BIOLOGICS, a label that hadn't been used for over a decade.

The next shelf held similar containers. He climbed over the pile of olive green covers to reach the last shelf. There it was! He cradled the power unit in his arms and started to leave, but stopped with surprise.

Jake stood in the doorway with a look of disbelief as he surveyed the mess on the floor. "Hold it, right there!" he said, pointing a shaky pistol.

Daniel started forward, smiling sheepishly.

"I said freeze."

"Jake, what are you doing?"

"I mean it! Chief rang the security alert. Ordered me to get here on the double. I'm supposed to prevent anyone from entering or leaving."

"But it's me."

"Especially you, Daniel," he said as a final warning.

"I've known you for a long time, Jake. You're not going to use that on me." He advanced slowly, eyeing the classic Colt revolver.

"No, maybe not." Jake lowered the revolver. "But I will use this." He raised an aerosol can in the other hand, a chemical incapacitate known in the security trade as SpraySTOP.

Daniel took a step back. A single drop of that chemical on a man's skin could ruin his whole day, leave him quivering for hours. A direct blast from the nozzle could even be lethal.

"Easy, Jake, you don't really want to use that either. See this Tacdrive I'm holding? It's very fragile, and very expensive. You squirt that and I'll drop like a rock, taking this with me. You want to explain to the Chief how you rescued ten kilos of scrap metal? Well, do you?"

Jake squinted in a frown. "I don't wanna explain nothing. Why don't you put that, that gizmo down real careful like. Then step over to the wall. We'll let the Chief figure it all out when he gets here."

Daniel nodded, taking a casual step forward and bending over. As he set the power unit on the floor, he computed the distance and exact position of Jake's hand. If he missed, he'd wake up tomorrow in the Chief's office, or Bio-Med.

He couldn't stop to think about it. He had to trust his instinct. As he straightened, he launched out with his right foot, breaking fingers and knocking the can free to bang against the wall. Before his next heartbeat, the second kick sent Jake flying through the door to land in a heap in the hallway.

"Sorry about that, Jake. I really am."

# # #

The door to the launch room opened before he had a chance to knock and revealed Thomas' scolding face.

"You said immediately, what took so long?"

Daniel pushed past him into the room. "Fire up the transformer, the Chief knows, alright. He's already called a security alert."

"You want to make the slip now?"

"I have no choice. They'll be here any minute."

"It's your funeral." He walked over to the workbench, opened his briefcase of electronic gadgetry, and made the link-up onto the main net as Daniel installed the power unit.

Neither one talked much as they hurried to complete their tasks. They didn't know how much time they had left. Daniel wondered if Jake was seriously hurt. What if he woke up too soon? He should have tied and gagged him. How long before Security was knocking down the door?

"Is VAL ready to monitor the power?" he asked.

"Everything's set. I've programmed the entire sequence, almost. Once I initiate the cycle, nothing can stop it." He began typing the last set of instructions into his portable terminal. "I'm not sure about the duration of max velocity phase. I'll make it twenty-six microseconds longer this time. That should land you close to the exact time you left the future."

"I thought you said you had the formula all figured out."

"I do, sort of. There is a failsafe override inside the capsule that will delay launch once I engage it. Ten seconds after you reset that switch, you're gone."

Daniel reached for the tube opening and pulled himself up. He struggled into the access hatch and crawled into the tiny cockpit. Thomas came over to pull the safety harness snug. He glanced over the harness assembly and tugged again. Satisfied, he gave a slap on the arm.

"Good luck."

Daniel tried to sound sincere. "Thanks, Tom. I couldn't have done this without you."

"Yeah, I know, you owe me one. We can discuss payback in about two minutes."

Daniel nodded. “It’s time for you to get out of here. As soon as you’re out, I’ll launch.”

Thomas lowered the hatch and tightened the bolts. He pressed the engage button on the terminal and ran to the door, which opened before he reached it. He jumped back, startled.

“I should have known you would be involved!” Chief Todd’s scornful eyes narrowed in authoritarian glare.

“You don’t understand.”

“I understand everything,” He said gruffly. “It’s over. Security, escort both of them to my office.”

“Chief, I’m more than ready to leave.” Thomas pointed over his shoulder. “I don’t want to be standing here when that tachyon drive fires off!”

Chief Todd stared at the capsule. “He wouldn’t dare endanger everyone.”

Thomas tried to twist free of the security guard gripping his arm. “He knows you’re not stupid enough to stand here and expose yourself. But he’s determined to go, regardless of the cost.”

Chief Todd continued to stare in disbelief. “He wouldn’t dare …”

A deep, throbbing hum filled the room.

# # #

Inside the capsule, Daniel waved to his friend, then rendered a hand salute to a disconcerted looking Chief Administrator. There would be hell to pay for what he’d done, and he was leaving his friend behind to pay it. But he had to go through with it. He flipped the override switch to RESET and a low vibration filled the cockpit. When he glanced out the window again, they were all gone.

Seconds later he was gratified with an instant surge of power that crushed him deep into the cushioned seat. The pressure hurt. The guilt hurt. Yet, he felt relieved. He was finally going back to where he belonged.

Chapter 35

He awoke to darkness.

The instrument panel's faint reddish glow faded and went out in the inky blackness of the capsule. He remembered his chest tugging against the harness, the skin being pulled from his face by the tremendous force of deceleration. He remembered squinting hard when eyes felt as if they were being yanked from their sockets. That was all. He looked out the blackened hatch and couldn't remember how long he had been sitting there.

He groped his way through the scratched tube to the exit port, found the emergency release, and fell to the floor. He rubbed his eyes, but it didn't help; he was still in the dark. Maybe he was blind!

He started across the room, but kicked something with his boot and heard it skitter across the floor. He held his breath, but heard nothing but his beating heart in the silence.

He bent over feel around the floor and discovered a searchlight. Had he left it before, when he had tried to destroy the capsule? He couldn't remember.

A weak beam crawled through the dusty air. Tiny dust particles sparkled as they drifted through the faint beam. It should be brighter than that, he thought. He gave it a gentle rap on the butt. It didn't help. Just a bad battery, he decided. That was strange; they were PermaStores®, guaranteed to hold a charge for at least a decade after their initial use.

He looked around the room. The emergency exit sign above the door was dead. His footprints in the floor, fresh intrusions disturbing the fine layer of dust, were mingled with others. They were different, not as distinct as his, almost obscured by the thin layer of dust.

He had to push hard to open the stubborn door leading to the corridor before making his way to the surface.

# # #

After leaving the subterranean world of the Complex, the midday sun was a welcomed harshness. His flashlight had given out, forcing him to climb four flights of stairs blindly. He looked around to ensure the same, unchanged semi-arid landscape which he knew so well. He knew it from two separate times. There was the now abandoned road which he had traveled countless times between work and home, and then there was the path by foot across the open savanna, which crossed the flats and grassy meadow where bounty hunters would lie in wait for careless warriors. The warm, dry air smelled reassuring. This was where he belonged.

He ran down the road, skirting the cracks that crisscrossed the bleached gray asphalt. He ran the entire way. He had to reach Grotto Cave. He had to find the Clan, his clan. He had to find Lauriel.

Within a few minutes he approached the cave entrance and wondered if the police were still there. Had they left? How long had it been? The entrance which was dark and cool, damp with moist air drifting up from below. He ran inside and inhaled the cool air in deep gasps. It smelled clean and refreshing. Something deep inside stirred to the subtle aromas. He was home.

At first, the vista from atop the sloping ramp seemed unchanged. Lighting panels still rimmed the giant room, casting their bluish white glow on the on the cavern floor below. Clusters of shacks and shabby tents huddled around the small clearing, crowding around the Lodge that still sat with dignity in the center. Then he noticed the difference.

The village was empty. There were no people scurrying back and forth between the dwellings, no children laughing and playing, no old women stirring their cooking pots. The dwellings looked older, more decayed. Even the cavern itself seemed dimmer than before.

He ran down the ramp and found no sign of the recent struggle, no burned shacks, no trampled tents, and no bodies lying around. He called out repeatedly, trying to raise a response as he passed dozens of dwellings on his way to the Lodge. He heard no response but his own echo. He stopped in front of his Lodge and noticed the heavy flap was missing from the door.

"Hello? Lauriel, I'm back!"

The main room was bare of furnishings. Even the painted animal skins that used to hang from the wall were gone, leaving ghostly squares of unstained wood. In the center of the floor, a few unburned coals remained in the fire pit, but mostly ashes.

He grabbed a dusty lantern from the doorpost and headed to the rear of the cavern, toward the burial chamber.

# # #

He raced through the low hanging narrow tunnel, ignoring the multi colored reflection of the lantern. Finally, he came to the small room where he had last confronted the riot police.

The room had been partially cleared of debris, the floor almost swept clean. A large boulder still rested defiantly where it had fallen, sealing the only path to the burial chamber. He searched all around anxiously, feeling around the sides and top for a crawlspace. It was useless. The passage was sealed tight.

As he climbed down off the boulder, he noticed a small parchment spiked to the limestone wall. It was yellow and brittle, encrusted with dust. He carefully blew the dust off, revealing an inscription. He recognized the top symbol and its religious significance to Atira, the Earth Mother. Below the faded symbol lay the familiar prophesy:

# # #

The visitor comes from afar … to defeat the undefeated
… to lead his people to freedom
… with great magic, the warrior sacrifices himself for those not his own
emissary to the future … leader of clans … the Supreme May'r.

# # #

He had remained there, holding the brittle parchment, for over an hour hoping someone would show up. Finally he decided to go to the city and search for answers there. He considered taking a short cut across the open prairie, but stayed on the road just in case an airbus might be making a late run. There was no use walking any farther than he absolutely had to. Yet, the long walk had stretched on.

The retreating wisps of clouds thinned into pastel feathers of pink and red. Lengthening shadows draped the sandy plains as the last traces of twilight vanished. He heard a faint whine from behind and turned. An airbus was approaching at high speed. He waived his arms to catch the driver's attention, but the headlights came up, cast a sweeping shadow around him, and passed overhead.

"Hey! You lazy Perf …" His shout was drowned out by the passing whine.

Unexpectedly the bus halted a few meters away. Its large ramp flipped outward with a rush of air and extended a polished set of boarding steps. As Daniel scrambled up the floating ramp he noticed this bus was free of scars and dents. It seemed different in style too, larger and newer.

"Almost didn't see ya," said a smiling Hispanic driver. "You're a long ways from nowhere." He sped onward, flinging Daniel backward into a seat. "Better hold on, Brother. Last run o'the night, and I'm headed home."

Daniel glanced around the bus to find half a dozen passengers. Two Blacks sat midway back on his left. Two Hispanics, or Asians, it was hard to tell in the faint glow of the coach light, shared a seat in front of them. An older man, with a prominent nose ridge and high cheekbones, reclined half asleep directly across the aisle. None of them seemed to pay any attention to his choice of seating. Relaxing a little he leaned back and realized he had sat down beside someone, an older woman with coarse black hair. She stared out through the window, unaware of his presence.

"Mind if I sit here?"

She turned around slowly. "What?" Her expression softened, finally greeting him with a brief smile.

"I can move," he said. "I wasn't expecting the driver to take off so quick and I …"

"No, it's all right. I don't mind," she said.

The aisle lighting went out. He caught only a glance. She was in her sixties, but still retained a specter of lingering beauty. Her long black hair flowed gracefully over her shoulder, complimenting a dark complexion that concealed more than a few wrinkles. Like most Native Americans, she displayed the high, defiant cheekbones of a race that could not be broken. He thought he might have seen a hint of green in her eyes, but the dome light had blanketed them in darkness once more.

"Do I know you?" she asked, leaning closer.

"No, I don't think so. I'm from …" He forced a smile. "I came from afar off."

"A stranger, huh?" she said, continuing to stare.

"Yeah." Even in the dark he could feel her penetrating gaze. For some reason it made him uncomfortable.

Her thin lips revealed a fragile smile hidden by the shadows. "I knew a stranger once …" she said, her voice trailing off as she turned to the window. She stared out through the passing night and whispered, "He, too, was from afar."

Daniel looked around the bus again. "There doesn't seem to be any rules to the seating."

She turned back to him. "I'm sorry, what did you say?"

"I mean, no one's in the back."

"Why should they?"

"Well, they shouldn't, I guess. But isn't it expected?"

"Of course not." She gave a weak laugh. "We passed that a long time ago. My, that was in the Forties. No, Thirties, during the first yars of the Great Struggle."

"The struggle?"

She had returned to staring out the window. Daniel slid closer to hear her soft voice.

"Yes, for liberty. You young'ns don't remember the struggle, do you?"

She spoke whispers of yesterday, speaking more to herself than to the stranger beside her. "I'd almost forgotten. Those were difficult yars. Organizing the different clans. Spreading the knowledge He had given us. Trying to unite the Brotherhood to stand up and speak out against the injustices. The old Perf society. They wanted to blame someone, but the true guilty were gone. Already punished."

Daniel tried to keep up, but could barely hear her over the whine of the airbus. There was something about her voice. He glanced behind, scanning the dark aisle of shadowy seats. He didn't know what he was looking for. Answers maybe. Maybe he was trying to escape the old woman's nonsense. She was obviously senile, but something in her voice bothered him, a familiar tone from a stranger.

"I was very active back then, during the early yars," she said, becoming more articulate. "A pioneer of sorts, or maybe just a rebel. It was exciting to travel from clan to clan, leading rallies, organizing marches. A few times I even spoke to the assembled brothers, reminding them of the Great Sacrifice." Her voice faltered.

"It was hard that first yar after he left. Being the first wo'am May'r was very difficult. I knew it would be, but assuming leadership over entire tribes …"

"What did you say?" Daniel had been thinking about where he would go when he got to town, but mention of the word *May'r* had startled him.

"Oh, I know. There's been several now, but back then it was, well, unheard of. I guess you're too young to remember the old ways."

"You were a May'r? A clan May'r?"

She nodded. "Back when the tribes lived in isolated clans."

"Which one? I mean, which clan?"

She pointed to the darkness behind them. "They used to live back there, in Grotto Cave."

Daniel swallowed hard. "You know them, the Grotto Clan? Where did they go?"

"Where?" She smiled condescendingly. "Everywhere. To the city, mostly. A few moved to new lodges, I mean cottages, in the country. They tried to continue the traditional life."

"The city? But it was outlawed, how could they hold property?"

She gave a look of astonishment. "Where'd you say you were from? Those laws were repealed in the forties."

"The Forties!"

Daniel slumped back in the seat, stunned. Thomas had adjusted the control settings by only twenty-six microseconds for compensation. "I figured I came back a little later, but …"

"What are you talking about?"

"What year, I mean what yar is it?"

She eyed him strangely. "2171, of course."

"But that's impossible!" He didn't notice her expression as the realization hit him. He had returned forty years too late. The police attack, the Clan's escape, and the deep underground wandering were all history, old history. He had risked everything, and for what? Nothing.

He sat brooding in silence as the airbus continued down the road and the old woman stared out the dark window and seemed to recall memories of an earlier life. Daniel had protected his heart from all other women, but one had been special. She still was.

"Excuse me, ma'am," he said to get her attention. "You must've heard about the police raid."

"The raid? You mean that night after the first rally?"

"Yes! The Clan, or most of them, tried to escape. They wandered deep into the heart of the mountain."

"Yes," she nodded as if remembering. "And came to a large domed room with no way out?"

"Yes! Then their leader, well, he disappeared. What happened then?"

She turned to study him again. "So, you have heard of the Great Sacrifice? That was a long time ago, but I still remember. I always will. Legend claimed him."

"What do you mean?"

"The Great One did something, he gave himself somehow …" Her voice failed again. "There is truth and there is legend. I still don't know the truth of what happened. But when my people gather each year around the council fires, they tell this story. The old medicine men say that he willed himself to the mountain to free his people. I don't know; legend and truth become hard to separate after so many yars. I was there and still don't know what to believe. I will admit there was powerful magic that night."

"Magic?"

"This one saw it. No warrior has ever shouted to the mountain and commanded stone to move. But the Great One did."

"What are you talking about?"

She took an unsteady breath and patted his hand like a slow pupil. "My people believe it was sacrifice of prophecy. Whatever you wish to call it, it shook the very mountain itself. The rocks crumbled and the wall collapsed to open a small fissure, a passage leading out to the surface. The journey was over. My people have always been superstitious, even now with education they still cling to the old stories, but their favorite is how the Supreme May'r gave himself to the mountain." She wiped her eyes and looked back to the window.

"Please, go on." Daniel didn't want to contradict the old woman with an explanation of timequake dynamics. Actually her version portrayed him more as hero instead of a bumbling time-traveler.

"This one never held much with tradition." She grinned impishly as if she had revealed something about herself. "But their reverence of the unknown did help a great deal. It gave many the strength to hold on when the struggle was the hardest."

Daniel studied her face in the darkness, trying for a clearer view of her eyes. "You say you were there, that means you passed through the Well of Souls?"

"Yes, this one led them out of the mountain."

"You? You led them?"

"Yes. Well, me and him." Her words held no false pride, only a statement of fact mingled with pain.

A knot was growing in his stomach. There was something in her voice. It was older, more sophisticated, but no longer the voice of a stranger. Light from a passing building glimmered in her eyes, catching a reflection of green in her eyes.

His throat tightened. It couldn't be; she was too old. And the chances of stumbling into her on a bus. It couldn't be her, but he had to ask.

"Lauriel?" he whispered hesitantly. He waited, hoping she wouldn't answer.

"How, how do you know my name?" she asked.

His heart sank. He reached into his pocket. "I think I have something of yours."

She seemed hesitant, still unsure of his intentions.

Daniel spoke softly, as he placed the feather into her hand. "Do you remember this?"

She took a light from her purse and examined his gift. It was red and downy soft.

"Amazing," she said with a gasp. "This looks just like the one I wore a long time ago as a rebel warrior. Just like the one I gave to ..." She flashed the light into his face. "Where did you get this?"

"I promised to return it. I didn't think it would take this long."

She leaned close to study his face, then sat back. "No, of course not. Tell me, who gave this to you?"

"You did." He could hardly believe the words himself.

"No, I gave this, or one like it, to my first chosen one. Over forty yars ago." She looked closely again. "You have his eyes ... are you his son? Tell me, young one! Are you Danon's son?"

He took her trembling hand in his and whispered, "On wings of pleasure, remember?"

Her eyes were now framed by wrinkles, but they could still harden to a penetrating stare that matched the tone of her voice. "He would never have told you that!"

"No. You're right about that. I would never have shared that with anyone else. Just like I could never share my rainbows of pain."

Her eyes widened in amazement and disbelief. "Danon? No, of course not. Is it really you?"

"I'm sorry, Lauriel. I tried to come back sooner. I failed."

She studied the face of the young apparition as her eyes watered in the dry night air. "This is not possible. After all these yars ... It is you. With no beard."

He grinned. "It didn't look good on me, made me look too dignified."

"I liked it," she said. "Even though it scratched when we kissed." She stopped with a sudden sigh. "Is it really you?"

He tilted her light upwards to reveal more of her weathered face, but she took it from him.

"Please don't. Is not the face you remember."

He caressed her chin, his voice soft and sincere as his eyes filled with tears. "I still love you, Lauriel. You were the only one."

"And in my heart, I have never forgotten the chosen one of my youth. For many moons after you left, I prayed that Atira would bring you back. Of course I didn't believe she would. I still can't believe ... now, and after so long. And why haven't you aged!"

Daniel smiled as he cleared his eyes. "Yeah, this is kind of weird. I'm sorry. I guess for you it's been a lifetime, but not to me. Only a few weeks ago I held you close and promised to spend forever with you." His voice started to crack.

"Don't," she said, pressing a slender finger to his lips. "Do not regret the past. You were the love of my youth, the first. And you have always walked special path in my heart. But, as you said, that was a long ago. This one has lived a full life and done all I'd ever hoped to do. I made my contribution to the Clan. I was there in the forefront of the struggle, and have earned a place of honor in our history.

"Really?"

"My name," she said with a twinkle of pride, "is mentioned at the ceremonial fires. At the annual gatherings when the elders honor the bravery of famous warriors, and when they recite the lineage of Clan may'rs, my name has been added to yours. I have known the joys of raising a child and playing with my grandchildren."

She stopped to smile at his surprise. "Yes, grandchildren. They have become successful adults in this new and different world, a world without the sanctioned bigotry and prejudices of the old Perf Society. We haven't arrived yet, but we are so much farther along than when you were here last. And we owe so much to you, my young Danon."

"Me?" His laugh was bitter. "I failed at everything I touched."

"No, it was you who taught us about equality and civil rights. You showed us how to regain it. You were—You are the greatest May'r who ever lived. It was your destiny to unite all the different clans into one ethnos. We no longer live under the guilt of Bios."

"I only gave you the idea. It sounds like you did all the work without me." He leaned closer. "Wait a minute, children? Did I, did we …?"

"No, my first chosen one," she said. "You're not derelict father. I said you were my first, but not my last. There was someone else, much later. We had a good life together, even if he never did fully understand me. You were probably the only one who did, except my father."

"Who is he, your husband?"

"You never met him, a warrior prince from the National clan. He returned to the Earth Mother a yar ago," she said, wearing the same stone face from her youth.

"Sorry."

"Don't be, you and I will both join him some day."

Daniel nodded. As a warrior he had been willing to walk that path. "But I'm still lost. What happened after the attack and the Clan's escape? Where did they go?"

Lauriel patted his arm and sighed. "I told you. Your disappearance, whatever it was, opened a passage in the cavern wall that led us to the surface. Dazjon and I led the Clan out. We spent the night out in the open plains, where they spent most of the night telling and retelling exaggerated versions of your sacrifice. By dawn, you were well on the way to legend status, having fulfilled all the fragments of prophecy.

"Prophecy? That stuff about the Supreme May'r? Like you said, that was just some old legend, remember? That wasn't me. I couldn't take care of just one clan without screwing up."

"Father recognized the signs before anyone else. The old medicine man, Benon, tried to warn me, but this one could not believe, not until I saw your spirit disappear into the cavern wall. Like it or not, that is what you became. The Supreme May'r of all clans. Sometimes legends are more powerful than heroes, and we needed one."

"Whatever, go on with your story. You went back?"

"Yes, we went back to the cave, began cleaning up and burying our dead. Some had survived the attack by hiding. And they had additional stories to add about your bravery and defense of the Clan. The other may'rs and I went public with the account of the police attack, and several major news stations carried the story. Some countries, when they heard, sympathized with our cause. Eventually they added pressure, in later yars, imposing economic sanctions against the Americas. Most importantly, the massacre served to unify the different clans. It gave them the solidarity which you sought."

"They needed that more than anything else," he said.

"Yes. Then more and more brothers chose to stand, clans this one had never heard of before. They defied the restrictions placed upon us. Some sought education; others filed grievances in the courts. Sporadic demonstrations occurred in major cities all across the country as word of the struggle spread. Occasionally there was an outbreak of violence, like when Father was murdered. Sometimes the violence was from our side, but on the whole, your memory was honored."

"My memory?"

"When other clans across the land heard about you and the great magic you worked. Your sacrifice. They learned of your teachings about peaceful confrontation. Because of their superstitious nature and the story spread by the other may'rs of your mysterious departure, they soon revered you. Many other leaders and may'rs understood the danger of an aggressive rebellion. They soon realized that only peaceful tactics would gain the sympathy of the less radical majority. And we did!

"It wasn't easy. You had warned that. And it wasn't done quickly. At first many of my own clan, and some others, did not the like the idea of following the leadership of a wo'am, but I wouldn't give up just because I was not born mano!"

He smiled. "That's the Lauriel I remember."

She nodded gracefully. "Dazjon was the last surviving warrior and he went with me to the other clans and helped convince them how important it was to continue the struggle. He argued that I was not the leader for them to follow, but that you were. And in time I wasn't the only wo'am to rise to leader status. Over the last thirty yars I have lived to see many changes. There are no longer any laws restricting us from owning property, or living within the city, or preventing formal education. Many of our brothers have become carpenters, lawyers, and even a doctor or two!"

Her face brightened with pride. "My son is a civic lawyer."

Daniel didn't like hearing about a son that could have been his. "So, families moved out of the cave and into the city?"

"Yes. Gradually, as each could afford it, the migration began. I stayed for a while, as May'r to those remaining. Judging disputes and officiating a few ceremonies. But after a while, government aide came. You know, biotics, food supplements, and clothing. Within a decade, Grotto Cave held only a handful of families living by the old ways. With assistance from the Unite Ethnic Poverty Association, we started a housing project on the outskirts of the city. Many families migrated from the Data and Midway and Grotto clans. They have their own local government, and they have their honor."

"And Grotto Cave …?"

"Is only memories now. A former way of life that is spoken of beside the annual fires." She turned to look out the window once more. "That's why I was out here." Her voice again sounded distant. "This one was visiting the old path again."

She turned back to grip his hand enthusiastically. "But I didn't expect to find one of those memories in the flesh!"

Daniel tried to pull away. "Maybe it would've been better if I hadn't come back."

Again her tender fingers touched his lips. "No. Whatever you are, spirit or mano, I think you needed to find out. Do you think it is only by chance that we would both be here, on this night? It was meant to be. You had to discover your destiny. The spirits could not rest until you knew."

She cupped his cheek in a wrinkled hand. "I hope you can find peace with these answers. Remember the rainbow? This is not the end of your path, but a new beginning."

Finally he put his arms around her. As he held her tightly, he went back. Behind closed eyes he saw her; not the old wrinkled woman, but a younger, slender apparition. The rugged she-warrior who wore the crimson feather of bravery. He saw her walking, gracefully defiant beyond the flames of a tribal fire. The image of the Lauriel he had loved.

"I think I'd better go now," he said, wiping his eyes.

"So soon?"

"I need to be alone," He said, signaling the driver to halt. "Destiny isn't all it's cracked up to be."

She squeezed his hand one last time. "This one believes that your destiny continues. As long as you walk the path, there is something that must be done. I will pray that the Earth Mother walks with you. Good bye, my young Danon."

His throat tightened as he tried to utter the words he thought he'd never say.

"Good bye, Lauriel."

Chapter 36

Daniel walked alone in the dark.

He followed the road, often stumbling over the edges of crumbling asphalt. He shuffled aimlessly in the black moonless night, but he didn't care. He heard her words over and over.

"As long as you walk the path, there is something that must be done."

He stirred from his reverie to notice that the brush-covered countryside had become strangely silent. Then he heard something out of place, a low humming sound. He looked all around, yet, found nothing. The humming grew stronger, stirring vibrations under his feet, and he understood. Although he had arrived only a few hours earlier, it was time to go. Thomas was right about the vortex snapping him back sooner. He was ready. He didn't belong here anymore. Danon was the legend, the Supreme May'r of the past-future. Daniel was still just a visitor.

He closed his eyes in surrender as the second timequake struck. Somewhere in the distant darkness he heard the soft whine of the drive unit shutting down. Next came a faint scrubbing sound as the capsule, no longer supported by the waning energy field, skidded to a halt. He gritted his teeth as the forces of reentry pulled at him. When he awoke, he was back home, where he belonged.

# # #

Chief Todd stood in front of the warm tube, waiting for an explanation.

"You look pissed," Daniel said as he crawled out.

Chief Todd looked around at what was left of the launch room. Dust swirls and particles of insulation floated helplessly. Dozens of ceiling tiles littered the floor, and barren patches mottled the walls where plaster had once been.

"Are you quite through?" he asked.

Daniel nodded silently. He had broken confidences, involved others in his scheming, and risked a promising career. All for one more trip into the future. He realized the Chief wasn't so much angry as he was disappointed. So what, that made two of them.

Chief Todd turned to flash a glaring threat to Thomas. "I'll deal with you later." He returned to Daniel. "I shall see you in my office. Now."

# # #

Daniel had sat in the soundproof office for half an hour, as the Chief's tirade continued without a sign of finishing.

"I can't tell you how disappointed I am in you," he said. "And you were doing so well. Don't you understand? A Chief Administrator is expected to know the meaning of discipline. He must make a commitment to loyalty! There are priorities at work in this Complex which you know nothing about. Well, have you nothing to say?"

Daniel nodded. "No. I understand. I'm sorry I disappointed you."

"What?"

"I said I understand," he repeated. "About commitment. More than you can realize." Daniel almost smiled as he quoted Nathon's explanation. "One who truly understands the burden of leadership does not eagerly seek it."

Chief Todd nearly spit the unlit cigar out of his mouth. "Is that so? Well, I must say you've done extremely well at hiding that great insight. If you understand so much, why did you blatantly disregard my orders?"

"Because of the code," Daniel said as he searched for a better explanation. Was it just for Lauriel, or for a more noble reason? He thought about his journey as visitor, warrior, and brief leader. His blood oath to the code. He remembered here words about walking a path, and slowly smiled.

"Maybe it really was my destiny." He stood up. "It was something I had to do, but it's over now. I finally did some growing up, so if you're not going to banish me from the clan, I mean complex, I'm ready to finish the commitment I made with you."

Chief Todd replaced his cigar, then threw it away. "Is that so?"

"You are running out of time to appoint a successor. And unfortunately, you have no one else you can depend on to do what must be done around here."

Chief Todd seemed confused by Daniel's truthfulness.

"Is it my imagination, or the tachyon radiation? Do you think you can still become a good administrator after all?"

Daniel grinned. "I'm sure Ms. Jenkins wouldn't share that opinion. But we have no other choice. Go spend a relaxing weekend with your wife, and start making plans on how you're going to spend your retirement. Monday morning I'll start taking over your duties. This time for real."

Chief Todd seemed to relax, as if the headache had finally departed. He reached for a fresh cigar and lit it. "Doctor says I should give them up. He says they're bad for my lungs. Hell, I'm dying anyway."

Daniel started for the door, but paused. "Oh, about Thomas ..."

Chief Todd growled like a tiger releasing dinner. "Don't worry, I don't hold him responsible for your influence." He took a few satisfying puffs. "But I'm not going to tell him that, not until Monday morning. Then it's your problem."

# # #

Daniel drove along the empty highway, slower than normal since he had no specific destination in mind. He was in no hurry to go home to an empty house, and he didn't really feel like talking to Thomas. The long stretch of asphalt was a good place to be alone with his thoughts.

This was the time frame where he belonged, but it didn't feel like it. Memories came and went like the fence posts on the side of the road. Christina holding her negligee as she stood in front of a romantic dinner grown cold. The funeral. Lauriel walking defiantly around the council fire. Standing in her bonding dress. Holding her bow with remorse.

In the seat beside him lay the warrior's dagger. An anomaly stranded in time. It didn't belong in the present, but it no longer belonged in the future past. Just like him. He rested his hand on the dagger, with the prophecy tucked away in its handle, and wondered what he should do with it. He had tried to uphold the tradition of a noble line of may'rs. He had failed, yet somehow succeeded. Then he realized his destination.

After a short drive, and a solemn walk through the empty cavern, he stood in the circular chamber. He studied the barren shelf that would someday become hallowed ground. It would be a while before any of the clan fathers would arrive to claim their resting place. He fought off a shiver of realization. He was the first to stand in the burial chamber as a May'r before any of them were born. Somewhere, maybe on a reservation in Oklahoma, lived a young Cherokee boy who would one day lead his people into this cave.

As a token of brotherhood for that future warrior, he laid the dagger and buckskins on the shelf and left.

Epilogue

Monday morning Chief Todd entered his office to find his protégé already waiting, leaned back in the padded executive's chair with his feet propped up. Chief Todd put away his overcoat and proceeded to his desk where he rapped a crutch over Daniel's feet to move them.

"I'm sure Anita briefed you concerning the top secret visit from Washington."

"You mean Ms. Jenkins, the bull terrier guarding your front door? Yes, she's very efficient. She also doesn't approve of me."

Having regained his desk, Chief Todd began scribbling a few notes to himself which Anita would clean off his desk, but faithfully remind him of later.

"She has been here for quite a while," Chief Todd said with a smile. "You'll have to earn her respect. Just like I did."

Daniel wondered how much raw meat it would cost him. "She wouldn't give me any details. What does this spook from the Pentagon want?"

"Don't know. He hasn't arrived to tell us."

"Come on, you must have some idea."

"Mr. Nichols has visited this office before. Each time he has brought a request for research and development of some specific item. Exclusively for the Department of Defense, of course. Whatever it is, rest assured it is classified to the fullest extent of military bureaucracy and will not cure world hunger."

"Do we really need to deal with them? I mean, if it's military it's probably some sort of weapon. Can't we make enough money dealing with major corporations?"

"You tell me. You like sitting at my desk, you can decide if it's a worthwhile proposal. But remember, it isn't actually the money that we gain from government jobs."

Daniel waited for the bad punch line.

"It's the favors. Like a blind eye from the proper official when needed."

Daniel nodded understanding as he recalled another version. "… for the good of the Clan." He noticed the Chief's questioning look. "Skip it."

The Chief might have pursued the remark had not Ms. Jenkins' voice rang out abruptly over the intercom. "Mr. Nichols is here to see you!"

A short man with thin mustache and narrow, black eyes stepped into the room. He carried a black briefcase, attached by handcuffs to his wrist.

"Good morning, Chief Administrator," he said, showing deference to the position of power, while giving Daniel less notice than a chief servant.

"Mr. Nichols, this is Daniel Williams, he is taking over the position of administrator."

"Indeed?" He offered the limp handshake of a political candidate. "I don't believe we've met before. Congratulations on your appointment to this position of such authority."

Daniel returned a fake smile. "Actually it's a step down from my last job."

Chief Todd pointed to the beverage tray prepared by his executive assistant. "Please sit down. Coffee?"

"No, thank you. I'd prefer to get straight to the point."

Mr. Nichols sat his slim case on the desk in order to retrieve a golden key which released the handcuff. Entering the combination into the briefcase's cipher lock, he delicately raised the lid.

"This is the subject of our proposal."

Daniel peered over the desktop. Two slender vials of brushed aluminum were strapped securely inside on a bed of foam padding.

"What's that?"

"This is one of our latest strains, SMP-203." The man seemed proud. "Virulent little bug, according to the DARPA scientists."

"Strain?" Daniel asked. "Of what?"

"Well, bacteria, of course." Mr. Nichols answered as if Daniel should have realized the obvious. "Smallpox, actually. This variation has a nasty bite. The most promising aspect about this strain is its flexibility. It can be tailored for a variety of specific genetic targets."

Chief Todd had to sit down. "What do you mean by genetic target?"

"I think I know," Daniel answered. "He means that they hope to breed, or rather have us breed, a few mutations of their biological weapon. Strains that will be specifically tailored for an individual ethnic group, like Asian. Or Scandinavian. Or maybe even the great white Russian. Isn't that right, Mr. Nichols?"

"Russians?" Chief Todd said. "I thought they were our friends now."

"Well, the tactical aspects cannot be discussed at this time. Its exact purpose has yet to be determined. But we must always be prepared for any contingency. However, your assistant seems to have a keen insight on the situation."

"It doesn't take a rocket scientist to guess its purpose," Daniel said, feeling his fists harden. "And smallpox is caused by a virus, not bacterium. Pestilence, Famine, and Plague are also transmitted by infectious little viral creatures."

Mr. Nichols stepped back, surprised but not intimidated. Chief Todd started rising from his desk to intervene, but Daniel continued.

"Creatures like you, Mr. Nichols, who casually plan the death of millions with arrogance. You display the seeds of holocaust with pride."

Chief Todd leaned on his desk for support and spoke softly. "I think you've said enough."

Mr. Nichols turned his attention from Daniel to address Chief Todd. "And what do you recommend for this?"

"You can stuff it!" Daniel answered. "Just take those appropriately shaped little tubes and stuff them where the sun doesn't shine."

"Daniel!"

He turned to Mr. Nichols. "I apologize for my colleague's enthusiasm, but I'm afraid he is correct. Inform your superiors that we are not interested in this project."

Mr. Nichols straightened his jacket and spoke directly to the Chief. "You're sure you won't reconsider?"

"Don't push your luck," Daniel answered.

The man closed his briefcase and reattached the handcuff to his wrist. Then with the same businesslike tone displayed when he arrived, he bid them "Good day."

Chief Todd watched the government liaison depart, then turned a burning stare to Daniel. "I think you have some explaining to do."

"Me? He started it." He turned away to stare at the fake window, trying to decide how he could stop the inevitable.

"We've worked in the field of biologics before. Sometimes we have to do things which are, well, necessary."

"Yes, we do," Daniel said in total agreement. He headed for the door. "If you'll excuse me, I have business to attend."

"Business?" Chief Todd seemed confused, glancing down to confirm their now empty day planner. "What business?"

"Like you said, things which are sometimes necessary." His voice hardened. "Mr. Nichols and his friends have to be stopped."

"What exactly are you planning to do?"

Daniel flashed a look as cold as warrior steel. "Only what must be done."

# # #

THE END

Printed in the United States
130704LV00004B/157-174/P

9 780595 512195